Symphonic Etudes

Boris Asafyev (Igor Glebov)

Symphonic Etudes

Portraits of Russian Operas and Ballets

Boris Asafyev

Edited and translated by
David Haas

THE SCARECROW PRESS, INC.
Lanham, Maryland • Toronto • Plymouth, UK
2008

SCARECROW PRESS, INC.

Published in the United States of America
by Scarecrow Press, Inc.
A wholly owned subsidary of
The Rowman & Littlefield Publishing Group, Inc.
4501 Forbes Boulevard, Suite 200, Lanham, Maryland 20706
www.scarecrowpress.com

Estover Road
Plymouth PL6 7PY
United Kingdom

British Library Cataloguing in Publication Information Available

Library of Congress Cataloging-in-Publication Data

Asaf'ev, B. V. (Boris Vladimirovich), 1884–1949.
   [Simfonicheskie etiudy. English]
   Symphonic etudes : portraits of Russian operas and ballets / Boris Asafyev ;
edited and translated by David Haas.
      p. cm.
   Translation of: Simfonicheskie etiudy.
   Includes bibliographical references (p.   ) and index.
   ISBN-13: 978-0-8108-5700-1 (hardback : alk. paper)
   ISBN-10: 0-8108-5700-6 (hardback : alk. paper)
   ISBN-13: 978-0-8108-6030-8 (pbk. : alk. paper)
   ISBN-10: 0-8108-6030-9 (pbk. : alk. paper)
   1. Music—Russia—19th century—History and criticism. I. Haas, David Edwin.
II. Title.

ML300.A8513 2008
780.947—dc22

                                                                    2007022973

POLICE EXECUTIVE RESEARCH FORUM
1120 Connecticut Ave. N.W., Suite 930
Washington, D.C. 20036
Phone: 202.466.

www.P
Toll-Free Publication

Translator's Preface

*S*ince most of the text for *Symphonic Etudes* originated as program notes, the practical intent of the author most certainly was to use the opportunity to put his psychological and stylistic musings into the heads of a Russian audience who were about to see a performance of *Ruslan and Lyudmila* or *The Queen of Spades* or *Sadko* or another of the some twenty-eight Russian operas that were staged in the theaters of Petrograd (St. Petersburg) during the 1921–1922 season. Bearing in mind that original set of circumstances, one can understand the rationale for writing an often copiously detailed series of commentaries without a scholarly apparatus: any self-respecting regular ticket holder would have enough firsthand exposure to make superfluous any extensive point-by-point listing of act, scene, and measure number references. By the same token, if anyone were unaware of a particular past or present Russian painter or poet mentioned by way of analogy, that information could have easily been obtained during intermission.

With that original audience in mind, I have set the goal of being that generally knowledgeable acquaintance whom one seeks out in order to receive a few sentences' worth of information about a musical passage, a literary reference, or a biographical matter. And if most of the readers of this translation are unlikely to be in the situation of that original audience—that is, about to hear a familiar Russian work performed for the third or fourth time within a short interval (unless, of course, a recording is involved)—then the reason for my decision to supply additional endnotes to the author's original set will be self-evident. Since my audience is also different from that of the book's second edition, which was published in 1970 and edited by Elena Mikhailovna Orlova, I have chosen not to translate her notes; however, specific information taken from them has been duly acknowledged where appropriate.

The majority of the endnotes are indeed references to musical scores. The dedicated tracker of musical examples is encouraged to keep the appropriate volumes of the following standard editions at hand: (1) Nikolai Rimsky-Korsakov [Rimskii-Korsakov], *Polnoe sobranie sochinenii* [Collected Works] (Moscow: Muz. gos. izdatel'stvo [superseded by Muzyka]: 1946–1970), vv. 1–15 and 29–43); reprint: Melville, NY: Belwin-Mills, 1979–1982; (2) Pyotr Tchaikovsky [Chaikovskii], *Polnoe sobranie sochinenii* [Collected Works] (Moscow: Muz. gos. izdatel'stvo [superseded by Muzyka]: 1940–1990), vv. 3–10 and 34–42; (3) Modest Musorgsky [*sic*], *Boris Godunov*, full score [conflation] of 1869 and 1872 versions, edited by David Lloyd-Jones (Oxford: Oxford University Press, 1975); (4) Mousorgsky [*sic*], *Khovanshchina*, vocal score, completed by Rimsky-Korsakov (Paris: W. Bessel, [19–?]); and (5) Alexander Borodin, *Knyaz' Igor* [Prince Igor], vocal score (Leipzig: M. P. Belaieff, [19–?]). Readers not inclined to seek out a particular score will find frequent short descriptions and comments to the passages in question included in the notes, sufficient to follow the author's point.

The remainder of the notes are mainly explanations of topical references. With a music-minded audience in mind, I have provided merely general glosses to Asafyev's allusions to mythology, religion, philosophy, history, literature, art, architecture, campanology (!), and various other areas of knowledge. Out of respect for the author, I have refrained from taking issue with his arguments (except to correct an inaccuracy) or proceeding at such length so as to commandeer his book. My own views on the significance of *Symphonic Etudes* as a work of operatic criticism will be found in the introductory essay.

By way of a prefatory glossary, I would like to introduce and define nine Russian terms from this book's vocabulary, which I have transliterated instead of translated, either because the nuances of the best English cognate or other equivalent were misleading or because they were too restrictive.

The noun *déistvo* [pronounced "dyéist-va"], like its modern replacement *déistvie*, shares a root with the verb *déistvovat'* (to act, to influence). In Asafyev's usage, the antiquated word *deistvo* connotes not only sacred plays—for example, the medieval Russian Oven Play [*Péshchnoe deistvo*] taken from the Book of Daniel—but also any sort of ceremony or ritual with a dramatic component. Most often, he has in mind various types of regional ritualized drama, for example, of the seasonal *khorovody*. On the other hand, readers may be interested to learn that a native speaker of Russian is capable of characterizing Wagner's entire *Ring* as a *deistvo*.

The precise meaning of the literary term *skaz* [skahz] has been a matter of debate since Leningrad's Formalist critics (and Asafyev's colleagues) began to investigate the topic in earnest. All agree that the noun *skaz* is derived from the verb *skazát'* (to tell). Opinions differ, however, as to how or even if the essence of oral narration can be preserved in a text. In Asafyev's usage, *skaz* refers simply to the story*telling* aspect of a Russian tale or *skazka* in prose, traceable to the *personalizing* or *oracular* devices employed by the author to provide the reader with a memorable impression of the narrator as an individualistic and idiomatic speaker of the language. Mark Twain's tale "The Celebrated Jumping Frog of Calaveras County" is sometimes cited as an English literary equivalent, while Mikhail Zoshchenko's stories are the unrivaled Russian exemplars of the 1920s.

The *bylína* [pl. *bylíny*] is a category of epic folk song, averaging 300 to 400 lines in length, that is thought to have emerged from the 10th to the 11th century. The typical *byliny* from the Kievan cycle are concerned with the exploits of the *bogatýri* (see below) in their attempts to serve Vladimir, Grand Prince of Kiev, by vanquishing internal and external enemies of the realm; the many victories awarded to the noble *bogatyri* contradict a less-rosy historical record.

Protyázhnaya and *protyázhnaya pyésnya* refer to a category of Russian folk song that is justly renowned for a long-breathed lyricism that results from a melismatic intoning of the text. The melodic stretching out of syllables often has a developmental and not merely ornamental character. Pyotr Ryazanov (1891–1942), a younger colleague of Asafyev at the Leningrad Conservatory, enthralled Dmitri Shostakovich and other young composers with his insights into the melodic structure of the *protyazhnaya pyesnya*.

Whether translated as "countervoices," "under-voices," or something else, the term *podgolóski* refers to the melodic outgrowths that a trained singer of Russian folk song improvises to adorn the main tune; it is as natural as "singing harmony" to a 20th-century pop tune, but with the emphasis more on adding a somewhat independent linear variant than on sustaining sweet consonant intervals.

Khorovod [pl. *khorovódy*] refers to a wide range of circle dance games in which dance, song, game, and symbolic drama are united. They are categorized by season, by occasion, or by song title or lyrics.

The term *prisyádka* now refers to the familiar squat-and-jump figure of Slavic dance; it should not be confused with the dances themselves, for example, the Ukrainian *trepak*. In an *Academic Dictionary* of 1822 published in St. Petersburg, *prisyadka* was defined as a "type of dance in which the dancer by bending or spreading [the legs] to the side squats and jumps," with the latter motion providing the greater challenge.

A Russian *bogatýr* is a legendary or semi-historical ancient warrior, typically of greater than normal stature and girth, whose reputation usually rests upon the accomplishment of several miraculous feats. Among the most famous are Sviatagor, Ilya Muromets, Dobrynya Nikitich, and Sadko, the *bogatyr*-bard.

Skomorókhi are the jester-entertainers of medieval Russia. The introduction of *skomorokhi* into a Russian opera, whether chronologically defensible or not, proved to be a useful device for providing a contrary point of view, a reflection of protagonists and events in the "curved mirror" of satire, and an incidence of Bakhtinian carnival.

The customary word about transliteration must now be given. In all honesty, there is no such thing as a single all-purpose transliteration system. For this translation, I have availed myself of the customary set of *three*: (1) the Library of Congress transliteration (without diacritical marks) to facilitate electronic retrieval of the few Russian-language sources cited in the notes; (2) a hybrid system (with stressed syllables accented) for the transliteration of verses and a few Russian terms (Russians will forgive—that is, can *understand!*—a foreigner's mispronounced vowels, as long as the stresses are properly placed); and (3) the usual eclectic, unsystematic, yet familiar array of spellings for surnames: for example, Tchaikovsky, not Chaikovskii; and Chaliapine, not Shaliapin. With regard to the surnames of the author and his friend, the eventual composer of the opera *War and Peace*, I deviate from the norm, for the reason that *Asafyev* and *Prokofyev* will prevent a grating mispronunciation that results from the more common *–iev* alternative.

It has been my pleasure to receive invaluable advice and assistance from a number of people. First, I wish to thank Dorothea Link for providing so much expert advice throughout the early stages of the project. My thanks are due as well to Bruce Phillips and Caryl Emerson, for beneficial early interest and evaluation. At Scarecrow Press, Renée Camus, Jessica McCleary, and their colleagues have been patient with me and conscientious in completing the many tasks required to bring the manuscript into print. I also wish to express my appreciation for the book subvention awarded to me by the University of Georgia Research Foundation.

I am truly grateful to Olga Haldey of the University of Maryland for agreeing to verify the accuracy of the translation. Thanks to her, baroque syntactic knots were unraveled, unattributed phrases traced back to the middles of poems and plays, and meanings not found in any dictionary were not lost in translation. Among faculty colleagues at the University of Georgia, Elena Krasnoshchekova was kind enough to share generously of her professional and personal knowledge of 19th-century literary and cultural backgrounds. Marianne Koshkaryan, Yuri Balashov, and Maria Rubens each provided insights into matters of philosophy, aesthetics, and metaphor. Thanks to the following persons, I was reminded of the difference between literal translation and one that was more grateful to an English-speaking audience: Dorothea Link, David Schiller, Kevin Kelly, Kristin Thomassin, and Jeffrey

Tucker. I owe a special thanks, too, to three of my students who offered both encouragement and sage counsel: Lisa Jakelski, Joanna Hastings Smolko, and Terry Dean.

Although they were not directly concerned with this project, I wish to acknowledge John Wiley and Natalya Challis for the mentoring they gave me at the University of Michigan and the fine example they set in their own translations and research. Finally, I wish to thank my wife, Marigene, and children, Lennon and Natalya, for supporting me—yet again—in many ways over the course of a project that consumed a considerable amount of my time and energy.

Introduction: Igor Glebov and the Audiences of *Symphonic Etudes*

*W*hen the original readers of *Symphonic Etudes* leafed through the opening pages of the first Russian edition, they found neither an explanatory subtitle nor a preface to provide a rationale for the book's curious title. Pianists among them would have been correct to surmise that it was a conscious borrowing from Schumann's unusually named *Etudes symphoniques* of 1837. After acknowledging as much in the book's final "etude," the author offered a personal interpretation of Schumann's title and a justification for his own appropriation:

> [My] method is that of the great creators of "symphonic etudes" (Schumann, Chopin, and Liszt). They took a particular technical matter within the realm of pianism for their starting point and through creative intuition raised their stylistic intention to a level of profound artistic significance, . . . transforming "technical expertise" into the living tissue of music.[1]

The book's primary concern with the realm of Russian opera, if not the full scope of the author's "stylistic intention," is revealed in the table of contents. The Russian opera audience member of 1922—whether student, pre-Revolutionary *intelligent*, or newly empowered soldier, sailor, or proletarian—would likely have recognized the names of five Rimsky-Korsakov operas assigned to one series of chapters. The content of the fifteenth etude, entitled *The Queen of Spades*, is evident, as are the three other long etudes that assess the achievements of Rimsky-Korsakov, Tchaikovsky, and Musorgsky, respectively. Less is revealed, however, by the provocative first chapter title of "A Slavonic Liturgy to Eros," the three chapters merely designated as "Intermezzi," and the colorfully named "Incantations" and "Tale." The probable content of the penultimate etude, "Igor Stravinsky and His Ballets," is clear, but not its function in a book seemingly devoted to opera. At the very least, such a chapter would have immediately provoked a response, since this most renowned and controversial of Russian expatriate composers (since 1914) was no friend of the new Soviet regime.

With such a list of terse yet evocative chapter titles, the author hints at a further affinity with the collections of those piano etudes that he has dubbed "symphonic": this is not to be a "bloated survey" of Russian opera, any more than the artistically conceived anthologies of piano etudes composed by Schumann, Chopin, and Liszt were meant to compete with the systematic yet poetically void piano methods of Clementi, Cramer, Czerny, and Hanon. Thus the reader of these *Etudes* will learn little about Russian opera before Glinka or contemporaneous with Glinka, nor very much about the operas of Rubinstein and Cui, nor anything at all about Stravinsky, Taneyev, and Rachmaninov as operatic composers. Instead this book is a brilliant and passionate critic's attempt to define and explicate a core repertory, an attempt all but impossible when members of the Mighty Five, their stalwart supporter Vladimir Stasov, and their renowned public adversary Tchaikovsky were all yet alive. While much of the repertory had survived, the author believed it to be imperiled:

> Russian art is a series of oases in the desert, like 15th–17th-century monasteries amidst impassable forests and bogs. Is it possible that Russian music, and especially Russian opera, has been fated to develop in the same way? The universal deafness to its beauty of design and emotional depths, in relation to the utter "facelessness" of its style in certain stagings leads to an eventual neglect and incomprehension of one of the finest pages in the history of Russian art. I fear that the time is coming, when those who are interested in the monuments of Russian operatic music will feel as if they are in Novgorod, in a musty provincial town, amidst the priceless and splendid creations of Novgorod architecture and iconic art, peacefully sleeping in *soundless*, museum quiet. Does not that same feeling appear when, amid the masquerade-like emptiness and the simpleminded connivances, you view productions of *Ruslan* and *Igor* that are deaf to the music, presented on a stage once held to be exemplary?[2]

The note of dire concern was already appropriate for 1922, in the immediate aftermath of the Revolution's social and ideological upheavals, a bloody civil war, and the harsh economic austerities of "war communism." Ten years later, with Lenin dead and Stalin an unopposed head of state, abject despair would be justified, as the process was well under way of forcing all the surviving operatic repertoire into lockstep conformity with socialist realist priorities. In the years surrounding Lenin's death in 1924, however, the situation was different. Constrained certainly in their range of topics, the notable critics of the 1920s were not yet obliged to sacrifice polemical fervor, personal opinion, and individual voice. Evidence of all three is found throughout *Symphonic Etudes*. It is not a mild book, any more than *Boris Godunov* is a mild opera or Liszt's "Mazeppa" a mild piano etude.

Whose was this new critical voice, one bold enough to praise Stravinsky openly, to wax poetic over the artistic treasures of the 19th century, yet avoid all mention of Marx, Lenin, the masses, and the October Revolution? The name "Igor Glebov" was a *nom de plume* that first emerged during the First World War and was originally attached to several reviews of productions at the Maryinsky Theater. "Igor Glebov" was the invention of Vladimir Derzhanovsky, editor of the journal *Muzyka*, as a means of protecting the identity of a new author he had contracted, who happened to be an employee of the Maryinsky Theater. Soon after, Glebov's outspoken advocacy of three modernists—Stravinsky, Prokofyev, and Myaskovsky—sparked controversy elsewhere, leading to scandal and his resignation from a second journal, the prestigious *Muzykalnyi sovremennik* [Contemporary musician], edited by Rimsky-Korsakov's son Andrei. Somewhat later Glebov appeared as the editor of two dauntingly complex tomes of broad musico-metaphysical speculation entitled *Melos*. By the time of the Revolutions of 1917, if not sooner, it was known that the prolific Igor Glebov was none other than Boris Vladimirovich Asafyev (1884–1949), a native of St. Petersburg and former student of both the St. Petersburg University and the Leningrad Conservatory, presently lecturing at the Russian Institute for the History of the Arts, writing criticism for public and specialists, and still drawing a paycheck from the Maryinsky.

The main body of the *Etudes* can be traced back to a series of program notes written in 1921 for productions at the Maryinsky Theater (now assigned the bland new-Soviet name State [Gosudarstvennyi] Academic Theater of Opera and Ballet, or simply GATOB). The thematic interconnections between them, however, Asafyev claimed to have worked out in lectures he delivered at approximately the same time within the Arts Institute. Behind it all and beyond it all a major study was under development, whose final form might have differed significantly from the set of *Etudes*. In any case, their author consistently expressed satisfaction with them, both on account of their subtle interconnections and deep significance to his own development. Within a year of their publication, he described them as his "dithyramb of Russian music."[3]

Like the etudes that were claimed as inspirations, the book offered a variety of challenges to its original readership. Much more is attempted in it than the rehabilitation of a threatened repertory or the restoration of original performance ideals. Rather, *Symphonic Etudes* invited its readers to consider each work as a unique aesthetic and psychological experience. As a means of promoting those experiences, the author drew upon a deep knowledge of the composers' biographies, individual compositional styles, and multifarious general sources of 19th-century Russian music, enhanced by his respectable erudition in literature, folk customs, history, and contemporary philosophy. Even though characters and vocal numbers are named, lines quoted, and dramatic events described, the focus remains on each chapter's chosen theme, for example, the juxtapositions of the real and the delusional in the St. Petersburg of *Queen of Spades*, or the coordination of the rhythm of the seasons with the rites of passage in human lives in Rimsky-Korsakov's cycle of "cusp" operas, or the interplay of good and evil in his *Legend of the Invisible City*. Meanwhile, in virtually every etude, the author confronts the issue of how topicality is achieved: that evocation of everyday life, everyday routines, everyday surroundings, all of which are encapsulated in the short and gritty Russian word *byt*, a word infinitely preferable to the vacuous imported abstraction *realizm*.

Asafyev's ideal audience may well have been those widely read and widely traveled members of the Russian intelligentsia like himself, possessed of a pre-Revolutionary education at the St. Petersburg University and firsthand experience of the city's rich cultural life. The musical points he makes rarely depend upon a technical knowledge of harmony, counterpoint, or form. On the other hand, the book is well stocked with references to the many indigenous musical sources of Russian opera: the individual styles of the composers, the romances of the gentry, the dances of the Court, Orthodox psalmody, and of course the wide repertory of regional folk song and dance. In each chapter, musical knowledge is enhanced by extramusical contexts. The surface references to Silver Age Russian poets such as the recently deceased Alexander Blok and the still emerging Anna Akhmatova, to the metaphysics of the University's Nikolai Lossky, and to performances of the celebrated Chaliapine prior to his 1922 emigration are sufficient to establish the book's origination in the post-Revolutionary Petrograd, as St. Petersburg was then called.

Of more interest to posterity are the tantalizing deeper undercurrents, some of which correlate well with the new set of issues that were finding expression in recent work of the Russian Formalist School and others. In his introduction to Rimsky-Korsakov's *May Night*, Asafyev addresses the inherent dramaturgy of *khorovod* round dancing, suggesting an affinity with the concerns of Vladimir Propp, whose *Morphology of the Folk Tale* would not appear until 1927. Asafyev's identification of a surprising number of discrete song types coexisting among the characters and within the musical discourse of individuals in Rimsky-Korsakov's *Christmas Eve* certainly invites comparison to Bakhtin's views of the innate polyphony of spoken discourse. Far more provocative (and therefore a prime target for Stalinist-period denunciation) are Asafyev's strong readings of *Ruslan* as marital mystery play and *Pique Dame* as surrealist nightmare.

The lamentable fate of the book can be initially attributed to the author's other competing interests. Neither the contemplated sequel[4] nor any subsequent development of the operatic issues first broached in the *Etudes* emerged in the 1920s. Instead Glebov/Asafyev devoted himself to other projects, including a Stravinsky monograph (*Book About Stravinsky*, 1929), a treatise on musical form (*Musical Form as a Process*, Vol. I, 1930), essays, concert reviews, and numerous other obligations. His chief achievement for Russian 19th-century opera was to lend his support and expertise to the world premiere of the first (1867) version of Musorgsky's *Boris Godunov*, on 16 February 1928, at GATOB.

By the late 1920s, new political pressures made any effort on behalf of a book such as *Symphonic Etudes* impossible. Stalin was now firmly in control of the Kremlin. His new programs for industrializing the nation, seizing control of agriculture, and safeguarding himself, his regime, and his ideology against all real and suspected threats would cost thousands and then millions their lives. The initial onslaught against intellectuals like Asafyev was carried out with tacit approval from on high, by tightly organized associations of "Proletarian" writers and musicians, under the guise of achieving a long overdue "cultural revolution." The campaign against Asafyev resulted in staged disruptions of his lectures and defamations of his work and character in print. By end of decade, Asafyev had resigned under pressure from both the Conservatory and the Arts Institute, thereby silencing the once authoritative pen of Igor Glebov, seemingly forever.

Ultimately, the reign of the Proletarian Associations in the arts proved short-lived. All of them together with their already scattered modernist foes were disbanded by the Central Committee's "historic" Resolution of 23 April 1932, entitled "On the *Perestroika* of Literary and Artistic Organization." In their stead, unions of composers, writers, and artists were created, each with its faction of Communist Party members reporting to higher authorities. In the beginning, Asafyev wished to be admitted into the union as a composer, not a musicologist (which was also allowed). While his (and everyone else's) scholarly career remained under scrutiny, Asafyev began to compose with marked facility in a variety of genres, ultimately gaining some respect as the composer of two staples of Soviet ballet repertory: *The Flame of Paris* (1932), set at the time of the French Revolution, and *The Fountain of Bakhchisarai* (1934), based on a work of Pushkin.

In order for any public scholarly career to resume, it was first necessary for Asafyev to show clear signs that he was a convinced Marxist-Leninist and had also distanced himself from his ideologically deviant writings of the 1920s. Even prior to the 1932 Resolution, Asafyev had announced that *Symphonic*

Etudes was among those works wherein his dual interests in "literariness" and artistic form had "tempted" him to produce a highly literary prose in which "the analysis of works and biographical research material were hidden beneath the poetic texture,"[5]—a more self-respecting alternative, perhaps, to confessing ideological deviation.

In fact, such a confession never emerged. Instead Asafyev as writer showed himself capable of adopting the jargon and mind-set of Stalinist-period Marxist-Leninism, at least in small doses. The few occasional pieces on 19th-century Russian opera composers penned by Asafyev in the 1930s were devoid of scholarly depth or critical insight but rife with ideologically accept-able platitudes, each of them pointedly reversing a position from the *Etudes*. Thus, *Queen of Spades* was no longer a tragic personal encounter with mortal-ity and the supernatural, but the expression of the previous epoch's "uncon-scious processes of class struggle."[6] And Musorgsky was no romantic at all, but the "supreme realist, dramaturge, historian, and narrator of the life of the peo-ple," for which he is deservedly "respected and deeply treasured by the Soviet nation."[7] In the meantime *Symphonic Etudes*, like so many original works of the 1920s, had become a banned book, its original Russian audience forced into an imperiled underground existence.

In the next decade Asafyev experienced a new burst of scholarly ambition comparable to that of his alter ego, Glebov, at the peak of his career in the 1920s. Sensing a new opportunity in the lessening of publishing strictures dur-ing the Second World War, he wrote a series of major studies, three of which involved both the repertoire and the approach of *Symphonic Etudes*. "*Evgeny Onegin*": *Lyrical Scenes by P. I. Tchaikovsky: An Essay of Intonational Analysis of the Style and Musical Dramaturgy* of 1944 is a brilliant and long overdue complement to the *Queen of Spades* essay of 1922, with an equally dazzling tableau-by-tableau analysis of melodic shapes, drama, pacing, and form. It was followed by a short monograph on Tchaikovsky's *The Enchantress* and a tripartite study of Glinka and his milieu. Glebov the opera critic had returned in spirit if not in name.

Boris Asafyev died in 1949, four years before his Conservatory classmate and friend Prokofyev, four years before Joseph Stalin. By the time of his death he had lost face publicly, having been targeted once again for denunciation as part of Andrei Zhdanov's nationwide crusade to purge the arts of formalism and other anti-Soviet and "antihuman" tendencies. Asafyev was, in addition, still shunned by the composers (who had never welcomed him as one of their own anyway), owing to his behavior during the previous decade's official cam-paign against Shostakovich and his opera *Lady Macbeth*. Nevertheless, for le-gions of students and readers, it was unthinkable that Asafyev's enormous scholarly and critical legacy be allowed to fade into obscurity either because of current fears of guilt by association with an ideologically suspect citizen or because of ethical questions. Strong evidence of a meaningful rehabilitation and continuation of the main lines of his numerous scholarly pursuits began when the USSR Academy of Sciences committed to publish a five-volume *Selected Works*, the fifth of which contained an accurate and unexpurgated catalogue of his writings running to nearly one thousand entries and a second list of more than two hundred musical works.

It is no accident that the Asafyev republication project coincided with the cultural thaw of the Khrushchev Era. Neither is it surprising to find that the monographs, essays, and reviews printed in the *Works* were chosen not to provide a true sense of Asafyev's many-sided career, but rather to underscore points of agreement with mainstream Soviet musical historiography. As a result, the putative "second edition" of the *Symphonic Etudes* consisted of approximately twenty-five pages of fragments from the original nineteen chapters, scattered throughout the first three volumes of the *Works*. Drastically reduced in quantity, this selection was also distorted in its content—purged as it was of the book's underlying currents of idealistic philosophy, religious content, supernatural speculation, despair—and its portrayal of Musorgsky not as social progressive but as unrepentant, lifelong Romantic individualist and aesthete.

Perhaps it was then that a young member of the editorial board named Elena Mikhailovna Orlova set for herself a goal of one day seeing the entire text of the *Etudes* reissued in an unabridged second edition. In the end, that project would take her nearly fifteen years. Along the way she managed to achieve quite a lot on behalf of Asafyev. In addition to her assistance with the *Works* and various essays and edited volumes on Asafyev as a scholar, she wrote the major study *B. V. Asafyev: The Path of the Scholar and Publicist*, published in 1964. Bereft of extensive discussion of conflict or scandal, it nevertheless does indeed provide the essentials on his biography, teachers, and influences as well as a general orientation to his main writings from all periods of his career and the recurrent aesthetic concerns behind them. Two more monographs would follow.[8]

When permission for a second edition of the *Etudes* was granted, it fell to her to write a preface appropriate for the epoch of Khrushchev's successor, Leonid Brezhnev. Reissuing a book from the 1920s in the late 1960s or 1970s—whether poetry, or a novel, or a criticism—still entailed some degree of compromise. The first priority for any editor-caretaker of a suppressed or discarded work was to make every effort to have it published in its entirety. Once such an opportunity appeared, one typically made certain personal concessions and wrote out a *pro forma* preface. The preface to a work of criticism typically would begin with a brief statement about the writer, an appropriate quotation from Lenin and perhaps Engels (no longer Stalin!), and a dutiful account of where and where not the book accorded with dialectical materialism and its Soviet aesthetic offshoot, socialist realism, as currently envisioned.

Having dispensed with the Soviet front matter, the writer would have a small opportunity to evaluate the book on its own merits.

Though the rudiments of the formulaic preface are all in place, Orlova's genuine enthusiasm is evident throughout. From the outset Asafyev is allowed to speak for himself, first about the significance of the book for his career and then, in an oft-quoted proclamation, about the unique glories of the Russian operatic tradition: "It is necessary, once and for all, to stop squandering valuables and proclaim to one and all: the Russian operatic style is an artistic treasure unto itself, deserving thoughtful investigation and careful cultivation."[9]

Upon reaching the point where Asafyev's criticism must be reconciled with current Soviet Marxist thought, Orlova provides a sampling of the usual catchphrases. A case is made that Asafyev continued the "democratic [i.e., proto-socialist] tradition in Russian 19th-century aesthetics." His work is relevant to solving the "aesthetic, theoretical, and psychological problems of contemporary musicology" and "materialist-based Soviet philosophy." And while young Asafyev did not manage to cite V. I. Lenin's classic *Materialism and Empirocriticism* even once (he had not even read it!), a recent authority has "established" that he was no different from many another one-time fellow traveler, destined to achieve prominence in the Soviet Union as a progressive thinker.[10]

Having dispensed with the requisite Soviet front matter, Orlova changes course, devoting her full attention to the main idea content of *Symphonic Etudes* as she understood it in 1970. Much of her commentary is devoted to describing the book's main units: Glinka (Chapter 1); Rimsky-Korsakov (Chapters 3–12); Tchaikovsky (Chapters 14–15); Musorgsky (Chapter 16); and Stravinsky (Chapter 18); and the three *intermezzi*, which serve as transitions. Along the way, she underscores a number of issues that forecast future scholarly concerns in the career of Boris Asafyev and Soviet musicology in general. Most significant is the doctrine of *intonatsiya*, Asafyev's contribution to the vocabulary of musical semiotics, introduced here in connection with Rimsky-Korsakov's *Christmas Eve*. She properly identifies the *Queen of Spades* chapter as an early example of holistic or integral (or gestalt) musical analysis, termed *tselostnyi analiz* in Russian and associated with Lev Mazel and Viktor Tsukerman of the Moscow Conservatory.[11] Of equal importance is the revisionist view of musical form not as structure but dynamic process. Implicit already in various chapters of *Symphonic Etudes*, it would later be explored in the two volumes of Asafyev's *Musical Form as a Process* (1930; 1947).

Orlova concludes her preface with an address to a new generation of Russian readers, all of them born long after Igor Glebov's heyday, many of them born after Boris Asafyev's death: "Now as we return to the *Symphonic Etudes*, several decades after their creation, they emerge before us as if in a new light, 'reintoned' and enriched with new connections and associations of content . . . The wealth of ideas that are set down in the *Symphonic Etudes*, the aesthetic issues raised, and the vivid, artistic imagery in the style of presentation—all attest to the true originality of this work within both Russian and foreign musicological writing during the first two decades of the twentieth century."[12]

Eighty years and more after Glebov's *Etudes* first appeared, it is natural to wonder why an acknowledged classic of Russian criticism has remained untranslated for so long, its wealth of insight locked away behind the enigmatic title. One need not confront the mighty handfuls of Russian-reading musicologists and critics of each subsequent generation. One need not subscribe to the unwarranted fear that classics of criticism are as untranslatable as Russian poems are held to be. Neither should we conclude that any appreciation of a book on Russian opera must be reserved for that select number of non-Russians who have delved deeply into Russian history, geography, folklore, religion, and the "Russian soul."

The problem lies not with the book but with the misapprehension of its subject. If Glebov, writing in 1922, had gazed back over a century of Russian opera only to conclude that, in the popular mind, there was no tradition at all but only a series of oases in the desert, outside of Russia the situation was far worse. For most of the 20th century there seemed only to be two or three outposts in a vast polar wasteland. Since the status of Tchaikovsky's *Onegin* as an opera has been questioned and Rimsky-Korsakov's *Zolotoi petushok* reduced to an orchestral suite traveling under the Frenchified name *Coq d'or*, only two works have defined the repertoire: *Queen of Spades*, which Mahler brought to New York on 5 March 1910; and *Boris Godunov*, which scored a spectacular success in Paris for Diaghilev and Chaliapine on 19 May 1908.

When a century's worth of a major genre from a particular geographical region is reduced to only two works, there is no tradition at all—only a polarity, which inevitably engenders false or overstated dichotomies. In the case of Musorgsky and Tchaikovsky they are all too familiar. Musorgsky, the most favored member of the Mighty Five, is assumed to represent the Slavophile; he miraculously fashioned his *Boris* entirely from native materials, stubbornly resisting foreign traditions, foreign tunes, and foreign technical training. In the end he produced a work of unquestionable power that has required considerable editorial intervention from others' hands in order to bring it to the stage. By contrast, Tchaikovsky is quite often portrayed as the slick, conservatory-trained "cosmopolitan" composer: a product of German musical forms and Franco-Italian operatic fashions. Despite its Russian setting and Russian literary source, *Queen of Spade*'s powdered wigs, Mozartean pastiche, French air, and other clever set pieces make of it an eclectic numbers opera, devoid of *l'âme russe*.

The modern reader may be intrigued to learn that Glebov wastes no time either with restating or debunking these commonplaces of Western musical thought. Neither does he concern himself with the other chief Western concern: determining how and to what degree any Russian operatic composer might be considered an ideological or musical "nationalist." In the *Etudes* each work discussed is properly assumed to have an equal birthright, a separate but equal complement of cultural, psychological, and musical merits, and a distinct role to play both within Russian tradition and on the world's stages.

Glebov's claim for significant aesthetic common ground among Russian operas is substantiated by a combination of recurring themes in his book and the occasional generalization not confined to the particular work at hand. The use of the Russian language and speech idioms, the regional settings, and, as exemplified by *Boris* and *Queen of Spades*, the composers' attraction to literary *masterpieces* as opposed to faddish plays are too obvious for comment. More insight into the subject and a better appreciation of Glebov's particular interests can be acquired if one is reminded that Russian composers tend to be no less avid readers of literature than of musical scores. While Tchaikovsky's *Onegin* counts as the only successful attempt by a 19th-century Russian composer to turn a major novel into opera, he was not alone in bringing a novelist's concerns to the craft of operatic composition.

Both *Boris* and *Queen of Spades* are clearly distinguished from many a Western work by their protracted psychological scrutiny of the human mind turned against itself. Since the musical results are at times overwhelming, one may well fail to take heed of a corresponding lack of the assassinations, executions, armed combat, and other sorts of external conflict that often serve to heighten the drama in 19th-century operas of the Western traditions. No less memorable is Rimsky-Korsakov's truly Dostoyevskian treatment of the traitor Grishka Kuterma in *Legend of the Invisible City*, from before his act of betrayal on to an eventual mental breakdown. For Glebov, this interest in the workings of individual psychology is axiomatic of the Russian operatic tradition, yet by no means limited to pathological states. In fact the paradigmatic Russian opera for him—that is, the work most illustrative of the tradition and most challenging to Western sensibilities—is a small-scale Rimsky-Korsakov setting of a Ukrainian tale by Gogol, a work lacking both violent external interpersonal drama and inner psychological torment:

> I consider *May Night* to be an entirely suitable object for an attempt at defining the fundamental lines of the Russian operatic style. I shall begin with the negative delineations. Might it be an "action-adventure" opera such as the operas of Meyerbeer and others that resemble them? Of course not! Is it a romantic legendary opera, of the type found in Marschner's and Weber's operas? No, despite the presence of this sort of element in the third act of *May Night*. Of the Italian operatic style in all of its aspects, in this case there can be no discussion.

Wherein lies the main distinction? In the absence of action, or so it is said. Yes and no. If action means the appearance of the actual will of a hero, directed toward overcoming externally present obstacles, then no. It would be ridiculous to consider Levko a hero, merely because his father did not agree to his marriage to Hanna. But internalized action, an intimate musical dramatism, unquestionably exists, even though we are in the habit of believing that if there is neither a struggle nor an outward manifestation of reality, then not only is there no theatrical-dramatic action, but no life either, for life is a struggle.

Here we touch on the cardinal point of the diverging views. What if *action* is not merely a struggle? What if the obstacles that stem from people would be cast aside and not reckoned with? What if man himself is an element entering into a harmonious whole, which is called life? And what if it is not he with all of his struggle that has value, but life itself as such in all its depth, breadth, and height? Man simply fulfills what it has predetermined, obediently accepting the commonplace, the miraculous, the real, and the unreal. *All of this is life* and man is merely a fragment. How petty then become all his escapades and the surmounting of them![13]

Setting aside the author's *fin de siècle* (Bergsonian) infatuation with a transpersonal life force pulsing throughout nature and humanity, we are left with a plausible explanation of how particular aesthetic priorities condition both plot and structure. According to Glebov, Levko and other typical Russian operatic protagonists are not larger-than-life individuals with a destiny to play out on a grand scale, but rather ordinary souls facing ordinary life thresholds. A rite of passage will usually involve gaining necessary insights into the nature of how one *belongs*, either to a particular social group, or the human race, or a universe comprising human communities, the natural world, and a supernatural plane of existence. Successful negotiation of the rite is often marked by a combination of choral song and ensemble dancing, both of which feature prominently in Rimsky-Korsakov's folk operas. In the very simple case of Levko, his assistance in righting a wrong in the spirit realm leads to the removal of the main barrier (his father's opposition) to his marriage. The opportunity arises in the course of a *khorovod* dance-game of mermaids: when Levko intervenes, he is no longer a spectator but a participant, whereas the *khorovod* itself is no mere divertissement, but an integral component of the dramaturgy.

Like a novelist, the Russian operatic composer strives to evoke realms of existence—the "commonplace, the miraculous, the real, and the unreal"— paying particular heed to their points of conjunction or disjunction. Glinka set an important precedent in his *Ruslan* for delineating these realms at the level of style and harmonic language by opposing a diatonic vocabulary with whole-tone and chromatic elements. In the post-*Lohengrin* era, other composers followed suit, none more systematically than Rimsky-Korsakov. Glebov finds an elaborate interaction of discrete harmonic languages in Rimsky-Korsakov's *Christmas Eve*, wherein ordinary diatonicism is contrasted with static passages of third-related major triads (signifying nature at peace) and unstable passages involving double-tritonal relationships (demonic disruption of the natural order). Similar juxtapositions are noted within Rimsky-Korsakov's *Sadko* and Stravinsky's ballet *The Firebird*.

The shift of focus from external action to the "invisible" bonds that tie protagonist to community and to the natural world obliges composer and commentator to ponder how community and world are to be peopled and how they are to be associated with specific historical periods and geographical regions. To this end, Glebov introduced the concepts of the *lyrical sphere* and *intonatsiya*, the last of which would become the single most important term for the later career of Boris Asafyev as a scholar. In the chapter devoted to Rimsky-Korsakov's *Christmas Eve*, Glebov can already give a fairly straightforward explanation of it:

> In an adaptation to opera, whose language is essentially nothing more than a musical transformation of the word, i.e., an *intonatsiya* within the strictly delineated limits of intervallic interrelationships—the approach from the general to the particular just now explained is expressed in the assignment of the acoustical speech of the *dramatis personae* within a predetermined vocal-instrumental channel.[14]

If operatic song is indeed an expressive musical act employing a musical language of "strictly delineated" intervals, then the *intonatsii* are the musically intoned *words* of the language.

The *lyrical sphere* then is an assemblage of meaningfully related musical *intonatsii*, offering to each character not merely a leitmotif but a personal vocabulary of vocal idioms, some of them shared with other characters, others unique to the one character. In the essay on *Christmas Eve* Asafyev laid out a truly encyclopedic variety of indigenous Ukrainian *intonatsii*, of which Rimsky-Korsakov could avail himself in composing the individual vocal parts. They are grouped under three broad classifications of vocal melody: (1) Categories of song and lyric (e.g., the "pure lyricism of song; lyricism with instrumental inflections [rhythms of Polish dances: polonaise and krakowiak; the Ukrainian national rhythm of the hopak]; the lyricism of the [urban] romance"); (2) Categories related to the epic (e.g., "sacred verse, epic folk ballads [*dumy*], ecclesiastical recitative, historical songs"); and (3) Categories inspired by instrumental idioms (e.g., "riffs, improvisations, every manner of instrumental ornaments [figurations], and dance incipits").[15] In the actual opera, songs of praise predominate: praise for the Christian God, praise for pagan deities, praise for the maiden Oksana, praise for a witch, and finally, praise for Nikolai Gogol himself in Rimsky-Korsakov's choral epilogue.

In the *Queen of Spades* chapter and elsewhere, Glebov offers insights on how formal unity is achieved in a Russian opera. In all cases, operatic unity is the result of a combination of factors and not merely the result of harmonic, formal, or leitmotivic schemas in the music. While he does acknowledge the existence of operas "composed in the old manner of fragmentation into arias, ensembles, etc." and others written "in the new 'Wagnerian' manner of division according to scenes and episodes," such a general classification does not hold the key to the unity. Neither do the closed forms that may be employed for individual numbers. In the case of Tchaikovsky, he suggests that they are crude approximations at best of a deeper sort of form:

> Wherever the composer himself makes it possible, by means of a rationally composed design, to grasp the internal architecture, the essence of the entire conception, there it is comparatively simple to find the end of the thread and untie the knot. But where the composer did not even consider how that which is visible on the surface and measurable would reflect the *music*, but instead directed its impulse into a channel delineated, as is customary, in accordance with either predetermined or spur of the moment, *ad hoc*, serendipitous schemas; where these schemas at times do not at all correspond to the true form but offer only a crude outline of it—therein lies the difficulty and the risk of making shortsighted conclusions.[16]

For Asafyev, the "true form," or *form behind the form-schemas*, is inaccessible to an analytical method based on keys, cadences, and measure counts. Bearing in mind the psychology of the characters and the unfolding of the plot, one must instead seek out the dramatic peaks: these are the "nerve centers" of an opera, when it is conceived as a "living organism." Once the nerve centers are chosen, the analyst can then "untie the knot" and comment either on the narrative strands extending to and from the center or on the consequences of the moment for a particular character's psychological growth. Though he successfully applies the method to Rimsky-Korsakov's operas, far more of its potential is revealed in the two chapters devoted to Tchaikovsky's operas, a set of works that on the whole constitute the "most difficult problem" within the "psychology of musical style, form, and the evolution of musical language."[17]

Ever wary of losing a general audience by lapsing into technical analysis, Glebov nevertheless avails himself of charts, musical examples, and a considerable amount of score-based descriptive detail in the *Queen of Spades* chapter. In it the reader will find practically nothing about the children's songs, choruses, or the clever Mozartean cantata of Act 2. In the weird day-for-night ambience of Glebov's interpretation, these manifestations of the visible everyday world are not only irrelevant to the "invisible" psychological processes, but deceptive and illusory. In this way he presents a dichotomy analogous to the one he proposed between the closed forms and traditional operatic numbers listed in the score and a deeper, more extensive form conceived as an ongoing process. Setting aside the closed forms, he instead seeks out the nerve centers that coincide with the turning points of the characters' inner states of being. The first tableau contains three of them, each marking a stage in the progress of Hermann's obsession (or, in Glebov's alternative hypothesis, a phase in the process of a malevolent power to seize control of Hermann). Here and elsewhere in his exegesis, Glebov is receptive to a range of musical evidence, including changes in rhythm, fragmentation in a particular character's melodic line, shifts of timbre, and recurrence of keys.

Most significant are the motives, their affinities, and their transformations. In Tomsky's ballade introducing the legend of the three cards, Glebov hears the relationship between a previously heard motive associated with Hermann's desire for Liza and the three-note motive of the cards as an implicit musical confirmation of Hermann's fatal shift of focus. His fate is sealed when that same motive is associated with the countess's "ascending sequence of anapests." Throughout the remaining encounters with the countess—encounters both real and surreal—the motive of the cards vies for attention with other music associated with the events of the external world until the "crescendo of horrors and frights" of the fourth tableau registers Hermann's complete break with reality.

In the final chapter, Glebov offers his *Queen of Spades* commentary as an example of how stylistic analysis and a psychological approach can be combined to produce insights into "the psychological foundations of both the [musical] language and the style."[18] More than a brilliant program note, Glebov's remarkable sustained integration of psychological interpretation and multidimensional musical description is a model of an operatic analysis responsive both to music and drama. Since no other opera is treated at such length, one finds a similar level of stylistic detail only in isolated paragraphs, some of them containing promises or pleas for a continuation at some future date. A lack of sustained analysis is not surprising, however, given the book's provenance. Moreover, any initial dismay at the brevity or thrust of certain chapters may fade when one notices subsequent references to a particular opera's characters and, more importantly, the further developments of issues that befit a truly *symphonic* composition in prose.

Even though Glebov's original audience with its particular complement of common interests and perspectives have all but disappeared, his uniquely symphonic conception of the Russian operatic tradition, of operatic form, and of operatic criticism has not outlived its appeal. Rarely has a small volume of music criticism provided such a range of cultural contexts and aesthetic apprehensions, while maintaining a compelling unity of rhetorical tone and methodological intent. Neither the breadth of cultural references nor the unifying idea content can be adequately summarized in an advance paraphrase, any more than the aesthetic experience of a Russian opera can be preserved in a plot summary. Like Hoffmann and Schumann a century earlier, he has taken criticism to the point where music and literary prose meet, where commentary about the music not only conditions the musical experience, but becomes an integral part of it. At these moments, perhaps, one is best able to comprehend the Glebovian connotations of *symphonic* and its relevance to subject, book, and author.

NOTES

1. Chapter 19, p. 304.
2. Chapter 19, p. 303.
3. Letter to Alexander Petrovich Vaulin, 30 March 1923, cited in: E. M. Orlova and A. N. Kriukov, *Akademik Boris Vladimirovich Asaf'ev* (Leningrad: Sovetskii kompozitor, 1984), 142.
4. Elena Orlova found evidence of a planned sequel, including a table of contents, in a letter of 11 July 1922 to Pavel Lamm. Asafyev suggested the following chapter titles: "I. The Sources of Russian Opera; II. *A Life for the Tsar* and *Prince Igor*; III. The Problem of the Real-Life and Psychological Drama: *Rusalka*, *The Enchantress*, *The Tsar's Bride*; IV. The Romantic-Historical Drama: *Boris* and *Khovanshchina*; V. The Tale: *The Nightingale* and *The Nutcracker*; VI. Truth in Expression: *The Stone Guest*, *The Marriage*, *The Gambler*." See Elena Mikhailovna Orlova, "*Simfonicheskie etiudy* v puti Asaf'eva—issledovatelia russkoi muzyki," in B. V. Asaf'ev, *Simfonicheskie etiudy*, 2nd ed. (Leningrad: Muzyka, 1970), 13–14.
5. "Biograficheskoe [late 1920s]," reprinted in A. N. Kriukov, *Materialy k biografii B. Asaf'eva* (Leningrad: Muzyka, 1981), 31.
6. "Pikovaya dama," cited in *Akademik Boris Valdimirovich Asaf'ev*, 197.
7. Cited in Orlova and Kriukov *Akademik Boris Valdimirovich Asaf'ev*, 197–98.
8. E. M. Orlova and A. N. Kriukov, *Akademik Boris Vladimirovich Asaf'ev*; E. M. Orlova, *Intonatsionnaia teoriia Asaf'eva kak uchenie o spetsifike muzykal'nogo myshleniia* (Moskva: Muzyka, 1984).
9. Cited in Elena Mikhailovna Orlova, "*Simfonicheskie etiudy* v puti Asaf'eva—issledovatelia russkoi muzyki," in B. V. Asaf'ev, *Simfonicheskie etiudy*, 3.
10. Orlova, "*Simfonicheskie etiudy*," 6.

11. For a Western perspective on their work, see Ellon Carpenter, "Russian Music Theory: A Conspectus," and Carpenter, "The Contributions of Taneev, Catoire, Conus, Garbuzov, Mazel, and Tiulin," in Gordon D. McQuere, ed., *Russian Theoretical Thought in Music* (Ann Arbor: UMI Research Press, 1983), 51–54; 329–44.

12. Orlova, "*Simfonicheskie etiudy*," 14.

13. Chapter 5, p. 52.

14. Chapter 8, pp. 82–83.

15. Chapter 8, p. 83.

16. Chapter 14, p. 151.

17. Chapter 14, p. 151.

18. Chapter 19, p. 304.

• 1 •

A Slavonic Liturgy to Eros

$\mathscr{T}$he writer Nestor Kukolnik[1] (a boon companion to Glinka, who worshiped him and delighted in his genius), in describing one of the frenzies that occurred at the time when the librettists were discussing the plan for the opera *Ruslan and Lyudmila*, recalled the Russian proverb involving the figure of speech "seven nannies" [Eng.: "too many cooks."]. He could hardly have realized how prophetically he was forecasting the gist of the opinions on the design of the opera and laying in the axle around which the opinions and disputes of the "Ruslanists" and their enemies would glimmer in rapid rotation. Meanwhile, Kukolnik's judgment, like the stamp of a conviction imprinted in a passport, like the mark of the Antichrist, distorted the profile of a great work and bolstered that atmosphere of lazy and unending carelessness that enshrouded the general impressions of *Ruslan* as a composition that was scenically hopeless and structurally unrealized, notwithstanding the genius of the music. Glinka's contemporaries, both friends and foes, assumed this tone, acting as experts: one magnanimously forgiving, another presumptuously patronizing a brother-in-art, another maliciously and spitefully tittering. Little by little, this initially none too harmonious chorus attained concord, and even an ardent champion of "Ruslanism" like Vladimir Stasov ceded in part to the general opinion.[2] Meanwhile fairy-tale and storybook productions (with "personal touches" from the real world) of the long-suffering opera multiplied, obscuring the sense of it in every way and killing living tissue with dissection and vivisection (cuts!). The producers still blunder about in three directions (fantasy—story—real world), improving and pruning a work of genius by the greatest Russian musician without attempting or even setting the goal of finding the meaning in it: its spirit, its secret, its inner action. The last of these need not be lacking, for while the visible schema may be

1

confused and chaotic, the real essence of the composition is evoked by an inspired and creative spirit and by a genuine heartfelt need for self-expression, intuitively seeking paths of realization.

The entire structure and stamp of *Ruslan* are a stamp and structure inspired; and I feel that an intoxication with the riches of his own imagination transported Glinka into a state of rapture during the time of composing this miracle of Russian music (especially in the final days). It is no wonder that *Ruslan's* wisdom eludes those who have reasoned out the unquestionable advantage of entering a house through a door rather than climbing through a window, the factual certainty that heated water boils, and other visible and tangible truths. One who has never contemplated how mere accumulation differs from growth, even though both involve a material enhancement, cannot understand the secrets of creativity and its illogic. Indeed, we stand now in bewilderment before another remarkable Russian musical tale: the mysterious *Golden Cockerel*. We painstakingly reproduce the "milieu" of Dodon's kingdom and seek out more and more engaging stunts drawn from "everyday life," so as to give "depth" to the problem of "Dodonism," overlooking what is important: the sheer wizardry of the tale. And I have always felt the Astrologer deeply justified in sticking out his tongue (to be blunt!) at the most honorable assembly of the populace, when the action concludes, to say: "But you have still missed the *point*."[3] No doubt every production of *Cockerel* calls for preparatory sessions and assessments in the very manner of those that are found in the opera's first act, in the State Duma of Tsar Dodon, whose rich content was long ago pointedly set forth by the State clerk Kotoshikhin.[4] It is the same with *Ruslan*, and many have been seduced by just this attitude. Indeed, how can one not be seduced? How can one grasp the logic of this brilliant music, if it cannot be situated within the customary schemes of logic found in life?

In fact, already in the folk tale "Eruslan Lazarevich"[5] a solution was provided for a particular problem that was somewhat akin to that of *Ruslan*: how to render the psychological problem of heroism as a power unto itself in an artistic fashion, i.e., in a work of art. "The soul craves great deeds"—there it is in full, without any explanation! The unquenchable thirst for sensations and deeds is quite understandable in the nature of any human being who is not yet bound by civilization but is quite sated with the fullness of life perceptions, and whose will is languishing in inactivity. The boundless expanse of the plains beckons and attracts. Man seeks to expend the energy accumulated within him. Such is Eruslan. Ruslan shares his traits ("Give to me, Perun!") as does Ratmir ("Oh, warriors, make haste to the open field"); yet a satire of heroism is also at hand (in Farlaf).[6] The essence of the character of Lyudmila's lover is unveiled more profoundly in other moments that are not suggestive of Eruslan: in the first half of the aria "Oh field," in the duettino with Finn ("I thank you"), and in that most expressive arioso of jealousy: "Oh joy of my life, youthful bride."[7] The sketches of characters in Glinka's *Ruslan* are remarkably vivid and pliant: they are living profiles in flesh and in spirit. The environment in which they act is sumptuous and resplendent. The theatrical viability of *Ruslan* is therefore beyond doubt.

What motives and sources might indeed have spawned it? Here we come to the root of our carelessness. The fact of the matter is that up to now, that wonderful monument to an epoch, *Memoirs*, has not been deciphered from the standpoint of ordinary everyday life and has hardly been digested in any way.[8] Above all, it has not been studied psychologically, with the aim of deciding whether everything in it has been uncovered; or why it is that what *has* been disclosed unfolds in the tone of a frivolous, often trivial and Philistine, "everyday" narrative, with the sort of nuances that leave no doubt about an undisturbed consumption of life—of a heady Russian epicureanism.[9] Glinka's was a remarkable nature; he knew how, when, where, to whom, and to what degree to reveal himself. His lack of religion and amorality are questionable. Poring into the *Memoirs*, comparing their style with that of Glinka's older and younger contemporaries, one begins to understand that the riddle of his life and psyche—of some if not all of the many aspects of them—must mainly be sought first, in the decoding of the characters, actions, and habits of thought of the "confreres" and other individuals who came into contact with him; and secondly, via a reconstruction of the Russian musical environment, in the capital and in the country—from the middle of the 18th century through the end of Glinka's epoch.

Glinka was wholly a part of his milieu, and this milieu is at the root of the *Memoirs*. We know nothing at all, worst of all we may never learn anything (other than the names), about the people who assembled the plan for *Ruslan* that later came to light. What was their worldview? What were their tastes? There might be surprises here. When studying the nature of a personality of genius such as Glinka's and a work so very remarkable as his *Ruslan*, one cannot overlook any single detail: it is necessary to pick up every crumb, to gain insight into every allusion. As often happens, underneath an apparent blandness and triviality in the notes and diaries, what is significant has been hidden or seems inadvertently omitted, whereas the inconsequential leaps to the eye with marked effrontery. Occasionally, amidst a mess of everyday notes, Glinka would toss in observations of life and remarks that profoundly reveal his acutely impressionable artistic nature. Had his friends possessed more searching and sensitive feelers, they might have managed to draw forth rich and psychologically valuable pronouncements from Glinka's heart. At times, one senses that Glinka himself was moving toward a greater openness (for example, in Serov's reminiscences of him[10]), but, apparently, having encountered misunderstanding or condescension from intimates, he withdrew into himself. . . .

Thoughts of *Ruslan* are, for me, always linked with a conception about another great work, a product of Mozart's genius, which is nonetheless also "dissolute." In both technique and style, Glinka's music and the music of the "profligate flâneur" [*prazdnyi guliaka*[11]] have many points of contact. The fairy tale of the *Zauberflöte* compels me to add to the number of present-day conceptions of the structure of action in *Ruslan and Lyudmila*, one that emerges from intuitions into the psychological foundations of the musical style, from a probing into the worldview and character of Glinka and a belief in the unquestionable unity and conceptual depth of this work of genius.

I have always been struck by the lack of harmony in the scenic productions of Glinka's great "feat." There is no coherence to productions of *Ruslan*: the conceptions are not only too poorly imagined but also lack even the simplest restraint and practicality; the traditions have vanished, indeed I believe they never existed. Based on the memoirs of Glinka himself, of Serov, and other contemporaries, one can gain a fairly clear idea of the full psychological situation when the opera was written, and of its transfer to the stage, the rehearsal process, and performances of the first season.[12] At this time, mundane squabbles and the muck of gossip had yet to finish Glinka off, but the intellectual poverty and spiritual destitution of those around him (including the "Kukolnik bohemia" of confreres) had already muddled to a fair degree his clear and harmonious spiritual world.

Glinka was a genius, a musician, an artist, but not a thinker. He was unable to create an armor of ideas around himself, with which to inculcate his ideology and compel a submission thereto, such as Wagner achieved. But then, there are indeed essential differences between the cultures and not merely in their characters! In Germany the resistance to Wagner emerged from a tradition, out of past achievements. In Russia, given the deplorable habit of paying homage to a decayed past (the ideology of Russian "provincial" conservatism), not even an organic sort of struggle existed: Glinka simply went unnoticed by those who did not wish to notice him, for some of them on account of an innate boorishness; for others, due to a lack of maturity. And if the image of Pushkin's nanny be poetic, so the continuous presence of the "uncles" who surrounded Glinka seemed to be a vital necessity: the great originator of new revelations in the world of sounds was mired in an ooze of the mundane. Even the mind of Pushkin stood in need of the intuition and kind heart of Nashchokin;[13] Pushkin, though, was more fortunate in his friends. All the more were love and devotion, or at least sympathy or even simple attention, craved by the hypersensitive soul of Glinka, he who always subsisted on impressions of sentiment and sensuality, taken to the highest cultural plateau.

The social standing and spiritual makeup of Glinka's "uncles" were quite varied, but the benefits that came from them were only minor and of an internal sort. The exceptions were the German Dehn and Glinka's sister, Lyudmila Shestakova.[14] The Russian dilettantes among Glinka's younger contemporaries probably pestered him far more about "eight-hand" rattling on two pianofortes, than they could nourish and stimulate his imagination. I say this, giving all due respect to the memory of the pioneers of Russian musical culture, yet remain completely convinced that, aside from sincere admiration, they had nothing to offer Glinka.

Sometimes in letters and in conversations he would make the vain attempt to impart to them the musical significance of the discoveries made in *Ruslan*. It is enough to read through Serov's *Memoirs* to see with what frivolity and even a bit of haughtiness that Glinka's very few pronouncements (so valuable to us now) were received.[15] Nevertheless, during the process of creating *Ruslan*, he passed the test: with firmness and fortitude he wrote the opera, amidst a disagreeable life and without a good "literary" advisor (a chaos of "geological detritus" weighs down the libretto). He wrote with a kind of intuitive grasp and conviction and completed a deed of genuine importance, one that was necessary yet understood by him alone.

When rehearsals began, each day the burgeoning snowball of scandal, intrigue, complete indifference from some, and blind incomprehension from the others struck at the heart of the composer. He could not endure "everyday" pressures and therefore allowed anyone who felt like it to importune him with advice on how to improve the opera; moreover, he conferred on a frivolous but arrogant dilettante, an "expert with the knife," the right to cut out and stitch together his score *ad libitum*.[16] People brought Glinka to the point where he began to doubt himself and doubt his conviction that *Ruslan* was in fact the great work that he had tentatively begun to consider it. The early history of *Ruslan's* staging was, in essence, one of shameful lack of understanding. Later, of course, there were brilliant revivals of the opera and even special commissions convened to assess the plan and details of its scenic rendering. But all of the "commissions" always bypassed the question of how to justify the essence of it and give a philosophical foundation to this inspired, yet "incoherent" opera. Consequently no one has succeeded at getting to the heart of its perplexing content.

Ruslan and Lyudmila is music of genius. All of us sense that this assertion is justified and realize the truth of it (Larosh's article is among the most lucid proofs of it[17]) and yet, upon hearing this *mass* of music in the theater, many are nevertheless overcome with a strange sensation of dissatisfaction: there remains an incomprehensible element and a trace of exasperation. If someone were to succeed at convincing us that the significance and praises for *Ruslan* all lay in the distant past, that we have created a mirage, a nonexistent oasis, then things would be simpler. But such a seducer is not to be found: the freshness and *jubilant* splendor of the material, the crystallized characters, the eternal novelty of the craftsmanship are so overwhelming that one can only concede unconditionally. It has always been a perilous undertaking for Russian composers to proceed in the wake of *Ruslan*, when taken as a work for the stage. In a naively and myopically understood "Ruslanism" there are dangerous whirlpools: *Ruslan* as stage work is an *island of Sirens*. Its statuesque quality— the stasis of legends—has led to confusion and given birth to undramatic and unstageworthy plots.

But all of this has passed away, so that now, during the present epoch of our musical conditions and our musical psyche, we simply must accept *Ruslan* as a great achievement, as the alpha and omega of Russian music, and as a work deeply rooted in the folk (as Larosh emphasized), for the song-essence of its melos and the predominance of variation structure in its forms make this assertion incontrovertible. The richly drawn personages and the graphic characterizations, the plasticity of the images, and the breadth of the conception (plan), the picturesque quality and the depth of perspective all point to a scenic and theatrical quality. It is incumbent on us now to justify *Ruslan* as both opera and theatrical work and discover an approach toward its scenic realization.

1

In the autocratic Russia of Nicholas I, a work of enormous epic nature was created: a "gigantic undertaking" in the words of Odoyevsky.[18] Like an epos it was created, with a slow gathering of materials—not, of course, in an ethnographic sense—from all the corners of the Russian nation. Once many life impressions and much material had accumulated, Glinka became exasperated with waiting on the librettists.[19] Having hastily cut out the text for the scenes still lacking, he proceeded to complete the music in a state of self-obliviousness. He became content and tranquil, it seems, only when he had utilized all the accumulated fund of musical material on hand, along with the full strength of his creative energy. The overture became a brilliant synthesis. Impressions of the Caucasus (formed in distant youth), Finland (a chance excursion, which probably produced a profound contrasting impression on the passionate "southern" nature of Glinka's soul), and Ukraine intertwined with the influence of Southern and Western Slavic elements, especially the Polish, together with the impact of Italian music, which is practically omnipresent, albeit brilliantly transformed. One senses the breath of German music, too, albeit by way of the Slavicisms. Finally, behind it all, as background and essence (melos and rhythm), Russia resounds.

One does not sense Petersburg: it is not the bureaucratic and official, but the formerly feudal Russia that is revealed. Glinka probably had no sense yet of Petersburg's "phantasmagoria." However, the style of the Russian vocal romance of Petersburg in the 1830s and 1840s, and also, perhaps, the pomposity of imperial parades and feasts, which preserve in part the spirit of bygone times and traditions, doubtlessly exerted their weighty influence. . . .

In a country where despotic will produced a great orb of state officialdom and where the deep heart of the country lived by itself, on the basis of its own and not an imported culture, it was quite difficult for a national consciousness and justification of the state's purposes to emerge, a consciousness that was deeply rooted, organic, and experienced by the people themselves either in revolution or reform, instead of as an abstract development of the heads of state. No wonder that *Ruslan*, as national-state epopee, would turn out to be a work so luxuriant in material, richly nourished by the juices of the Russian soil in all its tremendous dimensions, but so wanting in ideology, even though warmed by heart's blood. . . .

In the epopee of *Ruslan*, the music may be glorious but it is ideologically incomprehensible how it is all brought together. How are the diverse cultures fused within actually united? There can be only one answer: through the musical genius of Glinka. Therefore it is not an epopee either of the Russian state or of Russian soil. The essence of *Ruslan's* everyday reality is not unified by a single idea: it is by all accounts an anthology of various songs, brought into harmony through the great talent of one individual. Hence it is still quite far from a true epopee of the state, especially during an epoch of state officialdom. An approach to *Ruslan* emerging from the social environment and epos yields a series of ethnographic tableaus, intermixed with a fabulous fairy play, but nothing more! *Yet that is how Ruslan is staged.* And that was how it was staged in the past. No one wants to sense and comprehend that such an approach was the greatest of blasphemies. Yet it is better to turn aside from *Ruslan* as a theatrical drama than to realize it so superficially and unworthily. Many wonder silently in their hearts: Why must one listen wearily to such a great work in its entirety at the theater? *Respect* necessitates, however, that one not display such a state of mind. *Ruslan* continues to remain a riddle: *it is the Egyptian Sphinx on St. Petersburg's Embankment.*[20]

2

Does the cause for all the apparently nonsensical structure not lie with the subject matter itself? No. Not with the subject on its own, but in the significance that we assign to it, not comprehending its role with regard to the style of the work. Naturally, if Pushkin had written the verses for Glinka, then the work would have benefited; but the subject would have remained the same. Let us recall Alexander Pushkin's poem *Ruslan and Lyudmila*.[21] Can the issue here really be the subject matter and not the seventeen-year-old adolescent genius's view of life? In evaluating the poem's subject, deep-thinking critics became angry with the poet, being unable to see, thanks to their own shortsightedness, that the subject was the outline and the poem itself, a *lyrical epopee* of an adolescent's view of life. Glinka's opera, though, was *a lyrical epopee of a great musician's view of life*. We will not confuse ourselves with the textbook precepts that allege that everything lyrical is subjective, whereas everything epic is objective. Let us allow that the "objectification" of one's own soul is possible, an objectification of the personal, i.e., of the subjective element by the very individual who is creating an "artificial" world. For Pushkin, the poem was a witty and playful synthesis of youthful erotica. Glinka was more *mature*. During the period when *Ruslan* was composed, he had outgrown the "pleasures of youth." I recall here again that remarkable book—*remarkable*, only if it not be approached from the predetermined stance of those who study the *greatness* of the greats—namely, the aforementioned *Memoirs*.

Many took offense at Glinka and even grew disenchanted with him, as they read the *Memoirs* in disbelief. A great man should express only great truths and lead a serious life, but here (what a trial for the pedagogues of school and the mentors of life!), all of a sudden, a narrative unfolds that is rich, colorful, and filled with life—a narrative of everyday surroundings, of life's quandaries. Sometimes, along the way, there is talk about some sort of music, but more than anything, it is about women and the *admiration* of them.[22] Glinka was entirely rooted in the everyday, deeply and inextricably immersed in ordinary relationships; and he is not to blame if, at the time he lived, the pure wellsprings of everyday reality were already sullied. He lived from these wellsprings, and when they were eventually polluted, he fled to Dehn.[23] They said it was on account of the great idea of studying counterpoint. He even convinced himself that he was going "to wed the fugue to the modes." I believe the issue was far simpler: weary flesh desired comfort; plain and ordinary warmth, a serious and "industrious" *German* tranquility and leisure, after the Russian nonsense.

In music, he had no love for the "rude coaches of solid German labor"; and in life, it was only with effort that he could endure a ride even in the finer coaches, whenever his own carriage was unavailable: yet having sampled the charms of a Russian society hemmed in by gossip, he began to crave even foreign surroundings, since everyday surroundings were the vital support of his life: its foundation, its nourishment, its strength. For Glinka, the compositional process was not a diary, but a squeezing out of rich, aromatic, velvety wine, a wine that had been maturing for a long time. These periods of self-containment and maturation required comfort and *warmth* (from friends, and most importantly, from women). Contemplation of beauty was a constant stimulus in Glinka's life; it was an infatuation with beauty, neither abstract nor asexual, but alive: the touch and feel of the beauty of a woman's flesh. I will add that this was no knightly cult involving an abstract representation of the ideal in the form of a lady for the heart alone. Glinka was no sentimental troubadour. *He was a Hellene, a priest of Eros*. His pliant melos and the rich, elastic charm of his harmonies are imbued with the linear rhythm of antique sculpture. The appeal is a manly one, not at all exhausted, decrepit, and ornate. Clarity is the creed of all his works, and they are suffused with it, both in their relationships and in repose. Every moment of Glinka's music is equally splendid, whether we perceive it in time—in motion—or in a state of rest, at a stopping point. The horizontal and the vertical lines always move in a harmonious relationship and complete connection. Glinka profoundly *understood* the harmony of life, and sensed that forces of light directed it, that from them emanated the joys of sowing and the festivals of harvesting. One cannot help cherishing Glinka for the integrity and harmony of the life reflections, and, having done so, never fail to understand that his perception of the beauty of woman's flesh never did and never could hold anything in it that was cheap, adulterous, or trashy.

Pore into his music, read the *Memoirs* and correspondence: his soul will be laid bare, if only one senses that the statistical count of his infatuations is one thing, but the powerful sense (grasp) of life and beauty is something altogether different. I realize that the essence of such a comprehension of life through intuitive sensation—not from sentimentality or sensuality—by which Glinka lived is difficult to grasp and embrace. People live under such intricately interlaced ideas of hypocrisy on the one hand, and cynicism on the other, that it is nearly impossible to perceive life in its entirety as did people of Glinka's sort: one must just believe them and, in believing, *sense* it, which is not difficult to do, especially with the help of music. In fact, one need only have faith and detect the aroma of the fragrant wine of Glinka's erotica in order to engender in the soul an admiration for such a person and see the question arise: Why is the knowledge of life out of an intuitive sense of beauty inferior to the knowledge of the mind? Why indeed, when this knowledge is imbued with life, inspired, and transformed into the most harmonious music? Glinka's music recognizes neither good nor evil, being created as if prior to the banishment from paradise, but it does know languor and ardent expectation, voluptuous ecstasy, burning intoxication, the delights of possession, and the jubilant ecstasy of sweet pleasure. Yet it all comes without torment, for this music is on the whole as radiant as a clear, sunny sky.

Music of the heart is not gloomy, because its lifeblood is penetrated by the sun: *as wine-of-the-blood, it conceals within the energy of the sun's rays*. Its architectonics and its incarnation into tangible forms are controlled by an intelligence enriched by vital knowledge of the sources of life and not by knowledge obtained from the contemplation of abstract ideas: an intelligence, possessing a knowledge of harmonic proportions, which in Glinka never become lifeless schemas, since he knew the laws of structure to be forms of living flesh. Indeed, the body is the border between Sun and blood: the Sun without, the blood within. Is this not why Eros—the connection between blood and the Sun—is two-faced? Turned to the Sun, he is resplendent, but when the face is turned toward the blood, to the heart, he spreads languor, pain, and passion. These are the *bases of contrast* in the music of Glinka, and of the spells and hypnoses; here is the impulse of its secrets, its *liturgical aura*. Indeed, in the latter concept, humanity has hidden all that is most dear, most *secret*, most treasured. Spring dies as it is transformed into summer. Maidenhood is forcibly violated for the sake of fertilization and maturation of the fetus. Why in any case bring up the mythological symbols that for so long have been cherished by humanity, singing of one and the same secret of creation, the secret of the seed's sprouting in the soil, to be warmed by the Sun's rays, the secret of maternity and nativity? One need remember only this: spring is ever the eternal virgin.

3

Why indeed did Glinka take a poem about Ruslan for the plot-outline of his lyrical transports? Was it really on account of Ruslan's feats, for the sake of heroism, for the sake of the strange epic, which is seemingly ridiculed by Pushkin in the poem itself? That Borodin would take for his subject *The Song of Igor's Campaign*[24] is understandable. Authentic historical fact was transformed into the poetry of *The Song*, something which did transpire. Moreover the fact was of the real-life, historical sort that not only extends into ordinary reality and life relationships, but expands into a genuine epic, since the seed of this growth is buried within it: the magnificent depiction of the struggle between the idea of state-sponsored settlement and the unbridled, rapacious wilds of the steppes. There is nothing similar in *Ruslan*: Glinka seems to survey the Russian land in song, in music. If one takes the subject matter to be the goal, then for consistency's sake, one must reach the conclusion that Musorgsky wrote his *Boris* in order to convince one and all of the real political fact of Boris's murder of Dmitri and to describe in music the servile condition of the Russian people. For the sake of ancillary reasons, one may employ such conceptions of operatic works, but such a method merely addresses the ideology behind the work and not the basis for the choice of subject. So it was with respect to *Ruslan*. It is a well-known fact of basic psychology that when the point of view toward some phenomenon or other is altered, not only the knowledge of it but also the perception of it changes. That which is long and uninteresting will come to appear quite normally developed and imperceptibly extended in time, while something vague can become clear and well founded. Does not the attempt to change the point of view toward *Ruslan* as scenic drama promise the very same?

The subject is not the point here, but rather a means of expressing an internal creative conception, just as unseen internal processes of our life have at their disposal an infinite series of expressive means, beginning with the organic construction of the body. For them, this is the "subject." In order to express a personal attraction to a homeland, to a milieu, to the spiritual drama of a man prepared to sacrifice himself and, in this way, to display an accumulation of musical material that was based in part on folk song—it was possible to dwell upon the legend of Ivan Susanin.[25] *Ruslan and Lyudmila* is something else. If interest in visible action is indeed lacking, instead Glinka expressed in *Ruslan* his life credo and life essence: intuitively we sense the greatness of the work and stubbornly proclaim it. Only out of misunderstanding do we express a reservation: "Yes, the music is genial, but the libretto is edited badly and therefore all manner of adaptations are necessary." Let us ignore the poorly edited libretto, the epic story, and the fairy-tale aura. Let us observe the development of action in *Ruslan* from inside, on the basis of the view of the subject matter just now set forth: the meaningful intensification of Glinka's life process, the empathy for a beauty that is alive, incarnated into the images of theatrical music. This then is what the action expresses.

4

Within the "mysteries " of yore, the person designated for veneration, in attaining step-by-step the highest degree of perfection, overcomes the onslaught of antagonistic material forces. By analogy, conceptions of life beyond this world and of peregrinations *over there* are formed (in Egypt, for example, or in our folk legends about great labors). The realization of the "peregrinations" in whichever images and forms is contingent on the quality of the poetic expression, but the substance of the idea is not altered thereby. Marriage is the mystery of mysteries. One must not forget that even the Christian church, under the powerful influence of an ancient trend, was obligated to acknowledge that marriage was a mystery. In not sanctifying the union of the sexes, it had risked losing any connection with life and handing over an essential sphere of life-relations to the natural regulators of the processes of sexual union.

In the mystery of marriage, as in any other mystery, there are two forces: an active, masculine force to overcome inertia and an opposing force fated to surrender itself, i.e., a feminine force. Since it does not surrender without a struggle, one cannot consider it to be entirely passive and inert. It is passive to the extent that it delights in being in repose, but active in its resistance (its dynamism), culminating in a spiteful stubbornness, having instinctively sensed that in surrendering, it will relinquish a portion of its vital properties and be transformed into a new union. All the philosophy of life that is expressed by the folk in the poetic images of myths and tales speaks to this. So, too, do our Russian Princes Ivans chasing about the wide world after brides attest to the same thing with their exploits. The distinction between the legends of various peoples and times are to be found in the shadings and not in the essential content. Doubtless there is a significant difference between conceits found in the myths of Adonis and Demeter, the philosophy of love espoused by Pushkin's Finn, and in the tale of one Ivan or other, dreaming that sooner or later he will roll about on a warm cot with his "princess." Thus, on the one hand an active impulse is present, and on the other, a sacrificing of virginity, a surrendering of the self. Resistance to the sacrifice is natural, for any bride is also an innocent [Russian: *nevesta, ne-vesta*], who does not know, is unaware, and only has a premonition of a man's right to coercion and to sacrifice (on her part) and will thus resist while surrendering (e.g., Brunnhilde and Siegfried). A struggle ensues between the element that establishes and affirms life and the stagnation of ignorance. Between the two extreme points of the process—the lure of sacrifice and possession thereof—the poetic imagination places a series of trials and feats, i.e., a triumph over inertia. The genius of Pushkin astounds us by having inserted into his poem about the conquest of Lyudmila a ballade of the unsuccessful love of Finn, for it is in fact a philosophy of love.[26] The erotically playful but keen mind of the poet here cunningly ridicules the idea of a triumph over virginity, stubbornly and strongly safeguarding itself by dragging out the struggle over an extended period of human life. Once he had decided to write an opera on the subject of the poem, Glinka composed the ballade among the first numbers, making use of variation form in a stroke of genius.[27] This ballade is the center and key to the opera, for Finn, this benevolent sage, is companion to Ruslan throughout the latter's traversals (during the "peregrinations") of the "mysteries" of love. The music transforms the mischievous, dramatic impulse of Pushkin into a lyrical, contemplative narrative with tragic overtones.

The first trial of Ruslan, the first feat that he is required to accomplish, is that of surmounting the danger of an overly protracted struggle.[28] Finn reveals this symbolically to him in the ballade. The beautiful Lyudmila is gone. The fairy-tale visage of the fantastic Naina has replaced her, as the blizzards and winds of winter replace the countenance of spring, when it is concealed by evil powers. To what does this long *concealment of beauty* lead? The encounter with Finn gives an indication. The following scene with Farlaf—a scene suggestive of *skomorokhi* with deep folk roots—ridicules the idea of a feat in general. Let us not forget that the role of *skomorokhi* both in wedding and funeral rites was quite intricate and essential. Moreover, the juxtaposition of impotent but lascivious old age with the full potency and vital, masculine voluptuousness of a young lover extends back to ancient times, and even now makes for merry intrigue in the stock characters of the Italian *commedia dell'arte* and in *opera buffa*. Thus Farlaf's scene takes on the significance of a comedic intermezzo between the "rites of passage" through the mysteries.

The next feat of Ruslan is the scene with the [disembodied] Head.[29] It appears to be a purely fairy-tale episode, but the "symphonism"[30] of the introductory music to the aria "O field, field" and the tragic overtones in the tale of the Head deepen what is visible into the symbol of a new mystery to overcome. The pathos of the introduction to the aria and also its first half are a profound grieving and despair of solitude in the unpopulated, boundless steppes. The image of Lyudmila for an instant seizes the imagination of her groom and introduces the joyful expectation of a rendezvous, but the surrounding desolation and the hopelessness of the struggle distract his will from an active overcoming of grief and coax him toward passive contemplation. The feat in the desert—the overcoming of temptations of thought and inactive contemplation—is an archetypal image in mythological tales. Glinka's music is of such an inspired profundity that there can be no talk of fairy tales for the scene in the field, i.e., of the fairy tale being the goal for its own sake.

The third temptation and the third surmounting of the soul's stagnation and sloth is a struggle with voluptuous visions, arising as a result of inactive contemplation of beauty.[31] If jealousy is an impulse to act (recall the episode after the ballade in the scene with Finn), then the expenditure of the will's energy in the pursuit after mirages of the sentiments dissuades the will from actual power over a woman in order to impregnate her. The scene in Naina's castle presents the temptation of an aesthetic, unproductive contemplation of beauty: the attempt to exchange the goal with the means is a tarrying for the sake of sweet moments. The reappearance of Finn is the awakening of consciousness: contemplation of beauty alone cannot be the goal for a hero. Any stalling will lead to the point when the evil mask of Naina the hag will gape behind the face of youthful beauty. Finn is that wise and good angel who guides the soul through the labors and breaks the fetters of voluptuous visions just in time. The third-act finale portraying these complicated states of mind is developed extremely well. It is apparent that Glinka composed it with affection and was greatly fond of it. Moreover, the action of this act is choreographic.

The elasticity and rhythm of the dance are the bases of movement in it. And, frankly speaking, the sensory delusions of the "swarm of living visions" in Naina's castle are more captivating, pungent, and honey-sweet than the piquant aromas of the flowers in Klingsor's garden.[32]

In the fourth act, the action is momentarily interrupted, or more precisely, transferred over to Lyudmila. Like any other maiden, *she* must now face the temptations of luxury, riches, and erotic bliss.[33] A most tender and languid music (developed by Glinka almost in spite of its "scenic tedium") intoxicates and lulls Lyudmila to sleep. The sumptuous brilliance of the kingdom of the dwarf Chernomor, bereft of an actual creative will, cannot confuse Lyudmila and replace for her the vital and fertile power of Ruslan's love. But there is a profound and essential difference between the temptations stemming from Naina and Chernomor. Naina's intent is to dissipate the element of will by exchanging the passionate attraction for a beloved creature with infatuation and languor amidst phantasmal feminine forms. In such languor, masculine procreative energy is sapped. The intent of the temptation directed from Chernomor toward Lyudmila is to turn her away from an instinctive inclination to sacrifice her maidenhood to Ruslan and pervert the meaning of woman's love by exchanging it for the infatuation and contemplation of wealth and luxury. These are two of the greatest temptations (as we can also see in life), and those who are chosen or summoned to surmount them are nigh to sainthood and mystery. Lyudmila is intoxicated, but her will is not perverted.

The fourth temptation of Ruslan arises after he has ended an active struggle with a rival, with an evil power attempting to turn Lyudmila from ardent attraction and awaken in her unfruitful coquettishness.[34] The forces of life congeal in Lyudmila as on Earth during wintertime, when it is a fossilized, cold mass. Ruslan is faced with the trial of overcoming the resistance of ossified matter, which no longer radiates the magnetic current of love. Lyudmila is a bride: not a loving bride, offering herself under some resistance, but a cold and indifferent bride. Ruslan is confused. He is afraid of her sleep and of the violent force of Chernomor's spell over the sleeping unconscious beauty. The evil power that exploits his confused spiritual state has stolen Lyudmila anew. An awareness of the feat is aroused in Ruslan, and life energy increases therefrom: Finn hands over a magic talisman to Ruslan—a ring, the symbol of union. The creative will and ardent attraction of her husband reinvigorate Lyudmila as the Sun's rays penetrate into the Earth. Maidenly ignorance is transformed into the most sublime knowledge in the life of a woman who has sought insemination. Who else but the Earth, in experiencing the birth process, can know life? . . . In the music of the opera's finale, various themes are gaily juxtaposed, but at its foundation sounds the all-triumphant hymn to the Sun and to Joy.[35]

5

In wedding laments, rituals, and in all wedding rites of the Russian people nowadays, the religious *deistvo* and its rituals have apparently not been preserved as focal points. The pagan cult of marriage among the Slavs could not help being linked to the idea of fertilization and growth, with the mystery of the birth of life. At present, the Christian marriage ceremony stands at the center, while the wedding ritual carried out before and after it emerges as an entirely mundane ritual, associated with the interests and relationships of family, relatives, and the home. All of this is now abased and draped over with historical residue and local particulars, with a multitude of folk beliefs and superstitions, with drinking bouts and cynical details. Only in the bride's laments can one catch the idea of sacrifice and doom, while at the reception of the young pair with bread-and-salt and the strewing of oats, hops, and grain, there is an allusion to the association of the mystery of marriage with the nurturing soil. It is only a hint, since more than anything it is a symbol of domestic contentment and abundance in the future household of the newlyweds. On the whole, the wedding ritual is as fine as any other dramatically coherent act, especially in its remarkable songs and laments; but in essence, it is still an entirely commonplace phenomenon. Therefore, to introduce weddings rituals into a stage realization of *Ruslan and Lyudmila*, conditioned by everyday surroundings (moreover, with details of later provenance), is a grave error.[36]

Glinka's opera, being nurtured and reared by the artistic culture of folk creativity, stands apart from ordinary relationships and particulars. To construe a production of *Ruslan* out of a hodgepodge of everyday surroundings, epic, fantasy, and legend is senseless. Glinka's intention is more profound, more ancient, and the inner essence of it is the mysterious and religious source of life. In the aura of the hallowed one's rapture, in the idea of *ill-fatedness*, in the surmounting of an ossified milieu and the enmity of matter, in the gradual rising up toward the light—simply put, it is necessary to peer into the cult of "mysteries" and on this basis affirm the depth and greatness of *Ruslan*. Then, not only will individual sections of the music (especially the sunny finale) acquire teleological sense and significance, but the entire opera will be illumined by the light of Reason and appear to the world as a materialization of the sublimity of Oneness and Beauty, confirmed in the transformation of carnal desire and in the belief in the sanctity of the creative act, in the secret of the birth of life. Setting aside the libretto and surveying the action as a stimulus toward transformation through the surmounting of trials, we can unveil the opera's priestly ritual as dictated by the music.

The first act unfolds like a gigantic, majestic prologue in "oratorio style" (the first part of a liturgy), in which the following take place: (a) the sacrificial victim's preparation to offer herself for betrothal, which therefore gives occasion for laments: farewells to family, father, and friends, which would never, however, be understood in purely everyday garb. Parallel to this is: (b) the contemplation of beauty before the dedication of oneself to it, the contemplation ("examination") of virginal Lyudmila before the marriage mystery, from the standpoint of three representatives of masculinity: Ratmir, the aesthete of lust, in whom admiration and infatuation dominate over authentic masculinity; Ruslan, the courageous knight of life; and Farlaf, the symbol of a lazy but vain impotence. The three of them appear to weave together three ages in a man's life, three differing attitudes to feminine beauty. Next come the moment of blessing (dedication) and the oath of fidelity in love on the part of the hallowed ones. Svetozar was certainly not a historical prince, but a priest and holy man. With his prophesy, the action reaches the threshold of the mystery. The recitation of the blessing, the oath of the chosen man and woman, finally the choral prayer of the priests and priestesses ("Mysterious Lel"): it is all a marvelously formed ritual liturgical action.[37] Most striking here are the growth in the dynamics of the sound (the priest's shout, the duet, the ensemble followed by the chorus, emerging as a herald of the "mystery's" encroachment), and the astonishing rhythmic transformation (compare just the moments of the languor of the wedding couple and the mystical, holy palpitations of the supplicants). Finally, there is a contrast, albeit a mild one, in tonal coloration: E-flat major and B major. Had this merely been an ordinary wedding, then no more theater would have been required. The action should conclude when Ruslan and Lyudmila are led into the bedchamber. On stage, the feast might have continued, with Russian dances brought in, the tomfoolery of the *skomorokhi*, etc., etc.—all the effective means used in operas of everyday life.

Therein lies the monstrous misunderstanding of *Ruslan* and the blasphemous stance toward Glinka's genius. One recognizes him to be a great musician, finds innovation in *Ruslan*, yet simultaneously situates the opera into a kind of "median" position between two domains, i.e., between drama and symphonic music, as a two-sided work, which can never be placed in one or the other. And what is worse: since it is an "unsuccessful" work and yet also a great work, one must—like it or not—adapt it for an "impatient" audience and present *Ruslan* as a mélange of everyday milieu and fantasy, with a pointless finale, stretching out to no real end that does not appear to give the artists anything to do. Oh, how awful for the artists without "anything to do!" It's as if to say that when there *is* something for them to do in truly dramatic operas, then they genuinely recognize it and can do it. However, it is not only the artists and directors, but everyone: composers, conductors, set designers, and critics all have gone astray. So great is the temptation and immeasurably deep the intuitive intention of Glinka! The magic of art lies in the mystery and in the *unconscious* revelation of an *idea*, even though the illusion of free will and reason claims the opposite—as if we always create that which we desire! Such is the lure of subject, of plot. . . .

After bringing the action to the point of erotic ecstasy, to the mystical terror of the priests and supplicants as they face up to the act of presenting the sacrifice, the composer's intuition compelled him to cut short the desire just now attained, together with the accompanying satisfaction. The subject matter, being a means seized by intuition, holds within it a fitting schema: Chernomor kidnaps virginal Lyudmila. As in a mystery, the attraction is aroused to the utmost and passion is raised to a greedy intensity, through the contemplation of a desired Beauty. But the virgin vanishes, just at this impassioned instant. The hallowed one must overcome a series of trials, and only by the gradual attainment of degrees of purification can he become worthy of the attainment of truth. Desire and jealousy are aroused out of contemplation of her, but only in deeds and in the overcoming of inactivity is strength tempered. The abduction of the virgin is depicted by Glinka with brilliant laconism: through the power of the momentary hypnosis of a six-note scale of whole steps, which had not yet been exploited to the point of familiarity, the listener is suddenly transported into the plane of another world of sounds.[38]

The ancient myth of Persephone, of the eternal Virgin Spring kidnapped by Hades, enters into the action. The cyclic return of the seasons has taken its designated flight. In the introduction to the opera, a quite remarkable event attracts attention: the wonderfully sumptuous chorus along with Bayan's soothsaying strangely anticipate the wedding itself, i.e., the blessing and veneration of the wedding pair; the feast itself precedes the act of marriage, preparing for it. Is that not strange? But we hear it in the music: in its propriety, "solidity," in its depth and abundance, in its contentedness. Out of this kind of feast, a feast of adulthood, a feast of autumn harvest, a feast as celebration of the gathering of fruits, a wedding will quite naturally emerge, as it has long since been in those human communities whose life was closely tied to the rhythm and change of natural phenomena, and as typically occurs now in rural life. The fated departure of Persephone—if we may return to myth—is carried out at that imperceptible moment when autumn sinks to earth, when the earth offers its fruits to people, when, out of weariness, it sinks into sleep and peace. Cold and gloom begin to reign over it. There is an end to growth: the goddess of fertility (Demeter, Ceres) herself goes to seek her daughter. Winter ascends to the throne (Hades's Kingdom)—Lyudmila has been taken away. Ruslan enters into the sphere of the hallowed. Along with him, two other seekers desire to meet the test.

The action moves into a second phase: the liturgy of the Chosen, if one might employ the terms of liturgical structure developed in Christianity. I have already explicated the manner and course of the veneration in this phase of the action. The temptation to have seen the attainment as futile—due to the rapid passing of years and extended length of the deed—results in the tragedy of a delayed rendezvous, as was revealed in the fate of Finn and Naina. The temptation of despair over solitude, of the desert (the unpopulated steppe). The temptation of lust leading to oblivion (the garden and castle of Naina); and finally, the actual struggle with the demon of spite and the last temptation resulting from the coldness and indifference of the beloved woman (Lyudmila's sleep or unconsciousness under the intoxicating spells of Chernomor). Ruslan attains the highest level. His two rivals do not withstand the test: Farlaf is lured by the promise of receiving what he seeks without risk and worry (stagnation of the soul), while Ratmir, though captivated by Naina's maidens, upon the disappearance of the blindness caused by them, returns to his former life: to erotic bliss and the tranquility of the harem (Gorislava).

The action is entering into the last phase of development: the liturgy of the Faithful. In Svetozar's kingdom there is winter and sorrow. Lyudmila's lament is taking place: it is a *panikhida* [requiem], according to the accurate determination of Stasov, who had intuitively surmised the issue at hand. I would add: not a *panikhida*,[39] but rather a burial ritual (with priest and chorus, laments and burial hymns). Ruslan approaches, full of power and masculine will, with Finn's talisman as a symbol of triumph over the trials and the end of his experiences. Farlaf, the servant of ossification, loses his power over the bewitched maiden. The loyal bridegroom becomes a husband. The maiden is transformed into a woman, knowing the joy of the sacrifice that leads to renewal, since dynamic beauty, unveiling itself as it comes into being, is more vital than a frozen beauty, conceivable only in eternal contemplation. The melos of Lyudmila, as she awakens and returns to life, differs in coloration from all of her previous melodies: a spring morn's freshness and a brilliant vivacity emanate from it.[40] The grand and powerful, sunny D-major finale (the day awakens!) unfolds in the music, like an elemental fire spreading out and seizing without constraint an immeasurable expanse of sound. Light and joy, rapture and ardent exultation resound over the earth as on the Day of Resurrection. Praise Eros!

6

The pagan element of Slavic music, when infected with boundlessness and rootlessness (the protracted existence among the steppes, fields, and plains), occurs now in images of unchecked "drunken" merriment (a Mother Earth as nourisher), now in an austere, protracted moaning over an immeasurable distance (the Desert Mother). Ukraine and Poland in their lyricism (both vocal and dance-instrumental) soften these extremes: the former, thanks to the tender lyricism of loving relationships, unspiteful humor, and a good-natured smile for her own contradictory qualities; the second, thanks to a proud, self-infatuated delimitation and noble competition with Western culture, which permeates it without ever overcoming the Polish rhythm of life. Russia is cognizant of both primary extremes and, in addition, knows of malicious derision.

Glinka sensed the wealth in Russian culture that was tempered in colonization.[41] The stark and severe Russian vein in his creative art apparently aided him in heightening the extremes and the temptations, not just those surfacing in the ancestral influence but also in the culture of the West. He passed over a romanticism that was foreign to him on to the great knight of music, to austere Gluck and to the inspired master of composition nourished by the Italian melos, to Mozart; he returned to them and embraced them as an equal. Judging by the *Memoirs*, Glinka's rigorous study of Mozart and Gluck also continued after the creation of *Ruslan*. At the end of his life, he was striving yet further and deeper: toward the austere gothic strength and ardor of counterpoint. He overcame his natural effeminacy and the undefined vagueness of the Slavic element, being endowed with a remarkable instinct for harmonizing style and material. With regard to the latter, he had the well-developed elastic sense of touch that is germane only to a sculptor. His point of contact with antiquity, with Hellenism, emerges here. Glinka did not know Greece, but the general shift of his personal cultural milieu can be understood if one can merely sense a sculptor's pliancy in his music's melos and harmony and a pull toward classicism, to an irreproachable clarity of lines, a harmony and rigor in their intertwining and an unquestionable rule of mind over material and over the emotions. Even the wondrous coloration of Glinka's music is not a self-willed element, but merely a visible and audible wafting of air and light around priceless sculptures: turquoise waves of heaven, enveloping the marble statues of the gods.

Why is it acceptable to compare music to architecture, when its lofty humanity draws it toward the anthropomorphism of a Greek sculpture? Glinka was a great sculptor who found in music an audible instrument or obedient means for revealing the movements of his spirit. The image of a beautiful statue of a Greek goddess is the best analogy to the music of Glinka, since the sounds in it, of such lucid plasticity, could not arise outside of impressions from a contemplation of the body's beauty. Yet it is a dynamic contemplation, attained in a process of touching, of carving out the stone. A sculptor, in carving, already envisions the desired form, one suggested to him by the perception of life and known by intuition. But in the carved form, nothing remains of the feeling and no trace either of anything chance or mundane. All is directed toward the revelation of a well-reasoned, creative conception by imposing rhythm on the material, leaving no place for arbitrary choice, since the existence of every sculpted line, of every moment of sound is justified by a relationship with preceding and succeeding stages of sounding music. Such are the architectonics of *Ruslan's* "mysteries." The remarkable transformation of various spontaneous and fundamental influences that preconditioned Glinka's nature and organization, given the spiritual inclination in him toward sensitivity, tenderness, and erotic bliss, evokes both respect for his genius and amazement. Did he not chart out his own path of spiritual testing in the *odyssey* of his *Ruslan*? Evidently, the goal of the "ascents" was the unveiling of the most valued qualities of life and spiritual inclinations, which were squandered in vain on everyday life. A *rhythmicalization* of the soul: for Glinka, art, too, was such a sacred act, and by no means a diary.

The sense of all the venerations and preparations for the partaking in the "mystery" is always contained in the confession, the cleansing of the self, which is like a refining ("polishing") of a precious stone of spirituality. The mystery of marriage for humanity's chosen ones has always been one of the loftiest and deepest, being associated with the secret of the birth of life in general and the sanctified secret of fertilizing the soil, which offers the bread of life. The idea of overcoming grew naturally out of a contemplation of the struggle of the sun's rays with the cold and out of the farmer's labor over the field. The idea of "sacrifice" emerged from the natural gravitation and inclination of every organism toward crystallization, toward a stable occupancy of a single familiar state. Life surmounts any inclination toward ossification. Then beauty tempts. Man wishes to halt the passing of spring: in his blindness, he thinks that when something is brought to a halt it might live on without changing. A girl instinctively clings to girlhood, sensing her coming fate: the exchange of a girl's springtime beauty and youth for a woman's summer maturity. But in tarrying in girlhood, she grows old fruitlessly. The sun's energy overcomes the earth's cold, snowy shroud (underneath it the earth was warm!). And the active force of love wisely overcomes the mirage of eternal youth and, in violating virginity, chases away that sweet deception, the mirage of eternal bloom. Such is the growth of life and the path toward death, to a natural death, from the fulfillment of a cycle of life's destinies: to the death of a Hellene, but not to the death of medieval man, so terrified of Hell.

In art, humanity found an escape, found happiness, by preserving images of beauty in perpetuity. Everything that gives joy or grief to a human being can be transformed into pure human creativity and called to life through a reflection over the forms of art, at any desirable moment. But the core and essence of any religious ritual (emerging from the period of primordial animistic conjurations) and, especially, the kernel and vital significance of liturgy, and behind that, theatricality in general, lie considerably deeper: through the contemplation of images of veneration, the preparation for the mystery, the step-by-step ascent, and the presentation of the sacrifice, to guide the spirit to a knowledge of the meaning of life. This is the point of contact between the spheres of religion and art: of that which is invisible but wishes to become incarnate and that which is visible but transient, with the desire to become immortal. Although an active religion demands a genuine feat, a definite entering into the mysteries, in a Divine service the *mystery* is revealed in *images*, in the beauty of speculation. Art preserves in liturgy the beauty of sublime religious revelations in imperishable form: through art we can attend the mystery's fulfillment. What a powerful impulse for a feat! . . . Therefore the significance of music in liturgy is profound, productive, and full of meaning. And if *for those not chosen* the theater was a passage into contemplation over that which was demanded of the chosen and the venerated, in reality and concretely, then the significance of the idea of liturgical practice in relation to the link between religion and art and the concept of the liturgy as a form, wherein the religious act and the "artificial" artistic *deistvo* are merged and interpreted, becomes completely clear and an entirely logical connection between liturgical tragedy and opera can be observed. Then, too, the "Florentine reform" of music ceases to be a chance, contrived phenomenon. But this is another matter. . . .[42]

The liturgical quality of Glinka's *Ruslan* is certain to me. Otherwise all the greatness of this music is a mirage and a conjuration, while its significance is paltry and transitory, for music cannot be great, when it only deceptively draws near to the secret of how the sun's rays are transformed into the juice of grapes but, in actual fact, is blasphemously indifferent, removed from the mysteries of life itself and raised to an abstract symbol of fleshless and fruitless play of sounds. Such a pronouncement would be fraught with terrible consequences for the philosophy of Russian music and for Russian music itself with respect to its foundations, pathways, influence, and the character of future achievements. The extremes of fancy designs and "psychologism" are incompatible with the creative genius of Glinka. He gleans images from within the mysteries of life, and therefore he is deeper and more archaic; although he stands near to the sources of Romanesque European culture (albeit without gothic asceticism), he is too much a Hellenist in spirit and, in addition, a naive Siegfried of the North in the body. It seems that Glinka was not unfamiliar with aestheticism and craved just to conjure up, summon, and sense living Beauty at any desirable moment through the magic of sound. But beauty in music, when summoned and made incarnate, like a ripe fruit and rich fiery wine, bubbles and boils, drawing our spirit into a contemplation of life's growth, flourishing, and maturation. It does not wish to be captive to the architectonics of sound, not having been created for the pleasure of the experts of moribund schemas. The intensity in the music of Glinka stems from Eros, and to him is dedicated the chief, the supreme achievement: *Ruslan and Lyudmila*. After a long procession of centuries, a grateful Scythian has honored the memory of his teachers, the Greeks. *Ruslan* is a Feast of the Sun.

NOTES

1. The poet and playwright Nestor Kukolnik (1809–1868) was introduced to Glinka in 1835. In addition to giving much advice and moral support, he provided lines of text for *A Life for the Tsar* and was initially the composer's choice to write *Ruslan*'s libretto.

2. In his essay "Mikhail Ivanovich Glinka" (1857) and other writings, Vladimir Stasov's main complaint about *Ruslan* (a work he referred to *A Life for the Tsar*) had to do with the drama, which he considered to be both ineffective and fragmented, two faults easily blamed on the libretto.

3. The parting words from the resurrected Astrologer in *The Golden Cockerel* occur in the opera's epilogue, forming a symmetrical albeit cynical close to a work that began with his invitation to the audience to listen to a moral tale.

4. The reference is to Grigory Kotoshikhin (1630–1667), a civil servant and ambassador under Tsar Alexei Mikhailovich, then traitor, emigrant, writer, and murderer. His innocuously named tell-all chronicle *On Russia During the Reign of Alexei Mikhailovich* contains a satirical account of the Boyars' Duma in session.

5. Narratives involving the *bogatyr* Eruslan Lazarevich date back to 17th-century Russia, at which time an initial adaptation was made from a tenth-century Persian epic poem describing the exploits of a hero named Rustem, who at one point is transformed into a lion [*araslan*]. Most Russian sources include the encounter with the still animate severed head of a giant that was preserved by Pushkin and placed in the opera's second act by Glinka. As Asafyev indicates, the Eruslan of legend was a two-dimensional warrior, defined merely by heroic acts and competitive zeal.

6. Asafyev quotes lines from the rivals Ruslan and Ratmir found in *Ruslan*'s second act aria (No. 8) and first act finale, soon after Lyudmila's abduction (no. 3, fig. 49 + 13). Third rival Farlaf's cowardice is a running theme in the opera, culminating in the buffo aria "The hour of my triumph is near" (Act 2, no. 7).

7. The duettino (Act 2, no. 6) following Finn's ballad of protracted, unrequited love expresses anxiety along with bravado. And it is a crestfallen Ruslan who sings in the Act 4 finale (no. 22), after he discovers that he is unable to awaken Lyudmila.

8. Glinka's *Memoirs* span the years from childhood until 1854 and were first published in 1870. An English translation by Richard B. Mudge is available, published as: Mikhail Ivanovich Glinka, *Memoirs* (Norman: University of Oklahoma Press, 1963).

9. Blessed with Onegin's range of interests, equal wit, but documentably superior gifts for languages (not least, Persian!), poetry, and music, Glinka made for good

company, both at home and abroad. Numerous passages in the *Memoirs* attest to the expert musician's knack for extracting telling details from scores and performances; others reveal his obsession with health and a cavalcade of ailments. The following extracts are representative of his "Russian epicureanism." Concerning a visit to the Caucasus, he recalled: "My companions and I moved into a modest little house. Life was pleasant: my friend had brought a supply of books and the kitchen was in good order. Excellent mutton, chicken, game, and superb fruit enabled our cooks to feed us well, while bottles of Santurino wine (which I still like to drink) replaced the expensive bottles we had brought with us" (*Memoirs*, 25). And from Granada: "Meeting a pretty Gypsy girl one time I asked her if she could sing and dance. She said yes, so I invited her and some of her friends to a party. Murciano made all the arrangements, and also played guitar for us. . . . I tried to learn how to dance myself from a local dancing girl named Pello. My legs obeyed all right, but I couldn't manage the castanets" (*Memoirs*, 201).

10. Alexander Serov first met Glinka in 1838 or 1839 and maintained the acquaintance until Glinka's death in 1857. Serov's *Memoirs of Glinka* were first published in 1860; a reprint with commentary by Vladimir Protopopov was published in 1951.

11. Salieri's epithet for the Mozart of Pushkin's "little tragedy," *Mozart and Salieri.*

12. Orlova's note from the second edition of Asafyev's *Etiudy* points the interested reader to the transcription of Glinka's initial plan for *Ruslan*, together with comments, to be found in *M. I. Glinka. Literaturnoe nasledie*, v. 1 (Moscow–Leningrad: Muzgiz, 1952): 315–39, 438–39.

13. Pavel Nashchokin (1801–1854) was wealthy, generous, eccentric, convivial, and therefore a source of fascination and pleasurable company for his friend Pushkin.

14. The Berlin-based theorist Siegfried Dehn (1799–1858) was Glinka's revered teacher for approximately five months, beginning in 1833. Glinka's younger sister Lyudmila Ivanovna Shestakova (1816–1906) supported her brother both emotionally and at times financially. In 1854 it was she who insisted he write his memoirs. After his death, she continued to promote his works, appear publicly at commemorations, and accept visits from prominent members of the next generation of Russian-born composers.

15. Although Serov's *Memoirs of Glinka* contains excellent descriptions of the older composer's singing and piano playing, as well as firsthand impressions of *Ruslan*'s premiere, he allowed precious few of the older composer's actual words to make it into print. Moreover, Serov's insistent polemicizing, which is all too evident throughout the book, may explain why Glinka walked away from him at parties (*Memoirs*, 57–58).

16. Orlova identified the editor as Mikhail Wielhorski, 1788–1856 (*Etiudy*, 255, n. 8).

17. Herman Larosh's lengthy essay, "Glinka and His Significance in the History of Music," was published in 1867–1868.

18. Prince Vladimir Fyodorovich Odoyevsky (1804–1869) was a writer and critic with a Hoffmannesque range of interests. His two reviews of *Ruslan* were published in 1843 and 1858.

19. Glinka's composition of *Ruslan* began late in the summer of 1837, even though the librettist Valery Shirkov was commissioned to draft a libretto only in the spring of 1838.

20. The two pink-granite Egyptian sphinxes on the Neva Embankment were excavated by an archaeological expedition of the 1820s and imported to St. Petersburg shortly thereafter.

21. Pushkin wrote the mock-epic poem of nearly 3,000 lines in 1817–1820. Though drawing on Russian folk motifs from the Eruslan stories and elsewhere, the work is also a response to Ossian and to Ariosto's *Orlando furioso*.

22. A representative reminiscence of his 1832 stay in Varese, Italy: "The arrival of Emilia Branca incited me to work still more; she was an unusually well-built girl and quite pretty. She pleased me, and it seems that she, for her part, did not find me unbearable, so that the time passed pleasantly in friendly talks, walks, and divers occupations" (*Memoirs*, 74).

23. The reference is to Glinka's final trip abroad, which gave him the opportunity to reacquaint himself with Dehn, initially for the purpose of studying the counterpoint of Palestrina and Lassus.

24. *Slovo o polku Igoreve* [The Song of Igor's Campaign] is an 861-line poem written in 1187, chronicling a 12th-century prince's defeat by the Kumans. Its main content survived 16th-century editorial corruptions and the loss of the manuscript during the burning of Moscow in 1812.

25. A passing reference to the peasant who gave his life for (future) tsar and country in Glinka's first opera.

26. The tale of Finn takes up lines 310–529 of Pushkin's *Ruslan*. After repeated rejections from Naina over a period of years, he finally resorts to sorcery, only to discover that he no longer loves the now aged sorceress.

27. The main part of the ballade (Act 2, no. 5) is a strophic song (with episodes) in A major, beginning in m. 67, justly renowned for its changes of orchestration and affect.

28. Since there is no action in the first part of Act 2, Ruslan experiences this first "trial" vicariously as old Finn recounts his sad story of a protracted struggle in vain to win the heart of Naina (No. 5: Finn's Ballad). In the next scene the poltroon Farlaf meets Naina herself, then sings his comic rondo in anticipation of the triumph he envisions.

29. The setting for the final scene of Act 2 is a boundless battlefield, where Ruslan will be presented with the spectacle of a huge disembodied head (its voice produced by a unison men's chorus), belonging to a giant who is brother to the dwarf Chernomor. Ruslan becomes passive and self-doubting (revealing the main challenge of Asafyev's second "feat") in the introduction to his aria "O field" (No. 8). Courage is regained during the cabaletta section, which includes a theme familiar from the overture.

30. By 1922, Asafyev's term *simfonizm* was a central concept within his evolving musical aesthetics, drawing attention to the quality of "musical stream of consciousness"—i.e., developmental process, not schema!—that was best exemplified by the symphonies of Beethoven and Tchaikovsky's Sixth, yet was also present in other music not scored for orchestra. In the usage here, however, it may refer merely to the appearance of an untexted orchestral act prelude.

31. The setting of Act 3 and Ruslan's third feat is the magic castle of Naina. First Ratmir and then Ruslan are seduced by bewitching maidens (for whom Glinka composed the opera's first set of dances, No. 15) until both are rendered passive and oblivious of their larger concerns. Eventually Finn will arrive to break the magic spell and rescue both Ratmir and Ruslan.

32. Asafyev refers to the flowers in the garden outside the magician Klingsor's castle, as depicted in Act 2, scene 2 of *Parsifal*.

33. As Asafyev states, the captive Lyudmila must face temptations of her own as she resists enticements of wealth, power, and erotic bliss in the castle of her abductor Chernomor. These events take up most of Act 4; her fortitude registers most in the series of exchanges with a rather insipid chorus of maidens occurring in the extended "scene and aria" (No. 18), structured as an elaborate cavatina-cabaletta with chorus. Thereafter a march (No. 19) establishes Chernomor's infernal power, and a set of three "oriental" dances (No. 20: Turkish, Arabian, Lezghinka) his extravagant wealth.

34. Asafyev found a fourth temptation for Ruslan to overcome in the finale (No. 22) of Act 4. Reappearing with the beard of the vanquished foe Chernomor, he is stunned to see Lyudmila be absolutely unresponsive to him. Although he rallies his sinking spirits in the brisk concluding march, he will not see her awaken until the penultimate number in Act 5, where once again Finn's magic will come to his aid.

35. With bride and bridegroom reunited, the opera can conclude with a celebratory ensemble finale in D major. The main thematic material is taken from the first theme group and coda of the overture, with the tempo accelerated to a blazing *prestissimo*.

36. Margarita Mazo's article, "Stravinsky's *Les noces* and Russian Wedding Ritual" (*Journal of the American Musicological Society* 43 [1990]: 99–142), contains much material that would pertain to Asafyev's notion of Russian folk wedding rituals.

37. Svetozar's blessing of the wedding couple occurs at the outset of the finale (Act 1, no. 3). The addition of voices changes a matrimonial duet into a quintet, both in E-flat major. When the chorus enters (no. 3, m. 90: singing in stark octaves) to invoke the god Lel, the key changes to B major; the tempo to a driving, pulsating allegro; and the meter to 5/4 time.

38. As fascinating and gripping as the descending whole-tone scale in *fortissimo* trombones (no. 3, mm. 166–71) are the various dissonant nontriadic sonorities and prolonged (31 mm.) tonal ambiguity that Glinka composed for Lyudmila's inexplicable abduction by an unseen and unknown entity.

39. The *panikhida* can be considered a Russian Orthodox requiem service.

40. After some perhaps half-conscious echoing of Ruslan's phrases, Lyudmila finally awakes (no. 27, mm. 225–26) and, in the very next phrase, ascends by accented eighths to a high C, then A, B-flat, etc.

41. In 1970 Orlova considered it necessary to note that Asafyev did not employ the term "colonization" in its present-day sense, but meant instead the "development and organization of a culture" (*Simfonicheskie etiudy*, 266, n. 17).

42. Asafyev revisits the origins of opera in Chapter 16, p. 234.

• 2 •

Intermezzo I

Ba! Chto v gólovu pridyót, To i
skazhú byez predugotovlénya
Improvizátorom lyubóvnoi pyésni

[Bah! What comes to mind,
I will speak without preparation
As improviser of songs of love]

—Pushkin, *The Stone Guest*[1]

In my opinion, this is the best characterization of Dargomyzhsky's *Stone Guest*.[2] It is an improvisation: magnificent, concise, driving, free musical speech, not contained in a schema and flexibly following the verse. There is no need for comparisons to Wagner, nor talk of reform. However much the argument is prolonged, when held up to Wagner's grandiose and philosophical musico-poetic realizations, Dargomyzhsky's conception remains a hothouse plant. And it is certain that no benefit will come to the Russian musician from concluding that, with the German master, all the expressive force is contained in the orchestra, whereas here the center of gravity is found in the voices, set to a transparent orchestral accompaniment, but still with identical content. Far from it! Once and for all, we must agree: in Wagner there is symphonism, in Wagner a power and grandeur of conception, an unbounded development, musical and poetic. For him there was something to reform but also something to outgrow and leave behind as he went his way. And here with us? Did Glinka stand in need of reforming? For Dargomyzhsky, he remained an unattainable ideal, and it could not be otherwise. At the same time, for a Russian composer to reform either the mistakes or the stereotypical devices of Italian opera would have amounted to chasing windmills.

The greatness of *Stone Guest* is not found in the grandiosity of the reforms that it supposedly engendered but in its uniqueness, unrepeatability, and particularity. Dargomyzhsky, it is said, prepared the way for Musorgsky. This may be true, but not in the sense of the schools of the great masters of painting, where the student would inherit the *techniques* of the teacher, at first living off of them and developing on the basis of them. When Dargomyzhsky was still alive, Musorgsky went his own way already in *The Marriage*, speaking a language that had nothing in common with the language of *The Stone Guest*.[3] The idiosyncrasies of this work by Dargomyzhsky, completed just before his death, are so striking, fresh, and *unrepeatable* that there is nothing to compare it with and no conclusions to draw from it. A unicum, therefore, and nothing more; or, if you like, a miracle, the outcome of an overwhelmingly bold conception.

This is the essence of the *distinction*, but not the ideological foundations of this work, viz., *the principles of a chamber style transferred to opera*. In this respect, *The Stone Guest* is perfection itself, for, in spite of its sheltered and hothouse qualities, it resolves the problem of characterizing an opera's *dramatis personae* with the aid of the most intense development, not broadly but deeply: not by increasing the means of expression, but reducing them. In place of consolidation there occur a deepening and enhancing of each individual's undertakings in the drama and an inspired utilization of the energy that is contained in each actual element of the action. The result: a supple characterization of actions and experiences emanating from the creation of highly detailed inflections and nuances in the vocal language for each of the *dramatis personae*. Each character intones a manner of speech peculiar to himself, profusely enriched with emotional shadings, whose perception offers unbelievably rich satisfaction: yet only in the act of perceiving, as in the examination of a miniature. The powerful impression is enhanced even more since in this case there can be no talk either of a strict structure or of a formal and strictly logical development. All of the organically proportioned succession of sounds is achieved only through a *vivid* use of the timbres and nuances of the human voice, apart from the demands of schematic form. I repeat: it is a brilliant improvisation. And the Stone Guest himself acts here as *deus ex machina*, cleaving through the *commedia dell'arte* intrigue, but not in the spirit of that Stone Guest whose mysterious presence and aura in Pushkin are felt everywhere from the first scene on, directing all of the action like an invisible yet vigilant force.[4] In Dargomyzhsky, the Stone Guest is a ponderous mass, immobile in his "whole-tone-ishness,"[5] and not at all a genuine temperament, so that the very idea of the Stone Guest presents itself in the opera as a mechanical resolution, but not a *basis of the action* as in Pushkin. From a purely stylistic standpoint, it could not be otherwise, for in order to offset the supple transitoriness of speech in all scenes, some sort of a foundation or a fulcrum needed to emerge—not among the human beings but in the sphere of the next world—a statue-like element, which turns to ice the impetuosity of aspirations. It needed to emerge, if not as a mystical imperative, then as a stylistic necessity. In Pushkin it leads and sets the course. In Dargomyzhsky, it only weighs it down.

In the latter's *The Stone Guest*, however, one quality is perhaps the most significant and salient. It is a deeply nationalistic work, conceivable only in the Russia of the 19th century, where the reign of the purely vocal element had not yet come to an end. We are not accustomed to reckoning for ourselves its might and splendor, even though we well know that in folk music melos is everything. In the boundless ocean of its manifestations, one can distinguish between pure melos—melody proper—and *skaz*,[6] i.e., musical speech in all degrees by which it is manifested, from church psalmody to hawkers' cries. Herein lie the roots and sources of Dargomyzhsky's musically authentic speech, here the reason for the *isolation* of his most important work, a work incomprehensible both to foreigners and to many Russians. It is the isolation of greatness. . . . Not in an ethnographic sense and not in an imitative sense, but for its manifestation of a single element of expressivity: *The Stone Guest* is a work deeply rooted in the folk, since it emerges out of the vocal (song) element that is recreated within the realm of *skaz*, speech, and recitative. By this I do not wish to say that Dargomyzhsky's *Stone Guest* is a stylization of one or another type of *skaz*. No, the point is that without a flourishing and development of the *skaz* in highly organic folk music, Dargomyzhsky would not have had the instinct to devise such a conception. And were it to have arisen only out of the intellect, then the composer would have been obliged to erect a house in the sand, i.e., one lacking support from within, and he would have needed to import foreign elements.

One must avow that the *musicality* of Dargomyzhsky, the creator of *Stone Guest's* melodic-arioso style, and the *musicality* of the folk, elaborating the flexible, succulent, and brightly colored intonational world of the real-life *recitative*, the *skaz* of the *bylina*, and *sacred verse* do not stand infinitely far apart from one another and could not remain foreign to one another. Somewhere in the psychic depths of each there is a shared tendency engendering an expressive common ground. The roots of *The Stone Guest* lie in the Russian musical *skaz*, although it is certain that under the influence of personal tastes, recent impressions, and an inclination toward expressivity aided by far from archaic means, Dargomyzhsky progressed quite far, thanks to a refined ear and instinct. The *chamber* quality and intimacy in the style of this work make a flexible following of the text a requirement, yet these enclose the work in the confines of restrictions and conventionality, no matter how paradoxical this latter claim might seem. *The Stone Guest* is inaccessible precisely because of its artistic aristocraticism: its melodic-recitative speech and its detailed nuances, proceeding without restriction, demand a colossal intensity of attention, for though the contours of this speech are sharp, the points of reinforcement differ and are found elsewhere from where we are used to encountering them: such is indeed a property of the structure of the improvisation.

In the end, this work is exemplary with regard to stylistic integrity and with regard to psychologically expressive characterizations, a work guided not by way of a purely symphonic but by an exclusively vocal-intonational method of realization. Just as a spring from the bowels of the earth may feed a fountain that sparkles under the sun in a luxuriant artificial garden, so did *skaz*-recitative from the folk come to life in a work that appeared unexpectedly. This is not a reform but a synthesis of possibilities hidden from view.

Borodin's *Prince Igor* is a Russian operatic unicum of an entirely different kind. There can be no talk here of improvisation. Borodin is immobile and ponderous. His thought was formal and solid. He applied his thoughts to uncomplicated but taut and tightly joined schemas. The plot of *Igor* was for him an accommodating means for revealing the fundamental contrasts of the Russian soul. The vastness of the steppes, the broad unending fields give birth in the soul both to a wild thirst for freedom and to a fearful apprehension before the vast distance: hence, a holding back in comfort for the time being. Prior to his victories and recognition, the hero Ilya stays put for thirty-three years, as strength gradually builds up within him.[7] Another example is even more to the point: that mystical genius of Russian art, Vrubel, has a painting showing an aged hero stock-still together with his mount in the middle of the field: the earth has swallowed up and consumed him; an inert force has overcome the energy of motion and achievement.[8] The epos *Prince Igor* initially proved to be the expression for Borodin of a great "nomadic" power not yet addressed in music: with the vital untamed rhythm of his ingenious "Polovtsian Dances" the composer "trampled" the earth. Nevertheless, through calm, good-natured contemplation of the nobility and beauty of the human soul alone, he could not conquer that other power—the force pulling him down. Thus he did not complete his task, did not pull himself together and, like Vrubel's hero, he became bound to earth. Thus it was not the impetuous forces in his nature that gained the upper hand, nor the wild Polovtsian freedom, but rather a constructive and colonizing foundation.

Step by step, year by year, like ancient Russian princes, Borodin conquered untouched virgin lands. The prologue he created for his opera was ingenious in its concentration of human energy and Handelian in scope.[9] And he painted like no other musician the hard but familiar picture of the ravaging of the native soil ("How downcast all around") and described it as would a chronicler, succinctly and expressively.[10] Over this ravaged plain he shed bitter tears—and sang a long-breathed Russian song, like a resounding moan (the renowned *a cappella* peasants' chorus in the last act).[11] With the utmost fervor, he created authentic Russian song, not a stylization or arrangement of it: a song of staggering expressivity.

Borodin also knew the other qualities in the Russian soul. A hidden force can be intuited there, as in the depths of the earth, but one that is malicious and scornful. Such a force is vividly expressed in the cynical and licentious music of Vladimir Galitsky and his sidekick *skomorokhi*, the rebeck players Skula and Yeroshka.[12] When suppressed or unsuccessful at revealing itself, this force can disguise itself as toadying complaisance and servility, even to take the side of what it has slandered. Borodin knew of this as well and could present it in brief (in the scene with the rebeck players in the last act of *Igor*).

But the beauty in the composer's soul is most vividly and fully revealed in his bright, flowing lyricism, especially in the realization of the character of a Russian woman—mistress of the Russian land, proud and majestic in her loyalty to the duty of a princess—and in evoking the enchanting quality of a woman in love (Yaroslavna's celebrated lament).[13] Every instance of Borodin's lyricism is a jewel. And a jeweled necklace lies before us: from Yaroslavna's premonitions (the first act arioso), to the song of a Polovtsian maiden and Konchakovna's cavatina, the "serenade" of the young prince, the lyrical "pauses" in Igor's aria, Yaroslavna's recitative and lament and, finally, the concluding duet.[14]

Strength in tranquility and the force of rage (the prologue and the finale to the Polovtsian act); the power of *deception* and *disbelief*, insolently ravaging the surroundings in drunkenness and outrage (the scene at Prince Galitsky's); and the strength of piety, concentrated on restraining and safeguarding (the boyars and Yaroslavna): Borodin felt it all and like no one else made it real.[15] Moreover, he intuited the mysterious connection between natural phenomena and the rhythm of the people's lives, and he knew that a visible disruption to the usual order of events in the heavens has a powerful influence on people and shakes up their customary impressions and life regimen. With a few brilliant strokes in the opera's prologue, he portrays ("paints with sound") the solar eclipse and does so with so much expression that the impression remains indelibly imprinted on the mind. The chords for the eclipse truly freeze the action; appearing only once, they impose a mystical stamp on all that comes after them, carrying an element of tragedy with them.[16]

The rhythmic flow in Borodin's music is for the most part calm and smooth. Healthy and radiant is this music. It indicates a positive nature, a harmoniousness and fundamental monism in Borodin's worldview.

Everything transpires in a single indivisible stream or process. The life force is all one. Peacefulness or debauchery are only varying degrees of its manifestation. There is no evil power in the world. There are, however, varying *degrees* in the revelation of humanity as well as varying levels of life energy. There are also differences in temperament (Polovtsians and Russians), as well as differences in character (Igor—Konchak—Vladimir Galitsky), but each of these "differences" is not established as a force unto itself: each emerges only in the course of one or another type of relationship. Everything progresses according to a logical order. Neither irascibility nor spiritual distress have a place in this music. Yet the force of talent and the charming freshness of the material that is called to life are such that the regular, steady light that has spread throughout all the music, its "engorgement" or satiety with vital juices, its steady regularity and robust health will exercise an irresistible influence and seize the soul to its very depths and do so quite differently from the "positive heroes" in literature.

I consider *Prince Igor* a work profoundly of the people, on account of the authenticity of its approach to the task at hand: not from the standpoint of action ("drama") as externally conceived, but founded on the concept of an elemental force and on the constant contact of the people with natural life. The calm, concentrated, well-contemplated life experience of Borodin offers a more or less objective approach to life through music, as opposed to distorting life by means of nervous palpitations and despair. Borodin is a poet-chronicler. *Prince Igor* is an epic poem, permeated with a lyrical temperament, suffused with melos and the beloved breath of life's aroma, and with the birth, growth, struggle, and downfall of interchanging "forces." A mature, equanimous approach to life emanating from a person of ardent heart and clean thought: such is the impression, both indelible and indispensable, that one takes away from Borodin's music. Yet still that image of Vrubel's *bogatyr* will not vacate the memory. Perhaps it must be so: the will of one who remains undisturbed by that which is transitory but continues on in the contemplation of life's profundities, who does not contradict fate but faces misfortune like the boyars in *Prince Igor*, who does not object to the laws of the world, who is content with the lot of a human being—the will of such a one must sooner or later unite with the will of those forces it contemplates and transform itself into them: thus, perhaps like Sviatogor, to take root in the earth.[17]

Like an oak uprooted by the storm, Borodin died, seized up by the hurricane of death that suddenly tore him from life without any sign of illness.[18] Everything that constituted his self, his single and indivisible individuality, was consumed in an instant; having failed to outlive its utility, it vanished as does every countenance in order to merge into the infinite and impersonal order of all things. In the music of Borodin the Cosmos prophesies.

NOTES

1. When Pushkin's Don Juan speaks the quoted verse in scene 3, he stands in the cemetery where the Commendatore is buried, planning his second seduction of Donna Anna (whom Pushkin turned into the victim's now celibate widow, not daughter). Hence an analogy is suggested between the character's spontaneous (yet rhymed) speech and Dargomyzhsky's through-composed (yet metered) arioso.

2. The work that Asafyev calls an improvisation was an attempt at turning Pushkin's eponymous "little tragedy" in verse into an opera with only minimal use of closed forms and form-shaping key centers. For a partisan, Dargomyzhsky achieved more than sustained generic arioso. Using little more than the rhythms and intervallic shapes of the vocal lines, he created atmosphere, personality, and emotional flux, not to mention matchless setting of the text.

3. Since Dargomyzhsky worked on *The Stone Guest* from 1866 to 1869 and Musorgsky finished the eleven scenes of *The Marriage* in 1868, Asafyev is correct to claim a relationship of concurrence, not derivation. The conceptions and styles are also dissimilar, since Musorgsky's opera is an adaptation of a prose play set in non-lyrical recitative.

4. Asafyev must be reacting to a sparse staging of Pushkin's play, since the Statue speaks a total of fourteen words, all on the last page of the play.

5. Even though Glinka's association of the whole-tone scale with a supernatural character and supernatural events in *Ruslan* is the indisputable precedent, Dargomyzhsky's usage has the distinction of being both more protracted, developmental, and hence, more akin to the Wagnerian leitmotiv.

6. It is curious that both of Asafyev's discussions of musical *skaz* were sparked by operatic adaptations of rhymed and metered Pushkin texts, whereas his colleagues Shklovsky and Eikhenbaum at the Russian Arts Institute initially focused more on prose. For further comments, see Chap. 10, n. 1.

7. For his first reference to a *bogatyr*, Asafyev chose Ilya Muromets, an invalid from birth until his miraculous cure at age 33. Thereafter he fought the Tatars at Chernigov, slayed the "Nightingale" Bandit (he of the transfixing whistle), and joined Prince Vladimir's knights in Kiev. Muromets was also the inspiration for a programmatic symphony by Gliere, composed 1909–1911.

8. Mikhail Vrubel (1856–1910) was both a painter and a set designer for several Rimsky-Korsakov and Tchaikovsky operas; he would later figure in Diaghilev's *World of Art* circle. In his painting *The Bogatyr* (oil on canvas for a decorative panel, 1898), a massive, motionless, squat knight in full armor sits on a massive, squat horse, the pair of them dominating the painting.

9. Asafyev here draws attention to the drama and scope of the opera's large multisectional choral prologue, not to stylistic particulars.

10. Asafyev quotes the opening words of Yaroslavna's Lament.

11. The SATB mixed chorus (No. 26, "'Twas Not a Stormy Wind That Wailed") precedes the final duet of Yaroslavna and Igor.

12. Under the assumption that the *skomorokhi* of Russian history originated somewhat later than the 12th century, the rebeck players Skula and Eroshka of *Prince Igor* should not be classified as such.

13. Yaroslavna's Lament (No. 25, "Ah, Bitterly I Weep") is heard in Act 4.

14. The seven vocal numbers (which by no means exhaust the lyrical "jewels" of the opera) are as follows: (1) Yaroslavna's arioso (Act 1, no. 3); (2) the chorus of the Polovtsian Maidens (Act 2, no. 7); (3) Konchakovna's cavatina (Act 2, no. 9); (4) Prince Vladimir's recitative and cavatina (Act 2, no. 11); (5) Prince Igor's aria (Act 2, no. 13, e.g., the D-flat-major center); (6) Yaroslavna's Lament (Act 4, no. 25); and (7) Yaroslavna's recitative and duet with Igor (Act 4, no. 27).

15. Asafyev has referred to the following four numbers: (1) the prologue (Act 1, no. 1); (2) the Polovtsian finale (Act 2, no. 17); (3) the scene at Prince Galitsky's (Act 1, no. 2); and (4) the finale to Act 1 (no. 6).

16. The four chords in the winds alternate with pedal points in string tremolo, beginning 14 mm. before fig. H in the Prologue.

17. The *bogatyr* Sviatogor, a curiously ambivalent fellow who never accomplished the usual feats of valor, dwarfed all the other *bogatyri* in size, yet suffered the fate of being buried alive in a giant casket underneath the Holy Mountains (Svyatye gory).

18. Borodin's death on 15/27 February 1887 from heart failure occurred seconds after he collapsed during a grand ball sponsored by his medical academy.

· 3 ·

Nikolai Andreyevich Rimsky-Korsakov
(1844–1908)

$\mathcal{T}$he professional pursuits and creative output of Nikolai Andreyevich Rimsky-Korsakov encompass a finely balanced multitude of diverse overlapping and interwoven life inclinations, directions, and achieved goals.

No other Russian musician (excepting, perhaps, Sergei Taneyev[1]) reveals to us over the course of his life such a striking picture of a fully conscious approach to art as a vital undertaking and, consequently, as a moral imperative of deed, duty, and instruction. The three ramifications of moral purpose (deed, duty, and the teaching profession) can only become life-transforming and be realized when two fundamental imperatives for the self, for will and thought, are present in the individual consciousness: strict discipline (i.e., a lifestyle that permits no chance deviations from the path that is laid out once and for all) and ceaseless labor, both in the sense of spiritual self-fulfillment and the development of one's talents, as well as in the procuring and consolidating of purely technical skill, in order to become an experienced master in one's craft, freely taking charge of any given material.

Rimsky-Korsakov structured his life strictly and harmoniously. Creative work was a duty for him, since he was obligated to develop the talent bestowed on him and to work out the dictates of his creativity, making note of everything in it that was incidental and immature. This he attained. Being a great master, he did not disdain to be a craftsman, working out in the minutest detail the technical devices and methods (the means for the most productive control of the material under study) of musical composition, i.e., of the process of transforming irregular sound masses into well-shaped patterns and forms.

Life for him was a deed, since he was obliged to move step-by-step toward the achieving of his true calling and position as a composer, not being satisfied with an ill-defined existence in the realm of the dilettante, i.e., when it is not a wholehearted personal devotion to art, but only a "leisure time" activity. Labor and work were the catalysts in the life of Rimsky-Korsakov.

Possessed of an idiosyncratic and wholly individual musical talent, so that even in his earliest works he immediately distinguished himself as a personality and individual, not an imitator, Rimsky-Korsakov nevertheless took on the study of the works of the great masters from the past, replenishing the stock of sound material already under his control with the experiences of previous pursuits and achievements.

A hidden danger lay therein, that of becoming an imitator and an arid collector (anthologist) of alien ideas. But Rimsky-Korsakov knew how to assimilate: he developed the musical legacy of Glinka, for example, in such a particular and idiosyncratic manner that it would be inconceivable to see only cold and passionless mastery of the craft.[2] He commanded a special acuity for the organization and fusing together of elements, i.e., for the proper articulation and interactive juxtaposition of various sound combinations that he found to be in existence prior to him either in isolation or else released *in vain.*

Predisposed to a precise form of thought, suspicious of anything incidental, Rimsky-Korsakov gave no respite to any useful theme that came into his head, until he had exploited it to the limits of the possibilities hidden within. Keeping all the while to his own path, i.e., working out the given material in his own way, he could with impunity remain a sort of magnifying glass, gathering in the devices from the creative output of Glinka and his comrades Musorgsky and Borodin, as well as the Western masters, including in particular Liszt, Schumann, and Berlioz. Rimsky-Korsakov also mastered Wagner's works, annexing to his own style (form of thought, quality, and manner of expression) everything that captivated him in the musical thought of that great German.[3] In addition, Rimsky-Korsakov made an idiosyncratic interpretation of Russian folk music in his own work.[4]

Rimsky-Korsakov occupies a most prominent place among that series of composers who elaborated one or another means to best utilize song for the sake of its further development in the context of general European musical craftsmanship: all of his music, which is instrumental in essence (even the operas) is permeated with song modes and song roots.

This "clever craftsmanship" in creativity, i.e., a profoundly conscious and extremely economical and consistent use of musical treasures, gave Rimsky-Korsakov the opportunity to reveal himself in a multitude of compositions, differing in intent and realization, while expertise and technical skill grew incessantly due to the abundance of musical material. In his early compositions (the symphonic picture *Sadko* [1867], *Antar* [1868–1869], the first three operas), Rimsky-Korsakov was a mad spendthrift in comparison with his manner of using the material over which he labored in *The Legend of the Invisible*

City of Kitezh (1904) and *The Golden Cockerel* (1907). In *Sadko, Antar*, and others, nearly all the fundamental elements (components) are present, with whose help the grand edifice of Korsakovian musical thought was erected, a structure that was built up brick by brick over the course of forty-five years (1861–1908).

Yet in addition to purely creative activity, teaching played an important role in the life of Rimsky-Korsakov, since from 1871 until his very death (with a minor break in 1905[5]) he held the post of professor in the St. Petersburg Conservatory, where he established a particular course or trend of unquestionable significance whose influence is far from exhausted, and which might be conceptualized overall as the *Rimsky-Korsakov school*.[6]

Several generations of young composers have been trained under the influence of the pedagogy (the teaching) of Rimsky-Korsakov. In his teaching activities he introduced the same demands that he applied to himself. The strict adherence to a plan and the awareness and sense of duty or rigorous accountability to art were to inspire anyone to work who was bold enough to enter into music. Intense study of one's craft and mastery of one's technique were the main goals of a composer, regardless of the degree of one's talent. Without a doubt, Rimsky-Korsakov taught the techniques and methods according to which he himself composed, those which he had mastered. In this regard he could not be impartial. In addition, being possessed of a strong will and the firm conviction that all that he had achieved in the realm of musical knowledge was indisputably according to law, since it was based on a fully acquired mastery and derived from the compositional practice of great musicians, Rimsky-Korsakov thereby set about teaching as if he considered it his duty to educate the young on the basis of the "musical truth" that he had come to know. Teaching was for him a duty and a great accomplishment. He felt obliged to propagandize the dogmas in which he believed with all his soul, whose veracity he never doubted. Indeed, how could he have doubted that which he taught, since he himself had passed through all of it, having learned it through *personal* experience?

Undoubtedly, it was not vanity and pride that turned Rimsky-Korsakov into the head of an entire school and the stalwart apostle of well-defined academic precepts: a passionate faith and a firm conviction as to the permanence of the truths he had assimilated made him thus.

The full intensity and rigor of Rimsky-Korsakov's professional activity with its uncompromising demand that duty be carried out both by oneself and by others were mitigated and illuminated by his radiant and warmhearted, wise and reserved inner self, i.e., that indeterminate and intangible, yet nonetheless deeply felt aggregate of life phenomena, which constitute the person, the profile, and the personality of a particular human being and distinguish him from others. A kindness and an understanding of others' woes shone through the stern face of the composer. From his well-proportioned, stately figure, unbent by age, breathed a vigorous spirit of courage, while eyes aglow revealed an eternal flame. In order to comprehend and truly evaluate the music of Rimsky-Korsakov, one must never lose sight of this cold, strict constraint and integrity of aspiration, protecting the chastity, modesty, meekness, and childishly accepting naiveté and timidity of Rimsky-Korsakov's spiritual world.

With the eyes of quiet and meek Snow-Maiden, the great composer gazed at the world and listened attentively to the songs of people and the music resounding in nature.[7] And to the song warmed by the heat of a human soul and to the sounds overheard in the coldness of a forest's quiet and the boundless expanse of the ocean, he granted equally fond attention, transforming them into harmonious successions of musical combinations, linking them together around the subject that unifies them. Thus did he create his fairy-tale operas, epic operas, and magical sound pictures and visions.

If they be judged only by the "literary" data—according to the poetic legends, stories, and tales that served Rimsky-Korsakov as a basis, by which his *emerald*-bright, intricately patterned sound embroidery spread forth—then all of his works represent a tranquil juxtaposition of human existence and natural phenomena, governed by mysterious forces of deified elemental forces, ruled by a sun deity. This pagan outlook manifests in musical realizations of folk traditions, legends, incantations, ceremonies, and games, in the depiction of all kind of fairy-tale wonders, transformations, of the intrigues and wiles of dark powers, of seductions, temptations, etc., etc. The fairy-tale world, together with the everyday existence of human beings, constitutes an integral whole, each being in contact with the other within the same environs, so that when, for a time, an evil element casts its net, the struggle is inevitably brought to an end with a victory of light, warmth, and the restoration of universal equilibrium. The entire ancient pagan outlook that was once customary for the Russian folk music, in connection with natural phenomena, found its musical realization in the creations of Rimsky-Korsakov: in *Snow-Maiden* we observe ceremonies and actions associated with the emergence and regal ascendancy of spring, in *May Night*, with Trinity Week (and Mermaids' Week), in *Kashchei*—nature's autumnal dying off, in *Mlada*—the dances and divinations of Kupala, and in *Christmas Eve*—Christmastide and ceremonious songs associated with the divine names of Kolyada and Ovsen.[8]

Russian everyday reality found its most striking realization in such operas as *The Maid of Pskov*, *The Tsar's Bride*, *Sadko*, and *The Legend of the City of Kitezh*.

In the musical tableaus *Sadko*, *Antar*, *A Tale*, *Scheherazade*, *Capriccio espagnole*, *Russian Easter Overture*, in individual episodes from the operas (the flight of Vakula the smith in *Christmas Eve*, night on Triglav Mountain[9] in *Mlada*, the procession in *The Golden Cockerel*), in the depictions of the three wonders in *The Tale of Tsar Saltan*, in the underwater kingdom in *Sadko*—everywhere the spirit of the popular tale-telling imagination spreads out and reigns, transposed into the world of musical representations, into the realm of orchestral (instrumental) creativity, which is no less magical than the tales themselves.

The power and fascination of Rimsky-Korsakov's music lie in the transparency of the sound, the inexhaustible wealth of its instrumental ideas, for they reveal the intricate iridescent play of light and shade, the bright and dark hues, and the exchange of motley, purely oriental designs and lovely resoundings, light as air, hovering in heavenly azure.

Nikolai Andreyevich Rimsky-Korsakov was born in the city of Tikhvin, Novgorod Province, on 6 (18) March 1844, where he also spent his childhood (until age 12). Household musical education (instruction in playing the piano began when the boy was six) led to the study of simple pieces and the initial acquaintance with the music of Glinka. Of course, as is customary with great musicians, a creative talent began to emerge all on its own, apart from anyone's concern, care, or advice: the nine-year-old greenhorn was taking a try at composition on his own. The duet "Butterflies" and the attempt to compose an overture, i.e., a work in a complex form, were the "starting points" along the path toward a future inclination.[10] In 1856 Rimsky-Korsakov was sent to the St. Petersburg Naval Academy, from which he would graduate in 1862, after which he was sent on a three-year sea voyage around the world. Barracks life under the conditions of the harsh military regime during the grim Nikolayevan years provided Rimsky-Korsakov with few musical impressions, but did temper his will and character, accustoming him to iron discipline. Musical studies proceeded with more success when the fine pianist and enthusiastic admirer of Glinka's music [Théodore] Canille was appointed instructor. He became more or less sufficiently satisfied with the ardent inquisitiveness of his pupil, playing through at the piano with four hands the most outstanding musical works and explaining why and wherefrom such and such musical structures arise and are put together. Through Canille, Rimsky-Korsakov became acquainted with the composer Balakirev, entering into the circle of young musicians, wherein Balakirev marshaled and directed the development of taste and the techniques of authoring music. Balakirev, Cui, and Musorgsky constituted the kernel of this circle (Rimsky-Korsakov joined it in 1861, and Borodin after him). It quickly grew into the Mighty Five that would bring such splendid sonic riches to Russian music. At this time, Nikolai Andreyevich had already begun to compose a symphony modeled after works by German composers, one "modeled after Beethoven" in particular.[11] He had to wait to complete the symphony until after the round-the-world cruise, which left a strong impression in the soul of the composer throughout his life: more than once in his works he presented a sound image of the "Ocean-Sea," its boundlessness, and the starry veil spreading above it.

The young naval officer's symphony was performed for the first time on 19 December 1865. It was given an amicable reception. This supported the hopes of the young musician, and, beginning in 1866, a series of fresh compositions suffused with talent emerges, immediately defining his persona, his style, traits, and idiosyncrasies: the Overture on Russian Themes (1866); *Sadko*, a musical tableau based on the eponymous Novgorod epic (1867); and finally, *Antar* (1868)—a luxuriant oriental symphonic tale, displaying the young composer's capacity for remarkably varied representation, especially with respect to uncommon sounds.

In 1868, the composer set about creating *The Maid of Pskov*, a dramatic opera, revised more than once subsequently, but unchanged at its core: through it he found thoroughly uncommon devices for the structure of operatic speech, sharply outlined descriptions of the everyday life of the folk (e.g., the famous scene of the nocturnal assembly), and precise representations of human characters (especially Ivan the Terrible himself and his daughter Olga).

The two next operas of Rimsky-Korsakov were the tender, dreamy *May Night* (1878), enveloped with the bright atmosphere of spring, and the well-known tale, *Snow-Maiden* (1880). Both are touchingly young at heart and unfaded to this day: Rimsky-Korsakov infused them with all the freshness, naiveté, and immediacy of his lyricism. Though a shy recluse and hermit, secreting away from people the inner world of his soul, here in these springtime stories, he revealed the charm of heartfelt natural purity and gentle, wise humility. The character of the quiet, sorrowful, girlish Snow-Maiden cannot fail to move people, even in days of hardship and harsh struggle for existence.

The composition of these two operas was preceded by a profound spiritual upheaval in the life of the composer: after being offered a position as professor of orchestration at the St. Petersburg Conservatory in 1871, Nikolai Andreyevich, upon assuming his duties, also took on the persistent and onerous task of thoroughly mastering musical technique and fluency in craftsmanship. Nearly all of the 1870s following the completion of *Maid of Pskov* were devoted to musical self-education and self-edification, since Rimsky-Korsakov had clarified for himself that with mere "squandering away" of musical material, even when especially valuable, one could never move ahead and that in order to exploit to the fullest all sides of one's talent, every artist and musician was obliged to become a master craftsman, to command the technique of one's art and reveal one's ideas without hindrance.

Having finally retired from maritime service in 1873, Rimsky-Korsakov resolved to devote himself wholeheartedly to music and make a living as a composer. Given the conditions of Russian life, this aim was not among the easiest. It befell Rimsky-Korsakov to assume posts (e.g., inspector of military orchestras of the fleet, director of the Court Choral Cappella), which, together with his teaching at the Conservatory, deprived him of considerable time. But thanks to this individual's willpower, discipline, and ability to apportion time economically, this kind of occupation not only did not prevent his purely creative achievements from following their calm course, but even proved to be of benefit to him. The inspection of military orchestras led him to a study of the most detailed idiosyncrasies and qualities of wind instruments, while service in the Cappella induced him to research the very rich legacy of Orthodox Church psalmody, which undoubtedly exerted its significance during the composition of *Russian Easter Overture* (1888) and the creation of *The Legend of the Invisible City of Kitezh* (1904).

The professorship at the Conservatory, doubtless both burdensome and tiresome, continued on to the final months in the life of Nikolai Andreyevich (the spring of 1908): teaching was his calling. But neither personal creativity nor pedagogical feats would satisfy him entirely. Above and beyond this, he considered it his duty to assist musician friends by advising and cooperating with them while alive and, most of all—concerning himself with the works after the death of their authors.

Thus, just after the passing of Dargomyzhsky, he orchestrated the latter's opera *Stone Guest*, as well as Musorgsky's *Khovanshchina* and *Boris Godunov*.[12] In 1887, after the death of Borodin, he and Glazunov together took on the completion of the opera *Prince Igor*, which had remained in an incomplete state, as "sketches."[13] In 1902 Rimsky-Korsakov orchestrated *The Stone Guest* again, painfully aware of his dissatisfaction with the first orchestration. In addition, he collected, studied, and harmonized Russian folk song (two anthologies) and then occupied himself with researching the style of church psalmody, producing a series of excellent arrangements of Orthodox chants.[14] Nikolai Andreyevich was also drawn to conducting activities: as the director of the Free Music School, founded according to the ideas and thanks largely to the powerful will of Balakirev, and as the director of Mitrofan Belyaev's Russian Symphonic Concerts, Rimsky-Korsakov attempted to master the secret of how to exert influence on an orchestra. However, in this area he was not fated to progress and achieve brilliant results.

The manner in which Rimsky-Korsakov could continuously develop his own composing, amidst such diverse professional musical activities, will neither be grasped nor understood without knowing how much strength of will and iron fortitude were inside of him! In 1880 *A Tale* appeared, a fascinating work thanks to clever orchestral beguilements; in 1882, the Piano Concerto, in 1884 the delightful little symphony (Sinfonietta) on Russian themes; in 1887, one and all were illumined and dumbfounded by the radiant *Capriccio espagnole*—an outstanding instrumental piece consisting of five of the most ingenious and colorful episodes: "capricious" tableaus, both whimsical and fantastic.

The brilliance and splendor of this sonic firework can blind the unaccustomed listener, but also beguile and captivate. The delicate fourth movement sounds especially alluring as, first of all, there occurs a sort of *contest* among individual instruments, consisting of presentations from each of them of their characteristic abilities and most effective sounds, followed by the growth of a sharply outlined Spanish theme (tune), beckoning ever more charmingly and intensely toward a passionate, fiery dance. In the fifth movement, this dance finally bursts forth like a sudden downpour, spraying forth blinding rays of shimmering hues. Only the sharply defined meter (a regular succession of accented downbeats) restrains this headlong, rushing torrent of sound! . . .

The piece *Scheherazade* is somewhat different in disposition: a symphonic suite (a succession of pieces in contrasting characters, unified by a single narrative idea or perhaps by the unfolding of a preconceived musical idea, for example, that of presenting a series of dance meters and juxtaposing them). In *Scheherazade* the composer set a goal of realizing in an orchestral retelling certain descriptions and events from the Arabian tales of Princess Scheherazade, *The 1001 Nights*, which had captured his imagination. In the four movements of this cleverly interwoven tapestry of sound, one may hear and see wonders. As in a broad, sweeping panorama, the world of the fairy tale spreads out for the attentive ear, not in words but in sounding and resounding images, exchanging and alternating with each other according to someone's all-powerful incantation.

Initially (in the first movement), just after the little tune that seems to sketch a profile of the tale-teller herself, the boundless sea heaves smoothly and majestically before us. A single vivid theme (idea) governs and reigns here, the tune set in opposition to it lacking an independent significance and development. In the second movement, a fantastic oriental tale unfolds (of particular interest is the first main idea, which is stated in the unique timbre of a woodwind instrument, the bassoon). The calm, leisurely, "nasal" voice is gradually replaced with the growing hustle and bustle of the crowd, here announcing itself with shrill and even savage trumpet calls, there rustling in timid fear.

In the third movement an atmosphere of languishing erotic bliss and caressing stupor spreads forth, interrupted by a light but distinct dance melody (tune) that hovers in the air. This undertaking was carried out by the composer with remarkable delicacy (without a single crude or shrill timbre to disturb the integrity of the "scene") and, at the same time, with quiet and wise naiveté: neither passionate, lascivious whispers nor voluptuous rapture! . . . In all the love duets and women's dreams (*May Night, Sadko, Kitezh, Tsar's Bride*), purity of heart and a child's soul did not allow the composer to violate the boundary of bashful maidenhood. The feminine images called to life in his works prior to the creation of the Queen of Shemakha in *The Golden Cockerel* are charming and touching at one and the same time: In the transparent depths of their heartfelt melodies, allures and languorous calls resound, but no greedy carnal diversions are to be found. Sin does not hold sway over them; they pass through life's temptations, sensing them in advance, but not partaking: hapless Marfa in *The Tsar's Bride*, tender and frail Volkhova in *Sadko*, the coquettish and crafty, yet still ingenuous Oksana in *Christmas Eve*, radiantly feminine Servilia, penitent Kashcheyevna, and, finally, meek Fevronia in *Kitezh.* . . .

In the fourth and last movement of *Scheherazade*, a motley, noisy, and brilliant festival, imbued with the rumble of the crowd, is sketched. Here a dance with distinct rhythm reigns, now whimsically meandering, now dispelled in drumming, now persistently stamping. . . . A picture of the sea majestically supersedes this onslaught of frenzied whirling. The sea rages, the storm rises. The growth of sound leads to cataclysmic plummeting, as if bringing to pass something fated and preordained. With the sacrifice accepted and the limit of agitation achieved, the water element is placated and becalmed.

Scheherazade was written by the composer in 1888, in the middle period of his longstanding and many-sided career. To this day, it has not stopped captivating listeners as one of the most fascinating legends of the East in Russian music.

It was followed by a series of distinguished operas (*Mlada*, 1889–1890; *Christmas Eve*, 1895; the epic tale *Sadko*, 1895–1896; *Mozart and Salieri*, 1897; *Vera Sheloga the Boyarina*, 1898; *The Tsar's Bride*, 1898; *The Tale of Tsar Saltan*, 1900; *Servilia*, 1900–1901; *Kashchei the Deathless*, 1902; *Pan Voyevoda*, 1903; *The Legend of the Invisible City of Kitezh*, 1904; *The Golden Cockerel*, 1907). Each of them fulfills its unique inherent aim and deserves its own sketch and review. Unfortunately, several of the Rimsky-Korsakov operas—these revelations in sound of the everyday life of the Russian folk and the folk's world outlook—have yet to receive careful study and broad renown. The fortune bequeathed by them to the Russian people still awaits appraisal and appreciation.

NOTES

1. Sergei Ivanovich Taneyev (1850–1917) pursued a multifaceted career in which composition, scholarship, teaching (and administration) at the Moscow Conservatory, and piano performance intertwined. An obsession with exhaustive precompositional exploration of his musical material's potential taxed his mentor Tchaikovsky's patience.

2. Already at age 16, Rimsky-Korsakov owned piano scores of Glinka's works from which he began to make arrangements. According to Rimsky-Korsakov (Rimsky-Korsakoff, *My Musical Life*, trans. Judah Joffe [New York: Tudor, 1936], 250), the "considerable degree of virtuosity and bright sonority" revealed in his *Capriccio espagnole*, *Scheherazade,* and the *Easter Overture* were attained "without Wagner's influence, within the limits of the usual makeup of Glinka's orchestra."

3. Rimsky-Korsakov's study of Wagner began in earnest after a Prague company under the direction of Karl Muck gave the Russian premiere of *The Ring* at the Maryinsky Theater during the 1888–1889 season. The first fruit was a reorchestration of the polonaise from *Boris Godunov*; his own *Mlada* followed thereafter (1889–90).

4. *See especially* the discussions in Chapters 5 (pp. 53–57) and 8 (pp. 82–85).

5. The gunning down of civilians by the tsar's guardsmen on "Bloody Sunday" was the focal event of the 1905 Revolution. Rimsky-Korsakov's support of student sympathizers led to his dismissal from the St. Petersburg Conservatory in March 1905. He was reinstated to the faculty in December to serve under Alexander Glazunov, who succeeded him as rector.

6. By 1900, Rimsky-Korsakov had established a program of study for composition students at the St. Petersburg Conservatory; the program consisted of at least two years of harmony, courses in strict and free counterpoint, orchestration, and form. The curriculum would not be challenged until the middle 1920s, when newly appointed instructors—including Asafyev—successfully argued for a change to a less standardized studio approach.

7. "You've no cause to call me cold / Shy, yes, and tranquil but not cold" (Ostrovsky, *The Snow-Maiden*, Act 1, sc. 1).

8. Asafyev provides more of a context for Rimsky-Korsakov's pagan calendar or "seasonal cusp" operas at the outset of Chapter 8.

9. Triglav Mountain is the legendary site of nocturnal demonic revels, which Rimsky-Korsakov used as the setting for *Mlada*'s third act.

10. Rimsky-Korsakov wrote the duet "Babochki" [Butterflies] in 1855 at age 11. The unfinished multisectional Overture for Piano dates from the same period.

11. The first version of the First Symphony was composed 1861–1865.

12. Rimsky-Korsakov completed his first orchestration of *The Stone Guest* in 1869–1870 and then reorchestrated the work in 1902; his work with *Boris* occurred in two phases: 1892–1896 and 1906–1997.

13. Rimsky-Korsakov and Glazunov together completed and orchestrated *Prince Igor* in 1887–1888.

14. A first collection of 100 songs and a second of 40 were published in 1877 and 1882, respectively. Rimsky-Korsakov's arrangements of Russian Orthodox psalmody were made in 1883–1884, when he served as Balakirev's Assistant Director at the Court Cappella.

• 4 •

The Maid of Pskov

$\mathscr{T}$he magnificent stylist Rimsky-Korsakov strove for his entire life to find the expressive means and methods by which every subject taken up by him would be graphically revealed in sounds corresponding to its language. Thus, in *Sadko*, the composer developed devices of *bylina* tale telling; in *Kitezh*, parallel to the language of the *bylina*, there flows a layer of religious lyricism, spiritual verse, and church psalmody; in *Christmas Eve*, the living speech of ritual and everyday reality; in *The Tale of Tsar Saltan*, the parlance of Lubok prints[1] and of legendary tales; and in *Mlada*, the measured tread of epic tableaus. Both the vocal and the instrumental elements in folk music provided him with the richest of material and the full possibility of strikingly rich inventions, approaching the living, pliant musical speech of the folk. With respect to stylistic integrity, *The Maid of Pskov*, being Rimsky-Korsakov's first opera, was somewhat inconsistent and uneven. Apparently, the composer sensed this, for the form of the work in which it is now performed differs considerably from the first version. The opera was conceived at the end of the 1860s. The epoch of romantic attraction toward Russian historical reality and the "freedom-loving" centers of our history (Novgorod and Pskov) probably played no insignificant role in the choice of subject.[2] But the musical language necessary to realize Mei's drama[3] was not easy to discover, especially for a composer who still did not command all the technical means in the fullest measure. In addition, the very development of the subject contained a dualistic tendency, whose expression throughout the entirety of the conception would mean discovering a completely unknown realm of lyric musical drama.

Two main characters are present in the play: Tsar Ivan the Terrible and his daughter. In each of them, two conflicting tendencies are realized. Olga is a girl who has fallen into selfless love with the leader of the "independence movement" in ancient Pskov and, at the same time, senses within a mysterious, mystical attraction to the character of cruel Tsar Ivan (her father). The tragic struggle of the two elements in Mei's conception was given stronger dramatic emphasis than in the opera: Olga betrays to the tsar the spot where her lover, the governor's son Mikhailo Tucha, is hidden. But a musician's intuition instead suggested to Rimsky-Korsakov a more profoundly lyrical expression of the divided love and, consequently, a more natural and tragically conditioned death for Olga as fated sacrifice. In Mei, Olga stabs herself, having heard of Tucha's demise, but in the opera she is thrown into the fiery fray of battle between the freedom fighters of Pskov and the tsar's Oprichniki,[4] dying from a stray bullet, i.e., involuntarily, but inescapably: life between the poles of the twin attractions would be senseless for her in any case! Nevertheless, she dies as a martyr to Pskov, as the daughter of a free city that has lost forever its freedom. In a stroke of genius, the composer joined together in concluding the chorus the funeral of Olga (not found in Mei) and the fate of Pskov with the fate of the daughter of Pskov and of Tsar Ivan!

The latter's character is likewise given in a twofold guise. On the one hand, it is Tsar Ioann Vasilyevich, brought to life as he is portrayed in the Third Chronicle of Novgorod: "And the Tsar and Grand Prince proclaimed himself, and showed himself as the Great Autocrat of all [Great] Russia, and all the heathen lands were seized with fear of him, and he was wise beyond measure and brave-hearted, strong-armed, strong in body, and light of foot, like a panther."[5]

He is certain in the sanctity of his political mission (the struggle with the enemies of a unified Rus) and only doubt in his powers sometimes clouds his spirit. The unexpected meeting with daughter Olga and the memory of young, passionate love for a while enchains the tsar to the sources of true life and its joys, a life not to be seen from the eyes of a political idea firmly carried through with iron and blood. "Let the killing cease; great is the bloodshed! We will dull the swords on the stones: May the Lord preserve Pskov"[6]—Ivan the Terrible was brought to this point, thanks to a meeting with a shy girl! But Olga perishes and, with her, vanishes the ray of light from another life for the tsar, apart from violence and blood. He will again resume his dark deeds, sensing himself to be fatally called by history to the role of a great tyrant and, in minutes of pained deliberation, pining away under the weight of this burdensome lot. It is not easy for a human being to realize that people consider him to be the Beast of the Apocalypse, "who will show no mercy for age or sex."[7]

The interrelationship of these two main characters, the tsar and his daughter, develops against the background of Pskov's struggle for freedom. The composer attains tragic depth for this background: The grand scene of the *véche* [public assembly] with its overwhelming expressivity sounds like a requiem to Pskov.[8] The song of the departing freedom fighters oppresses the soul. Quieting underneath the peal of the final assembly bell, it fades in the air like the funereal singing of the retreating procession. The greeting choruses to the tsar in the third tableau of the opera—the forced eulogy of frightened residents—contrast sharply, especially in rhythm, with the musical moods of the *véche* and with the boldness—the mournful and lyrical boldness—in the song of the Pskov freedom fighters. With the approach of the royal procession, anxious triumphalism resounds in growing sound masses: three distant tonalities (D-flat major, D major, and C major) alternate with one another in the predominant theme of the chorus, which bears the character of a universal prayer of lamentation.[9] At the moment of Ivan the Terrible's appearance, the motion of the music comes to a standstill: the choral theme sounds in augmentation, while underneath and penetrating through it, heavy, crushing triplets in the strings and woodwinds on the note G emerge, with a rigid, harsh, regular pulsation. Such an *encounter* does not occur in Mei, and neither does the concluding chorus—the *requiem* to Pskov's self-will. Rimsky-Korsakov wisely brought depth to the action and created—in opposition to the political inclination of Moscow, which was powerfully vindicated by the poet in the person of Tsar Ivan—a musical *chronicle* of the last days of Pskov, uniting the fate of Olga, daughter of Pskov, and Tsar Ivan, with the fate of the city.

If *Sadko* be an *epic* opera and *Kitezh* a *legend* opera, then *Maid of Pskov* is a *chronicle* opera. Its language is that of concise, concentrated and compressed, but precise and accurate characterizations, linked with pages of everyday life narration. It is risky to designate *Maid of Pskov* as historical drama, for its drama is not the customary drama of conflicts deliberately chosen by a poet. Rather, this is the drama of Russian chronicles, a drama emanating from a *perception* of the narrative, which on its own flows ever calmly and dispassionately as it describes the horrors of rampant death, famine, fires, and with the same austerity, restraint, and sublimity that it gives to the rare happy events.[10]

The characterization of Tsar Ivan in music is based on an ancient hymn tune and is elaborated throughout the entire opera by means of quite interesting variations of this fate theme, plainly and precisely implanted in the harmony.[11] One may consider such a technique of characterization to be that of icon painting, as it calls forth from memory the rhythm of the lines in old Russian icons and presents to us the countenance of Ivan the Terrible in that saintly aura, on which the tsar himself always relied, seeing himself as messenger and dispatcher of the orders of a higher will, which had laid upon him the burden of imperial power (letter to Kurbsky[12]). In the music of *Maid of Pskov*, the theme of Ivan the Terrible reigns like the *dux* of a fugue: it sounds here in augmentation, there in diminution, here gently imitating, there angrily snapped off, here plainly exposed with unisons and octaves, there emerging from behind clouds of slowly creeping harmonies. (In this respect, the slow introduction to the overture is magnificently structured.)

Olga's image is *melodically* sketched: the flowing gait, the soft and pensive speech, the timid glance; all the motives accompanying her appearance speak to this. Rimsky-Korsakov accentuated the struggle between a shy, maidenly first love for Mikhailo Tucha and the mysterious attraction for Tsar Ivan that was already conceived in the child's dreams by means of an especially successful technique: the nature of Olga's speech is gradually enhanced in depth and emotion over the full course of the opera—from the first duet with Tucha to the moment when she stands in the camp of Ivan the Terrible and reveals her maidenly reveries and prayers.[13] During her rendezvous with Tucha, Olga speaks in the language of song, an everyday language, for she has yet to separate herself as an individual from her surroundings, from life in the tower. During the conversation with the nanny on the square, as she languishes in awaiting the imminent meeting with the unknown tsar, she unveils the dreamy lyricism of her soul. In the first encounter with Ivan the Terrible, Olga blossoms like a tender spring flower and conducts her speech on the basis of a wondrous and radiant, smoothly flowing melody of love (which is actually the second theme of the overture).[14] In the duet with Tucha in the forest,[15] which is usually omitted on stage, a struggle ensues in Olga's soul between the two attractions: in her words addressed to Tucha an anxious lover's lament is heard, but during her recollection of Ivan, the melody just mentioned emerges anew in a broad wave.

Finally, in the last tableau, in the tsar's camp, the prayerful, mystical tremors and tender joys of a girl's ecstatic contemplations are revealed in full. All the charm and sense of the profoundly meaningful dialogue between Olga and Ivan the Terrible lie in the struggle of two powerful wills. Ivan's *demands* exude an air of harsh interrogation. Try as he might to soften them, cruel habit betrays him. Yet Olga's words firmly and steadily guide the tsar into a world of quiet contemplation, to a realm of maidenly ecstasies, woven together out of saintly, prayerful worship, frail premonitions and desires, and an unexplained but sweet inclination toward loving. The sufferings of Ivan the Terrible over the corpse of his slain daughter attest that Olga's dreams temporarily conquered the tsar's anger and that Pskov will not be threatened with making restitution for the willfulness of the *fighters*. The city was granted a free, not a violent, demise![16]

Thus in *Maid of Pskov*, under the cover of historical dramatic legend, an idea is revealed, one familiar from other Russian operas, of the involuntary predestination of the Russian woman's soul to consume itself in love, an idea of patient martyrdom and the sacrificial deliverance of self. It is a profoundly enhanced conception of the myth of Iphigenie.

The brief history of the creation of *Maid of Pskov* is as follows. The first thought of it came to the composer in 1868, while envisioning the imminent trip that summer into the wilderness, the interior of *Rus*, to the estate of I. N. Lodyzhensky (Kashinsky District, of Tver Province). The opera was not completed and orchestrated until the end of 1871, the overture in January 1872. It did not come about without censorial prohibitions, truncations, and changes, especially in the assembly scene; but finally, thanks to the intervention of Grand Prince Konstantin Nikolayevich, the opera was given permission to be produced and performed in the Maryinsky Theater. The first production took place on 1 January 1873. The opera was received by the public with great success.

Work on musical technique and a thorough acquaintance with the scores of Glinka led Rimsky-Korsakov at the end of the 1870s to become dissatisfied with the technical scoring of *Maid of Pskov*: "I realized that my compositional technique at that time was not commensurate with my musical ideas and the splendid subject."[17] Apart from technical and stylistic musical changes and improvements, the opera was greatly amplified with insertions and additions: new characters were introduced and additional scenes written in, including a prologue, a scene in the Pechersky Monastery, a royal hunt, etc. By 1878 the new version was complete, but in this form it never appeared on stage. Moreover, even then, the composer himself sensed that in its new reworking, *Maid of Pskov* had become "long, dry, and rather heavy, despite the fine scoring and the noteworthy technique."[18] Convinced of this, he resolved to make other use of the new material that was introduced in this second version, assembling from it music for Mei's drama *Maid of Pskov*, without, however, abandoning dreams of a new reworking of the opera, which he indeed fulfilled during 1891. Masterfully reorchestrated all over again and thoughtfully reworked with respect to form and style, the opera finally acquired that final splendid form in which it is given today. In 1897, the *Prologue to Maid of Pskov* was reworked into the "lyrical monologue" *Boyarina Vera Sheloga*. I call it a lyrical monologue because the chief interest for this work is its basic seed: the wonderful poetic tale of Vera Sheloga, one of the finest exemplars of Korsakovian lyricism! . . . In the 1903–1904 season, *Maid of Pskov* in a definitive version, together with the prologue, was produced at the Maryinsky Theater under the direction of Napravnik.[19] With the brilliant realization of the role of Ivan the Terrible by Chaliapine and *Maid of Pskov* itself, a series of rapturous and radiant legends were entered into the chronicle of Russian music.[20]

NOTES

1. Lubok prints were cheaply produced illustrations made with woodblocks or copperplates. Originally circulated among the nobility, by the 19th century they had reached the masses; with the addition of religious texts, folk tales, and poetry, they became a means for fostering literacy.

2. Prior to the Muscovite annexations of Novgorod (1478) and Pskov (1510) and to their continued misfortunes under Ivan III (reigned 1462–1505), Vasily III (1505–1533), and Ivan the Terrible (i.e., Ioann Vasilyevich "Grozny," or Ivan IV, ???–1584), followed by Boris Godunov and the Time of Troubles, both Novgorod and Pskov were thriving, politically autonomous mercantile centers enjoying lucrative trade with the Hanseatic League. By the 19th century, they served as democratic symbols throughout the nation.

3. The poet Lev Alexandrovich Mei (1822–1862) completed *Pskovityanka* [The Maid of Pskov] in 1859, yet its Moscow premiere was delayed on account of political sensitivities until 1872, by which time Rimsky had finished the first version of the opera. Like Pushkin's *Boris Godunov*, it is a chronicle play with a similarly large cast and even larger time span. The premise that Ivan the Terrible spared Pskov the grisly retribution that he inflicted on Novgorod in 1570 on account of a love child is likely the writer's invention.

4. Ivan IV's *oprichniki* were the guardsmen attached to the *oprichnina*, a special state within a state, cordoned off from the other regions controlled by Moscow. Six thousand strong in their peak years, they served as primary agents of his state terrorism, inspiring numerous legends and eventually literary treatments.

5. Asafyev quotes from an 1872 transcription of the *Third Novgorod Chronicle*. See also note 9.

6. Closing lines to Act 4 of the drama (Act 2 of the opera), spoken by Tsar Ivan.

7. In his arioso from Act 3 (fig. 190), Tsar Ivan seeks a reaction from Olga to a song in which he is characterized as the Beast of the Apocalypse. Note: The score references for this chapter are taken from the vocal score of the opera's *third* version (*Complete Works*, v. 29B).

8. In addition to the situational affinity, Asafyev's comparison to a requiem would be based on the formulaic quality of Tucha's verses, the responsorial setting of the text, and the passages of imitative polyphony.

9. Act 2, 1st tableau, figs. 106–9. The modulations occur in Asafyev's ordering.

10. Asafyev's characterization of the literary style would apply especially to the "northern" Russian historical chronicles produced in Novgorod during the time of the drama's events.

11. The chant-like tune appears first in the overture and is later associated with Tsar Ivan. Neither Asafyev nor Rimsky named a source.

12. Tsar Ivan's astonishing epistle, dated "year 7072 [i.e., 1564] from the creation of the world" and sent to the "cur, serpent, Church-destroyer, belcher of poison, devilish schemer, Herod, devil-spawn," etc. Prince Andrei Mikhailovich Kurbsky (1528–1583)—if authentic—was provoked by that nobleman's futile appeal to a tyrant's conscience. In addition to demonstrating that the ruler was deranged in the extreme, it attests to a formidable level of biblical and historical erudition, mainly wielded to give precedent and Higher Purpose to the actions Kurbsky found objectionable.

13. Cf., e.g., Act 1, figs. 41–50 and Act 3, figs. 182–97. While Olga's earlier arioso phrases modulate freely, her final duet with her father Tsar Ivan presents a richer linear chromaticism, more impulsive rhythms, and a greater range.

14. On its first occurrence in the overture, the broad and lyrical theme is pitched in A major and assigned to solo horn; in the Act 2 encounter between Tsar Ivan and Olga, a subtle F-major restatement in the orchestra underscores mere small talk between the characters, yet initiates a longer process of reconnection.

15. Act 3, first tableau, fig. 155.

16. In other words, Pskov's putative armed resistance to Moscow's unwarranted repression did not end with the bloodbath just suffered by Novgorod.

17. English translation from: Rimsky-Korsakoff, *My Musical Life*, trans. Judah Joffe (New York: Tudor, 1936), 149.

18. Rimsky-Korsakoff, *My Musical Life*, 151.

19. The new "definitive" third version produced at the Maryinsky Theater contained not only the prologue based on the first act of Mei's play but also a new third-act aria ("Bygone joy and passion") written especially for Chaliapine.

20. Chaliapine's interpretation of Ivan the Terrible for the revival of *Pskovityanka* at Savva Mamontov's private theater was as defining an achievement for his career as his portrayals of Philip II, Mephistopheles, and Boris Godunov.

• 5 •

May Night

If it is possible to establish the essence of Russian opera and its distinction from Western European, then here is the work, in which the sought-after essence is graphically distinguished and the boundaries between the European operatic style and ours clearly demarcated. But let us agree that before marking the boundaries, it is necessary to set forth an axiom: Russian opera is a unique world of sound complexes whose musical worth is unquestionably outstanding. If this simple truth is not accepted, if one cannot cease gazing upon the riches of Russian opera with a condescending smile, then one can never progress at all in determining the roots of its style and one had best admit that the broad swath of our culture that materialized in musical works for the stage simply does not exist—merely a failed attempt and nothing more! Of course, anyone who holds Russian music dear will be shocked by such a conclusion. I welcome this shock. But shock alone counts for little. It is necessary, once and for all, to stop squandering valuables and proclaim to one and all: the Russian operatic style is an artistic treasure unto itself, deserving thoughtful investigation and careful cultivation.

Let us admit that with few exceptions, everything done on behalf of Russian opera in Russian theaters stems either from the usual Western European clichés or from a correctly surmised but still accidental, instinctive comprehension of its unique beauty. In the first case, Russian opera was adapted to familiar prototypes, eliciting complaints over its unsuitability for the stage, while in the second, out of the desire to make its realization the finest possible, it was subjected to fashionable decorative or production trends, which did not at all proceed from the music, without considering what the score has to say and without comprehending the expressivity of the musical language.

I consider *May Night* to be an entirely suitable object for an attempt at defining the fundamental lines of the Russian operatic style. I shall begin with the negative delineations. Might it be an "action-adventure" opera such as the operas of Meyerbeer and others that resemble them?[1] Of course not! Is it a romantic legendary opera, of the type found in Marschner's and Weber's operas?[2] No, despite the presence of this sort of element in the third act of *May Night*. Of the Italian operatic style in all of its aspects, in this case there can be no discussion.

Wherein lies the main distinction? In the absence of action, or so it is said. Yes and no. If action means the appearance of the actual will of a hero, directed toward overcoming externally present obstacles, then no. It would be ridiculous to consider Levko a hero, merely because his father did not agree to his marriage to Hanna. But internalized action, an intimate musical dramatism, unquestionably exists, even though we are in the habit of believing that if there is neither a struggle nor an outward manifestation of reality, then not only is there no theatrical-dramatic action, but no life either, for life is a struggle.

Here we touch on the cardinal point of the diverging views. What if *action* is not merely a struggle? What if the obstacles that stem from people would be cast aside and not reckoned with? What if man himself is an element entering into a harmonious whole, which is called life? And what if it is not he with all of his struggle that has value, but life itself as such in all its depth, breadth, and height? Man simply fulfills what it has predetermined, obediently accepting the commonplace, the miraculous, the real, and the unreal. *All of this is life* and man is merely a fragment. How petty then become all his escapades and the surmounting of them! Only life itself reigns to the fullest extent.

What then must man do? Carry out what was predetermined and rejoice in life. Contemplate the beauty and the power of it. Take delight in all its manifestations in every place and in every hour. The interest is shifted from man to that element by which he lives. Man has value specifically because there is life within him and not because he directs it at his discretion.[3]

It is not so much the dramatic intrigues and adventures as ends in themselves, nor even people, their conflicts, and their attractions that interest Russian composers as much as life itself, quite regardless of the hues in which it presents itself for comprehension. Against the background of life, people stand out in bold relief on massive planes, as if marked out by it, precisely in the way that the visible profile of a human being reveals the internal emotional world. After this short but unavoidable introduction, we shall attempt to glimpse the qualitatively intense development of the musical action in *May Night*. Right away we will notice something out of the ordinary.

The opera opens with a chorus and *khorovod* based on the well-known old Russian song, "As we sowed millet."[4] This *khorovod deistvo* is associated with representations of spring sowing, spring shoots and early sprouts, and also with the springing and blossoming of romantic relationships, with the stealing away of young girls and spring weddings.

Beginning the opera in this way, Rimsky-Korsakov immediately brought the listener into the everyday surroundings of the action and to its religious essence. The emergence of the *khorovod* can be traced far back to a prehistoric vanishing point. Well-known evidence of them in Homer (*Iliad*, canto XVIII) appears to generalize an array of evidence that has come down to us (including depictions on vases) of a significant development of the *khorovod deistvo* among the Greeks.[5]

A range of historical sources also attests to the presence of the *khorovod* among the early Christians at the time of feast days honoring martyrs.

Here in Russia, the information about the *khorovod* is quite extensive. We find abundant material touching on *khorovod* songs and descriptions of *khorovod* games in Sakharov, Tereshchenko, and Shein.[6] From this is it is evident that the *khorovod* is a dramatic *deistvo*, in which scenes corresponding with the text are played out, accompanied by singing, revealing the most vivid aspects of how everyday life is lived. Naturally, the main interest is concentrated on whatever life itself has made most appealing and dear to people, that which preserves an indestructible connection with nature: on love, love relationships, marriage, and family life. The text of the songs usually creates a symbolic representation of it all in lovely poetic images, in which the inexhaustible riches of the folk imagination are reflected. Gesture, i.e., the game itself, reveals what the text is singing about, in pantomime, body motion, and dance.

Of this kind of *deistvo*, I offer the following list of the most entertaining: scarlet dawn (a girl's pining for freedom); "little wreaths" or the seeking of the bride, the choosing of the bride ("Bridal Pillow"); the examination and catching of the maidens ("Near the Valley a Nightingale," "On the Path to Town," "Yartyn-Grass," "Son of Tsar and King," "Radiant Prince"); matchmaking, gift giving, i.e., the "bridal dowry," the newlyweds' relations ("Near Town She Went," "Shining Gold"); a woman's love, familial discontent ("Little Deer"); jealousy, the hard lot of women ("The Weaver"); domestic bliss, the town assembly (i.e., reunion of acquaintances after a long separation). The *khorovod* also expresses various moments in agricultural life: the sowing of flax, the harvesting of flax, "millet sowing," "horseradish planting," "poppy growing." A *khorovod* may possess the purely aesthetic character of merry amusement, of free play. Among these: "Nikolshchina," "Baidan," and "Run, Run!"[7] I wonder why it is that even now this important and substantial side of folk creativity, encompassing the whole sphere of the Russian folk's relationship to everyday life and surroundings, still awaits complete and thorough investigation? And why has the *khorovod deistvo* not attracted the least attention for its own sake, but only been introduced as a component in various dramatic works?

In this regard, *May Night* awakens an unwitting curiosity, since the *khorovod* occupies an important place in it. The introductory chorus ("Millet") creates a type of background: spring *infatuation* of the whole community. Already from this there emerges a personal element: the love of Hanna and Levko. The furthermost development of the *khorovod deistvo* (or its reflection) is given to us in the third act, the scene of the mermaids, amidst the *nezhit* ["un-living" spirit beings]. The *nezhit* are creatures who did not live out their lives. They are those who perished from a violent death either by their own or another's hand. Mermaids belong among the *nezhit*. For them, spring is especially burdensome and bleak. When life impetuously reveals its force all around, even the *nezhit* appear to sense the power of life's energy upon it and will linger on the earth throughout the spring, especially until the moment of its luxuriant flowering during Trinity Week, in that happy time, poetically nicknamed "Green Holy Days."

"May Night" is also one among the nights of "Green" or "Kleshchalnaya" Week.[8] The tempestuous growth of life fills all of nature and all people with a springtime intoxication of joy and delight. Only the spirit world grieves. But even it acts in memory of life in the same way it once acted in life. In the *khorovod*, in the very idea of it, is concentrated much of what is most important and significant for young girls, associated with the best time of life, with life's spring, with the awakening in the soul of the delights and languors of spring love. The *khorovod* of the mermaids is a ghostly *khorovod*, a *khorovod* of remembrance. Rimsky-Korsakov sketches them in sound with soft, intertwining melodic lines and colors whose vividness is softened and diffused. In these amusements of mermaids the meaning and essence of the *khorovod* ritual are revealed more fully than in the introductory chorus.

Every *khorovod* comprises three parts. First, there is the invitation—a calling in, a commencement or gathering. Then comes the *deistvo* itself, and, at its conclusion, a parting or dissembling. Based on this, *khorovod* songs can be divided into songs of *gathering* or *recruiting*; songs for *enacting*; and songs of *dissembling* or *parting*. In Rimsky-Korsakov's "Millet," the place of the gathering and parting songs is occupied by the merry and expansive opening and closing instrumental strains.[9] In the mermaids' *khorovod*, the ritual action is developed much more broadly and fully. It begins with the calling in, gathering, and the cry of "Gather around, maidens, gather, pretty ones, we will lead the *khorovod*, we will plait the wreath."[10] Only after this introduction is the main *khorovod* tune to be heard ("Oy, at the time of midnight"). The verses signify an address to the moon, in order that it light the way for the beloved young man and not shine on the "old man, the unloved groom."

The second or subordinate *khorovod* tune is sung over an unchanging, repetitive text: "Little wind, little wind / Always stirring cattails."[11] It plays the role of a refrain and, as such, deepens and reinforces the fundamental idea. The girl languishes for her dear one, awaits a reunion: this is at the core of the present *khorovod*. The further development of the song concerns the fact that the dear one did not come, having forgotten his beloved. The refrain emphasizes one thing alone: how the beloved kisses, fondles, and speaks so brashly. The fact that the refrain remains at all times unchanged has great stylistic significance. Such a technique signifies the "unreality" of what is described in the song concerning the wait for the beloved and the change in his behavior: it is play, theater, and the transports of amorous dreaming themselves, here rejoicing with hope, there lamenting in doubt. The conclusion of the *khorovod* is an invitation to "unplait the wreath." The mermaids throw the garlands in the water and make predictions about the intended and their fate, just as they did when they were living young girls walking the earth:

> *Ven-vénochek, uplyvái,*
> *Krásna dévka, propadái*[12]
>
> [Little wreath, float away,
> Pretty girl, you're done for, too]

As is apparent, here the *khorovod deistvo* has two tendencies: one, to lead, and the other, to confirm (the choir's two sections). This is the old, old custom of so-called antiphonal singing, wherein a personal element (experiencing, enacting) is always placed in opposition to a communal element (establishing, commenting on the course of action, confirming its essence). Two choirs may be put in opposition to one another, or two sections of a choir (as here) or a solo voice against a choir. In the *khorovod*, the personal element usually reveals itself in action, i.e., in pantomime and gestures of the actors (youth and maiden or two maidens), during which time they do not sing, but translate whatever the choir is singing into their acting.

In a *deistvo* such as the present mermaids' *khorovod*, which is lyrical in essence, there is no need for revelation in pantomime of the idea behind the *khorovod*. Its meaning here does not contain a dramatic element. As often occurs, a *khorovod* may more likely express not an action but rather a lyrical mood: oppression, suffering, melancholy, joy, merriment, infatuation, displays of beauty and affection, etc. As I have already noted, the mermaids' *khorovod* ends with the tossing of the wreaths into the water. It is the most significant moment in all the games and *khorovody* of Trinity Week.

The twisting of the wreaths, the sisterhood ritual of the girls through the wreaths twisted from branches of birch trees bent toward each other, the predictions about the intended and her fate based on the garland that was thrown into the water, the *khorovod* danced around a tree dressed in springtime raiment, games and entertainments linked with the friendship customs, the untwisting of the garlands, and the examination after the garlands (whose withered, whose did not?) are also linked with the predictions of fate. Finally, the triumphal procession with the young birches to the small towns and villages as a sign of bringing into life the symbol of spring's flowering—all of this is closely fused with the joyous atmosphere of vital renewal, which envelops the human soul with a feeling of rebirth and the delight of young love. The growth of nature, its greening and flowering, its vernal *music*, when the noise and hubbub will not subside even for a moment, when everywhere is sensed the presence of life energy intensely pouring forth, these ensnare a human will and subject it to the will of spring.

In *May Night* everything is naturally expressed with great charm. The games of the girls with the wreaths, in particular, are maintained as one of the primary elements throughout the entire opera. At the center of the first tableau sounds the delightful maidens' chorus, which keeps to the old manner of setting counter voices [*podgoloski*] to a main melody, to which a transparent orchestral accompaniment is added. It is a highly original Slavonic pastorale or else an ornately patterned embroidery. This chorus ("I will weave a wreath for all the Holy Days") corresponds to the nighttime stroll of the girls into the forest at Semik for the plaiting of the wreaths and the sisterhood ritual.[13] All the night, they frolic and gambol, fraternize and tell fortunes, returning when it's nearly morning to the village, adorned with garlands and flowers. The mermaids' *khorovod* and games in the opera correspond exactly to these maidenly rituals, and the meaning of the entire action is closely linked with whatever transpires in life. An impression arises of the inseparability of elements real and phantasmal when, once again, at dawn is heard the spring song of the maidens returning from the forest (at the beginning of the opera's finale). The lads come forth to meet them, singing of spring carols, and already the communal *khorovod* is assembled. Since a marriage contract has now been tied up with the merriment associated with the apotheosis of spring and since, in addition, everything takes place at sunrise, the opera's finale acquires an even more joyous meaning from the glorification of spring, a young betrothal, and the sun. A characteristic aspect of the finale is the brief commemoration (the requiem for Pannochka) that is closely joined with the custom of remembering the dead in the Week of Semik (i.e., the seventh week after Easter).[14]

Thus a *deistvo* based on everyday existence is developed handsomely and expressively in *May Night*. From the first *khorovod* ("Millet") through the chorus of maidens heading off to twist the garlands, and the pranks of the lads introducing confusion into the tranquil course of a May night, the action leaps to the nocturnal *khorovod* and games of the mermaids, which correspond to the selfsame rites of humans. It is all brought to a close with praise for spring, happiness, and the light at sunrise.

This is the background that is so richly exploited with respect to music, especially in the masterful design of the *khorovod* choruses and the interweaving of the spring carols of the maidens and youths (in the finale). Against this background the tender love of Hanna and Levko blossoms like an embroidered pattern. When the first *khorovod* has dispersed, lovely and exquisitely tender music accompanies the appearance of Levko. Song could not help breaking out in such an entrancing spring evening. And unwittingly it springs forth from the heart: Levko sings a call to Hanna based on a motive from a familiar Ukrainian song ("The sun is low"), which is delightfully stylized in gentle, caressing tones that envelop and captivate the ear. Suffused with a still timid if winged lover's passion, the song insistently entices the girl. Hanna comes out to Levko. Their duet is divided into three stages: a lyrical mutual affection–infatuation and contemplation of the dying away of nature in the hour of the wondrous southern night blanketing the earth; next is dialogue: the lively coquettish speech of Hanna and the embarrassed confusion of Levko; and as a conclusion of their rendezvous, the ballad tale of the fate of hapless Pannochka.[15] This story introduces the charming fascination of night's mysterious quiet into the action, together with the trembling, guarded beating of the human heart. It can intuit the presence of mysterious, unknown powers since, in the night, away from daytime thoughts and the noisy flaring up of tiresome matters, faced with feelings that can grasp the very life of nature, her soul—her psyche—is laid bare, as if a man might hear the growth of life and the respiration of the plants, might touch the sources of life, might intuit the effluent springtime attraction of creatures for each other, and, with an inner eye, might see how the flowers blossom and the trees spread forth. But why indeed should one restate that which has been expressed with perfect knowledge and inspired wisdom in the poetry of Fet and Tyutchev and transformed into music by Rimsky-Korsakov?[16]

The idea of concluding the duet not in a shameless baring of passion, but in the chaste proclivity of human feeling when faced with a mystical, unknown element that is overcast by night's falling and linked to the story of the terrible event in a noble's home, is an idea acceptable only to a Russian artist, for whom mere scenic effects do not exist, for whom life has a secret, powerful and vast, which can be gleaned only through art in all of its manifestations. The lyrical and mystical moments in the duet-dialogue of Hanna and Levko resonate with great charm. We should not forget that *May Night* was, for the composer as well, a wedding song and song about the springtime of life. The idea for it arose at the beginning of the 1870s, the time of the composer's engagement ("My wife, when she was still my fiancée, often tried to persuade me to write an opera at some time on this subject. We read the tale together on the day when I proposed to her"—Rimsky-Korsakov, *My Musical Life*[17]). The opera was then composed during the years 1877–1878.

The duet is interrupted by the aforementioned Trinity song of the maidens and by comic scenes drawn from everyday life (drunken Kalenik; then the wooing of Hanna by the Village Head; and, at the conclusion of the first act, the swaggering song of the youths). The further development of the lyrical element takes place only in the third act. It begins with a magical sound sketch: a symphonic tableau of a May night in the springtime. Rimsky-Korsakov achieves here a moving combination of simplicity, natural expressive charm, and, at the same time, precision in illustration, using the most delicate roulades of aural adornment. No distinct colors are found here, but instead the subtlest and least perceptible of nuances in the dissemination of reflected light and in the soft, gently shifting shadows of this "moonlit" music![18] Here the light softly flows, instead of rapidly spilling forth, and in the gentle stream of moonbeams, silence itself sounds, brightly and transparently. *Silence sounds*: I can find no better definition to render in words the impression of this musical moment.

In this silence, a man voices his song of love. Levko remembers and dreams of Hanna in the spontaneous and sincere lullaby, "Sleep, my beauty," sung with the tender admiration of a masculine will confronted with a young girl's beauty. His dreams are met with the emergence of a world of ghosts. A sad, mournful, frail, and crystalline tune rings out in the air—the voice of Pannochka, pining away.[19] Her languor, her softly spreading sadness resounds, entices, and allures. In Pannochka's singing, the composer brought forth the eternal suffering and the dream of an unknown life of sweet delight, a mood so familiar to Russian maidens. First, Hanna, suffused with life, surrounded by the warmth of love; and after her, the ghostly form of despondent Pannochka, woven out of moonbeams and silvery streams of water: these are the realizations of the Russian dream of the eternally beautiful sanctity of femininity.

Korsakovian composition has a remarkable quality to it: in spite of the harmonic instability and undulation, the wonderfully changeable roulades of timbre, the unwavering instinct for color—and by this means, the steadfast and meticulously underscored fondness for the coloristic quality of the sound— nevertheless, at all times, an astonishing precision of outline is always maintained, so that the music never becomes blurred in a whirlwind of splendors, never allows a spot of color to acquire an independent structural significance or become a controlling element. The compositional plan emerges from the outline, and that outline directs all the rhythmic patterns of color and all the changes of timbre.

The remaining unused space between the *khorovod deistvo*, the lyrical states of infatuation, and the aural sketch of a nocturnal atmosphere is filled in with everyday scenes and expert graphic characterizations of Gogolian personages: the Village Head, the clerk, Kalenik, and especially the distiller—four sharply distinguished characters in all. To each one there belongs a quite particular, idiosyncratic, and rich "sung" language and an ingenious instrumental characterization, whose delights cannot be rendered in words. I need only recall such moments as the distiller's tale about the mysterious newcomer choking on a dumpling, the vainglorious tall tales of the Head and his awkward and agitated amorous speech;[20] the appearance of the clerk against a background of a march subjected to humorous treatment, the drunken entrance of Kalenik and the drunken beat of his hopak, some precisely characterized speech intonations of all four; and finally, the scene in front of the shed, with its outstanding musical humor. To these one must add the no less vivid person of the sister-in-law, especially on account of her ferocious assault on the Head, who becomes flustered by the onrush of her words. Lifelike verisimilitude[21] and simplicity, clarity and distinctiveness, sincere and gentle laughter, together with genuinely witty inspiration—these are the main character traits in Korsakovian characterizations, reinterpreting in music the heroes' personages from Gogol's heartfelt tale.[22]

May Night is an opera in chamber style, an opera of intimate poetry, where significance is found in the tiniest details of the twists in the intonations and the instrumental colors, so accurately reproducing the reflection of the stream of reality and the change of spiritual states. *May Night* is an opera of fragile, crystalline sounds and gentle interlacing of rhythms, an opera of soft contrast of melos (the melos of life, nature, and spirits), an opera of the delicate dreamy lyricism of love. On the whole, the work is a musico-poetic *deistvo of spring*, individual and inimitable in its formal and stylistic particularities and, of course, having nothing in common with operas wherein man and life at high tide, in its ebb and flow, are less significant than dramatic intrigues and adventures. It is not to deny a place for operas of this cast but in order that artistic worth be acknowledged not only in them, but also in Russian operas, which are so unique both in conception and realization, that I am now dedicating my research.

In Russian operas, external dramatic intrigue may not exist at all, since it is not the intrigues and adventures that create the action, but the opposite: the action, proceeding from *internal* sources, from the spiritual life of the individual, from religious or poetic-philosophical speculation, is responsible for the presence of a dramatism appearing on the *outside*—in the subject matter and in the relationships *of everyday existence*. The latter occupy a significant place in the composition of Russian operas, and along with symphonic sketches in sound and the moods of nature or episodes from life, emerge either as an

organically implanted fabric of the *whole* or as an inevitable and essential stylistic *device* (as, for example, in *The Tale of Tsar Saltan*). Indeed, the scenic and
theatrical essence and significance of Russian opera is revealed in part in the
khorovod deistvo. But that is another topic.

I have shown how various elements in the composition of *May Night*, being tied together in a complex, yet classically lucid and clear manner, comprise
in their entirety its musico-poetic and dramatic mold or mode. That which lies
behind the mold and mode and which nourishes them, the creative imagination and organizing thought, are irretrievable in their secret core. Their presence can only be intuited and sensed according to the degree of their appearance in the work created. And if *May Night* strikes one as a radiant "*deistvo* of
spring," then one cannot help seeing in it the expression of desires and outbursts of a youthful imagination inspired by life's springtime and striving toward spring, in the joyous vernal flight of thought that soars.

NOTES

1. Asafyev has in mind the *grandes opèras Les Huguenots, Le Prophète*, and others celebrated for the staging of action as well as ceremony.

2. The more common English-genre designation for such early 19th-century stage
works as Weber's *Der Freischütz*, Marschner's *Der Vampyr*, and *Hans Heiling* is German
Romantic opera. The incorporation (and orchestral depiction) of a supernatural element in *May Night* led Asafyev to the speculation on influence.

3. In her preface to the second edition, Elena Orlova identifies Henri Bergson,
Theodor Lipps, and Andrei Bely as likely *fin-de-siècle* sources for Asafyev's musing over
teleological life forces and the intuition by which they can be sensed.

4. The melodic material in the sowing song, "A my proso seyali," has been traced
back to several 19th-century collections; a variant appears as No. 48 of Rimsky's first
folk song anthology of 1876.

5. The relevant passage from Homer's *Iliad* concerns the images Hephaestus forged
on Achilles' shield ("the wedding song rose high / And the young men came dancing,
whirling round in rings" [Book 18, lines 576–77]).

6. I. P. Sakharov, A. V. Tereshchenko, and P. V. Shein were all ethnographers and
folklorists whose work was known to Rimsky-Korsakov. W. R. S. Ralston's *Songs of
the Russian People* (1872) is a treasure house of material on the customs and rituals behind Russian *khorovody* and other folk songs, based in part on the above-mentioned
Russian sources. It is currently (2007) available in a full reprint on the Web at
http://www.sacred-texts.com/neu/srp.

7. Asafyev's listing demonstrates the range of *khorovod* topics related to wedding rituals, agriculture, and entertainment. The song titles he lists from memory are representative examples of once broadly familiar titles, which were not tied to a single geographical region.

8. Asafyev's alternative designation *Kleshchalnaya* may be a derivation from *kleshchevina*, i.e., Palma Christi, the castor-oil plant.

9. Rimsky-Korsakov's choral arrangement of the "Proso" [Cottonseed] sowing song is the opera's first vocal number as well as the first *khorovod*. The untexted opening refrain consisting mainly of falling thirds in rapid eighths achieves a modulation from E to G, at whose arrival the curtain rises to reveal the *khorovod* already in progress.

10. The mermaids' *khorovod* (Act 3, no. 13-c) begins with a single soprano calling the others to her, which serves as the "gathering" portion. The chorus enters with the main tune at m. 28 [full score: fig. 20], whose text soon identifies this as a courtship *khorovod*.

11. The main refrain of the second *khorovod* tune, consisting of two 4-bar phrases of parallel structure, emerges at m. 43 (full score: fig. 20 + 15).

12. The concluding section of the *khorovod* begins at m. 269 (full score: fig. 30) with the quoted lines of text, while the previous refrain sounds in counterpoint underneath.

13. The choral arrangement of "O tie the wreaths" that overlaps the parting of Levko and Hanna is the fifth number of Act 1 and (as Asafyev describes below) accompanies the new spring bonding rites of friendship

14. The passage that Asafyev likens to a requiem mourning Pannochka's tragic death (fig. 65) is a chant-like, delicate duet sung by Levko and Hanna (who are indebted to her for their betrothal) and accompanied by flutes, harp, and *divisi* strings playing harmonics.

15. Levko's ballad (Act 1, no. 4, "It happened long ago") introduces the supernatural dimension as well as a key plot element and two important themes, all of which invite speculation over an influence from German Romantic opera.

16. Both Afanasy Fet (1820–1892) and Fyodor Tyutchev (1803–1873) are renowned and revered for their nature poetry.

17. Rimsky-Korsakoff, *My Musical Life*, trans. Judah Joffe (New York: Tudor, 1936), 158.

18. The 34-mm. orchestral prelude to Act 3 is launched by a horn call, a gesture traceable to Weber's *Oberon*. Contrary to Asafyev's assertion, the horn's timbre is both distinct and pervasive, despite a veiled proto-impressionistic texture of chromatically sliding accompanying string tremolos.

19. Pannochka's initial response to Levko's singing occurs two bars after fig. 8 with harp glissandi registering as her leit-timbre.

20. [Author's note:] The musical portrait of the Village Head is remarkable in this exploitation of extremes in the tempo of intonation: either a slow, dull-witted, and haughty speech or else rapid patter, i.e., the expression of his feelings in a voice, gasping from excitement.

21. [Author's note:] Verisimilitude even when the realism of the moment is so difficult to produce, as in the domestic conversation of the Head, the distiller, and the sister-in-law (Act 2).

22. The musical caricatures cited by Asafyev all occur in Act 2's four numbers. The vivid characterizations are achieved through such tagging gestures as tritone leaps, chromatic thirds, distinctive rhythms, and melismas.

· 6 ·

Snow-Maiden

(A Tale of Spring)

For all who hold our native art dear, the name of Rimsky-Korsakov's *Snow-Maiden*, that delicate flower of Russian opera, rings no less convincingly than the great names: *Ruslan*, *Prince Igor*, and *Boris Godunov*. Though perhaps not equal in value, it is still convincing as a *sui generis*, unique, profoundly original and wholly spontaneous work. The distinct temperament of *Snow-Maiden's* music, its freshness, its affability and simple wisdom are as engaging now, forty years later, as back then, during that serene period in the life of the late composer, when he conceived and, in a burst of youthful ardor and enthusiasm, brought his idea into being: an opera on the subject of Ostrovsky's play *Snow-Maiden*[1] (in Stelevo, during the summer of 1880, the opera was sketched in two-and-a-half months). The magnificent subject material was certainly a powerful impetus and served as a foundation for both the schema and the outline, even though one may state with conviction that this material, both on its own and in Ostrovsky's elaboration, by virtue of its fiery paganism and passion, would allow for a raising up to the level of myth and to the heights of myth's transformation into music, such as were attained by Wagner. Simply put, Rimsky-Korsakov's *Snow-Maiden* is not the one and only solution to the problem of Snow-Maiden as presented in Ostrovsky's story.[2] I say this, not to belittle the music, but in consciousness of its *otherness* and the beauty of its charms, which are so captivating that one forgets, while contemplating the soft light and delicate hues of a spring sun at dawn and dusk spreading through the music, about the unflinching severity and the conceptional strength of the story itself.

The main guideposts of the conception are these: after spring must come summer, after first bloom, maturity, after infatuation, a fervent and greedy impulse. Earth and humanity await the sun. All that has flowered must fall off, with a ripening of the fruit commencing in exchange. The tender, delicate blossoms of snowdrops, violets, and lilies of the valley, fearfully hiding in the grass from the burning rays of the sun, melt and disappear. Any passivity or refusal of struggle, of tempering will be persecuted, and woe to a creature that does not carry within a fertile seed waiting to be sown: the sun will burn it without mercy. Such is the law of life, the change or turn of life's evolution. And that is as it should be. But, in his eternal and incessant aspiration, man wishes through art and by means of art to consolidate and safeguard for perennial and unforced admiration all that captivates *him* in nature. And if some musical creators move on, along with the mighty stream of life, not thinking of any crystallization but nervously and impulsively dredging out their thoughts, dreams, and experiences, not considering the isolated worth or lack it of each moment for the ear but only the emotional veracity and sincerity of what has been created (Wagner, Tchaikovsky), there are others, who, on the contrary, though they do not love life any less, go out to *meet* it, to choose fond and favorite instants, in order to transform them lovingly into sounding shapes and, through the power of love, place them forever into their personal universe of creative ideas.

Every musician knows how difficult it is, when listening to Wagner's music, not to surrender oneself to the forceful summons of his will, when the intellect is in no position to pause to contemplate the beauty of one or more isolated groups of sound on their own account. In contrast, the charm of Rimsky-Korsakov's music lies in the constant contemplation of the beauty of the sounds.[3] The composer himself adored and cherished every sound and every chord. Their delicate and intermittent interweaving in his works is always elaborated before the listener in the most captivating colors and illumination. Not a single property is forgotten, provided it can augment the aural value of the sound pattern and prepare delights before the wondrous beauty of resounding vistas and expanses. A wise economy of means and prudent frugality in its dispersal should give no cause for dismay: they stem not from the stinginess of the skinflint Pliushkin but from the Miserly Knight's infatuation with the fiery gleam of metal![4]

With respect to *Snow-Maiden*'s subject, the difference in approach leads to a strong difference in its treatment. A realist and lyricist of everyday existence, Ostrovsky draws us onward toward the sun and summer. With him, with Berendei, with Bermyata, and all the people of Berendei's kingdom, we await the exchange of spring for the time of ripening, in hopes that the sun might transmute its anger into kindness:

Dárui, bog svéta, tyóploe lyéto,
Krasnopogódnoe, lyéto khleboródnoe![5]

[God of Light, grant a warm summer,
Fine weather to grow the grain!]

Snow-Maiden dies; for indeed, the snowdrop must die as well, no less than the just a bit longer-lived lily-of-the-valley. (It is not without reason that Tsar Berendei compares Snow-Maiden to a lily-of-the-valley.[6]) Mizgir perishes just as anyone does who wishes to live only in springtime, by means of the spring, in expectation of an eternal existence of spring alone. He has betrayed summer and the shining of the sun: a strong and powerful man whose commitment is to fertilize life, he sallies forth contrary to nature and expends his passionate energy on phantasmal appearance! But Kupava and Lel deserve to live on, and it is with good reason that, contrary to formal demands, the play's conclusion tells us nothing of their eventual fate: still to come for them are summer, fall, and winter.[7] They live with nature. This is the idea ("Praise to the Sun!") of Ostrovsky's *Snow-Maiden.*

Another attainment radiates from Rimsky-Korsakov's *Snow-Maiden,* from the story now retold in music. In it is revealed the purely and profoundly human (even in its opposition to the eternal flow of all that is bestowed on nature, deeply human) inclination that love summons to awaken the spring of life—an inclination to preserve and imprint into music all the enchantments of nature in springtime, the nature that is so familiar, so near, northerly, and dear to us, to Russians. If in the opera Tsar Berendei, as a hierophant and priest of the god of the Sun, announces that neither the sad passing of Snow-Maiden nor the demise of Mizgir should disturb anyone; and if the magnificent ritualized final chorus praises mightily the coming of spring, all of this will still not deceive the listener: the mournful tale of the life and death of the girlish Snow-Maiden on the one hand and, on the other, the beguiling transformation into sound of the caress, the bliss, the grief, the languor, and the fleetingness of spring moods against the background of a remarkable musical sketch of nature in springtime cannot fail to produce such a deep and lasting impression, so that no sort of triumphant ritual and no amount of conviction that all comes to pass as it must and is taking its proper place can convince us as to the justice in the Sun's retribution, of the necessity of summer's coming, and of the fact that all of the opera's music is leading us to this "Slava." We *grieve* for Snow-Maiden, for the passing of spring with its tender dawns, its soft evening light and timid, pale lilies-of-the-valley. How can people help sorrowing for spring, since, no matter how wonderful summer might be, fall will certainly follow! . . .

The great significance and unsurpassable beauty of Rimsky-Korsakov's tale of spring glow namely in its *springlike quality,* which resonates with a magical conviction and appeal.[8] The composer leads us from the first breaths and calls of springtime, from the first step of awakening life, when "the early spring flowers have only just shown themselves on thawed patches," from a shy and vague rumbling toward the spring chanting of nature and toward the spring songs of human beings. Spring and the life of nature in springtime form the substance of this music. Snow-Maiden is the incarnation of fragile, fleeting beauty and of poignant spring laments, laments over the inevitability of death. Rimsky-Korsakov's inspiration lends its warmth with an even light over the entire opera, but in such moments as the introduction (the flight of spring); the second arioso of Snow-Maiden with its "lark-like" roulades (the gentle languor and anxious calls of nature in the spring); the third arioso of Snow-Maiden (foreboding of death's inevitability); the first arioso of Tsar Berendei (contemplation over spring's lily-like beauty); the spring night and morning in the mysterious forest, Snow-Maiden's gravitation toward the sun (a love duet, so softly transparent); and, finally, her melting away—in these moments the music achieves great depth, reaching to the innermost recesses and sources of life, those which can only be *heard*, concerning which, words, being chained to reality, must unwillingly keep silent.[9]

Thus music alone can transform Ostrovsky's tale, so as to suspend the natural *gravitation* of the action toward the Sun, *substituting* its quite miraculous presence in the world with the *eternal desire for spring*. And if, in all of the sounds of music, humanity aspires not only to reconstruct the eternal evolving of all things, but in a reflection of the phenomenon of crystallization in nature, also to imprint the ever-flowing world of phenomena into patterns of sound, then in *Snow-Maiden*, that latter goal was achieved by Rimsky-Korsakov in a most desirable and attractive form: through song (for song permeates the entire opera) and through a springlike, soft, and transparent vividness in the instrumentation, where the fragility of crystal and a thawing softness of sounds are remarkably brought together with a distinction and lucidity of line and where the wafting of serene springlike tones is juxtaposed with the mysterious transparency of the fantastic forms of unknown creatures of legend.

Yet all along, parallel to nature, "Berendei's folk of both sexes and all ages"[10] move about and act or, rather, cowering in fear, follow the behests of nature, religion, and existence. Among those distinguished as individuals are Tsar Berendei, the foreign trader Mizgir, and the girl Kupava. The tsar is a contemplative sage, masterfully characterized by the composer, his sagacity showing in his awareness of the sense behind everything that happens. No fear of death, no despondency, no weariness! A good-natured smile and gentle humor permeate all of his relations with people, while the sober and austere (out of simplicity) wisdom of a pantheistic pagan infuses his contemplation. Only *beauty* calling forth delight in the presence of her revelations can engender in Berendei lyrical bliss and sweet languor! . . .

Mizgir and Kupava are two passionate creatures, ecstatic from their passion and scornful of ordinary rules and customs—yet their passions are contradictory. The powerful Mizgir is captivated by Snow-Maiden, whose coldness he wishes to overcome, not suspecting that her coldness is her essence, and no passion is hiding underneath a cover of modesty. In the passionate Kupava, there is nothing for him to overcome: she herself surrenders to him. Hence, Mizgir, still craving triumph, goes forth to meet the daughter of spring, at a time when both people and nature have already set out to greet summer: Mizgir, of course, dies; and Kupava enters into union with radiant Lel.

Lel is a demigod and not an individual.[11] He stands in the same relationship to the sun as Snow-Maiden to spring. Over the course of the entire story, his speech-songs become more impassioned as if to turn crimson; he awakens in girls the desire of love, just as the sun, striking the earth with its rays and warming it, engenders in it the energy of fertilization.

Encircling the *dramatis personae* like a *khorovod* chain, other people take measured steps: measured, since life for all of them flows in accordance with the natural chain of events and is united by the pantomime of custom and existence. Shrovetide celebration, the stroll in the mysterious forest, and the wedding sacrifice on Yarila's Day[12]—these are the tableaus of religious rites, which include the last chorus: the adoration of the sun. The ransom (or, rather, the abduction) of the bride, the lamentations of Kupava, the herald's cries, the judgment, the welcoming and seeing off of Berendei—these reflect the rites in worldly existence in relation to the tsar and those near to him. In the music, it all flourishes and is revealed in the traits that characterize the unique talent of Rimsky-Korsakov. It is not found in the austere grandeur of myth but in that gentle countenance revealing a kindhearted infatuation with poetic images, a faith in the past and a transformation of the images into vital, concretely perceptible *life forces*, suffused with the spirit of paganism. On the other hand, blind secularism and crude formalized relationship toward God, toward life, and toward existence are whimsically ridiculed in the amusing musical characterization of the courtier Bermyata.[13]

Thus, the music of *Snow-Maiden* encapsulates the tightly closed circle of an integral worldview. The essence of Snow-Maiden's tale as retold in music, i.e., the center of the circle, I repeat, is found in the unsurpassable delight of spring. Hence the indisputable significance of the opera lies with the fact that the composer has managed to render nature during springtime into sounds and to reveal, within this aural transformation, the awakening and growth of vital forces and the blossoming of springtime. And if we might only wish it, we can always gain a sense in the music of *Snow-Maiden* of springtime and youth, for the power of music's charms is limitless, provided that the composer himself believes in what he has created. There is no reason to doubt this, for any passage in *Snow-Maiden* confirms better than any words the profound sincerity and veracity in all the music—music of the Russian spring.

NOTES

1. Alexander Ostrovsky (1823–1886) completed *Snow-Maiden* in 1873. As myth-based verse drama, it marks a considerable departure from the realist drama *The Storm* and the later historical plays.

2. Even though the themes explored by Ostrovsky could be developed into a philosophical music drama, Asafyev suggests that Rimsky-Korsakov instead used the play as a vehicle for an evocation of the Russian spring, while he meanwhile focused on the emotional drama.

3. In Chapter 8, pp. 73–74, Asafyev will posit a similar contrast between Tchaikovsky as an exponent of teleological form and Rimsky-Korsakov, once again, as an early producer of what will later be called *Momentform*.

4. Pliushkin was the archetypal miser visited by Chichikov in Gogol's *Dead Souls*. By contrast, Pushkin's knight is covetous of vast riches.

5. The excerpt is from the closing chorus of play and opera, which accompanies the apparition of the handsome young sun god Yarila, garbed in white.

6. Cf. Mei, Act 2, sc. 5; and Rimsky-Korsakov, Tsar Berendei's cavatina (Act 2, fig. 7).

7. In fact, the merchant Mizgir commits suicide after realizing that he cannot protect Snow-Maiden from the sun's rays. The shepherd Lel, however, is able to relinquish her and pledge his love to Kupava in the finale to Act 3.

8. A stronger yet still plausible claim would be that Rimsky-Korsakov used the orchestration not merely to evoke spring generally, but to follow the libretto in tracing the season's progress from equinox to solstice, i.e., from the hushed, low A-minor pedal that opens the opera to the fully scored, choral-orchestral blaze of the final chorus. Knowledge of the compositional task at hand is a step toward understanding how and why Rimsky-Korsakov's tone-poetic orchestration differs markedly from Wagner's. For some prominent timbres and gestures, see note 9 below.

9. A list of distinctive timbres found in the seven passages identified by Asafyev should attest to the variety in instrumentation employed by Rimsky to evoke impressions of spring: (1) Introduction, mm. 20–60: string tremolo, whirling figures for (arco) violins punctuated by pizzicati, woodwind calls; (2) prologue ("I heard, mama, I heard"): chromatic oboe solo with woodwind trio; (3) Tsar Berendei's cavatina (Act 2, no. 7, "Mighty nature, full of wonders"): cello solo, then violin, accompanied by muted strings; (4) spring night (Act 3, no. 5): extended bass clarinet solo, later polymetric string texture; (5) spring morning (Act 4, no. 2): flute, two violins, harp; (6) a love duet (Act 4, no. 5, designated "finale" in the score, mm. 27–122): a Korsakovian (not Wagnerian!) orchestral tutti; (7) the "melting away" (Act 4, no. 5, mm. 216–64): chamber scoring with woodwinds and strings.

10. The onstage chorus is so designated in the *dramatis personae* listing for both play and opera.

11. The shepherd Lel is indeed a Slavic demigod, broadly familiar after Afanasyev's 19th-century anthologies of Russian folk tales.

12. Yarila's Day traditionally coincides with the summer solstice and is associated with St. Peter's Day (June 29); hence it marks the end of spring.

13. Buffo leaps, heavy brass and percussion scoring, and flourishes akin to those characterizing Baron Ochs make the intent of musical caricature unmistakable.

· 7 ·

Incantations

 $\mathcal{T}$ he music of Rimsky-Korsakov does not wield savage, primal energies in full revelation. It is not known, and perhaps need not be known, whether the composer himself experienced primal, elemental phenomena in his soul; yet certainly outside, in the world of sounds revealed by him, elemental energy is pacified and becalmed. This was not necessarily achieved because of a vagueness or indifference to the currents of impetuous will that agitate life. Otherwise, there would be no images of the elements in his music; indeed they do exist and are almost constantly at hand in any opera by Rimsky-Korsakov. Moreover, there are operas whose conceptions are closely tied to the expression of an element, e.g., *Sadko*. Here the element of water resonates like a powerful kingdom, controlled and directed by a single will, taking on the character of the King of the Sea. The principles of control and direction are quite characteristic of Rimsky-Korsakov's creative method. "It came out thus" or "it was created so" will almost never do for him. "It must be so" and "one needs to compose it so": this is what his brain tells him. It is not an instinct of will per se, as an end in itself, that stimulates his music and is revealed in it, but a willed *principle* standing apart from the work, in the creative act, a principle that controls the development of the sound images and directs the course of the sound.

It is the magic of the astrologer, who not only makes predictions based on the constellations, but rules them: and not only the constellations, but the elements, too, as does the sorcerer Prospero in *The Tempest* or, more precisely, the Astrologer in *The Golden Cockerel* (an indelible image!).[1] With such people as these, one can never know if god or devil takes precedence in their souls. Yet it has been given to them to disseminate creative energy in any direction and subject their will to any phenomena, to summon forth any character that they desire, whether it be Kaliban, Ariel, Miranda, the Queen of Shemakha, Fevronia, Kashcheyevna, Kashchei, Berendei, or Salieri.[2] Call forth but do not reproduce yourself! Colossal spiritual intensity is required, a strength of will and discipline, and the ability to govern one's own personal talent. An ever-lively consciousness is necessary and even a large dose of rationality in order to keep control of oneself and not allow the visions called forth to seize control of the will that summoned them.

The rationalism which, to a long-acknowledged degree, characterizes the art of Rimsky-Korsakov presents itself without a doubt as a talisman, an amulet, a protective device. One could hardly bring to life without penalty the meekness and wisdom of Marfa; the divine grace of Fevronia and the ardent voluptuousness of the Queen of Shemakha; the sacred knowledge and wisdom of Prince Yuri and the diabolical irony of the Astrologer; or the heartfelt simplicity of Levko and the abysses of spiritual instability of Grishka Kuterma. I'll confess that I sometimes saw the rationalism and schematic planning behind other constructions of Rimsky-Korsakov as bordering on indifference. The temptation must simply be too great!

Consequently, questions about the psychological origins of Rimsky-Korsakov's art are for me the most vexing: not questions about his style, for here there are no doubts, but the question about his creative psyche. And let the composer's faithful disciples not become angry with me now: a faith that has undergone doubts is stronger and firmer than one that comes cheaply. "Because I love, I suffer!" (Oksana in Tchaikovsky's *The Slippers*).[3] I say all of this to prevent any misunderstanding as I now proceed with the analysis.

In essence, the relationships between the composer and the elements that he contemplated were amicable. In the cycle of Rimsky-Korsakov's pagan operas, the elemental forces passing through the representations of folk poetry permeate the music as well: here as a background, there as a grandiose active entity. In *Christmas Eve*, it is air; in *Mlada*, fire and water; in *Kashchei the Deathless*, wind; in *Snow-Maiden* and *May Night*, earth as fructiferous power, awakening also in people (as creatures born of it) a current of ardent love. Outside of this cycle: in *Sadko*, water (the ocean-sea, Lake Ilmen, streams and rapids); in *The Golden Cockerel*, it seems to be air. The elements are realized either in a static, calm state (introductions to *Sadko*, to *Christmas Eve*) that occurs more often than not, or else they are commanded to stir something up (e.g., the mighty storm in *Kashchei*)—i.e., *a spell is cast* to summon them. Never do the elements act under their own power. On the basis of this distinctive and—from a psychological and stylistic standpoint—extremely *important* peculiarity in the structuring of action in Rimsky-Korsakov's operas, a series of remarkable musical moments emerges; at times the opera's entire musical development will be based on this quality.

I have chosen two operas in order to establish more concretely my stated conclusion by observing the course of action and the development of a stylistic aim: *Mlada* and *Kashchei the Deathless*. Their essence is incomprehensible without some disclosure of the idea of an *incantation* of elements and of governance over them. In the structure of a flower, a tree, of any organism or any creature, we notice amidst the general mass of matter primary centers, which are akin to strong points or nerve centers, where cell-complexes that guide, direct, or connect are concentrated, or guided, or directed or connected. It is the same with musical-artistic conceptions: motion proceeds from or is dispatched out of one fulcrum or focal point to another, sometimes along different routes or at different rhythms. If one takes as a starting point for comprehending *Mlada* the idea of a spell and incantation, then the action flows with a striking intensity and drive precisely when the subject matter, from a dramatic standpoint, does not show itself to be a synthesis of breathtaking theatrical clashes.

Let us look closer. In the first tableau, the action intensifies at the instant of dialogue between the old woman, Sviatokhna (she is indeed Morena, the goddess of dark underworld powers), and Voislava. What is its point? It lies in the *incantation*, the summoning of Morena, after Voislava, having delivered herself to evil, has received power over elemental forces. The charms take effect, just as Morena promised: Yaromir begins to forget Mlada. The chorus of radiant spirits is the first *counterspell*, the first warning to Yaromir.[4] The second tableau is a nocturnal folk festival honoring the sun god (a summer solstice; Kupala, Yarila[5]). The priests of Radegast, god of the sun, engage in divinations. The essential moment is the impassioned incantation of fire during the Kupala *khorovod*, which is developed with remarkable intensity. The amorous zeal enthralls and infects Yaromir: more than once he attempts to kiss Voislava. Corresponding with this and parallel with it, counterspells of warning follow: Mlada separates the kissing pair and, eventually, drags Yaromir away with her.[6] The third tableau: again it is Kupala's Night, but already among the unhallowed on Triglav Mountain. With the incantation of Kashchei comes a new temptation for Yaromir: before him is the image of passionate and captivating Queen Cleopatra. The cock's crow (the approach of morning) as a counterspell against unholy forces saves Yaromir.[7] The fourth tableau: divination and summoning of ghosts, demanding vengeance. Incantation of water (Voislava): the flood and demise of the city of Retra.[8] Equilibrium is restored with a rainbow, the victory of the sun, the appearance of the gods of light and the wedding of Mlada and Yaromir in the heavens! In this way the course of action meanders all the time from incantation to counterspell (warnings), with an extremely significant moment of seduction (temptation) on occasion standing between the incantation and the counterspell. It is characteristic that without the help of Mlada, Yaromir is powerless to endure a trial and triumph over a test, no less than Ruslan without Finn. The most expressive moments in the music of *Mlada* adhere in full to these situations.

Probing deeper into their essence, we can observe the following. In festivals honoring Kupala (St. John's Eve), it is difficult to comprehend who is being honored. Is it not fire in general being honored, as an element, with the leap through the bonfire as the spell casting? But which fire is it: fire from the bright sun or from Morena (the fire of the underworld, subdued in time, but always striving to burst out), Apollo's fire or Vulcan's? In our folk beliefs, these two differing materializations of a single element are more likely to arouse vague premonitions than to be sharply distinguished; thus, the essence of Kupala's Festival remains indecipherable. Connected with the moment of the summer solstice, with the moment of the sun's turning toward cold, and of summer to heat—i.e., when the evil spirits that had been tranquil raise themselves anew and when the flame of love more strongly blazes in the human heart—this festival conceals twin origins within it: farewells to the bright sun and appeasing of the unholy, and as a result, every manner of counterspells and incantations.

The flame of love comes from the sun but comes also from within and subject to sin. It is tempting to awaken and summon it, but one needs to know how to cast the spell, for a passion scorched by it is fatal (this can emerge quite independently of religious edicts). The underworld flame, the flame of Vulcan, is also fatal: the flame of an evil and destructive element. This is why the dark power lives *under* the earth. In *Mlada* a struggle unfolds between a shining fire—Radegast, god of the sun—and an underworldly fire: one purplish-crimson, that of the goddess Morena. Out of this struggle and its results, the fate of Mlada and Yaromir is predetermined. Thus any dramatic action in this opera would certainly be senseless, whether in an external sense or in the sense of internal psychic collisions. Consequently, this opera (like *Christmas Eve*) is, in essence, static, a kind of vicious circle of enchantment: the struggle takes place at the elemental core between the forces that rule the Creation, but not inside people; the acts of people and the change of phenomena are instead conditioned and predetermined by this internal struggle of elements.

The stasis of Rimsky-Korsakov's operas is one born out of preordinations in the sense that the change of years and seasons is preordained, a stasis of the unchanging rhythm in the sequence of phenomena! This stasis is cyclic. Of course, this does not take into account the qualitative difference that arises over the course of bringing to an end each cycle of phenomena, when viewed as a vivified path, a path of changes and transformations. The qualitative aspect of spiritual experience undergone; its inimitability evokes not the image of a circle, but that of a spiral. Eternal cyclic return was the invention of man terrified before eternal change, who had noticed the constant change in nature, desiring not to know that neither one day to another, nor one spring to the next are similar. And in his art, man introduced the dream of eternal return: introduced, so that he might, in accordance with his wish, summon before himself images of (unchanging) beauty. Then the quarrel arose, a quarrel without an end, over where true beauty is to be found: whether in images of a qualitative sort, realized in a plan of lifelike growth, or in images of a more quantitative sort, in which the number of accomplishments (deeds) plays a role, but not the development of character, wherein the change of phenomena is everything but the personality as an autonomous force nothing? Music of surmounting or music of surmounting achieved? If it be the latter, then Mlada and Yaromir are two forms of lasting beauty. In the phenomenal change linked with them, all is fulfilled, just as it was. When the cycle of phenomena changes, so too does their fate.

Can one say the same for the more active individual, whose will is not the fulfiller of what is preordained, but the creator of new relationships? Then, let us say, in the occurrence of two unaltered series of events the individual might, in the second case, act quite differently than in the first. In music there is a clear example: Oksana and Vakula, together with their fate. In Rimsky-Korsakov's *Christmas Eve*, they are closely tied to the environment that bore them, just as the environment itself is fused together with the rhythm of cosmic events. Under these conditions, they will always discover the very same fate. Their characters are eternal and qualitatively unchanging. Oksana and Vakula in Tchaikovsky's *The Slippers* act like a pair in love, quite independently of the environment, which does surround them but only as *background*. And the devil's mischief is his personal vexation at Vakula, magnified into the very incarnation of evil. In Tchaikovsky, Oksana and Vakula are individuals and therefore, within the same surrounding conditions, under the repetition of the cyclic course of phenomena, they experience everything differently. They are unique and inimitable archetypes.[9]

I now comprehend the *static* quality of the Korsakovian operas in the sense of what has been discussed above, but not in the sense of any alleged lifelessness, indifference, coldness, and impotence in his psyche. This structural stasis stems from a fond contemplation of the world, from the eternal temptation for human beings to stop time, to preserve in perpetuity a desirable phenomenon or image. For the one who sees and can find satisfaction at all times and all places, everything that makes an impression needs to become permanent. Life may harshly brush aside the dream, but such people transform life into "stations" in art, rendering everything beautiful that they found to be attractive in the world.

On the other hand, there are others who see nothing as permanent, nor do they wish to see. They live in restless forward momentum, in eternal dissatisfaction, in constant and intense searching. There, somewhere further on, in the distance, looms the image they desire. Such people will render only their "searching" into art. Hence, in every moment in which matter is overcome and images are crystallized, all that impressed them earlier seems pointless and unnecessary; they take pleasure only in what they create in the present moment: that is what seems to them—in their self-deception—to be a final achievement! . . . A vivid example of this is the technical process within Tchaikovsky's works.

I shall now return to *Mlada*. The action in it unfolds in a steady succession from spell (incantation) to counterspell while, in addition, a glorification of fire or "tending" of the fire lies at the foundation of everything. Yet fire lacks a fully autonomous will (as does water) and can only act upon conjuration, on call. This trait permits one to view the entire opera as an *incantation of fire*.

A stream of incantations is also contained in the conception of *Kashchei the Deathless*, but it develops more in a tragic than a fairy-tale or epic direction. Nature delivers herself into the arms of winter. Tired from giving birth and nourishing her fruits, she waits peacefully until the winds blow down wedding attire from the trees, and blizzards and storms bring in snows and with them blanket her naked body like a shroud. This is the moment at which the action of the "Little Tale of Autumn" commences, a moment ingeniously chosen for incarnation into music.[10] The wind has been contained in Kashchei's cellar. Now the time has come for it to fulfill what has been predetermined.

The power of the *incantation* summons it forth and directs it to act so at the pleasure of Kashchei's will. The symphonic portrait of the blizzard is the marvelous sound sketch of a master.[11] In the second tableau, Kashchei's daughter must accomplish her evil deed: to destroy the force of life (as embodied in Prince Ivan), the life that is kindling in a sleeping earth, so that winter would last eternally, so that there would be no one to liberate spring, which Kashchei has captured. The music is suffused with the piquant aroma of poisonous blooms, with the cold, dispassionate, evil will of Kashcheyevna.

Rimsky-Korsakov knew of the lyrical beauty of a woman's soul in love; but like no other Russian composer, he also sensed the evil nature of a woman when she lacks the feeling of love or, even more frightening, when she, playing the coquette to the utmost limits of voluptuousness, in essence scoffs at love! Kashcheyevna's character is sinister, but the character of the Queen of Shemakha is frightening and monstrous. In creating Kashcheyevna, the composer still had not reached his art's final destination, had yet to develop all that was concealed in Snow-Maiden's cold heart.[12] Kashcheyevna could still *show pity*, i.e., could fall in love, but the Queen of Shemakha *sins* without concern.

Nevertheless, Kashcheyevna's incantations are especially frightening when one realizes that their power, like the power of Kashchei's incantations, is directed against life itself. The composer probably knew not what he was doing, yes, and probably did not dare to for otherwise he would have stopped before confronting the horrific meaning behind the myth of Kashchei.

"A Little Tale of Autumn" is not at all popular. I believe that in time, its music will be valued and that people will understand how it both attracts and frightens. Kashchei's will is turned to evil: he turns everything to ice. His arioso, based on a cold, monotonal series of short sliding phrases, one after another, is shocking due to its impassioned rage. Cold but passionate, no matter the paradox! Indeed, Kashchei is an ideologue of an immortality existing apart from life or, rather, in a crystallization of life.[13] He is the enemy of a love stemming from life but not of *sensuality*: he is no defender of dispassionateness. And is it truly so small a paradox to have created and summoned to life a human imagination, especially with the help of music!? His—Kashchei's—incantations are terrifying, for their passion stems from their immobility: dissonances, stock-still and congealed![14] Kashcheyevna's incantations of flowers and the sword, however, are more sinister, since we hear therein how a woman's passion can be directed not along the natural path of love's rapture, but toward malevolent murder.[15] In every woman a mother is concealed, and, therefore, a woman who casts a spell on the force of life and murders it, frightens all away from her. The enchantment of the music compels us to relive all that is incarnated in the singing of Kashcheyevna with such a convincing expressive force. In such moments there is an unintentional desire to take refuge in the rationalism in the works of Rimsky-Korsakov, and thereby not disturb oneself with the question: should a composer, prior to the incarnation, experience for himself that which he made incarnate with such conviction, as something true and beyond all doubt?!

Yet, if we forget about the cold enchantment of autumnal decay and Kashchei's disturbing lack of sentiment and proceed to the radiant sphere of the opera's finale, at the moment when the force of life grants spring its freedom, when the powers of Kashchei's spells are broken and warm energy has vanquished the stagnation of winter, then an even more profound riddle awaits us. For anyone acquainted with Rimsky-Korsakov's structural schemas and typical methods for developing themes, or even upon merely listening, it becomes clear that the coronation of spring in *Kashchei* is incomparably weaker and paler as music than all that was "autumnal," "deathless," and "malevolent." The composer himself, in the intense throes of creativity, succumbed to the charms of Kashchei and Kashcheyevna and, having been worn down by them, turned them into fierce and sinister characters. The preponderance of dark forces is beyond question. The bright D-major finale is too little developed (even in the second version, which includes a choir) or, more accurately, coldly formalistic, to be in a position to engulf the tenacious power of the incantations.[16]

According to the subject material, *they* lack sufficient intensity to restrain the sun's power in Prince Ivan from uniting with the soft, gentle spring beauty of the Princess. Yet the music establishes the opposite. One might certainly console himself with the explanation that is usually offered: the inspiration ran out before the finale! Personally, I believe that inspiration almost always suffices wherever it is needed and always arises when necessary. The music of Kashchei and Kashcheyevna dominates because during the period of life when work on the little tale was under way, the composer's intuition probably demanded from him a completely different resolution to the myth of Kashchei than the one given in the tales and, in particular, in this reworking of the legend of Kashchei. Perhaps at the time his imagination was inclined to envisage an incantation of life itself as fully possible. Might it not be governed by one's own will? I may carry on if I so desire or else come to a standstill. If one is to believe the music, then one must conceive the problem of Kashchei the Deathless as a tragic problem. Goethe was mistaken if he thought that man yearns to bring only the beautiful moments to a standstill. In art one can and *does* bring any moment of life to a standstill. In the character of Kashchei, the pagan folk imagination was moved to call a halt to (cast a spell on) life itself—to the life force, its growth, and animation. This is the meaning of Kashchei's deathless state. Thus, it can never correspond to the representation of an eternal spring. Spring is growth; spring is aspiration. If one cannot believe in a *dynamic* deathlessness, then he can only imagine it for himself in the character of Kashchei: in a symbol of life come to a halt.

Being accustomed to controlling life without pursuing it in blind faith, Rimsky-Korsakov was able to call forth in his imagination the character of Kashchei and, having done so, empathize with him and make a vivid incarnation of him. The harmonic structure of the little autumnal tale is quite piquant, venomous, new and original. The work appeared not under the imprint of previously inherited methods, but with the mark of bold and unusual achievement. Is this not an indication that *Kashchei* should be assigned a more significant role in the works of Rimsky-Korsakov than it appears to have? The incantational impulse links it to *Mlada* and because of the character of Kashcheyevna, with the Queen of Shemakha, i.e., with *The Golden Cockerel*. *Kashchei* is an instrumental opera, through and through—even though, because of its title, it must be listed with vocal compositions. In this respect it is akin to *Mlada*, which may be pallid in its lyrical intensity but is inspired with respect to the posing and solving of problems of instrumentation.

NOTES

1. Both Shakespeare's Prospero and Pushkin's Astrologer (from "The Tale of the Golden Cockerel") are mortal, their magic learned, not innate. Prospero's mastery over the elements is apparent from the outset, when he manages a sea-storm with precision.

2. Asafyev's listing of three more Shakespearean creations from *The Tempest* and six from Rimsky's operas reveals a great diversity in character type.

3. Tchaikovsky, *The Slippers*, Act 1, no. 7, fig. 90 + 7. At the moment, Oksana is reacting to the probable loss of her suitor Vakula as a consequence of her teasing.

4. The first-act dialogue between the maiden Voislava and the old woman Sviatokhna (i.e., the dark goddess Morena in disguise) takes place in scene 2; Voislava's incantation (fig. 18) brings on a roar from the depths, fire, and wind, all of which unleash the full force of the winds and brass in Rimsky-Korsakov's now Wagnerian-size orchestra. The chorus of radiant spirits that Asafyev characterizes as a counterspell appears in scene 5 in the course of Yaromir's dream.

5. Kupala and Yarila are both Slavic mythological personages associated with the veneration of the sun. Yarila is a youthful pagan deity, often arriving mounted on a magnificent white horse, with a garland of flowers on his head. His season is spring-time, his festival falling in April to coincide with the spring planting. At the end of spring, the burial of Yarila is marked, within a week of Trinity Sunday. By contrast, Kupala is a less defined entity, more conceptual receptacle of seasonal traditions and preoccupations than god. In Christian times, the veneration of Kupala on or about the summer solstice merged with the Feast of John the Baptist (24 June, old style), which further reinforced Kupala's association with cleansing by water (the stem of Kupala relates to the verbs *kupat* [to bathe] and *kipet* [to boil]) as well as by fire (e.g., with individual or communal leaps through a bonfire).

6. Overlooking the introductory crowd scenes of the second act, Asafyev focuses on the *khorovod* ritual that brings the putative lovers Voislava and Prince Yaromir together, only to be separated by the shade of Mlada (portrayed by a dancer, not a singer). In Asafyev's interpretation, Mlada acts as a counterspell to Morena's magic on Voislava's behalf, thanks to Yaromir's still lingering love for her (i.e., for Mlada).

7. The opera's third act is largely taken up with a demonic festival, which offsets the celebration and praise of the sun god Radegast in the second act. Rather than a summoning, it is more of a spontaneous gathering of the dark gods, demons, and witches. The apparition of Cleopatra takes up scene 4. The counterspell of a cock's crowing (1 measure before fig. 47: muted trumpet call at *fff*) emerges unbidden by any character. The crowing and the dawn's arrival elicit predictable changes in the music: the chromaticism wanes, the melos turns diatonic, and triads establish the *roseate* (to Rimsky-Korsakov!) key of A.

8. In telegraphic prose, Asafyev lists the main supernatural interventions of the fourth act. Yaromir is visited by the shades of heroes (scene 3); Voislava, dying from Yaromir's mortal blow, summons Morena to wreak havoc on Radegast's temple (scene 5); sea-storms and an earthquake follow (scene 6, keyless chromaticism for full orchestra) until finally calm and key (first B major, then E) are restored and a rainbow of

seven colors (symbolized by seven contrasting triads!) appears, to illumine a procession of the gods of light.

9. The restating of Asafyev's psychological distinctions between the Gogol adaptations of Tchaikovsky and Rimsky-Korsakov (see Chapter 8) is appropriate here, first because Mlada as dancing ghost certainly does lack the full-bodied individuality of Tchaikovsky's heroines; and secondly because once again, the rhythm of natural events has greater cumulative effect on the operatic structure than do the emotional vicissitudes of the characters.

10. "A Little Tale of Autumn" is Rimsky's subtitle for a work consisting merely of a single act divided into an uninterrupted succession of three tableaus.

11. The plucking of an orchestral harp corresponding to Kashchei's onstage magic harp unleashes the snowstorm for full orchestra and offstage "invisible" chorus, an orchestral interlude developed out of various figurations of diminished seventh chords.

12. [Author's note:] The character of Snow-Maiden points to Marfa, to Kashcheyevna, to Fevronia, and to the Queen of Shemakha.

13. Kashchei's arioso ("I have grasped nature's secret," first tableau, fig. 26) reveals his uncanny state of being: an existence removed from the modalities of life and death, the secret of whose destruction is locked up in the frozen heart of his daughter, thus rendering him "deathless." The rigid, astringent melos of the arioso is blatantly defined by falling tritones and falling half steps.

14. The incantations themselves are, predictably enough, in recitative character, declaimed atop dissonant sonorities of uncertain key (e.g., first tableau, fig. 31).

15. Kashcheyevna collects the poisonous blooms and sword at the beginning of the second tableau (figs. 48, 51). The flowers are associated with a motive of chromatically joined falling thirds, the sword to an ostinato of four brusque minor triads (E, C, E, G#).

16. Even though the D-major tonality used to close the opera is amply prepared well in advance by diatonic passages in A and D assigned to Prince Ivan, Asafyev objects to its brevity (17 mm. total), a deficiency unremedied by the gain of chorus in the revised conclusion of 1906. [Author's note:] Indeed, the entire characterization of Prince Ivan is rather stereotypical in its "typically Russian" stylization.

· 8 ·

Christmas Eve

(A True-Life Carol)

The rhythmic element that imperiously controls all the manifestations of life, within the continuity and flow of life, nevertheless incorporates moments akin to foundations, to fulcrums or concentrations of force: zeniths and nadirs within the eternal alternation of ebb and flow, day and night, strength and weakness. The rhythm in the life of the world's peoples, life that is still not separated from nature, likewise follows the beating of a cosmic pulse that affects the course of life's most important paths. The four seasons in their sequence, in their full circle, demand an involuntary adaptation to them from human life and a corresponding accommodation. But within the seasons' eternally continuous succession, people have detected fulcrums, points of departure and arrival, around which—or more precisely *through* which—an eternal cyclic return is fulfilled: an eternal return to the point of origin. These fulcrums give birth, strictly speaking, to the rhythm of nature, i.e., to the differentiation of strong segments (ictuses, theses), without which rhythm is undifferentiated, since in a regular, incessantly flowing uniform mass or in a monotonous repetition of a sound of equal dynamic, pitch, duration, and timbre, rhythm cannot be perceived! Certain instants have been imprinted in the everyday existence and beliefs of the Russian people since time immemorial: the winter solstice—winter's turning to the cold ("the frost rages, sensing its irreversible demise"), as time moves ahead toward warmth; the vernal equinox—a restoration of rights to spring; the summer solstice—summer's turning hot as time moves toward the cold; and the autumnal equinox—that moment when nature, having delivered a ripe harvest to people, seems to congeal in expectation of a sleep unto death, allowing the winds to tear off summer's fine raiment and prepare to lay on the shroud.

In the life of the people, these conceptual moorings—moments of respite—serve as a concentration and amassing of life energy, not, however, for the sake of labor but in order to while away time in celebration—in a jubilant contemplation of the changing course of the divinities that guide human life. There are four main festivals, of which three have up until now not lost their pagan adornment: (1) the festival of Ovsen and Kolyada[1] (associated with Christmas); (2) a series of spring festivals from Shrovetide to Semik[2] (Seventh Thursday) inclusive, whose center is Easter, and within which one finds a mixture of ancient pagan and Christian beliefs that are almost inaccessible to analysis; (3) the Festival of Kupala, i.e., summer's prime, a celebration of fire and the sun.[3] The harvest festival (4) spreads out into a series of Christian festivals, including the three Holidays of the Savior, dissolving into the September feasts extending to The Feast of the Protection.[4] Of course, in essence the entire cycle is tied to representations of the struggle of good and evil (dark, unclean) forces, and the previously mentioned points signify various peripeteias of this struggle. With the influence of one force or another, a variety of beliefs are connected: customs, full-fledged *deistva*, and even liturgical ritual. And to all of this, in turn, are linked the offshoots of folk musico-poetic art: incantations, protective spells, laments, charms, various types of tale-telling, and the luxuriant flower that is lyric song; in addition, there are elements of dramatic art: games, dances, *khorovody*, rites of friendship betrothal, Shrovetide celebration, the burning of Kostroma,[5] leaps through the fire, and all possible types of divination and community games, including the thoroughly worked-out *deistvo* of the wedding rite. It all stands in such a close relationship to life and also to nature and through nature, and is so inseparable from the creative workings of cosmic forces, that it could not fail to enthrall a composer—assuming that urban culture has not destroyed in him those perceptions of life which respond sensitively to all that transpires and is attained in nature; which rejoice in the springtime at her resurrection and growth, and in wintertime, struggle with the chills and blizzards that freeze life. Since music as an art lacks images with concrete associations, it is therefore well situated to reproduce the interaction of the cosmic forces whose reciprocal struggle gives birth to life: music lives in motion, in full awareness of a beating pulse, in the regular exchange of beats, i.e., in *rhythm* that is both all-encompassing and unconditional.

Among Russian musicians Rimsky-Korsakov has, up to now, revealed most fully the idea of a cosmic rhythm in his compositions. The presence of an inborn feeling for nature and the stylistic tendency to master the offshoots of the folk's musico-poetic language helped him to realize an entire series of significant and worthy artistic conceptions. Among his operas, five are closely linked to the cult of nature and four of them to the rhythmic sequence of folk holidays. Here they are, beginning with the instant of the winter solstice: *Christmas Eve, Snow-Maiden, May Night, Mlada,* and *Kashchei the Deathless.* The central three are closely connected: from the first striking up of spring songs to Kupala's *khorovod!* An analysis of each of these operas in this respect would be a most interesting task, embracing the broad expanse and depths of folk life as conceived by a great Russian musician at the end of the 19th century. For the time being I shall dwell on *Christmas Eve.*

For its originality, for freshness and wholeness of poetic conception, for formal structure and juxtaposition of splendid material, for a laconic expressivity of language—this work counts as among the finest. It is more than acutely intelligent: it is wise. All the more vexing then is its fate, its rejection, and unpopularity. I shall attempt to reveal the meaning of the entire composition, which so undeservedly remains an unsolved riddle.

With due caution, I will touch on the problem of Gogol in Russian music. I would prefer to turn it into the question of how the schemes of Gogol's tales have so intensely entered into the lyricism of Russian composers, or, to narrow the range even more, how the souls of those heroes who have roles in *May Night* and in *Christmas Eve* or *The Slippers* glimmer in the music.[6] Heroes in tales, however, are merely a literary concept: music sings to us of people infused with warm breath.

One might state the matter in this way: Tchaikovsky—with the full naiveté and immediacy of his melodic gift in which so many elements of Ukrainian vocal lyricism are found, with the full richness and intensity of his harmonies—deepened the life of Oksana and Vakula and attained bold drama, suffused with passionate ardor, even though the subject did not extend the privilege to do so. And therefore, after the drama in the scenes of scoffing and cunning and of poignantly felt coquetries (the second and fourth tableaus of the opera), in which the character of Oksana is sketched so vividly and so well, there is nothing more with which to stock the action: a blissful wedding is too bourgeois an ending for so highly developed and profoundly experienced a narration in song of such an unassuming love story. The same could be said of the characterization of the remaining personages. Moreover, in Tchaikovsky's work, an evil power has stirred up the world and a bit of weather maliciously and in full earnest: one senses that the matter at hand is something far more important and disturbing than one might think from the tone of Gogol's tale. Does the tragic end to the latter's life not suggest that Tchaikovsky just might have been correct and that, if in Dikanka the association with an evil spirit ends unostentatiously—with a flight to Petersburg and back—then subsequently the devil inside Gogol not only stole the moon within plain sight, but all of God's world as well, leaving him only "dead souls" or virtuous living mummies of Kostanzhoglo's ilk for hire?[7]

Rimsky-Korsakov approached Gogol naively and directly, with a youthful freshness and even a fervor in that delightful opera of springtime, *May Night*. Its music is filled with tender caresses that are inexpressible in words; with warm, soulful singing; and with a witty realization of the comic spirit: it is a fascinating festival, a green-bedecked Springtide, a night-long's sacred vigil of spring, flowers, warmth, and joy. I cannot conceive of any more fitting, more poetic approach to the tale: and with no note of tragedy, of sadness and suffering, which darkens the Holy Night in Tchaikovsky's *The Slippers* and renders this splendid opera somewhat incompatible with its subject. I have purposely compared *The Slippers* with *May Night* first, instead of *The Slippers* and *Christmas Eve*, since in the former case an equally sincere, direct, and purely lyrical approach to the tales in both composers comes to the fore and a generalized method resulting from contemplative mental effort has not yet become the main priority.[8] Therefore, in proceeding to a comparison of *Christmas Eve* and *The Slippers* with regard to the lyrical impulse, it emerges that in *The Slippers*, living people endowed with individual passions, joys, and sorrows interact, whereas in *Christmas Eve*, the expression of feelings is stylized; each person in the drama is expressed within the confines of a manner of speech characteristic of the particular personality type: a type, and not a personal identity.

Here the approach to the characters proceeds not from the emotionally idiosyncratic uniqueness of each individual, but according to a generalization stemming from a preassigned *lyrical sphere* within whose boundaries a type of music is defined which is not as characteristic of a given personage as of his position in the community and of the conscious state in which he abides. It is an approach moving from the whole to the particular, from the community to the individual, to its member: thus it is in folk art, e.g., in laments, wherein it is not such and such a definite person under consideration but a husband, father, son, brother, wife, daughter, or sister in general—and the mourner designs her lament in accordance with a schema established since antiquity. This then is the vitally important dividing line between the dramaturgical styles of Tchaikovsky and Rimsky-Korsakov, and a particularly important characteristic of the latter's works, having great significance and exerting an enormous shaping influence on the character of his operas. We will therefore dally for a moment on the characterizations of the *dramatis personae* in *Christmas Eve*. The conclusions will lead us to a deciphering of the content of the entire composition. Naturally I will take up only the most striking features.

In an adaptation to opera, whose language is essentially nothing more than a musical transformation of the word—i.e., an *intonatsiya*[9] within the strictly delineated limits of intervallic interrelationships—the approach from the general to the particular just now explained is expressed in the assignment of the acoustical speech of the *dramatis personae* within a predetermined vocal-instrumental channel. That general channel, which results in a unity of expression and coloration, is in this case that of the Ukrainian song element. It is more precisely not an element, but a song *style* of the sort established in an environment of late 18th-century influences, which developed further both in Ukraine and far away from it, in Petersburg, having been imported by singers, church choristers, and composers of the Elizabethan and Catherinian epochs. The flourishing of this style provides the possibility of elucidating a series of musical *categories*, which in turn create means of expression that are quite characteristic of the entire array of *dramatis personae*.[10]

Categories of song and lyric include the following: the pure lyricism of song; lyricism with instrumental nuances (rhythms of Polish dances: polonaise and krakowiak; the Ukrainian national rhythm of the hopak); the lyricism of the romance (song transmitted through urban culture); lyricism of everyday life and ritual, including arioso laments that are not in the character of recitative; expressive lyricism (songs of particular strata of the population and the estates; comic and satirical songs; Cossack songs).

Categories related to the epic:[11] sacred verse, epic folk ballads (*dumy*), ecclesiastical recitative, partly historical songs, recitative from ordinary life (of bazaars and streets), the musical stylization of folk discourse; and in the dramatic sphere: incantations, games, and *khorovody*.

The instrumental element is found in: riffs, improvisations, every manner of instrumental ornaments (figurations), dance incipits, and finally, bell peals.

Song lyricism has the greatest significance in *Christmas Eve*. The entire characterization of Vakula in love (apart from the thematic instrumental riff that accompanies his appearances) is produced on the basis of one of its strata: the lyricism of the romance. Next, there is lyricism with dance inflections, based on whose elements a part of Oksana's characterization is conveyed (in the second tableau's scene of coquetry, during the second half the A-major aria, a polonaise rhythm appears[12]) and a ceremonial and everyday lyricism (carols, the songs of Chub and the Village Head, the song phrases of Solokha and the devil). Purely vocal ("long-breathed") Ukrainian lyricism, with its archaic or traditional tunes, is seldom encountered in this opera; more often there is an inherently false romance style or the generic Korsakovian melos. However, one finds splendid moments even of this sort, such as Oksana's second aria (with nuances derived from the folk lament).[13]

Speech of an epic cast is used inconsistently (with the exception of the sacristan's "inspired" and highly florid gloria in honor of Solokha, although here we are more likely dealing with a brilliant caricature and not with authentic epic speech).[14] The characterization of Catherine's court is exclusively instrumental (a sumptuous polonaise), which contrasts with the fantastic realm of flight. The dramatic sphere assumes pride of place through carols, games, *khorovody*, and, finally, the incantations of Solokha, the devil, Patsyuk, Vakula (one little phrase of sacred character is akin to a sign of the cross), the bell pealing and the chorus in religious style on the morning of Christ's birth like an incantation against the Evil One at the end of the flight. There is no complete representation of ceremonial or religious-ritualistic drama in *Christmas Eve*.

Such an attachment of *dramatis personae* and dramatic moments to a general channel, according to categories of vocal style, brings about a well-determined outcome, when the method of characterization is persistently followed. All of the characters and the full course of action do not appertain to themselves alone, are not treated as independent worthies; but are drawn into the sphere of action of a force, unknown to them, that controls them. Gogol's tale is thereby transformed into myth, into a true-life carol, concerning which one's own vantage point, i.e., whether from the standpoint of ceremony and ordinary existence (the true-life aspect) or from that of religion and the epic (carol-myth), determines whether it is to be a matrimonial *deistvo* (the devil disturbs the wedding, but a sign of the cross chastises him, commanding him to offer a service on the lovers' behalf) or a religious event: a warming turn of the Sun and the appearance of Ovsen and Kolyada. Rimsky-Korsakov's task was to underscore the mythological aspect and develop it in such a way that a most ordinary fact of life—Vakula's wooing—would lose its everyday quality and would be drawn into a kind of *game* of elements: into a struggle between light and dark powers. This is why Vakula, Oksana, and the others do not emerge as individuals with a dynamic cast of mind. Indeed, the love between Vakula and Oksana as *individuals* has no significance at all with respect to community and religion. Their wedding is important only as an act of union between a lad and a lass—representatives of the species, for the propagation of the species.

This is the fundamental point of divergence between Tchaikovsky and Rimsky-Korsakov as operatic composers dealing with a common subject, whereas it is completely insignificant that one creates *subjectively* and the other *objectively*. The perceptions and images of both are deeply subjective; however, the former opposes the individual and the world, whereas the latter connects personality with the world through an insertion of its *intonatsii* into the lyricism of folk song—meaning of course only the style of it, not an obligatory use of folk melodies or a chanting of songs "in the rough." Let me use a concrete example of how I comprehend this insertion. No matter how she *personally* senses the approaching moment of her wedding, every village girl will "lament" like all others, as is customary, based on a long since established motive, regardless of whether she marries out of love or by force. Such is Oksana in Rimsky-Korsakov: distinguished from among her friends, she still remains connected to them and "speaks" as do they all in the "style of Dikanka girls," as the composer intended to recreate them. Tchaikovsky's passionate, capricious, and skittish Oksana speaks for herself alone, and only in combination with Solokha's laments for a supposedly dead Vakula does she speak in folk intonations. Consequently, she makes a stronger impact on the listener and is perceived as a living character. But this is a mirage: Rimsky-Korsakov's Oksana is no less alive, even though it is necessary to view her life as emanating not from her personally but from out of a greater whole, of which she constitutes a part. This is the sense of the stylization.

I have allowed myself to dwell on the method of characterization for the *dramatis personae* that occurs often in Rimsky-Korsakov (one that holds for *Mlada, Christmas Eve, Kashchei, The Tale of Tsar Sultan*, Mozart in *Mozart and Salieri*, and very much in *Sadko* and *Kitezh*). It was necessary to do so, since an elucidation of how the individual and the life of the community are connected and then of how his or her life's path conforms to the life of the cosmos will deepen all the more the problem of *Christmas Eve*'s composition.

Having linked everyday actions with nature and inculcated the very same into the sphere of mythology, Rimsky-Korsakov needed to find an outlet for the idea in the corresponding musical structure. Otherwise, the skillfully constructed edifice would fly apart like a house of cards! A solution was found, one both clever and resourceful. A parallel procedure was incorporated, a method of parallel structures, based on the analogy between the psychological and the physical worlds, which is one stage of anthropomorphism. Here are the clearest examples: Vakula compares Oksana's eyes to the stars in the sky (arioso in the first tableau) and then, at the moment of flight, a *khorovod* of the stars is devised on the basis of this theme or on its motive, i.e., on its development.[15] The human carol corresponds to the demonic one. Moreover, the encounter of the Dawn Goddess and Ovsen in heaven parallels that of Oksana and Vakula on earth. In this way both a poetic and a musical connection were found on the basis of the distinctions, similarities, identities, and imitations between the two worlds: the real and the unreal, and between everyday (human) life and nature.

Let us look now to the world aboveground and to nature: to the interrelationship revealed within them. Here, once again, we will encounter a stylistic inventiveness both uniquely suitable and consistently carried through.

Of the three fundamental manners of connecting chords—namely [by] quartal/quintal, tertian, and secundal [motion][16]—the second of them, i.e., the tertian, creates the most stable, tranquil, and "positive" impression, even when the succession of chords is chromatic and not merely diatonic: in such a progression, the ear perceives each instant to have a firmly established link. This quality of tertian interrelationships inspired Rimsky-Korsakov with the idea of using a chain of triads, descending by thirds as a leit-harmony, symbolizing peace with nature (with this succession of chords, the music to the opera's introduction begins: "Holy Night") or an aerial expanse (s.v. the "flight"). Calm nature peacefully abiding within itself: this is the sense of the leit-harmony. If a series of triads with descending bass notes is set forth (for example, E, C#, A, F#, D, B, G, E) a circle appears: an eternal cyclic return within a closed sphere and therefore: *immobility*. Rimsky-Korsakov breaks this circle, taking the G triad not to an E triad but to a third-inversion seventh chord originating with the G dominant-seventh chord, i.e., with the note F in the bass.[17]

A dissonant sound arises, of extreme significance with respect to style: here it is simultaneous (within the chord), but in other cases as a leap in the voice by a pungently dissonant interval: by an augmented B–F fourth, i.e., by a tritone. This interval introduces confusion into the calm and regular interrelated succession of chords: with good reason did it carry the honored title *diabolus in musica* during the Middle Ages! In its concluding phase, the introduction to the opera leads again to a succession of the leit-harmonies of nature; but this time they cadence normally, i.e., with a bass motion beginning at E and reaching an E one octave lower (the point of departure = the point of arrival: an E-major triad in both cases). A similar device, present already in the introduction, leads one to wonder: does not the consistently applied principle of disrupting the tranquility of a tertian chordal succession through a tritonal leap serve to stir up a sluggish and inert harmonic mass? Leafing through several pages of the score, one observes a curious fact: the appearance of the devil is symbolized with a motion of a diminished fifth in the voice, i.e., by a tritone employed in the manner of a leitmotive for the evil power, which introduces an element of fermentation into the calm sequence of events. Further on, one can easily follow how the devil's interval, beginning with the arioso "The old custom people have forgotten," will justify its reputation over the course of the entire opera.[18]

On the basis of the "demonic" harmonies and figurations thus engendered, fantastic sounds emerge, evoking strange and bizarre images in our imagination. These sounds make their mark on the work's harmonic texture, thanks to their ability to subject themselves to every possible tonal transformation and, through enharmonic exchange, to astonish the ear with unexpected modulations. As a result, the psychological significance of the interval coincides entirely with the stylistic import and with the full poetic and musical conception of the subject in Gogol as well as in Rimsky-Korsakov.

The fundamental core or center of the entire conception is most graphically revealed in the symphonic portrait for the scene of Vakula the smith's flight to Petersburg. Here an aural background can be perceived: a sojourn in the aerial atmosphere, undifferentiated and indifferent, calmly flowing and stretching out. The movement that can be observed in the flights of the stars (games, dances, *khorovody*) is, in essence, not movement but a shifting within the boundaries of a well-defined plane. At the foundation lies the leit-harmony of nature, already well known to us (for *Christmas Eve* it might be more correct to label it a harmony of the aerial sphere, of the aerial element or, simply, of air that is crystal pure, cold, and clear). By means of rhythmic and figurational changes, this *theme* is wonderfully varied and, together with the beautiful tonal coloration, offers a whole series of lovely, changing aural tableaus.[19]

As a contrast to the delights of heaven, the gray cloud of the Evil One is introduced and an evil power strikes up its carol. The Evil One fills up all audible space with its groans, drones, hoots, howls, crackling, and rattling. Sequences out of a sinister succession of an ascending chain of minor triads and second-inversion chords, joined together by augmented fourths (the familiar fickle face of the devil!), very fittingly underscore the essence of the diabolical onslaught with their astringent coloration: his bustling animation, rootlessly traversing heaven and earth, the confusion of tonal hues within the wild convolution, and, finally, his facelessness. The intense theme of flight for the witch (Solokha) and the devil, unleashing second-inversion chords in the figuration, moving incrementally by minor thirds (to make a diminished-seventh chord), heightens the gloom of the coloration.[20] But the motive of the demonic carol just beginning to sound seems to concentrate within itself the full power, the entire onslaught. With ever-greater insolence it rings out, gaining control over the expanse. With a whooping and whistling, the demons descend upon Vakula, who rides on the back of the devil; next an incantatory motive is brought to the ear with an original rhythmic gait: a sign of the cross to drive away the Evil One![21]

The magnificent court of Catherine II (the sumptuous polonaise) strikes the smith from Dikanka blind.[22] Having received the slippers, Vakula summons the devil: suddenly a leaping devil (in the form of a diminished fifth) destroys the charm of the radiant tableau. Again there is aerial space. Strange, shattered fragments of the Evil One's harmonies and motives scurry hither and yon, hovering in the celestial atmosphere. But they will assemble no more: the sunrise approaches, dispersing the bewitching illusions. The power of light conquers the sky. Tender music portrays the appearance of the Dawn Goddess, and after her the cortege of Ovsen and Kolyada: in the spellbinding coloration of roseate dawn, their theme is born, resounding more and more fully, itself seeming to blossom and give forth light. This theme presents nothing other than the theme of the Evil One's magic, transformed almost beyond recognition—one of the most astonishing miracles of Rimsky-Korsakov's stylistic mastery![23] Waves of sound grow and rise up as if from the depths: Dikanka becomes visible, proclaiming with church bells and sacred song an invitation to a feast on the day of great celebration for the

Star rising in the East: the light of Reason. C major enters triumphantly as a tonal synthesis and affirmation of light. The coloration finally is dispelled. The sun reigns over the earth.[24]

This is the center of action in *Christmas Eve*: a most expressive *poema* amidst the multitude of examples of symphonic depiction that characterize the works of Russian musicians. Prior to this tableau, the action was inclined toward the visible victory of evil power: the "evil" fifth plays an important role in distilling the confusion. The devil muddled Solokha and all her suitors, the smith, and Oksana into one giant confused mess. But the unraveling of it was not entrusted to human beings: a higher power, another sphere, reigns over ordinary existence: within it the struggle began, within it the dénouement is to be effected. Only after the sun conquered the foes and turned again toward warmth were the obstacles to a propitious fate for Vakula removed and a reign of peace restored to Dikanka: only then did the cosmological and psychological conceptions coincide. Thus, the circle was closed.

The composition of *Christmas Eve* can only be recognized as stylistically perfect. It is perfect to such an extent that this perfection, with an iron cohesion and consistently maintained thematic symbolism (the magical enchaining of reality and hallucination) detracts from the lifelike design of the work itself, from its lyricism, from its soul: from music, i.e., from a musical *foundation*. The latter will at all times and places elude an analysis, yet it envelops and permeates the structure like the atmosphere: without it, no less than without oxygen, the artistic organism cannot exist—assuming that the given work is not a mechanical, moribund complex of sounds but a unity, permeated with the current of life. In a deep sense this foundation might be designated the melos of the opera, its structure the mode. The melos, of course, is not identical to the sound material; and the fullness, richness, novelty, and freshness of the latter may still not presage a rich and intense melos. There is any number of works whose material is lucid, but hopelessly squandered, even when a logical distribution of it is present. Here lies a hidden secret not admitting of explanation.

Every work conceals within itself, in potential, the spirit and breath of the person who created it. It is inconceivable to imagine music without respiration. Not a single work can be performed unless respiration is brought into it. Respiration is the precondition for the intensity of song ("song" is used with the understanding that a *violin also sings*, for both the vocal and the instrumental elements in music are equally permeated with songfulness). It is the degree of the song's intensity or, if one might clarify more expressively—the song *energy*—that is the melos. Contrary to what is conceived and expressed in words (*logos*), melos emerges like thought (i.e., is both felt and comprehended), but is expressed in *intonatsii*, i.e., is *sung*, both with words and without them.

In concluding my analysis, I wish to recall this—let us say, *metaphysical*—side to the style of *Christmas Eve*. Rare qualities indeed are inherent in the melos of Rimsky-Korsakov.

Notwithstanding all his apparent and sometimes unquestionable conventionality and "stylization," these qualities are always inseparable from him: the tender caress, enshrouding the patterning and meandering of the melodic lines; restraint, stiffness, suppression, and a chaste reserve that does not permit shameless disclosure and a baring or exposing of the soul; hence, a cold and pellucid crystalline quality in the motives that accompany representations of winter, cold, chills, and a cordial stiffness and noble restraint, an affability and spiritual warmth in those motives associated with "sunny" representations: e.g., of light, warmth, soul clarity, goodness, beauty, and spirituality. A further rare quality germane to Rimsky-Korsakov's melos is his expressivity, not in the sense of raging dramatic expression and pathos but rather of a precision and brevity in the characterization. This quality probably explains the wit, restrained slyness, and good-natured laughter of Rimsky-Korsakov's comedy (especially in the opera *May Night*) and, on the other hand, the distinction and sharp relief of motives demarcating an event (for example, the annalistic style of characterizations in *The Maid of Pskov*). But behind it all the composer's soul is concealed, hiding out of modesty, comforting the world (even amidst the thorny dog-rose shrubs in the Queen of Shemakha's song garden). The pure lyricism, i.e., the "kernel" of Rimsky-Korsakov's melos, can almost never be found: he was too great a stylist for this. But if one compares the degree of immediacy in the melos of *May Night* and *Snow-Maiden* with that of *Christmas Eve*, one will sense in the latter a stronger inclination toward an instrumental timbre that was ever near and dear to Rimsky-Korsakov's heart.

There was a moment in the historical evolution of melos when technical refinement brought it into close proximity with the instrumental arabesque, a time when it became difficult to establish the boundaries between purely vocal and instrumental timbres in the melody. The clearest examples are Handel and Bach. The reign of homophony[25] elicited once again crudities in the structure of the melos, which was now not conceived as a goal unto itself but as something dependent on the harmony and, more often than not, conditioned by a dominant-tonic structure in the chordal relationships. In essence this melos, too, was of an instrumental sort (especially among the later Italians); however, one need not confuse melodiousness with melos, nor merely point to an innate natural talent to write comfortably for the voice, to assess the importance of a composer as a melodist! In Russian music Glinka's melos is of the greatest worth. All of his music is sated with the song principle, even his orchestra. Rimsky-Korsakov was fond of melos, because he adored folk song and strove to comprehend its language; yet at his core, he was an instrumentalist: just look at how he cherished the clarinet and how highly stylized were his instrumental phrases! Or how often, in the course of development, did he entrust the full ardor to the orchestra; but to the voice, merely the sustaining of a note amidst the harmonic background. There is nothing here deserving of censure: this is merely the composer's *way*—provoked, of course, by inner dictates.

In *Christmas Eve*, the voice almost always sings vocally conceived phrases; but the transfer of instrumental melody into the singing occurs rather frequently even here, yet only where a true melody has been composed and not where there is pure song or a romance with the character of song. The example of Volkhova in *Sadko* convinces us that such a method often has a profound significance for the underlying style: as long as she remains in the sphere of the water element, as long as she is a water maiden, she sings tunes and calls of an instrumental character. But as soon as she is penetrated by love and both humanity and spirit take root, then her melos is transformed and songfulness encroaches on her essential being. Something similar can be observed in Oksana: if one considers the two pinnacles of lyricism in her role: the first aria (in the second tableau) and the second aria (in the opera's final tableau), then the contrast between them is precisely of the aforementioned type. In the first case, Oksana sings "instrumentally," but in the second case with intimate songfulness.[26] Within Oksana herself, a profound change is effected: a capricious, willful, coldly self-assured beauty, delighting only in herself, her loveliness, and her maidenhood is transformed into one who loves with sincerity: genuine humanity is expressed in her heartfelt rumination. For a graphic contrast, there are the devil's *intonatsii*, which are thoroughly instrumental as is his entire characterization.[27] On the other hand, the carols from the chorus are pure melos.

The charm of *Christmas Eve*'s music and the enjoyment aroused by it are linked to the composer's attainment of clarity, crystal purity, and transparency in the musical process and the sharply defined presentation of ideas. The logic in the outpouring of complex harmonic waves and clever interweaving of melodic lines relies upon such natural, simple, and well-proportioned relationships that listening to the music of *Christmas Eve* produces an inescapable impression of the immediacy of intention and facility befitting a great master.

Already in the introduction itself ("Holy Night"), the thread of the entire development is given. In the cold air there are sparkles and a spreading stream of light to join the boundless, starry expanse with the cold, frosty Earth at night. Against a background of softly undulating sounds, the lovely phrases of a contemplative horn and a caressing clarinet glide about in stark relief: quiet and calm, not moribund, nor threatening, nor preparing for a storm, suggesting instead a *joi de vivre*, gratitude, a faith in life. There is calm but, instead of sleep, a gazing out into a world harmoniously unfolded and organically united. It is a state of wise activity, an abiding in contemplation of the world and acceptance of the world as a harmoniously organized space. Out of this comes that quivering, that trembling that fills the air: it is neither mute nor lifeless. It rings out, spreading about in the soft light beams that pierce through it. The starry heaven, the chill of the air, the silvery nocturnal light, the sparkle of the snowy shroud: all of this is what the composer overheard in nature and realized in that most concise and wondrous symphonic poem that is *Christmas Eve*'s introduction.

In the course of their clever and convoluted dialogue, the devil and Solokha chase away the nocturnal mood: you can already sense a truly diabolical plan, but at the same time will understand that the devil's escapades are not to be feared. His pranks can momentarily change the course of what is transpiring, just as his characteristic interval changes the hue and mode of the harmonies; but to alter the structure and order of the universe, to introduce discord into the essence of things—this, Dikanka's little devil was not fated to do. The music splendidly confirms this, not only in the flight of Vakula and its radiant conclusion, but even earlier amidst the everyday occupations: in the remarkably well-elaborated crowd scene of caroling (the opera's fourth tableau).

The introduction, the carols, the flight, and the brilliantly introduced finale in memory of Gogol (the concluding ensemble to the opera) are the most important fulcrums in the development of the entire design. The introduction—wherein the air reigns in splendid isolation—is no place to consider whether or not with an equal power of imagination Christmas Eve might be musically portrayed in another plane, the plane of everyday existence. Rimsky-Korsakov did just this, and perhaps by way of contrast—or, more likely, as a filling in of the introduction's "emptiness"—he developed the choral scene of carols with consummate mastery: thus the reverential mood of nature is juxtaposed—after a certain space of time during which the characters of the *dramatis personae* are delineated—with human merriment and joy. In the luxuriant music for this scene are concentrated the breathtaking intoxication from the boundless frosty night and the rapture from life, yes, of life itself: its process, the abiding within it, and the veneration of it. The stormy, irrepressible force of youth and health, of fortitude and integrity of spirit, the mighty authority of ordinary life relationships, the sense of a link between everything alive within man and the life of the air spreading around (for wherever even the light of the starry night is warmed, there music already is sounding, and life along with it): this is what is heard in the swelling, exultant songs of the chorus, pouring forth from everywhere. Life affirms itself here in all the sonorous fullness of human voices, in the deep mass of their sounds, in the waves of respiration, and the rhythm of a rising and falling chest! In breathing, man by himself fills aerial space, pouring out his spirit in song, permeating it and giving warmth to nature with the heat of his breath: like sunlight, the joy of song, caresses, and unbounded freedom bursting forth into soft rays of tenderly twinkling stars!

In the well-proportioned harmony of music glad tidings of ancient traditions are proclaimed to the universe: proclaimed in the heavens, "in celebration and wonder," and on earth, in merriment and joy, in a loving unity of people, joined since long ago in centuries of hallowed ordinary existence. And if we are captivated in *May Night* by a festival of spring, in *Mlada* by the passionate ardor of summer *khorovody* and the cult of fire, then in *Christmas Eve*, amid the tranquility and grandeur of nature, disturbed only a little by the mischief of the indefatigable devil, a rapturous cry rings out, spreads, and proliferates in the sonorities of the mass scenes: onward to the sun! And no matter how sound the frosty sleep that has overcome nature, with the arrival of the festival (the meeting) of Kolyada and Ovsen, she can already hear the cry, hear it even through the snowy shroud that covers her, and awaits only a greeting from the sun itself in order to be resurrected into new life.

NOTES

1. Ovsen is a male deity of youthful appearance, associated with spring and oats, who is venerated on March 1. Songs honoring Ovsen and the scattering of grains on New Year's Eve are welcoming gestures to the new sun in the hope of receiving new riches with the new year. Kolyada is a female sun deity venerated at the winter solstice with *kolyadki* or Yule carols.

2. Semik is a pagan holiday falling on the Thursday of Rusalnaya Week, which occurs in early May.

3. The approximate coincidence of Kupala revelries and the Feast of John the Baptist (June 24) led to an ecumenical confluence of holidays and symbols. See also Chapter 7, n. 5.

4. Asafyev refers here to the three feast days venerating Christ (August 1, 6, 16) that comprise the Dormition Fast. The Feast of the Protection (October 1) commemorates a tenth-century visitation of the Virgin Mary in Constantinople, during which she spread her veil to protect the assembled worshippers at Blachernae Church.

5. Kostroma is a vaguely defined female sun deity, whose burying or burning in effigy is a rite performed to mark the summer solstice.

6. Originally entitled *Vakula the Smith*, *The Slippers* is Tchaikovsky's setting of Gogol's tale, *Christmas Eve*. Asafyev's commentary is in Chapter 14, pp. 161–63.

7. Asafyev here contrasts the ultimately harmless pranks of the devil in Gogol's story with a hypothetically more malevolent real or imaginary entity whose tormenting of Gogol himself led him to create his darkly comic characters, e.g., the landowner Kostanzhoglo in *Dead Souls*.

8. Asafyev frequently makes an antinomy of spontaneous lyrical effusion and calculated systematic creativity, the latter being exemplified by *Christmas Eve*.

9. The connotations of *intonatsiya* would expand and evolve throughout Asafyev's career. His usage here holds a key to understanding a core aspect: in texted music, meaning is conveyed thanks to a confluence of the word and the specific vocal pitch idiom, which come into being and coexist in the act of singing (or an evocation of the act of singing).

10. The threefold typology of melodic materials that Asafyev provides is intended as supporting evidence for his major claim: that Rimsky-Korsakov peoples his Ukrainian village community with characters who are distinguished by their "lyrical spheres." The variety of melodic types, the specificity, and the cultural authenticity of the opera's intonational source material—or, as Russians would term it, of the *intonatsii*—all justify the serious claim that Rimsky did indeed evoke an everyday milieu by means of an obsessively planned vocal soundscape.

11. The "epic" source materials that Asafyev lists could also be seen as a conglomeration of recitatives and reciting tones.

12. See, e.g., Oksana's aria in the second tableau, mm. 75ff, with the tempo change to *Allegro non troppo e capriccioso*.

13. The nuances consist of short chromatic descents in the vocal line.

14. In the third tableau's scene 3 the sacristan woos the witch Solokha using a Rimskian parody of the phraseology and reciting tone of the ecclesiastical professions.

15. Cf. Act 1, first tableau, scene 3, mm. 264–65 ("Dark eyes like stars sparkling brightly") and Act 3, sixth tableau (the *khorovod*). The defining motive is an ascending fifth, followed either by an ascending sixth (first example) or a series of fifths (second example).

16. Asafyev is referring to the pitch interval by which chord roots are connected, e.g., a C triad to a D triad would be secundal, C to E, tertian, etc.

17. Asafyev has named the root pitches of the opera's opening chord progression. The pattern of motion by thirds is broken when the G falls to F instead of E, the F of a G7 chord in third inversion, which also breaks pattern by introducing a tritone, i.e., Asafyev's "dissonant sound."

18. The arioso occurs in the first tableau's first scene (mm. 97ff.). A melodic (harmonic) tritone is introduced along with the phrase *obyichai staryi* (the old custom). [Author's note:] Sometimes as a "pure" tritone, sometimes in inversion. From this stems the important stylistic role of third-inversion seventh chords in this opera.

19. For the first phase of Vakula's night flight (with the devil in his sack!), Rimsky restores the opera's opening key of E major, brings back an ostinato of quarter-note trills and then enlivens the passage with new figurations.

20. Before the striking change to a dissonant harmonic language registers, Rimsky has already changed tempo to *Allegro assai*, changed to triple meter, and brought back the G7 chord with its ominous F–B tritone (for the Demonic Kolyadka, mm. 6–29). Two full statements of the "tone-semitone" or "Rimsky-Korsakov" or octatonic scale result.

21. Vakula's sign of the cross to ward off the devil is marked in the music with the intonations of stately Russian Orthodox hymnody.

22. A polonaise in D major begins shortly after Vakula's landing in the Russian capital, which begins the seventh tableau.

23. Asafyev has in mind the transformation of the main theme of the Demonic Kolyadka (seventh tableau, Kolyadka, mm. 55ff.) with its nondiatonic harmonization into an andante theme in A major, celebrating the joyous cortege of Ovsen and Kolyada (eighth tableau, Cortege).

24. The appearance of C-major triads coinciding with Vakula's homecoming and Christmas morning symbolically resolve (and dispel) the many B–F tritones scattered throughout the opera.

25. I.e., the predominance of homophony in the classical period.

26. Asafyev's assertion is likely based on a combination of intervallic contour and rhythm. More than the various arpeggiated figures found in the earlier aria (which presents us with an Oksana preening in front of her mirror), the vocalise at mm. 67–75 imitating the violins makes a pointed transfer of an instrumental idiom; later on, the aria's concluding stretto is a polonaise (as noted above). Oksana's final aria, by contrast, is a tender romance, the text other-directed, the showy virtuosity absent.

27. Observe, for example, the predominance of tritones and other disjunctive leaps in the first-act duettino (mm. 246–95) or the dance refrains of the second-act duettino (mm. 133–97).

• *9* •

The Problem of a City Made Visible

*W*hen Rimsky-Korsakov, in a preface to his musical *bylina* about Sadko, appeared to apologize for an anachronism he had allowed—namely, the introduction of *skomorokhi* into the scenario he had developed (i.e., a social stratum or class of people who were established later in history than the posited time of action for the dramatization of the legend of Sadko[1]); when next, in reporting in his *Chronicle* about the work on this composition, Rimsky-Korsakov justified the appearance of an introductory scene (as it apparently was to him) involving Lyubava Buslayevna with the fact that he wished to compose an aria in F minor, i.e., in a tonality not yet used in the opera[2]—in all such explanations, one senses a desire to forestall those objections of thoughtless critics that are especially annoying to every author, or else to defend himself against them, against the objections, by means of explanations made *post factum*, i.e., after the creative act, after the genesis of the work. Sometimes such explanations (including so-called programs, placed atop the music) actually do correspond to the ideas that were chosen *ad hoc* for a particular work, but more often than not they are merely plausible conjectures, in which the author himself believes sincerely and to which the public is extremely susceptible. In such pronouncements "from the heart," the crowd searches for answers about the creative process that is so mysterious to them and a key to the understanding of a work, which releases them from the obligation to ponder the work's organic structure.

If indeed the author may be slightly more cognizant than others of the meaning of the creative process occurring within him, he will nevertheless think that since he is someone in close proximity to this process that he can elucidate more correctly than anyone else the inner meaning of what has been achieved and thus believe in his explanations. But, alas, he forgets that in the moment when he is explaining the work, he, the author of it, is not producing it: he is not the person creating, but one perceiving. The difference lies merely in the degree of perceptual intensity and in the greater share of partiality, relative to those who did not participate in the creative act. I am therefore allowing myself in this etude on the construction of the opera-*bylina Sadko* to bypass the composer's rationalizations, to forget about them, and examine *Sadko* as a fact of art, as one would, perhaps, a Gothic cathedral whose builders' names are unknown.

Based on its structure, the internal logic of its formal design, and the joins and associations of the musical materials, this work is among the most exemplary in Russian music. It deserves an analysis specifically devoted to the structure, apart from any consideration of the poetic conception that conditioned its design. Let us not forget, though, that the opera-*bylina Sadko* grew out of an eponymous symphonic tableau, which was created under the impulse of an entirely poetic intent and sated with the most vivid musical material from the period of youthful romanticism in the works of Rimsky-Korsakov.[3] Consequently, *Sadko* as an opera presents a fascinating example in the psychology of style, wherein musical material is transformed over the course of the life of one and the same individual from various points and angles of approach, with other methods of realization and with an enrichment of technical experience.

Mlada, Christmas Eve, and *Sadko* are operas in the "experimental style" of the "accumulative" epoch in the works of Rimsky-Korsakov, when with exceptional assiduousness, doggedness, and zeal he developed material that was molded in his youth and material that came later. This epoch displayed the greatest concentration of "methods," economy of material, and intellect. Directly thereafter, Rimsky-Korsakov again took in fresh tendencies and strove to realize bold new aims and ideas, on until the end of his life.[4] *Sadko* is in part a stylistic turning point: here the character of Volkhova is deepened, she who had not appeared in the symphonic poem, who anticipated the characters of the Princess (in *Kashchei*) and the Queen of Shemakha on the one hand, and on the other, Marfa (*The Tsar's Bride*) and Fevronia (*Kitezh*), since female characters are the main connecting thread in the works of Rimsky-Korsakov, i.e., the life current that suffuses them and unifies that which the intellect had taken apart (the women's sorrows in *Servilia* and *Pan Voyevoda* also connect them to the remaining operas). But this is another matter.

The structure of *Sadko* was conditioned solely by that spiritual disposition in the composer, wherein life experience and technique nurtured the craftsman inside of him and guided his thoughts toward the creation of grandiose conceptions based on conscious methods and manners, on the basis of a rigorous critique and selection of usable material: in a word, on the basis of conservative, academic principles, the principles that have built up classical art.

Such is the style of *Sadko*. Of course, the psychological sense behind the genesis of the opera lies with the poetic, romantic dream of Novgorod the Great, a dream that has appealed to numerous Russians and been put into song by them. In its craving to make manifest the secret life currents that fill the Russian everyday world and Russian culture, Russian art could not, indeed had no right, to await painstakingly verified scientific results and principles. Where inner spiritual impulses demanded realizations of foreordained tasks, one could not tarry until Russian ethnology and ethnography turned from the collection of material toward scientific generalizations; therefore Russian opera, being based on folk traditions and an instinctive speculation that one set or another of poetic elements played an enormous role in the life of and creativity of the people, revived and recreated them—not taking into account possible errors, thus asserting its style with all of its failings, but with a wholly sincere conviction as to the rightness and correctness of the chosen path. For indeed, at the heart of their musical-poetic conceptions, Russian composers were indeed profoundly correct in their beliefs and intuitions: faith and heartfelt conviction saved them wherever the material was wanting.

The matter stood approximately the same in the realm of musical-historical conceptions. To this day, the problem of Novgorod in all of its romantic charm contains much that is unexplained and unresolved. For his resolution of it, Rimsky-Korsakov relied on folk tradition and on the *skaz* found in the *bylina*, enhancing them and adding historical data; but fundamentally, in the logic of the formal design, he was guided more by the intuition of the artist who creates his own truth than by the mirages of intellect. It is essential to reveal this truth in examining the musical *poema* of Novgorod the Great, of its everyday existence and spiritual order, a *poema* created by Rimsky-Korsakov on the basis of the Novgorod *bylina* about that unusual *bogatyr* Sadko, who was praised not for his feats of arms, nor his strength, nor his guts, but for an artistic talent: "Sadko, the *bogatyr*-bard."[5]

Being a most convinced stylist, Rimsky-Korsakov was seeking for a musical transformation of the folk language of sounds in all of its resulting formations; he called his *Sadko* an opera-*bylina* because it was based on the defining idea of employing *skaz* from the folk *bylina* as a unique kind of recitative by means of which the work would be given unity, organization, and a cohesion of elements. The *bylina*-recitative (a stylization of the *skaz* of the *bylina*) indeed has a predominant stylistic role in *Sadko*. Without a doubt, it gives the opera its truly distinctive shape, making it a *bylina*-opera, just as *Kitezh* is a legend-opera, *Saltan* and *Cockerel* are story-operas, and *The Maid of Pskov* is a chronicle-opera (the latter, according to my personal conjecture).[6] But any such designations in our time remain in essence stylizations, which cannot embrace the full conception in all of its ramifications. So it is with *Sadko*. The structure of the *bylina* makes a definite imprint (let us say, that of the *epic*, no matter how conditional the designation!), but does not entirely subordinate nor unify the remaining stylistic strata: the lyric, the fantastic with its fairy-tale coloration, and the contrast-based dramatism.

The *bylina* as such fades away already in accordance with the sense of the poetic idea: Sadko is a *bogatyr*-bard (in his characterization, melos and lyricism or songfulness predominate), at times impulsively attacking (the relationship of Sadko to the rank and structure of Novgorod life), sometimes surrendering himself to the contemplation of an unrestrained element (the song at the bank of Ilmen Lake), at times captive to the charms of an unknown world (praise for the underwater kingdom), at times himself enthralling *them* (Sadko's playing the *gusli* and his *songs*, which uproot the entire sea kingdom[7]). And Sadko is also a hero: sometimes rakishly arrogant ("The heights, yes, the heights"), sometimes meekly bringing his achievements into his native city, aware that for the fulfillment of his great deeds he is only obliged to the intervention of a holy power (the opera's finale).[8] The commanding role of a lyrical-dramatic element in the person of Sadko sets forth in this opera a problem of which ancient Rus was already well aware: the interrelationship between the world (community) and an individual, a person, who is bound to it, i.e., to the world or the community. In the music alone there is a significant advance over the dispassionate epos and the world of the *bylina*.

Of course, *Sadko*'s finale, being somewhat calculatedly composed, leads the entire action toward a *bylina*'s sort of outcome: the hero bends his will to his native city, just as Ilya Muromets and other *bogatyri* brought prisoners to Prince Vladimir and always accomplished their deeds for his glory and, through him, for the "Russian land," which was ever the supreme idea.[9] But in music, any intellectualized formalism is dangerous, especially wherever an unbridled lyricism and resigned surrender of the self, united in a single character, enter into conflict. With regard to the philosophical conception and organic structure of the entire opera, the conception of *Sadko*'s finale is therefore quite complex; it is thus necessary to find the path toward a suitable expression and scenic realization, which cannot be resolved simply by means of prunings, truncations, and alterations.

With regard to the core truth and influence, of course, the song impulse at the words "The heights, yes, the heavenly heights," "Oh you, my dear dark grove," "I will stock my string of ships"[10] always prevails over the epic narrative. Thus, to the extent that *Sadko* in all of its rich ramifications allows elements within itself to manifest independently, those which produce an artistic effect independently of the entirety of the epic stamp—the opera becomes, with regard to psychology, an opera-*poema* and makes an effect chiefly as such, with a predominance at the root of its stylistic conception of the *bylina* quality.

The first and foremost contrast of the work's entire design appears before us as an opposition between world and hero, i.e., between the community with its stratified, long-established existence and political system—and the individualistically gifted nature of a particular human being: Sadko and Novgorod. Sadko reproaches the ossified people of Novgorod and wishes to try for some mercantile luck in foreign terrain at his own risk. Envy and malice counteract his attempts. Powers from the world beyond (dark and light) assist him: the former do so egotistically, under the influence of an amatory passion (Volkhova), the latter with the intent of a divine predestination and salvation for man (Saint Nikolai). Providence alters the course of events and directs them in its own way, acting against the destructive element. It utilizes Sadko's autocratic will in a sense useful to Novgorod (i.e., to the community), reveals to man the inescapable need to find a concord between his will and the will of Providence, and reconciles Sadko to the world of here and now, returning him to his native city and his own family (the meeting with his wife itself is the commencement of the opera's finale).[11]

Such is the basis of the *dramatic* structure. With respect to music, it provides a basis for the chief contrast: the element of everyday life (i.e., the chorus), its representatives (the elders) and intercessor before the Lord (Saint Nikolai)—and the *personal* element (Sadko's lyricism). It is presented in the opera's first act as a *proposition* (strictly speaking, in the prologue), developed in the market scene with considerable power, since this is the *center* of the entire action, and resolved in the opera's finale[12] with a general consensus: not relinquishing its rights, the communal world (existing in the city) is conscious of the significance of an enterprising individual will, accepts its gifts, and recognizes its right to exist within the city-state (which is the political system that we find in Novgorod during this historical epoch[13]). This fundamental opposition is revealed in the music by means of an entire series of clever contrasting architectonic structures in sound, which are unquestionably brought in with firm consistency. The musical discourse or language of the speeches of Sadko himself is differentiated depending on whether he uses the intonations of a law-abiding Novgorod citizen (the *bylina* character of his recitatives) or else of a loving, hating, suffering, admiring, or ill-fated human being. His speeches[14] at the feast in the first act are, in turn, profoundly distinguished from the speeches with which he addresses the representatives of the Novgorod social structure at the moment of his miraculous return to his homeland.[15]

Yet within the structure of everyday reality, too, as it is given in the music, the composer also effectuates the most significant parallel stratifications and contrasts. Everyday reality appears in both a social aspect (chorus, elders, Nezhata the gusli player) and a domestic one (the wife of Sadko). Adherents of every political unit, every worldly rank and system emerge, on the one hand as *protectors*: a higher heavenly power (here, St. Nikolai); the power mongers (the elders) and the exponent of their political ideals (Nezhata the gusli player); and on the other, as those who are *sustained* by them: the beggars, the pilgrims, those whose purpose of being is to awaken in the strong and the proud a feeling of compassion and to provoke an act of mercy, love, and charity. Juxtaposed with this milieu stands an opposition of strong, self-willed individuals (Sadko) and the destitute homeless (Sadko's comrades). A third stratum, parallel to these two fundamental layers, is that of the *skomorokhi*. This was an extremely important "critical" element in the structure of ordinary life and the state of Ancient Rus. It is the curved mirror, the satire of social relations, a kind of public opinion, a sort of press. They were a bribable folk, holding their noses to the wind, looking out for the predominant influence of one or another political party or individual agent; nevertheless, not even the least shift of the barometer in the realms of politics, religion, and morality could elude their vigilant eye, while with their keenly attentive language, they remarked on every life disturbance, giving vivid expression to everything of significance. By introducing them into the structure of his musical realization of Novgorod, Rimsky-Korsakov, the creator of a former system of Russian life, was profoundly in the right for, like it or not, they symbolized an ever-present social order, since indeed new designations often do conceal old relationships of ideas and interactions.[16] All of these ramifications within the manner of everyday existence are sharply delineated and correspondingly conveyed in the music. Stylistic layers therein are therefore distinguishable, as well as cellular formations, every one of which fulfills its own characteristic function, while on the whole, a harmonious social organism is created thanks to their effort.

I apprehend the following [intonatsii]: the *skaz* of the *bylina* (the speech of Sadko and Nezhata[17]); elements of sacred verse (the poor in the market scene, whose motive plays an extremely important role there, both in the ensemble and in the course of action[18]); laments (Sadko's wife); incantations (the sorcerers); instrumental riffs ("Sopelny mode") and tunes of the *skomorokhi*; the riffs ("gusli mode") of Nezhata; the powerful speeches (unisons) of the chorus, and finally, as counterweight to all of this, the free lyrical verse of Sadko's songs in their most varied aspects.[19]

Yet the fundamental contrast between community and individual occurs not only within, over a series of confrontations, but provokes them in the outside world. Juxtaposed with the everyday existence and order of human beings is the immeasurably rich (for the imagination creating it was indeed rich in invention!) world that lies beyond: the fabulous fantasy world of an underwater kingdom. Paradoxical or not, this contrast is built not on a reciprocal opposition (like the fundamental contrast between Sadko and Novgorod's everyday structure of existence) but on the extenuation or reflection of one world into the other. The very same always occurs in any utopian conception: the ideal design in which all the discontents find refuge unwittingly reflects the system out of which its own self was created, one which it either enhances or consummates. So it is here. The underwater kingdom is the mirror of the kingdom above the earth: despotism is there, despotism here, ritual there and ceremony here (the wedding of Sadko and Volkhova and a conjugal *deistvo*), there a feast according to rank and regulation and also here (but, of course, the dances of the *skomorokhi* are only humorous in comparison to the irrepressible dance of an agitated element). There, a higher power might, in the beliefs of people, alter the random course of events—and here, the cry of a saintly elder brings order in the place of a chaos that scatters and threatens destruction.[20] On earth there is loving and so, too, in the underwater kingdom. This is of the greatest significance: it is the cement that makes the action cohere. Volkhova's love charms Sadko: she attracts him to herself and serves as the main link between the two worlds. Novgorod stands in need of the help of the aquatic element. The union of Volkhova and Sadko symbolizes this help in the form of a touching self-sacrifice of Volkhova herself according to the idea of women's faithfulness.

Thus the opera's second contrast, which brings about a new flight of the composer's fancy, is based on the rapprochement, the reflexive fulfillment, and reflection of opposed elements or polarities (the Novgorod Republic and the Underwater Monarchy: Sadko and Volkhova). Here we come to the most remarkable and even somewhat enigmatic aspect in the structure of the entire composition. The interrelationship of the real world and the fantastic world, contrasting between themselves, gave Rimsky-Korsakov the opportunity to introduce two sound worlds into the opera, proceeding in *parallel* motion. One abides in the plane of diatonicism with all of its splendid ramifications, from the depths of folk song to reminiscences of Beethovenian themes. The other lies in the plane of refined chromaticism, with structures emerging out of sequential motions, elisions, juxtapositions, and concatenations of diminished-seventh chords, augmented triads, second-inversion chords, etc.—in a word, the full arsenal of dissonant harmonies, producing and provoking unsteady and unstable, perhaps disembodied sounds.[21] Their coloration, truly unique and sweetly seductive in moments of enchantment but sinister in moments wherein the elemental powers are revealed, depicts in sound, more expressively than ever before, the illusory reality of the underwater kingdom.

Consequently, we have before us a *deistvo* within the *parallelism* consisting of the action of two *contrasting* worlds: a *parallelism*, since the second of them is merely a mirror of the first, i.e., a refraction in the watery depths of earthly life's relations; a *contrast*, since we have before us two completely distinct planes of sound or, more precisely, we sense two completely different psychic states, existing in the real world and the fantastic world. The composer achieves this contrast with a sharp change in tonal, rhythmic, and melodic contours, evoking an entirely distinct, truly magical coloration. Nevertheless, over the course of the action, these two worlds are inseparable. And just as the fundamental dramatic contrast (Sadko and Novgorod) produces as a result a resolution, a reconciliation of the contending forces, so the contrast of coloration, created by fantasy, leads to a merger, a synthesis, but one that is more mysterious and profound. This is what I call the enigmatic factor in the compositional structure: *enigmatic*, since any synthesis will be so, when it emerges as the result of a merger or coupling of two opposing elements, no less than in closing the circuit between a positive and negative electric charge.

The inherent process within the increasingly passionate love of Volkhova and Sadko, in their developing association, in their "conjugal flight" up from the watery depth to the world above the waters (in the entr'acte-intermezzo that joins the tableau in the underwater kingdom with the concluding act of the opera[22]) leads to their merger for all time through the act of Volkhova's self-sacrifice. The beginning of this process lies in her promise "I will wait for you" (second tableau), the end in her words: "Into a light mist I will dissolve and a rapid river become" (seventh tableau of the opera).[23] The characters of the lovers Sadko and Volkhova are symbols of a reflexive coexistence: the entrepreneurial, mercantile, and colonizing spirit of Novgorod and the presence of the Volkhova River, providing an egress to the sea, to Russian and to foreign lands. Their union, their coupling, constitutes the thread, the vital current, and the nerve center of the entire work; and thus, the inner dramatic sense of the musical *bylina Sadko* is the development of the amorous attraction between the natural element born of the maiden Volkhova and the bard poet Sadko, who is formidable in his masculine will and filled with the fluids of the earth. This process also serves as a unifying link for the entire musical action: in it there occurs an organic merger of contrasts, through it is achieved a melting of metallic ingots made of sound and their metamorphosis into a priceless engraved chest of expert workmanship.

Having traced the course of this transformation in connection with the course of action for the opera as a whole, we can reveal its structure both in sequential development and in the interrelationship of the parts. The meeting and parting (or, rather, the element of reflexive coexistence) of Volkhova and Sadko is bounded by two events, emanating from the main dramatic contrast (Sadko and Novgorod). The first of these events (the quarrel at the feast and Sadko's departure to go and dream at Lake Ilmen), like a prologue, initiates the action. The second (the final scene: the meeting of Sadko with representatives of the Novgorod social structure and the offering, as a gift to his native city, of the *fruits* of his bold design) concludes and completes the opera, closing the *circle*, since social petrification and personal enterprise can hardly be reconciled forever! Thus, the main contrast conditioning the drama receives a formal resolution.[24] Between its points of departure and arrival, it flourishes vividly at first, then for a time comes to a stop. It flourishes, too, in the scene with Sadko and his wife (a juxtaposition of the individual and the family structure) and next in the market scene, wherein the greatest tension is achieved at the moment of fishing for the "fishes with the golden fins."[25]

In this setting (the everyday surroundings of Novgorod and the awakening struggle within it between personality and milieu), the amatory association of Volkhova and Sadko grows and develops, and does so with such intensity that everything else seems to be a backdrop. The impetus to their meeting is found in the moment of Sadko's banishment from the feast. He departs to reflect, to sing songs to Lake Ilmen, and to tell stories. Having failed to touch the hearts of men, Sadko's songs with their moaning and yearning for total freedom find an echo in nature: within the daughter of the watery element (second tableau of the opera: the encounter and birth of feelings of love). Here the new and most intimate contrast lies between Sadko's songful lyricism and Volkhova's.[26] At first it seems insurmountable: so different are the bewitching shouts and cries of the siren Volkhova from the earthly songs of Sadko that weigh upon the soul. But therein lies the task, instinctively accomplished by the composer in the creative process. In the gradual warming of the cold heart of the sea maiden, in her humanization, in the awakening of a soulful femininity, where magical charms and unknown, mysteriously alluring cries from the sea's abyss and deepest whirlpools hover—there an impulse for development is offered and the action can unfold. In Volkhova's phrase ("Your song has flown to the depths of Ilmen Lake") one can already hear human longing: here is the turning point, from thence begins the growth of the soul, the sparking of a soul's warmth inside Volkhova. The charms fall away from her (duet). Only when it is necessary to give aid to her beloved man will Princess Volkhova make use of them ("Cast the net, catch them up, and rich and happy you will be"); but, in essence, her transformation has already been accomplished. Under the influence of the warmth and light of human song, the sea maiden becomes a girl. Her humanization and spiritual influx is movingly expressed in music: especially in its final stage, at the moment when Volkhova lulls the sleeping Sadko (the lullaby in the final tableau, prior to the metamorphosis of Volkhova into a river: "Sleep, Sadko, my lord").[27] We may recall that "human songs" and their performer, the sun's poet Lel, also attracted Snow-Maiden and coaxed her toward people.

Just as the life-giving strength of the god of warmth and light is hidden in the juice of grapes and in wine, so in the sounds of song heated by the warmth of human breath are concealed the light beams of a radiant divinity, which, as they radiate out into space, draw into their sphere all who crave warmth and life.

In the myth of Volkhova, Rimsky-Korsakov revisited the myth of Snow-Maiden, but in a more significant and profound sense: not only is a human being born within her, but she, as a maiden in love, is led into an act of self-sacrifice. Since the manifestation of such a mystery is possible in music, the character of Volkhova in a musical transformation so authentically agitates and attracts, unifying and enhancing the poetic idea of the composition and connecting its many multifaceted elements. This character is presented in ceaseless development: from hovering in misty ripples (the initial calls and cries of the princess sound like an instrumental kind of improvisation) unto the radiance at the time of the full moon (with the melos of a lullaby). Of the full moon indeed: Volkhova and the lyricism of her soul accompany the sunny lyricism of Sadko and reflect it, thus recalling here the image of the moon at the moment of its most radiant ecstasy. And it is not for nothing that Volkhova, before she eventually pulls away from Sadko, in order to be with him and accompany him forever, melts (vanishes) into the mist or becomes one with the mist so as to be pierced by the fire of the sun's rays and spread forth as a river.[28]

Like a mighty, many-branched, spreading oak, the *bylina* of Sadko in Rimsky-Korsakov's musical transformation descends by its roots into the depths of the folk's vocal creativity; with its leaves, absorbs the warmth of the sun's rays; and, set afire with the flame of human love lyricism, becomes one of the most brilliant examples of a synthesis of contrasting elements and of the transformation of sound material that was skillfully laid out in balanced interrelationships: a transformation by the power of the human intellect and will into a harmonious, integral, and firmly welded organism.

NOTES

1. While the *skomorokhi* may have originated as early as the 12th century, they flourished from the 15th to the 17th century. Had Sadko been a historical figure, the details of the political, social, and economic structure in the *byliny* narrating his exploits would place him in medieval Novgorod, between the 12th and 15th centuries.

2. Asafyev is responding to the following comment from Rimsky-Korsakov's memoir: "It is laughable, but at that time I developed an indefinable longing for the F-minor tonality, in which I had composed nothing for a long time and which thus far I had made no use of in *Sadko*. This unaccountable yearning for the key of F minor drew me irresistibly to compose Lyubava's aria, for which I jotted down the verses on the spot" (*My Musical Life*, 299). Whatever the inspiration, the F-minor aria, which is introduced by F-minor recitative and concluded with a brief cabaletta in F major, is thoroughly integrated into the third tableau. Further along, the return of F (repre-

senting Sadko's wife) to dominate the seventh tableau pointedly clashes with the E tonality that represents Volkhova and her watery native realm.

3. The symphonic poem was composed in 1862, then revised and reorchestrated in 1869 and 1892. The G–E-flat–D motive that launches the opera originated in the orchestral work, as did the melodic material used for the sixth tableau's wedding song, the golden fishes' dance, and the dance finale.

4. It bears mentioning that by 1889 Rimsky-Korsakov had seen the complete *Ring* and made a thorough study of the harmonic language and orchestration.

5. There are more than a few *byliny* concerned with Sadko, who indeed lacked the *bogatyr's* typical superhuman strength, but could instead achieve comparable miracles through the power of music.

6. As noted earlier, Asafyev's typology is largely derived from the genre tags that Rimsky included in his operatic subtitles. The specific influence of the *bylina* on *Sadko* is discussed below.

7. Ripples in the lake emerge in m. 50, just after Sadko completes his song.

8. Asafyev is apparently referring to mm. 562ff., wherein Sadko acknowledges the intervention.

9. See Chapter 2, n. 5.

10. The score locations are as follows: (1) 4th tableau, m. 1208; (2) 2nd tableau, m. 23; (3) 4th tableau, m. 1128. They differ from the passages involving a reciting tone due to factors of meter, intervallic variety, and range.

11. In the score, the start of the Finale is placed more than 250 measures later, in m. 471.

12. Asafyev hereby reduces the essential dramatic conflict to three focal points: Sadko's initial proposition to the elders in the first tableau; the mixed response to Sadko's first return to Novgorod in the fourth tableau; and his triumphant final homecoming after twelve years in the seventh. At this point the opera's germinal motive no longer sounds as an interpolation against a Novgorod setting but is thoroughly integrated.

13. Thanks to a political independence movement led by the boyars and prominent merchants, the Novgorod Principality successfully removed itself from the aegis of Kievan Russia's Grand Princes in 1136. Under the rather unusual type of feudalistic regime that resulted, the highest authority was given over to a public assembly known as the *veche* [pronounced "vye-che"], as opposed to a prince, allowing an entrepreneurial spirit to flourish, which eventually resulted in trade agreements with the Hanseatic League.

14. [Author's note:] I speak of the speeches in a musical sense, i.e., of the intoning of sounds that are well defined with respect to pitch.

15. Cf., e.g., 1st tableau, mm. 506–17, and 7th tableau, mm. 446–65. Above all, the new disjunctive leaps match the exuberant mood of the final tableau.

16. Rimsky-Korsakov's technique for musically enhancing the *skomorokhi* verse is simple, direct, and consistently applied. With most appearances of Duda and Sopel, the meter changes to 2/4, the tempo accelerates, and simple *chastushka* melodies accompany the doggerel verse.

17. For the musical intonation of the *skaz* of his gusli-playing bards, Rimsky-Korsakov employed syllabic reciting tone formulae, both strict (e.g., 1st tableau, mm.

366–77) and free (mm. 378–95). The inspiration may trace back to Glinka's portrayal of his bard Bayan in *Ruslan*, since his instrument was also portrayed by piano and harp.

18. Asafyev is referring to the 4-eighths/quarter motive of Sadko's ragtag seamen recruits, which first appears in the fourth tableau, mm. 623ff.

19. The musical elements here symbolizing each stratum of Novgorod society identified by Asafyev are independently introduced in the first half of the fourth tableau; the numerous passages of choral polyphony suggest the "harmonic social organism."

20. The "here" of Asafyev's comparison of parallel worlds refers to the underwater kingdom as portrayed in the sixth tableau.

21. The greatest concentrations of Rimskian chromaticism occur in the closing Moderato of the second tableau (mm. 643ff.), during Sadko's plunge in the fifth tableau (mm. 358ff.), and in various passages of the sixth tableau.

22. Rimsky portrays the ascent to the surface with rising (obviously!) sequences. They remain chromatic (or rather, octatonic) and with a Wagnerian delay of cadence until a resplendent D-major chord at the beginning of the seventh tableau.

23. The score locations: 2nd tableau, mm. 604–6; 7th tableau, mm. 154–56.

24. From a harmonic standpoint, Sadko's return and reconciliation with his wife occur in the tonic major of Lyubava's F tonality, a character and key not yet introduced when Sadko left Novgorod for the first time.

25. Stark contrast underscores the dramatic conflict in both cases: in the third tableau, Lyubava's F tonality is answered by unfaithful Sadko's harmonic instability; in the market scene (fourth tableau), the incredible tale sparks a modulation away from the B-flat tonic of the Novgorod population.

26. The water nymph and her sisters "bewitch" by means of the not yet hackneyed sound of soprano range chromatic undulations, which contrast with the *protyazhnaya pyesnya* in E natural minor and the *khorovod* in D.

27. The *kolybelnaya* [lullaby] in F# minor sung by Volkhova in her newfound "surface world" diatonicism begins at m. 86 of the seventh tableau.

28. Volkhova's transformation into the watery element that can give Novgorod its trade route—i.e., into the Volkhov River—is marked by a return of chromaticism and octatonically based chord passages.

Tale

Góre sládko v pésne
V skázke mil i strakh . . .

[Woe in song is sweet
And terror in a tale is dear]

(From the final tableau of
Rimsky-Korsakov's *Tale of Tsar Saltan*)

 *T*he Russian tale is above all a *skaz*.[1] Nothing explains and determines the meaning of a tale better than this concept. Its goal is the narration of words: the stringing together of word after word, word to word, and image to image. The chain of words, of clever turns of phrase, and bold whims of the imagination is intended to while away the long winter evenings at home or on the road. The essence of a tale is also the very same thing as its style: the manner of composition and the cluster of its expressive means. The tale strives most of all to hold the attention, without respite. As soon as a gap in linguistic invention in the narrative thread is revealed, the attention dissipates. As a result, the Russian tale avoids extended descriptions of nature or the place of action or the characters. For this there are long-established catchphrase formulas, which spare the storyteller from the necessity of an extended exposition of details, leading instead from action to action, from fact to fact.

The tale is an improvisation, not so much in the sense of an invention of new images and wonders, as in the clever juxtaposition and combination of material that has long been at hand. The tale is an improvisation welded together from traditional sketches and schemes, within which the *skaz* flows along, proceeding like a pathway that capriciously twists and circles amidst the fields and forests that bind it: flowing rather in its own way, each in its own mode determining the way, but in fact concealing a regular design or mold, which is characteristic of a whole series, nay, of a multitude of such paths that shorten the distance between the distant prospects of Russia.

"A tale is a lie, a song the truth." "You cannot cast out a word from a song." Moreover, in a song, the metrical speech and rhythmical sounds are present at every moment, and thus it is not for nothing that "conversation shortens the road and a song the work" or "the tale by its structure, the song by its mode is beautiful" (see V. Dal, *Proverbs*).[2] In a tale there is free passage from post to post, from change to change in the adventures. In a Russian tale there is no obligatory presence of monsters and wonders for the sake of a *mystical* event. They may or may not exist. The issue at hand is not the wonder itself but its characteristic abridgement of the course of action. Wonder and witchcraft are above all stylistic devices. Hence the Russian tale is on the one hand fundamentally realistic, for indeed it does not convince anyone, nor does it frighten like Western ballades, nor does it instruct, like legends.[3] It is also formally abstract in its design, since all the means of realizing it are utilized like stylistic devices.

The musical tale (in Rimsky-Korsakov) brings together these traits. Above all, it transforms and colors them in a unique way, thanks to the special nature of the art of music. *Skaz* is here united with song. Consequently, lyrical moments are unavoidable at the very instants where the action turns, where the hero or heroine is moved, willingly or not, to express his or her feeling, pain, or joy. The tale in music is chained together by an uninterrupted regular rhythm. Portraiture and the depiction of nature and the everyday world do appear in it, but the musical tale need have no fear of wearing out the attention, since it has at its service the richest of possibilities in instrumental color, comprising all the intensity and power of influence, all the inventiveness of the idea.[4]

Pushkin transformed the tale into the metrical speech of poetry. Rimsky-Korsakov translated the tale into music and brilliantly overcame the stylistic difficulty of blending the improvisational essence of the tale with the strictly rhythmic mold of music, transferring the center of gravity from *skaz* to soundscape, producing two scores of remarkable stylistic ingenuity: *The Tale of Tsar Saltan, of his Son the Glorious and Mighty Prince Guidon Saltanovich, and of the Beautiful Swan Princess* and *The Tale of the Golden Cockerel*.[5] The first represents to me the *pure* tale, with a basis in a child's naivety, in simple-hearted action and narrative interest, merely for the sake of seizing the attention. I am devoting my commentary to it.

Every tale always aims to separate the goats from the sheep, the bad from the good. So it is with *Saltan*: on the one hand, the Swan-Princess, Prince Guidon, and Tsaritsa Militrisa; on the other, the Cook, the Weaver, and

Babarikha the Matchmaker. A struggle ensues between the Swan and Babarikha. The Swan is a creature imparted with knowledge of how all the world's phenomena will come to pass. She is therefore a Prophet Bird as well as a beautiful maiden. Wise is her riddle, directed toward Saltan:

> *Dlya zhivýkh chudés*
> *Ya soshlá s nebes*
> *I zhivú nezrímo*
> *V mílykh mne serdtsákh*
> *Svétel im so mnóiu*
> *Zherebii zemnói,*
> *Góre sládko v pésne,*
> *V skázke mil i strakh.*[6]

[For living wonders
I came down from Heaven
And live invisibly
In hearts dear to me.

With me their earthly
Fate is easy,
Even pain is sweet in song
And fear in a tale is dear.]

In these words lies the sense of the entire operatic tale—indeed, perhaps of all Rimsky-Korsakov's works as well. If this be the case, then what is *evil*? In the final reckoning, it is nonthreatening, existing only to "stir up" the world, in order to disturb inert petrification and to reveal the power of good. Babarikha the Matchmaker lays traps, but the Swan already sees them in advance and guides the action to a positive outcome.[7] The power of evil lacks prophetic knowledge and can only go blindly about, devising obstacle after obstacle, winning to its side such weak-willed oddballs as Tsar Saltan, or Militrisa's envious sisters the Cook and the Weaver.

Such is the naive, simple-hearted philosophy of the tale. With respect to style, it produces the fundamental contrast or conflict from which emanates all the dramatic strength of the work. The motives that characterize Babarikha the Matchmaker are concise but sharply drawn and prickly. Against a bright background of the remaining music they are etched with malice and when they appear, seem to sting everything that comes into contact with them. They sting like a nettle, which was born to sting.

One of the evil motives (it can be called the "ridicule" or "taunting" motive) whose origin traces back to the smirking trepak tune of the peasant Bakula in *Snow-Maiden* gives birth to a motive symbolizing the *barrel*, i.e., captivity and oppression, which the radiant Prince Guidon and his mother undergo during the period when he is growing up.[8] The transformation of this motive is one of the rhythmic and orchestrational wonders of this musical tale.[9]

On the other hand, the Swan's themes and harmonies are enchantingly smooth and mysteriously majestic. As Swan-*Bird*, she appears before Guidon in the second act against a background of exquisite harmonic sequences with avian cries and inflections ("You, prince, my savior").[10] As Swan-Princess, she is characterized by a broad and freely unfolding attractive melodic ribbon, encircled by whimsical ornamentation.[11] Between the Swan and Babarikha, like a sphere in which their influences are to clash, a mysterious land and country hold sway, with its city of Tmutarakan ruled by Tsar Saltan. In opposition to this inert, absurd, and slavish kingdom, the Swan has created the city of Ledenéts, a city full of wonders, in which Guidon rules: a type of fairy-tale heaven.[12] The contrast between the everyday world of Saltan's kingdom and the richly diverse storybook wonders of Guidon's land emerges in the opera as an element no less significant than the juxtaposition of the Swan and Babarikha.

It goes without saying that the wonders of the city of Ledenets present a composer's imagination with inexhaustible possibilities for a different sort of instrumental and timbral invention. At the root there are three wonders: the squirrel, the thirty-three *bogatyri*, and the Swan-Princess. But the city itself is a miracle: miraculous is its appearance on the location of an uninhabited island; and miraculous is the birth of the brightly resounding theme of Ledenets out of a figurational phrase in the minor mode (second act, at Tsaritsa Militrisa's phrase: "Barren and wild is the isle, / My son, only a lonely oak is growing").[13] Earlier yet, the bobbing of the barrel in the sea and Guidon's growth within it are miraculous: an instrumental entr'acte to the second act, where against the background of the evenly undulating sea and the brightly shining stars, Guidon's theme twice passes by, first in a clarinet's tender caress and then in the more masculine sounds of the horn.[14]

The squirrel is cleverly characterized with the song "Was it in the orchard, in the garden," which is transformed in several marvelous instrumental variations, most piquantly in combination with the rattling of the xylophone.[15] "The Thirty-Three Bogatyri" is a sharply rhythmicized, brightly ringing march set against the wildly roaring sea.[16]

It is pointless to relate how enchantingly magical the orchestra is during the tale's wonders, how bewitching the beauty of the sonorities, the contrasts, and the soft and subtle changes in shading. Like dazzling fireworks, the work of the creative imagination amazes by linking chosen combinations into an endless series of fabulous and wonderful musical images. One doesn't know whether to marvel more at the masterful use of timbral nuances among the instruments of the orchestra or at the gorgeous play of tonal relationships. Thus it is hard to say which wonder wins out. When Guidon, for example, is turned into a bumblebee, then flies after the ship, the music uses the opportunity to create out of the simplest of melodic, rhythmic, and tonal elements a truly magical tone painting: an instrumental embroidery in the form of an enchantingly scored scherzo.[17] The simplicity and prudent economy of expressive means accompanied by an almost naive illustration that generalizes the very essence as in folk painting engender heightened attention that is never broken for a moment: is this not a *genuine tale?*

No less wondrous is the characterization of the surroundings that the composer unfolds. First of all, there is a *tableau vivant* of maidenly rumors and gossip (the prologue to the opera, which commences with a fervent, ingeniously stylized song with *podgoloski* ["On Sunday morn I bought shoe hemp"]. Further on, there is an intricately colored march-procession for Tsar Saltan's advance into war, wherein clever subtleties along with the tiniest of details still do not interfere with the revelation of genuinely inspired instrumental conceits: here a master craftsman appears hand in hand with a prodigiously talented man endowed with an unfailingly ardent imagination. One cannot dismiss this march-entr'acte without recalling the presentation of the second E-flat major theme, so remarkable in its freshness (first in the horns, then in the violins, doubled by the clarinets).[18]

The stamp of the material, the delicate azure of the trimmings, and the intricately composed ornamentation in Rimsky-Korsakov make an impression akin to the carved doors of the Imperial Gates in the 17th-century churches of Yaroslavl. One finds a similar sureness of hand, clarity of purpose, logic and realization of them, as well as the selfsame confidence in craftsmanship.[19]

Just after the aforementioned entr'acte to the first act, the scene takes us to Tmutarakan, the capital of Tsar Saltan. The nannies and the mamas sing lullabies to the prince. Three times over the course of the middle of the act, a lullaby is sung; three times it shifts the tonality and the character of ornament: the prince is growing up. In due course, the entire audible and inaudible populace of the kingdom of Tmutarakan is presented to the audience and spectators: the *skomorokhi*, the old sage and tale-teller (the variations in the form of a humorous dialogue between the old man and the clown are ingeniously composed with respect to instrumental color); the wicked old sorceress (her lament-incantation during the lullabies is a plea for the prince's death); the nannies and mamas (the delightful use of the songs "Dear Hare" and "Clapping Song"); the stupid sacristan-clerks; the fifth courier; the welcoming chorus of the faithful and their general lament over the queen and prince. The most resplendent lyrical moment, with significance as a turning point in the action, appears in Militrisa's arioso, "To stay a spinster."[20] Thereafter, all of her laments ("You, my wave, my wave") are deeply moving when juxtaposed with the morose laments of the people on the whole, who seem to sing a prayer for the dying.

The aforementioned instrumental entr'acte with its most interesting soundscape takes us to the second act: to a deserted island. The prince rescues the Swan out of the clutches of the Sorcerer turned bird of prey. In exchange he receives a kingdom. The finale of this act is a broadly developed and richly sonorous real-life scene: the glorification of Prince Guidon. It is one of the most outstanding Korsakovian ensembles. The ecclesiastical character of the theme on which it is constructed enhances the magnificence and solemnity of the moment of glorification. With respect to style, I see here an employment of a concerted church style, similar in taste and conception to that of Maestro Sarti: with bell peals and cannonades, like the victory hymn *Te Deum laudamus* but in a fantastical interpretation![21]

In the introductory music to the first tableau of the third act, a musical poem of the sea again unfolds. Rimsky-Korsakov was fond of depicting this mighty element in all of its various states: from a measured and regular lapping, now like a caress, now urgent and severe, up to the fiercest storm. Many moments of his music are permeated with the rhythm of the sea: individual episodes as well as entire works (*Scheherazade*; *Sadko*—both as symphonic poem and opera; the episode *From Homer*; the cycle of romances *At Sea*; the flood in *Mlada*). Here in the *Tale of Saltan* the nautical element occupies a significant place. The entr'acte to the second act, the introductions to the first and second tableaus of the third act, as well as a series of individual moments within the drama are all flooded with it.

The sea in *Saltan* is presented in various aspects: in the hues of day and night,[22] in changing timbres, in the diminishment and augmentation of the diapason of rhythms, now fragmenting into sparkling pearls, now concentrating into powerful steady waves. It splashes majestically, flying up in spreading waves, and in an instant, as if by the will of the sorcerer Prospero, peacefully respires, softly and tenderly rocking, as if lulling itself with its own regular breathing. A fluttering breeze periodically disturbs the regular splashing of the aquatic element, giving rise to a broken rhythm: an agitated, nervous ripple spreads over the surface. But again there is calm, again the green waves play gently about, carrying off a faraway sailing ship. Or here again, a gust, a flight of the wind: furiously foaming, in a frenzied flood, the waves flutter to the shore, carrying with them the thirty-three knights and Old Chernomor. Or else, with great solemnity, in the brilliant sonority of a breathing orchestra's full chest, the sea sparkles in the radiant gleam of day, as the ship puts in to the dock of Tsar Saltan's capital. . . . But I sense that my description is saying nothing at all. I have given it only to rivet the attention of this tale's audience to the musical transformation of the rhythm of the sea's waves, since the *action* or *drama* of this opera consists of the stylistic transformation of sonic material symbolizing an *element* (water, wind), *natural phenomena* (dawn), the *everyday world* (encounters, receptions, celebrations, mourning, clownish tomfoolery, girlish talk, incantations), *fairy-tale wonders* (the squirrel, the knights, the Swan-Princess, the city of Ledenets) and, finally, the internal *spiritual world* of a human being—a world of brightly radiant lyricism (remarkable in this respect is the transformation of the Princess-Swan's theme in her duet with Guidon or all the many transformations of his main theme: "Ah, how sweet to be free").

One must regard the score to *The Tale of Tsar Saltan* as a priceless manuscript miniature with the most delicately colored attire or, rather, as an intricately braided pattern with the most refined coloration. To study it is to produce a correspondingly careful and detailed analysis of the style, thoughtfully investigating the provenance of every line, every colorful spot, as well as their connections with their surroundings. As the tale-in-words threads word to word, links image to image and saying to saying; as the tale-in-a-book (a decorated manuscript) elaborates the magically illumined strand of letter-petals, wavelike streams of stitchery and tender miniatures; as the tale-in-ornamental-design joins link to link, stroke to stroke, and ray to ray into a fantastic *skaz* twisting about all over the plane of lines, so the tale-in-music, in linking and combining shafts of sound drawn from the play of shadings, from the alteration of tonal and timbral coloration, from rhythmic breaks, from contrasts and imitations, and from the elastic texture of melos and harmonies creates a joyous world of sounds, occupying our attention during leisure hours and enriching the consciousness with the splendid gifts of a rich creative imagination.

The Tale of Tsar Saltan in Rimsky-Korsakov's recreation enters the sphere of music like a musical cosmogony. It depicts in sound the nascence of an audible world of rhythms, timbres, and melos by means of an entire series of newly conceived combinations (physical reactions) of sound material. Thanks to its ties to the poetics of the fairy tale in general and (through music) to a particular *symbolism* of the world and a *reflection* in music of the world's evolutionary process (since there reigns within it a rhythmic structure to the linkage of "sound-atoms" and, in motion, an emerging light or luminescence of changing tonalities and harmonies), *The Tale of Tsar Saltan* depicts in music a kind of cosmological process and itself emerges as a cosmogonical utopia, a case of *De rerum natura* in music.[23]

NOTES

1. A definition of *skaz* consistent with Asafyev's usage was given in the Introduction. The evocative prose performance of these opening paragraphs both explains and embodies *skaz* in its use of metaphors and word repetitions that bring to mind the content and manner of the storyteller's art.

2. The revered Russian lexicographer Vladimir Dal (1801–1872) was also a pioneer of folkloric *skaz* cast in stylized prose. Dal's *Russkie skazki* appeared in 1832 and were followed by four more volumes of folklore. An essay on Dal's use of *skaz* in the folk tales was included in an early anthology of the Russian Formalists: V. Gofman, "Dal's Folkloric Skaz," in *Russian Prose*, ed. Eikhenbaum and Tynianov, trans. Ray Parrott (Ann Arbor: Ardis, 1985): 181–201. Dal's *Proverbs of the Russian People*, from which Asafyev extracted the epigrams, was published in 1862.

3. The assertion that the folk fairy tale is "realistic" is based on an essential Formalist position that its primary interest lies not with the subject but with the formulaic elements of its style, many of which can be traced back to the oral traditions of a particular time and place.

4. Asafyev's primary challenge in claiming that Rimsky-Korsakov's *Tsar Saltan* should be considered an operatic *tale* comes down to this: how to account for the absence of a *tale-teller*, i.e., a ubiquitous onstage narrator. By stating that the composer has transferred the emphasis "from *skaz* to soundscape," Asafyev suggests that whenever no character is narrating, the orchestra itself is performing the role—as, for example, in those orchestral preludes and interludes to which verses quoted from Pushkin are pointedly appended in the score.

5. Pushkin wrote six fairy tales in verse over the years 1831–1834, of which *Tsar Saltan* was the third and *The Golden Cockerel* the last. Readers of Pushkin familiar with the richly characterized narrators of *Onegin* and the *Tales of Belkin* would find his *skazka* storyteller hardly personalized at all.

6. The Swan Princess's fourth-act address to Tsar Saltan, which includes the two-line epigram that Asafyev used as chapter motto, was written by the librettist Vladimir Belsky, not Pushkin.

7. The greater role assigned to the operatic Swan gives ample evidence of such supernatural powers as clairvoyance.

8. The musical association Asafyev makes with *Snow-Maiden* is based on a chromatic motive that underscores an exchange between the peasants Bobyl-Bakula and Bobylikha (in that opera's Prologue, final scene, mm. 17–27). In *Tsar Saltan*, the "barrel" motive is defined by a semitonal step conjoined with an octave leap (later a fourth) as, e.g., at Act 1, fig. 82 + 9 and fig. 90 + 5. Chromatic turn figures permeate the sisters' carping comments throughout Act 1 (e.g., figs. 58, 82). The final phase of Prince Guidon's "growing up" occurs *inside the barrel*, which was cast adrift into the "Ocean-Sea."

9. The barrel motive first appears in triple meter (Act 1, fig. 78 + 2) and undergoes pitch and metrical transformation throughout the remainder of the finale to Act 1 and the symphonic prelude to Act 2.

10. Rimsky-Korsakov evokes the dazzling beauty of the Swan-as-Bird (Act 2, fig. 115) using triads pointing to keys quite distant from tonic G; the delicate orchestration features harp, high woodwinds, solo horn, and solo violin.

11. The transformation of Swan-Bird into Swan-Princess occurs in Act 4, figs. 201–3. The "attractive melodic ribbon" unfolds in highly ornamented chromatic arabesques that are interchanged among flutes, oboes, clarinets, and violins.

12. The names of the two capitals are not found in Pushkin. In ancient times, a Tmutarakan Oblast existed on the eastern banks of the Sea of Azov. "Ledenets," the

Swan's city, means "lollipop" in common parlance; but the added resonance with Ledo, the swan of Greek mythology, may be more than mere coincidence.

13. Score location: Act 2, fig. 106. The "figurational phrase" that is first associated with the barren isle is an arpeggiated triplet pattern in barren octaves played by the strings. It returns in the final phase of the erection of Ledenets, at fig. 129, with a new meter of 9/4.

14. Score locations: Act 2, prologue, fig. 100 + 10 and fig. 102 + 14. The return of this same theme at rapid tempo during the central section of the "Flight of the Bumblebee" counts as yet another transformation, an effect perhaps resembling the caricature of a person as an insect with the human face preserved.

15. The variations featuring the xylophone occur in Act 4's symphonic interlude at fig. 216.

16. At the first mention of the mighty *bogatyri* (Act 3, fig. 181) and subsequently, a sixteenth-note ostinato in the strings creates the ocean's roar, and the loud brass the warriors' deliberate tread.

17. Originally in A minor and scored to highlight flutes, clarinet and violins, the famous "Flight" appears in Act 3, figs. 156–60, to close the second tableau.

18. S.v. fig. 28 (+15) and fig. 29 (+1).

19. At the altarpieces, on the walls, and on the Imperial Gates (used to close off a special alcove for royal personages), the churches of Yaroslavl, the "pearl" of the Golden Ring of southern Russian cities, display a delicacy and invention in woodworking that has inspired comparisons to lacework and tapestry.

20. Score location: Act 1, fig. 83.

21. Giuseppe Sarti (1729–1802) was appointed Director of the Court Cappella in 1784. The Te Deum in D (his sixth of seven) for double choir, orchestra, bells, and Russian horn band was composed in 1785.

22. The orchestral interlude preceding the miraculous unveiling of Ledenets provides the listener with the opportunity to muse over the composer's synesthetic fusion of musical tones and colors. Rimsky assigns the "dark blue" key of B major to the nighttime, modulates to the "rosy" key of A as the "first ray of morning light" appears, and then moves through the circle of fifths to his goal key: "green" F major.

23. Lucretius (99?–55? BC) is known for a single literary work, the philosophical essay in verse entitled *De rerum natura*, in which he expounds a materialistic utopian worldview that expunges fears of mortality and the gods. By implication, the musical utopia to be ruled by Guidon and the Swan-Princess resembles the utopia of Lucretius' poetic vision of a godless universe, since Rimsky-Korsakov's structures and processes can be disassembled into mere sound atoms.

The Legend of the Invisible City

Mílyi, kak byez rádosti prozhít,—
Byez vesélya krásnoýo probýt?

[Dearest, how can one live without joy—
How without radiant bliss can one abide?]

(*Kitezh*, first act[1])

*F*rom a psychological perspective, one might view the design of action in *Kitezh* as follows: from an imaginary point signifying the equilibrium of the human soul, the will, and the emotions—i.e., of an ideally balanced human being—two diverging lines extend: one of ascent and one of descent.[2] The *ascent* of Fevronia must never be construed as a feat of perseverance for its own sake. That would be naive. The depth of Rimsky-Korsakov's insight is evident from the way he wisely avoids the trap laid by mysticism on the one hand and by self-denying asceticism on the other. Fevronia's feat is neither a renunciation of the world, nor a nervous succession of ecstatic states, after which one returns heavily burdened to the ordinary conditions of existence. On the contrary, Fevronia's spiritual state is one of constant aspiration and, at the same time, a steadfast abiding in a condition of joyous contemplation of the world: of nature and of people.

Fevronia's spiritual *self* is profoundly characterized by her heartfelt *intuitive understanding*[3] of the harmony and oneness in the makeup of the universe, and as an inevitable consequence therefrom shows an acceptance of the naturalness and rightness of the close tie between human being and nature, along with the complete rejection and, so to speak, incomprehensibility to her of the ego-centricity and the alienation in purely human conceptions of the world. I will clarify this with an example. For Grishka Kuterma, *woe* is an unavoidable factor in the structuring of life. Nothing exists outside of the web woven by misfortune. All human relations emerge from the subjection of human beings to a slavish existence in a realm both sorrowful and bitter. All human sins and vices come from this. As a line of *descent*, such a worldview is, in this case, not gleaned from a contemplation of life in the natural world: it stems rather from the personal *everyday life* experience of Grishka. Of course, for Fevronia, such an "existential pessimism" is entirely unacceptable. It is a sin, a very great sin: the sin of doubting the order of the Creation; the sin of human pride in an existence that is separated from nature. Intuitively comprehending the unity in the development of everything from everything, Fevronia senses that any conception of *evil* as an independent entity can only be a human fabrication: the result of religious blindness and spiritual limitation.

Yet she does not comprehend the bright and joyous world as a mechanically finished whole, existing in an incessant recycling and repetition of its elements. She perceives it as unbrokenly flowing and enduring, eternally and tirelessly striving toward a vernal renewal and infusion of spirit. The fabric of life and spiritual fortitude in Fevronia are grounded in an unconquerable faith in the evolution of spirit *for the world as a whole* and in the inspired growth of human consciousness. Apart from the world's evolution, when kept aloof from it, human consciousness wanes and withers, like a plant removed from the soil that nourishes it. For Fevronia, even death cannot be conceived as either evil or as oblivion. Within the formative process whose goal is the surmounting of material mass through centrifugal forces (i.e., growth), death is merely that moment of transition, in which this surmounting is finally *being accomplished* and when a transition into another state will be achieved. It is the joy of harmonious unity, the joy of liberation from the dualism of matter and spirit, from the opposition of mechanical and organic elements: the joy in the knowledge of the entire evolution of the world toward oneness, toward a process wherein everything emanates from everything.

This conception of the formation of the universe is *imagistically* revealed by Rimsky-Korsakov in music, on the basis of the Russian folk legend of "The Invisible City of Kitezh."[4] The actual method of revelation involved here demands careful analysis *itself*, for it is this method that substantiates and explicates the worldview that was set forth above. Out of the two existing variants in the subject matter, i.e., a Kitezh concealed under water, or a Kitezh that continues to abide on earth but is invisible to the "unseeing," the composer chose the latter. This offered him the possibility of developing the action as a line of ascent toward a face-to-face beholding of Kitezh. Thus, an evolutionary process is born. The striving toward a full comprehension of the light, the spiritual infusion of consciousness, along with transfiguration and transformation—these are the actual intentional principles by which the action of *The Legend* develops and *grows*. Furthermore, the technique of parallelism, literary in essence, which is constantly employed by Rimsky-Korsakov in nearly all of his operas, is, in this case, thanks to the unique conception of the subject matter, raised to an extreme level of intensity and significance: namely, to a point where the inner unity behind the apparent divisibility of the world can be set forth. This monism, which is consistently carried out and developed in the music through thematic expansions, growth, and the transformation of elements, does not call for an obligatory approach to the subject, whether from a pagan-pantheistic standpoint, or an Orthodox-Christian, or one derived from mystical experiences. It is all offered *ad libitum* to the listener, in accordance with his personal psychological state or states.

The aesthetic gratification that emerges during the process of hearing *Kitezh* and after is rooted in the harmonious unification in this music of two eternally warring tendencies of the human "creative will": the process of revealing creative conceptions in abstract-schematic forms and in forms that are organic and of a natural concreteness. The first process at its most supremely inspired is found in Gothic art, the second in the Renaissance (earlier still, the first is found in Egyptian art, the second in Greek sculpture and architecture). In Russian art, there needed to occur a *sui generis* reinterpretation of these tendencies. If one accepts that the *origins* of our icon painting lie with Egyptian portraiture and that it then passed through the temptation of the more abstract Byzantine manner, then its *evolution* must be construed as a gradual overcoming of linear-geometric structure toward those creative impulses that Lipps introduced under the concept of "intuition" (Einfühlung) and which gravitate toward artistic designs based on the organic world.[5]

This is the added taste of its *own* that a Russian understanding brings to bear on religious art. In music, and particularly in the works of Rimsky-Korsakov, a most interesting struggle can be observed between the processes of abstraction and intuition. The composer was drawn to the former by the cast of his musical thinking, i.e., a speculation over colors of sound together with an incessant differentiation of material; i.e., its dispersion into the most minutely contrasted elements. He was drawn to the latter on account of the lyrical nature of his soul and his tender infatuation with the visible world, along with an inclination toward anthropomorphism. First one, then the other tendency dominates, and they do not always harmoniously combine. In this regard the following are all antipodes: *May Night* and *Christmas Eve* (or *Kashchei*); *The Maid of Pskov* and *Servilia*; *The Tsar's Bride* and *The Tale of Tsar Saltan*; and *Sadko* and *Mlada*.

The first group is overloaded with a lyrical impulse and an *intuitive* process, the second with an *abstraction* infused with spirit, a linear-geometric ornamentation, a rhythm of contrasting planes (or sonorous masses)—in short, a *process* stemming from the creative will's tendency to extract a particular object out of the eternally flowing and fluctuating development of the visible world and establish for it an absolute existence, independently of any connection born of causality to the phenomena of the surface world. It is an existence conditioned by a given artistic conception, based on an inclination toward *abstraction*, not *intuition*.[6]

For all its unquestionable achievements and all its charm, *Snow-Maiden* conceals a deep inner contradiction within it, since the composer's interpretation of the subject, his method of thought, and the musical conception of the subject all reveal a struggle between these processes of the self-asserting will as it creates artistic treasures. *The Legend of Kitezh* is the result of a lengthy creative path. It is a profound response to *Snow-Maiden*, the result of remarkable contemplation; for indeed, in addition to an undeniable lyrical impulse that cedes nothing to the youthful depth of feeling and clarity in the lyricism of *Snow-Maiden,* we find here the most perfect union of all the factors that ensure stylistic harmony, i.e., a unity of all the work's means of expression.

How was this achieved? The lyrical impulse was not taken as a value unto itself. Instead, it was given a dual interpretation, yielding both joy and suffering. The world can either be accepted under the belief of its transformation or be renounced under the belief of its servile subjugation to evil. This principle is entirely the opposite of asceticism, wherein the rejection of the world is based on the impossibility of its transformation and on the expectation of reward in heaven. Consequently, Fevronia's joyful acceptance of the world (the process of "intuiting" into the world, as it is especially displayed in the first act, in Fevronia's worship forest liturgy[7]) does not lead to the demise of her soul, but to the transformation of the entire world, to its growth and liberation from subjection to the law of gravity, which was ever the great dream of Gothic art. On the other hand, Grishka Kuterma's mournful rejection of the world leads to a subjugation to the burdens and sorrows of this world, to a sinking into evil and envy, into spiritual blindness. Thus, two tendencies of the artistic will are intertwined throughout the action of *The Legend*. Yet in the music of Rimsky-Korsakov their reconciliation is achieved. Preserving his exceptionally speculative and contemplative former approach to creativity, and not for a moment relinquishing his manner of thought (i.e., the principle of differentiation), he managed not to produce a mechanically formalized and "ornamental" work, but instead the most organic among all his compositions, one in which the two aforementioned and continually conflicting tendencies of his creativity are reconciled.

It is my deep conviction that this reconciliation was not achieved under the influence of mysticism (I am convinced that *Parsifal* must have been unbelievably alien to Rimsky-Korsakov) but was entirely due to the instinct of a great stylist, i.e., due to a purely aesthetic approach. There is no need to suppose that this claim removes all possibilities of a religious-philosophical significance of *Kitezh* or the presence of a religious-psychological impulse in Rimsky-Korsakov's soul during the period when the great work was created. But any religious-philosophical significance of *Kitezh* can only be derived from a religiously predisposed *perception* of the music, i.e., after a performance that bestows a concrete existence to the work and thereby stimulates the proliferation of an encircling world of ideas evoked by this particular phenomenon [i.e., the work]. The question of the religious significance of *Kitezh* is tied to questions of the work's vitality or the spiritual energy aroused by it. It is not a matter of the aesthetic essence of the work itself. As for the question of the psychological basis for the creation of *Kitezh*—whether religious experiences or a will to create artistic treasures—it is necessary to rule out the suggestion of a subjective impulse in favor of an impulse whose actual presence can be justified within the conception of the work and its realization as a stylistically unified entity. In *Kitezh* we seem to *apprehend the logic* of an organic process and *sense the organicism* of a process of abstraction, which elsewhere we perceive as things apart: the former in Greek sculpture and in Renaissance painting, the latter in Gothic art. It occurs to me that only the mysterious nature of music is capable of realizing such a synthesis!

In the first act of *The Legend*, as in a seed, all the further development of the action is contained in potential. One can think of this scene as analogous to a Vespers, or rather, an all-night vigil, i.e., as a religious *deistvo*, in which praise is sung to the Creator and to the Creation, i.e., to the Maker of the universe and to the universe. In this regard, the central point of this act is developed in Fevronia's "Great Doxology" ("Day and night we perform the Divine Rite").[8] A deep-set and unbroken thematic connection of this act with the process of "ascending into the City of Kitezh" and with abiding in it (i.e., with the fourth act) extends from the moment. Here Prince Vsevolod Yurevich, he who had struggled with the contradiction between the daring of youthful volition and the ascetic decrees of elders, enters into communion with the secret of an unclouded acceptance of the world through an indivisible worldly gravitation toward vernal renewal and joy. The renewal of spring is unveiled by Fevronia in a wonderful musical portrait ("The puddles and swamps are spreading"[9]) even before the "doxology." The dogma of a joyous acceptance of the world is set forth by Fevronia in the splendid lyrical arioso "Dearest, how can one live without joy?" Through this one observes a connection with Fevronia's deed that bears upon Grishka, the one who slandered her (in Act 3, when Grishka is liberated from his bonds).[10] The arioso is developed into a "prophetic vision": "Something never seen will come to be and all will be made beautiful." This music encapsulates and seemingly foretells the entire wondrous scene of nature's transformation in the first half of the fourth act. Thus from a story of the springtime renewal of nature through the "doxology" and affirmation of a "dogma of joy" there proceeds an unbroken growth in the music's intensity, thanks to a close thematic association and a method of gradual accumulation of the sound ("nature" is represented as a rustling background, as a neutral condition, in which and out of which "blossom" blooms of joy and beauty, of inner and outer renewal) and also to a touching lyricism in the melodic elements that are placed at the root of the thematic development.

Although tied to future development, this central moment itself—in its entirety—emanates from the introduction to the act (the orchestral introduction and Fevronia's monologue "Praise to the wilderness"), wherein religious folk poetry is idealized in a vocal-instrumental realization.[11] The harmonic background—a rustling and delicately changing effluence—beautifully creates the changeable yet eternal face of nature. As an adornment to this background, short melodic motives are sketched, signifying the meekness, spiritual simplicity, and *lowliness* of Fevronia. Twice this presentation leads to the establishment of the more expansive, splendid melodic motive of praise for the beauty of nature and of gratitude for her gifts. All these thematic shapes are closely linked with the development of action in *The Legend* overall and are flexibly transformed and converted according to a psychological impulse that emerges from each particular turning point in the action. Three purely lyrical moments ("of infatuation") set the boundaries for the scene of Fevronia's and the prince's conversation and infuse the cosmic plan with warmth from the emergence of human feeling: "Brave handsome stranger"; "You, maiden beauty"; "You, my love, wild bird."[12] All three coexist in a single thematic sphere. Attached to them are an episode of wound dressing (tenderly unfolding thirds like a ribbon, which will be encountered further on in Fevronia's lament in the Tatar camp and in the scene of the ghostly encounter) and the prince's declaration of love: the ecstatic hymn "Hail, sweet lips."[13]

Therefore, in the design of the entire act, four *fulcrums*[14] can be distinguished: (1) the periodically returning rustling of nature (the harmonic background); (2) three instants of amorous musing (based on the same theme); (3) a center of action—the setting forth of Fevronia's worldview; and (4) the intensive growth of a cosmic consciousness (from the lyrical verses "Praise to the wilderness" toward the prophecy about the fate of the world, i.e., toward the Apocalypse) and, parallel with that, of the warmth and light of love (i.e., the sphere of intimate human feeling). But, despite this internal connection and association with that which follows, this act would suffer from incompleteness had not the composer's intuition suggested to him a true psychological and logical outcome or concluding act and result of it all: namely, the appearance of the *theme* of the capital city Kitezh after the explanation of Poyarok, with whom Fevronia had come into contact.[15] The theme appears in F major, of course, but still over a second-inversion chord. Now Fevronia's fate is linked with the fate of Kitezh. Her contemplative life passes into the real world, into lifelong selfless devotion. Thus the prologue to the drama *reaches* its destination (culmination), closely linking itself to the succeeding act.

I just now remarked that the theme of Kitezh appears in F major, as it should. Indeed, this is the tonality that plays such a large role in *The Legend*. If we recall that in Rimsky-Korsakov's musical worldview the tonality of F major elicits an image of vernal renewal, of nature in springtime, of youthful scurrying and green shoots,[16] then all of the following make sense: the culmination of *Kitezh* in F major (the final tableau, in the inspired and transfigured Holy City); the persistent tarrying in F major in the scene wherein Kitezh is miraculously hidden from the "infidels" (Act 3, first tableau); the use of F major at the moment of the Holy City's reflection in the lake, as seen by both Grishka and the Tatars; and two fleeting but important appearances of this theme in the same tonality at the ends of the first two acts (at Fevronia's prayer, "Lord, make invisible the city of Kitezh").[17] By coordinating the growth of the fundamental idea of "transformation" with a key that he actually *saw*, Rimsky-Korsakov achieves a stunning depth in form and style. For indeed, with respect to form, a stable, steady, yet at the same time ever-expanding chain is created among all the most significant moments of the action (the theme of the city acquires significance as a sort of "subject" that directs the musical action). With respect to stylistic unity, an interesting design is produced, one based upon the apparent partitioning of elements within each self-enclosed sphere and on the joining of one landmark to another at the boundaries.

Musical motion in Rimsky-Korsakov is based precisely on this or on an impulse therefrom: within demarcated musical planes, motion increases, not on the basis of an intense development of a quality, but on the basis of a *quantitative* growth according to a progressive principle: usually geometrically, i.e., while the contour of the theme is preserved, the figuration that accompanies it "expands" in a gradual diminishment: at first the motion is in quarters, then eighths, and next sixteenth notes, whereas the tempo remains unchanged.[18] Examples are numerous. Among the most striking: the growth of the forest in *Snow-Maiden*, Nezhata's *bylina* in *Sadko*, and the second act chorus of the Kitezhan citizenry pursued by the Tatars ("Ah, woe is coming, people"), so overwhelming in its growth of terror and confusion.[19] Returning now after this digression to the matter at hand, i.e., to an explanation of the "synthesizing" significance of the F-major tonality in *The Legend*, we must further state that the "vernal" aspect or "mood of rebirth" engendered by this tonality can never be taken merely as a symbol: for Rimsky-Korsakov, the perception of F major as the color of spring verdure was a concrete phenomenon and an actual sensory experience. It matters not if the psychological conception of *Kitezh* is now thought to be subjective, for it is by this means that one establishes the integrity and harmony of the design and the unity of expressive means and assigns an objective value to the work, based on the logical form and harmonious style.

As a result of all the accumulated development striving toward F major, one notices the extremely rare and, for Rimsky-Korsakov, *daring* event of an act concluding with a question mark (i.e., with the interval of a diminished fifth). This occurs at the close of the third act, where the Tatars are terrified and confused upon seeing the reflection of Kitezh in the lake. This dramatic episode is brought about by means of replacing an F-major triad with a diminished-seventh chord on the note F and by a clever gradual lowering of the chord (over the characteristic Tatar theme in the basses) to the note B, i.e., toward a glaring instability.[20] No less noteworthy are the tonal relationships between the thematically conceived harmonic background ("nature") and F major. If in the first act this background is based on B minor, in the first tableau of the fourth act leading up to the transformation of nature it "blossoms" in D minor, i.e., into the relative tonality of F major, whereas B minor appears to be isolated from it by an extremely unstable interval.[21] Moreover, much of the episode of "blossoming" (Larghetto, D minor) is based on a prolonged transition from a D-minor chord in second inversion to the root triad of that same scale degree, i.e., on a very gradual approach to a firm establishment of the relative key of F major and the sunny parallel key of D major.

Another extremely important element that links together the course of action in *The Legend* is the sound of bells in several figurations, which are sometimes superimposed on each other and usually with the basic motive of Fevronia's "doxology" from the first act as well. Although it does not represent an active force, the pealing emerges as a symbol of a triumph of faith and of jubilant hope, and in this sense, like all the remaining stylistic elements of the marvelous *Legend*, it too can grow and be transformed. The pealing first *sounds* in the prophetic vision of Fevronia (first act).[22] It sounds as a joy-filled promise, not yet as a triumphant drone, a rejoicing that is akin to a paschal bell ringing. In the second act, at the end of it, Fevronia's prayer is structured from elements of the bell theme signifying hope.[23] Beginning immediately with the opening measures of the third act, an astonishing transformation of the bell theme appears before us.[24] It is given in minor, with heavy octave triplets, corresponding to the heavy, grief-stricken mood of the city as it awaits the enemy's approach. A frightening tableau unfolds before the audience: this act marks a kind of song of mourning, a parting wish, and a blessing before death. The pealing element here plays the most important role, and from the first transformation of the bell theme (G minor, triplets) until the moment when "the church bells by themselves began to drone," a painful, protracted drama ensues: a resigning of the self to death, to fate, whose final episode is the departure of Prince Vsevolod Yurevich and his troops to meet the foe in an unequal battle, with the singing of a woeful Russian song, at once despairing and bold:

> *Podnyálasya s polúnochi*
> *Druzhínushka khrestyánskaya,*
> *Molílasya, krestílasya,*
> *Na smértnyi boi gotóvilas.*
> *Prostí-proshchái, rodnáya vyes!*
> *Ne plach zhe ty, seméyushka:*
> *Nam smyert o bóyu napísana,*
> *A myórtvomu soróma nyet.*[25]

> [Rising up at midnight,
> Our own Christian forces
> Prayed, crossed themselves,
> And prepared for mortal battle.
> Farewell, oh native land!
> Do not weep for me, dear family:
> Death in battle is decreed for us,
> And the dead can feel no shame.]

Over the course of the drama's development, the theme of bell-pealing is transformed and transfigured several times, sounding nearly all the time, sometimes threateningly, sometimes as a promise of hope. Compare, for example, first the lines of the chorus: "God still protects great Kitezh"; and Poyarok's "Ah, one man has been found." From there, it develops onward to the words: "Woe to cursed Judas!" Further on, in Prince Yuri's stylistically remarkable, stringently restrained, archaic arioso "O glory, vain riches," the bell theme sounds during an appeal to the city, first as a tender memory (E-flat major), then proudly rising up (D-flat major).[26] After the first entreaty[27] and first vision of the youthful page, the very same theme is played more fiercely than at the beginning of the act: like a punishing will ("O, how terrible is the right hand of God! So the demise of the city is prepared").[28] After the second entreaty and vision, it sounds like woeful despair. After the third entreaty, the vision of the boy loses its menacing character and inspires hope for a miracle: F major is introduced, and therewith the bell theme resounds in smooth imitations between voice and orchestra.[29] The vision is interpreted by Prince Yuri as a "disappearance of the city." Prince Vsevolod sets forth with the troops "to meet the enemy" (again, the frightening funereal thirds from the first transformation of the bell theme). The song of the troops dies down. "A shining mist with flecks of gold quietly descends from dark heaven" is followed with: "The church bells peal softly of their own accord."[30] Here begins the consummation of the miracle of transformation and the spiritual infusion of the city: the bell theme occupies a foremost position, now timidly hovering in a soft rustling atop the choir's recitatives, now ascending like the smoke of incense, now sounding like a still cautious song of gratitude and hope. Little by little, countermelodies attach themselves to this main theme (rather, contrapuntal subsidiaries: for the divergent sequences in the basses and the theme of Kitezh diverge). The music congeals into a quietly jubilant drone, so that on the very same foundation it can awaken episodically in the following tableau (the Tatar's fright) and in full flourish rise up again in a mighty Eastertide ringing of the "passage into the invisible city."[31]

In the final tableau of *The Legend*, the pealing has already been linked simultaneously to the theme of "doxology and joy," and to the theme of Kitezh, and to the sequences of bell ringing. In this way the third act is linked to the concluding act.

No less evocative is the second act's connection with the entire opera, especially with its concluding moment. How interesting that it takes place in Lesser Kitezh as if on the threshold of the Greater, in this sense symbolizing the "passage into the invisible city." The entire act is devoted to the *everyday world*. It is based on the anticipation of the reception of the wedding procession of Prince Vsevolod's bride (i.e., Fevronia). The folk are satisfied with the choice of the bride. The "higher born" see it as an insult and bribe the drunkard Grishka Kuterma to cause harm to the "bride from the swamp." Grishka assiduously carries out the task and impertinently insults Fevronia. She endures his mockery with calm and forgiveness. The wedding procession continues on its way, but not for long: the wedding song is cut short, the sounds of horns are heard, and the panic-stricken crowd flees (there follows the aforementioned genial chorus, "Ah, woe is coming, people"). Such is the schematic design of the act. I have sketched it out only with the goal of establishing a link with what follows.

At the beginning of the [second] act, after the frolicking with the bear, a *gusli* (psaltery) player appears. His prophetic soothsaying-song points to the imminent destruction of Greater Kitezh (his theme enters as an instrumental tune between the song's strophes): "Ah, hard times lie ahead."[32] The lament of the Queen of Heaven over Kitezh is the basis of the song: by this means the entreaty of the Kitezh citizenry to her in the next act becomes comprehensible. As already noted, it is based on one of the beggars' phrases from the second act ("And they will find a dwelling-place"). . . .[33] The gusli player's song brings discord into the peaceful "everyday" course of life in Lesser Kitezh. The prince's wedding distracts the residents' attention, but the prophecy soon begins to come to pass. Like a storm, the Tatars' invasion descends. The wedding song remains incomplete until the final tableau, where the chorus of the Kitezhan citizenry, who are now radiant with joy, again pick it up: Fevronia and her husband are met by Prince Yuri, the father-in-law. The bell peals at first flow in gentle passages, then rise up like incense, then ring out in resounding triumph. In her modest way, Fevronia asks forgiveness of the people, who are still illuminated with the light of knowledge, and addresses questions to them (a stylization of the cosmic revelations of the *Dove Book*).[34] Radiant and wise, she enters with her husband into the cathedral, where the wedding ceremony is to be performed. With this *Kitezh* is thus brought to a conclusion, even though the seed of this act is rooted in the second act, in the interrupted wedding song. . . .

Hence there is an important conclusion to draw: Kitezh is the Earth, radiant and transfigured, together with nature, everyday reality, and the structure of human relationships, bestowed now in joy and harmony. This is not a resurrection for an eternal life in an "abstract" Heaven, but a transfiguration and transformation, the outcome of a gradual evolution of the will and consciousness. Thus the structure of the entire action of *The Legend* can be outlined as follows: in the first tableau, as in a seed, the process of nature's transformation is outlined in a prophecy and the tender, forgiving soul of Fevronia is revealed, deeply plunged into contemplation over the joy of the Creation. It is a simple soul, yet intuitively wise, for it has grasped the unity (harmony) of the Universe. And her humility is not the compulsory humility of the ascetic, but a free sort, which emerges from an unconscious, yet wise inner vision, so full of potential. The rendezvous with the prince links Fevronia to Kitezh and to its fate. Thus a current flows from the first tableau and throughout the entire action of *The Legend*, creating a close connection with the second tableau (the "wedding train") and with the moment when nature is transformed (the first tableau of the fourth act).

The invasion of the Tatars (second tableau) interrupts the peaceful course of the action leading up to the wedding and impedes its development along the lines of an "everyday life" drama, which, doubtless, would emerge as a consequence from the social inequality that is contained in this wedding (the "high born" bribery and Grishka Kuterma's provocations). Thanks to the Tatar devastation, the action is transplanted into a religious-moral sphere, the sphere of the real-life deed; and the postponement of the wedding to the music's final chords acquires another, higher meaning: Fevronia's life is redirected from the realm of quiet speculation and rejoicing contemplation into the realm of selfless devotion—not the ascetic sort, in the seclusion of the desert, but one born of "experience," amongst people. Her life acquires a new sense of efficacious enlightenment and illumination. Her wise presentiment of oneness and harmony must be turned into a knowledge born from experience, learned from the deed. In accordance with the enlightenment, she draws nigh to the "invisible city"; and along with her all the action of *The Legend* is guided toward the "passage into the invisible city." Because of style, then, out of a stylistic necessity within this conception, *growth* emerges, a pull toward development. The philosophical basis imparts a meaning taken from enlightenment and transfiguration through the deed to this idea of growth (elicited by stylistic necessity). The principle of formal unity conditions the musical development on the basis of precisely delimited material. The psychological impulses that take root in the depths of creative fervor transform mechanical development into an organic process and blanket all the created work with a lyrical pathos that penetrates the soul, for indeed one of the most profound merits of *The Legend* is its lyrical-melodic material: those melodic phrases, out of whose confluence and juxtaposition the entire musical fabric of the work is organized. One need only try to imagine the spiritual poverty of *Kitezh* if all Fevronia's themes, her benediction, her praises of joy, Grishka's painful cries, the songs of the Kitezhan populace and Tatars, and the bell-pealing were deprived of the lyrical intensity and plasticity that characterize them!

Whereas the second act reflects the entire developmental process of *The Legend*, at the same time it is closely linked with the third: *through the gusli player's prophetic song and Fevronia's prayer about Kitezh.*[35] These two important episodes portend the direction and the outcome, which will be given in the third act. Its dramatic power fluctuates between terror at the impending destruction and hope for deliverance. At the center is the entreaty to the Virgin, for here the two currents intersect: here the gusli player's prophesy is ready to be fulfilled ("Weep, Queen of Heaven, for Kitezh") and also the hope, known only to the audience, emerging from Fevronia's prayer, wherein the theme of deliverance (transfiguration) of Kitezh already was heard.[36]

The *enslavement* to horror and fright that hangs over Kitezh (third act), if not thematically, then at least psychologically, was already prefigured and conditioned by the soul-shaking chorus, "Ah, people, woe is coming," to which I have repeatedly referred.[37]

The third act's second tableau is linked to its first tableau by a stunningly expressive symphonic portrait: "The Massacre at Kerzhenets."[38] Here the clash of the Russian and Tatar thematic content (rooted in the Russian songs of the Tatar captivity) unfolds vividly and concisely. Formally and psychologically, it is the epicenter, where the everyday side of *The Legend* is reflected and where the energy of the Tatars' victorious offensive, emanating from the second act, achieves its highest intensity. After the "massacre," it diminishes and the Tatars' activity wanes (in the brilliantly conceived scene of the divvying up of the loot); for in the second tableau of the third act, the action is already concentrated, for the most part, on the relationship between Fevronia and Grishka Kuterma, who betrayed the city and defamed her.

I have intentionally put aside until now this most important aspect of the action, for herein lies the dramatic power of *The Legend*, and through this power the action receives a final impulse toward completion. The musical *deistvo* of a spiritual transformation of the world, conceived on a massive scale on the basis of *The Legend of the Invisible City of Kitezh*, contains within it several "little *deistva*," which condition the growth of the main one: a *lyrical deistvo*—the love between Fevronia and the prince and the inclination toward marriage: an *epic deistvo*—the stylized depiction (presented statically) of the real life of "Lesser Kitezh," destroyed by the Tatar invasion; and a *dramatic-moral deistvo*—the great sin of Grishka Kuterma and the moral deed of Fevronia.

All of these *deistva* are closely associated with the main one: the "passage into the invisible city"; and within each of them it is possible in turn to establish a crescendo and diminuendo in the intensity of the *deistvo* and, in addition, to observe the emergence of individual characters (in this respect I emphatically direct attention to the remarkable stylistic characterization of the strictly devout Prince Yuri Vsevolodovich) and of wonderfully descriptive moments. . . .

The characterization of the drunkard Grishka, so graphic in its lyrico-dramatic essence, almost does not yield to analysis in words, since it is so musically, psychologically, and stylistically flexible and prone to capricious change. Indeed it is based on certain deeply moving lyrical melodies and on dramatically well-considered juxtapositions and combinations of them, first in the voice and then in the orchestra.[39]

On the whole, they display the complicated diapason of spiritual states in the unfortunate Russian man who fashions for himself a religion out of the worship of woe and misfortune. There is nothing sacred to him, no thing that he could never desecrate, nor any transgression from which he could not escape. However—in inverse proportion to the mockery, the malicious daring, and sin—a fear of death grows in his soul and, far worse than that, an inescapable malefactor's anguish, a doleful disappointment over a life ruined and effort squandered for nothing. In the musical characterization of Grishka, one can distinguish (true enough, only in part, due to its instability) two fundamental motivic nerve centers: one set impudent, audacious, and provocative, the other painfully intense, like any genuinely Russian crackup. From the latter "series" of these motives, those that distinguish themselves and receive a broad application and profound transformation are heard in the second act in

Grishka's phrases: "To woe we're long accustomed; just as we're born to the world in tears, so not even in our last years will we have known our fate" and "Envious is cruel woe; it attaches itself to whatever it espies."[40] The more Grishka's reason is beclouded, the more his themes acquire a distorted and deformed imprint. New thematic layers attach themselves to them, beginning with a unique interpretation of the Kitezh bell pealing in the ears of the traitor and finishing with every manner of refined Korsakovian chromaticism, characteristic, too, of the Russian school in general (chords and harmonies of the augmented and diminished modes, creeping motions of augmented fourths and diminished fifths, and leaps of these intervals, special modifications to the minor mode by means of altered notes, etc., etc.).[41]

All of these purely stylistic devices result in the blackest musical depiction of insanity, unveiled in its incremental growth with momentary flashes of normal consciousness (when the motives appear in their essential, strictly diatonic form!). One could hardly conceive of a more intense, oppressive, and terrifying contrast to the full structure and growth of the action, or a more graphic image for the inert pull toward evil, toward materiality, counterbalancing the "ascension" into the holy city. Grishka appears as an image of the realization of evil[42] in a *weak-willed* (I emphasize Kuterma's weakness of will) human nature. And he *alone* opposes the full upward course of action: such is the power of *Russian* depression and passive acceptance of fate, whether evil or good. In this case, it is evil. But on Fevronia's side, both a willful striving and a faith in the inevitability of transformation are inherent in a real-world deed.[43] At the same time that the Kitezhan citizenry (with the exception of the prince and his troops) in contemplation and in prayer deliver themselves unto a higher will, Fevronia accomplishes a tangible good deed and through this conquers the inertia of evil. Thus a stylistic contrast is revealed and also a philosophical meaning (the counterbalancing of action and counteraction) in the juxtaposition of Fevronia and Grishka Kuterma, i.e., the bases of the inner drama and psychology of *The Legend*. Struggle and growth are found in the *development* of the music; on the whole, therefore, perception leads to consummation and harmonic unity, i.e., an unconditional aesthetic satisfaction (die höchste Beglückung) as a sign of the existence in this work of the realization of a vital and organic element (but not a lifelike verisimilitude).

Repeating what has already been said in the first part of the analysis, I must establish once again that the organic unity is achieved not by the method of coordinating the elements but by a method of differentiation and diffusion (of an ornamental design); and that, if in producing *Kitezh*, Rimsky-Korsakov did not deprive himself from his *rational* techniques over the course of the action, he mitigated the geometric quality of the formal conception as always with a lovely lyrical impulse. All the more amazing and inscrutable then, the achievement of harmony, accomplished through the bold casting of an arc (rainbow) from the first act to the fourth and the transmission hence throughout all of *The Legend* of the idea of growth and contrast in action and counteraction.

In the sharply contrasting musical juxtaposition of Fevronia and Grishka there is one moment of near rapprochement. It is the terrible moment of their common praying (Act 4, first tableau). All of the action between them drives toward this point: here is the final page of Fevronia's deed, after which the *deistvo* of nature's transformation and the passage into the invisible city commences. Let us examine the kernel itself, in the first encounter between Fevronia and Grishka (Act 2).[44] The speech of Kuterma is insolent and impudent. Fevronia's speech is grounded in the themes of her spiritual simplicity, humility, and meekness. Rimsky-Korsakov made the psychologically accurate observation that when an admonition is directed toward the sort of independent and freedom-loving people like Grishka Kuterma, the admonition has the opposite from the desired effect: it incenses them. So it is here. But amidst the impertinent speech one moment stands apart, in which Grishka cannot restrain himself but expresses his weakness: all of his fervor is merely sham and self-defense; and he himself, in essence, is a pitiful, unfortunate, weak-willed human being, a holy fool on account of suffering. It is here that he reveals his religious ideology: "Envious is cruel woe" . . . "We must bow to unholy woe" . . . The Tatars' invasion and the moment of Grishka's treason come thereafter.

Again there is proof of his lack of will (inertness): he betrays Kitezh not out of spiteful pride but out of cowardice. His quick mind suggests to him the idea of declaring to those he encounters that the city was betrayed by Fevronia, which blind Poyarok is also announcing to the people of Kitezh (in the third act), not suspecting that the strength of the prayer of a slandered innocent girl will save the city (this knowledge has already been given to the listener in the musical thematicism). In this way a clash of two opposing elements took place. Now the rapprochement begins: in the second tableau of the third act, Fevronia and Grishka are joined together by fate in the Tatar camp. Grishka is bound to a tree. Conscience has blinded him. He hears the incessant tolling but cannot see the city. The pangs of conscience are psychologically justified: I repeat, his malicious move stems neither from pride nor from revenge, but from the weak will of a humiliated unfortunate. It is the drunken Russian evil—misfortune's woe. Fevronia also is disconsolate, not about herself but about the prince, of whose demise she has overheard in the Tatars' conversation. Her lament is one of the most touchingly beautiful musical moments in all of *The Legend*.[45] Grishka begs her for deliverance. He turns to her as to a pure human being, fully aware of his own squalor. The impertinence has disappeared: his words are tearing our souls asunder! He confesses to Fevronia his slander of her. Frightened by the depth of the sin, terrified Fevronia asks: "Grisha, are you then the Antichrist?"[46] Certainly *not:* he is merely the "last of the drunkards," those who "drink bitter tears by the bucketful."

The strong compassion that Wagner ached to find, a compassion that during his work on *Tristan* in Venice (see the Wesendonck correspondence and the diary) was more akin to an *indulgence* that one strong in spirit and in possession of the wealth of wise and eternal knowledge of the essence of things would show toward the poor in spirit than to the *real compassion* for a neighbor, which is provoked by sorrow—something he achieved in *Parsifal.* The triumph over himself and his instincts guides Parsifal toward the healing of those who suffer from demonic temptations. *Demonic.* The full horror of Fevronia's situation consists of the fact that her struggle is in no way directed against a demon, against an element that would call for a struggle, but against those vile traits in a human being that can only inspire *contempt.* To surmount contempt within oneself and to say: "Do not grumble over a bitter lot: therein lies God's great secret"—means to sense inside oneself a cosmic consciousness, in which any personal innocence or guilt disappears. Fevronia accomplishes this deed and liberates Grishka. But freedom does not grant him peace: his reason is tortured by the incessant droning sound in his consciousness. The attempt to drown himself in the lake and the sighting of the city of Kitezh as reflected in the water send him into a yet stronger spiritual imbalance: "Where once there was a devil, now there are idols; where once was God, now there is nothing." The themes of Kuterma take on an all the more pitifully distorted appearance (especially the vocal melody that stems from the second-act phrase: "To woe we're long accustomed").[47] In the place of bitter woes and uncontrollable despair, he now emerges as devil and tempter. From a pure diatonicism, Grishka's thematicism tends toward an unstable chromaticism. Thus stylistic and psychological changes and transformations proceed hand in hand.

The third act ends with a question (over a diminished interval). . . .[48]

The first half of the fourth act reveals the burdensome spiritual state of Grishka Kuterma in the full amplitude of pliant musical means of expression. Pliant, since at no point does Rimsky-Korsakov the great stylist lose track of the idea of instrumental clarity and expressive logic. The theme that predominates here is the idea of sorrow ("Envious is cruel woe"), but in constant proximity to the chromatic motion of demonic visions. They alternate with moments of lucid consciousness: then the impudent and brazen tone returns to Grishka ("Your pride has grown, my little princess"). The sense and purpose of the relationship of Fevronia with Grishka are expressed in her words: "God, have mercy on Grishenka, send him *love,* just a tiny bit, grant him tears of tenderness."[49] Steadfastly, she follows her path. She succeeds in awakening in the soul of Grishka the desire for prayer. Here we are at the threshold of her deed, at her commingling with "woe-misfortune": with the god of Grishka. With the sensitivity of genius, the composer structures this prayer not on the themes of "doxology" and "joy," not on the theme of "praise for Mother Earth," i.e., not on the prayers of Fevronia herself, but on a vocal phrase of Grishka: "Envious is cruel woe."[50] Fevronia prays with him, not to a world of joy and light, *her world*, but to the world soaked with bitter tears, to the world of Grishka Kuterma and others like him. In her lips, this prayer, too, gradually begins to change into a doxology ("And on the virgin field, white as a shroud," etc.). On the other hand, in Grishka's mouth, the theme little by little loses its sense, becoming more fragmented as he plunges once again into even more bitter insanity: a vision of the devil and of worship of him through a wild dance and song, accompanied by whistling! . . .[51]

I know of no other scene so graphic in its psychological veracity as this scene of insane servitude to the force of evil expressed in music. The full horror of boundless cynicism, of outrage toward life, toward human dignity under the mask of impudent clowning is unveiled in this scene with soul-stirring boldness and realism, yet still within the guidelines of a harmonious artistic design, and not at all in the sense of imitating "true reality." The expressive force of this moment stems from the fact that it is conditioned by a will that is creating things of artistic value: a will, joining together things drawn "from life," yet without producing "ordinary life." In a fierce depression, with a yelp, Kuterma flees. An emaciated Fevronia lies down on the sward and sinks into contemplation. She has always prayed to the Earth in a state of joy, yet with Grisha has prayed in sorrow, to a sorrowful Earth.

A transformation of the Earth and of all the Earth's natural world will now be achieved, in accord with her prophetic vision (in the first act) and with her prayer. Fevronia stands at the threshold of Kitezh. Her deed has been accomplished. Contemplating the elated transformation around her, she delivers herself unto death, not in order to vanish but to find repose ("Come, my dear death, my dear welcome guest").[52] Over the theme of her "doxology," the ghost of Prince Vsevolod floats slowly and smoothly in the air. This meeting of Fevronia and her husband musically enhances and vivifies the meeting of the first act. The music brightens, becoming more and more transparent, concluding with a mystical Lento. During it, Fevronia passes through three states: there is a breaking of bread and bestowing of heavenly grace; a parting from the Earth; and a prayer for the dead—after which her ascent into the invisible city, together with her husband, begins. The music flows into a symphonic entr'acte (the transition to the second tableau of the fourth act), painting in sound this ascent and gradually overflowing into an exultant festive "ringing of the Uspensky Bell."[53]

F major (the hue of vernal renewal) is introduced as the main tonality and, together with it, an abiding state of eternal joy. I have already spoken previously of this concluding scene of *The Legend*. The action comes to a halt in order to be transformed into speculation: into contemplation within a state of joy.

The profound distinction of *Kitezh* from Rimsky-Korsakov's "pagan" operas is found in the liberation of his thought out of the confinement of a circle, from the eternal, periodically repeating cycle and return of the seasons. From *Snow-Maiden* to *Christmas Eve* he revealed the full cycle of religio-mythological views of paganism. Now his thought found another outlet: in the idea of eternal growth, in ascension, in the spiral (as a symbol), not the circle.[54] The pinnacles of contemporary thought gravitate toward this symbol as well. My attempt to identify the psychological and philosophical bases for the style of *The Legend* started from the evidence provided by the music, yet avoided purely musical analysis, since this would have led me to tiresome details of appeal only to the specialist. The riches of instrumental color alone demand a special essay, to say nothing of the harmonic fabric and thematic development. A multifaceted study of *The Legend of Kitezh* (and therefore *not* a textbook formal analysis of the harmonic plan and "leitmotivic" links)—is a matter for the distant future, since such an essay would demand a colossal concentration of thought as well as a thorough survey of the work's sources: both the internal organic ones and the external, those gleaned from literature and folk art.

No such work exists yet for Glinka and his *Ruslan*, i.e., concerning the threshold of the phenomenon whose final stage I see to be depicted in *Kitezh*. It appears that, with this, an epoch of national epic operatic works has come to an end. Such great achievements always serve as boundary points: as a synthesis of the past and challenge to the future. Indeed, from the intuitively inspired creation of *Ruslan* to the creative speculation, to the conscious "clever craftsmanship" of *Kitezh* an enormous trek has been completed. We who are close at hand are still powerless to demonstrate the place and the significance of this work in the future evolution of Russian culture. We can only sense the grandeur of the conception and bow our heads before the marvelous craftsmanship of its realization.

NOTES

1. Score location: Act 1, fig. 39 (mm. 473–80).
2. The psychological dichotomy discussed here is between the worldview of *Kitezh*'s protagonist Fevronia centered on human life as an opportunity and obligation

for spiritual growth and that of her antipode and antagonist Grishka Kuterma, whose life follows a course of spiritual decline ending in madness and death.

3. "Intuitive understanding" resonates with much fin-de-siecle metaphysical thought, e.g., Henri Bergon's intuitive metaphysics, Nikolai Lossky's intuitive episte-mology, the aesthetician Theodor Lipps' concept of *Einfühlung*, and various strains of German and Russian Neo-Kantianism.

4. Folk legends about the miraculous vanishing of an ancient Central Russian city under the threat of a Tatar onslaught served as source material for a number of 19th-century poets, writers, theologians, and philosophers. Of particular relevance to Rimsky's opera is the variant used by Pavel Melnikov (1818–1883) to establish a storied past for the present-day setting of his novel *In the Forests* (1871–1874), since the composer not only read the work, but went on to borrow essential details of the legend as related by Melnikov: "The city [stood] whole and intact, yet invisible: not to be seen by sin-ners. By the Lord's command, it was miraculously hidden when the godless Khan Baty, having ravaged Susdalian Rus, came to wage war on Kitezhian Rus. . . . For ten days and ten nights, Baty's minions vainly sought the city of Kitezh, but being blinded, could not. And to this day, that city stands invisible, to be revealed on the day of Christ's Last Judgment. But in a quiet summer evening one can see, reflected in the water of Lake Svetly Yar, the monasteries, princely towers, noble mansions, and the courtyards of the dwellers on the outskirts. And at night can be heard the deep doleful ringing of the bells of Kitezh" (P. I. Melnikov, *Sobranie sochinenii*, v. 2 [Moscow: Pravda, 1963]: 7–8).

5. According to Theodor Lipps (1851–1914), the essential response to art is the feeling of empathy [*Einfühlung*]. The impulse to project the self in order to enjoy the self led gradually to an art aesthetic that favored the reflection of the organic world over the creation of linear-geometric structures.

6. [Author's note:] Abstraction should not be understood as a tendency toward stiffness, or as creation that is nonliving or lifeless. Gothic art was a profoundly vital art form! The inclination toward abstraction is an intellectual process, born of the human spirit, a process that is the reverse of the anthropomorphic tendency, i.e., the human-izing of nature.

7. Words of praise for forest, nature, and God are never far from Fevronia's lips. Asafyev is likely referring to her hymn of thanksgiving (Act 1, fig. 8), spun out from a cantabile theme in D-flat, introduced in the orchestral prelude to Act 1.

8. Fevronia's second hymn, "Day and night," stemming from a horn fifths motive, begins at fig. 34.

9. Rimsky scored the delicate passage beginning at Act 1, fig. 28, for muted *divisi* strings, flute, oboe, and harp.

10. Cf. Act 1, fig. 39, and Act 3, fig. 236 + 6. Both a melodic phrase and a three-note "horn fifths" ascension motive return in Act 3, even though no explicit textual reference would justify it.

11. Asafyev has taken note of Fevronia's simply phrased sentiments, expressed in ar-chaic idiom and set to artless diatonic melody.

12. The entire encounter between Fevronia and Prince Vsevolod extends from Act 1, fig. 18 to fig. 65. Asafyev's three lyrical moments are at figs. 19, 26, and 51, all of

them cast in a flowing 6/8 meter and at larghetto tempo. The thematic links do not involve whole phrases.

13. Asafyev has observed the recurrence of thirds during Fevronia's dressing of the prince's wound (Act 1, fig. 25), as an accompaniment to her lament in the Tatar camp (Act 3, figs. 222, 223), and during the visitation of the prince's ghost (Act 4, fig. 298 + 8).

14. The term "fulcrum" [*tochka opory*] is fundamental to Asafyev's analytical approach to opera, as exemplified here and in the *Queen of Spades* essay. Simply put, fulcrums occur when a defining moment of the opera's unfolding drama is assigned a cyclic musical element of some sort (e.g., a motive, a theme, a thematic complex), which comes into sharp focus on its initial occurrence and is later reprised. The succession of fulcrums (and cyclic elements) in *Kitezh*'s first act is particularly complex due to the interweaving of the four discrete plot elements identified by Asafyev. Their coexistence (after a point) in Fevronia as evidenced by her words and the thematic interplay transform Act 1 into something more than an extended love duet.

15. The Kitezh theme consisting of a fanfare for trumpets atop a second-inversion triad first appears at the close of Act 1 (fig. 65), just as Poyarok names the city and the city's ruler: Vsevolod's father, Yuri. The emergence of the Kitezh theme at this point in its home key of F confirms by this symbolic use of key that Fevronia's act of committing herself to Vsevolod also ties her fate to the fate of the city.

16. In plainer terms, Rimsky-Korsakov's synesthesia caused him to associate the key of F with the color green.

17. Asafyev names five occurrences of F major that are associated with the city of Kitezh, its theme, and its transformations: (1) the transformation of Kitezh into heavenly Paradise (Act 4, fig. 325); (2) Kitezh made invisible (F major is attained at Act 3, fig. 181, as preparation for the miracle of the spontaneous bell-ringing; the Kitezh theme returns at fig. 186); (3) the reflection of Kitezh in the lake (Act 3, fig. 241); (4) Poyarok's first mention of Kitezh (Act 1, fig. 65); and (5) Fevronia's prayer of solicitation for Kitezh (Act 2, fig. 136 + 2).

18. [Author's note:] How awful if a conductor does not take into account this unique structure and increase of musical motion and allows at such moments cuts or accelerations in the tempo!

19. The analogous passages of a submetrical acceleration occur at the following locations: (1) *Snow-Maiden*, Act 3, "Scene with Snow-Maiden and Mizgir," mm. 185–92 and (2) *Sadko*, fourth tableau, mm. 657–97.

20. The transformation of an F-major triad into a diminished-seventh chord built on F occurs at Act 3, fig. 246. A prolongation of that dissonant sonority closes the act as the Tatars flee in terror from the reflection of a city in a lake that they cannot see on land.

21. Asafyev is describing a large-scale harmonic progression that is played out in Act 4 from fig. 273 to fig. 285.

22. Score location: Act 1, fig. 45 ("And from Heaven a mellow chime will ring").

23. Score location: Act 2, fig. 136 + 3.

24. Score locations: Act 3, figs. 138, 139, 141 inter alia.

25. Prince Vsevolod strikes up the battle hymn at Act 3, fig. 177.

26. Score locations: Act 3, figs. 157, 158. The keys that Asafyev names make for a stark tonal contrast with the arioso's main key of E minor.

27. [Author's note:] It seems almost to be an acathistus of the Queen of Heaven. We may note that the prayer themes emanate from the praises of the beggars for Greater Kitezh in the second act: "And they will find a dwelling-place." It is yet another example of the wonderfully realized dramatic connection!

28. Having been ordered by Prince Yuri to climb a tower and survey the environs, a young page reports on the destruction of Lesser Kitezh. A chromaticized variant of the bell theme returns thereafter, at Act 3, fig. 166. (Score location of the beggars' praises mentioned in Asafyev's footnote: Act 2, fig. 77 + 11.)

29. As the page describes the mysterious white mist over the lake, the bell theme returns in a stately, slower transformation in both the vocal line and orchestra (Act 3, fig. 172).

30. Score location: Act 3, fig. 181.

31. The Tatars' sighting of Kitezh reflected in the lake is accompanied by both the bell theme and the Kitezh theme (as mentioned above). Both reappear in counterpoint at the beginning of Act 4's second tableau (fig. 325).

32. The refrain-like tune occurs at Act 2, fig. 75, followed by a choral response with the cited text.

33. The plea for protection in Act 3 (fig. 171, chorus in imitative polyphony) traces back to the hymn verse sung by the beggars at Act 2, fig. 79.

34. According to a Russian Orthodox encyclopedia of 1913 (*Polnyi pravoslavnyi bogoslovskii entsiklopedicheskii slovar*), the adjective *golubinaia* [dove's] in *Dove Book* was probably a corruption of *glubinnaia* [deep], signifying a text of profound spiritual wisdom. The posing of questions is a traditional means of verifying an initiate's readiness to receive the wisdom. Such a book, apocryphal in content, appeared in a 13th-century list of banned books.

35. After an episode involving a trained bear, the essential drama in Act 2 begins at fig. 72 with the gusli player's singing a prophecy of Kitezh's destruction. Act 2 concludes with Fevronia's prayer that Kitezh be spared by being made invisible.

36. Faced with the impending destruction of Kitezh, Prince Yuri (Vsevolod's father) beseeches the people to pray to the Virgin Mary for deliverance (Act 3, figs. 170–72). When a tangible response to that prayer appears in the form of a strange mist rising to shield the city, the page describes the event (fig. 172) using the theme from Fevronia's prayer in Act 2.

37. [Author's note:] Thematically, this chorus is associated with the Tatars, since it stems from the gradual descending motion that characterizes the "Kitezh Tatars."

38. The battle music depicting the massacre of Prince Vsevolod's troops takes the form of a 222-measure symphonic entr'acte in which diatonic themes representing the Russians confront chromatic themes for the Tatars, with an additional rhythmic motive to evoke the sound of hoofbeats.

39. [Author's note:] The musical fabric (entity, body) of the operas of Rimsky-Korsakov is by no means created on the basis of the Wagnerian principle of combining leitmotives, but on the basis of the melodic unification of song melodies. This must

not be confused, for no matter how tempting the proximity to the "leitmotivic" analogy, the *origins* of the fabric for the two composers were entirely different.

40. Score location: Act 2, fig. 114. Grishka Kuterma sings the fateful words, "Envious is cruel woe," to Fevronia during their first encounter; the important motive consists of three pairs of repeated eighths.

41. Grishka's first breakdown occurs at Act 3, figs. 242–43 in response to his sighting of the hidden city of Kitezh's reflection in the lake. A chromaticized variant of the bell theme and a descending whole-tone scale accentuate the sudden shift of harmonic language away from the F-major diatonicism of the Kitezh themes that had just been reprised.

42. [Author's note:] One should not forget that this evil stems not from demonicism, nor from human pride, but from misery. It is not a Western European but a Russian "creation." A man has gone off the rails, has despised everyday reality and its rules, but does not see the light and does not possess the *will* to raise himself.

43. As Asafyev proceeds to explain, in the real-world plane of action, Fevronia's essential good deed is her attempt to confront the evil possessing Grishka in order to save his soul. The culmination of this process is their praying together in Act 4.

44. Score location: Act 2, figs. 111–17. Rimsky-Korsakov underscores the clash of personalities through his customary technique of juxtaposing extreme contrasts of style involving all of the fundamental elements of musical style.

45. Score location: Act 3, fig. 222. The lament portion of this arioso consists of a repetitive phrase in A minor harmonized initially with a simple pedal point.

46. Score location: Act 3, fig. 231 + 4.

47. Cf. Act 2, fig. 95 + 1, and Act 3, figs. 224–26. The recurring motive is subjected to numerous transformations with tritones and chromatic inflections frequent.

48. The diminished fifth is formed between B and F, both of them representing prominent key centers used throughout the opera.

49. Score location: Act 4, fig. 259.

50. The quoted phrase was sung by Grishka at Act 2, fig. 114, during his first encounter with Fevronia. At Act 4, fig. 262, she begins to teach him to pray using the same musical *intonatsiya*, thus showing that she can speak his language.

51. Grishka's descent into wholly delusional ravings is indeed achieved by degrees. At Act 4, fig. 264 + 8, his screamed G# is pitched at the interval of a tritone away from the last pitch sung by Fevronia. As his hallucinations continue, more tritones continue to infect his melos. A dance accompanied by Grishka's whistling begins at fig. 267, rooted in an obsessive ostinato. Thereafter come chromatic scales, whole-tone scales, and other key-destabilizing devices.

52. The quoted line establishing Fevronia's acceptance of death is found at Act 4, fig. 293, immediately to be followed by the appearance of the ghost of the martyred Vsevolod.

53. The adjective "Uspensky" yields a double significance, referring not only to the Uspensky Sobor [Cathedral of the Assumption] in Greater Kitezh but also to the Uspensky Sobor in Moscow's Kremlin complex and to the Uspensky Bell (forged 1817) that was used at coronations of the tsars and to ring in Easter morning when Rimsky-Korsakov was alive.

54. This is Asafyev's first reference to the contrasting paradigms of circle and spiral used in reference to the evolution of the universe. For the Symbolist poet Andrei Bely (1880–1934), the figure of the spiral served as the long-awaited alternative to the older linear and circular conceptions of the evolving world, since it united the experience of the present moment (the Real) with the participation in eternity and eternal truths (Ideals). The concepts are thematicized in his novel, *Petersburg*.

• 12 •

Kingdom of *Skomorokhi*

The Tale of the Golden Cockerel, Rimsky-Korsakov's most conceptually complex creation, is at the same time one of the most difficult subjects for the psychology of style. It does not surprise me that after *The Legend of Kitezh* an opera appeared that stunned one and all with its novelty and boldness of design.[1] The path into both the kingdom of Dodon and the princedom of Yuri of Kitezh emerges out of the kingdom of Berendei; likewise, Snow-Maiden leads both to Fevronia and to the Queen of Shemakha. If Snow-Maiden, after being resurrected, were to realize that it is possible to enjoy love not by loving but by teasing and stimulating human lust, so that then her heart would not melt, she would become the Shemakha enchantress.[2] Being a man infatuated with the phenomenal world—as a perspicacious observer—Rimsky-Korsakov had the authority to choose any image that drew his attention and permeate it with music—to smelt it in the furnace of sounds. He was an astrologer and magician and as such cast fortunes and concocted relationships between the powers of nature and of people in the combinations he desired, playing with forces of both light and darkness, while himself remaining apart from the life or above the life of his creations like a watcher and steward. Sometimes, such a character is introduced into the action itself: the gusli player Nezhata in *Sadko* and the aged performer in *Kitezh* are heralds and chronologers; yet Patsiuk in *Christmas Eve* and the Astrologer in *Golden Cockerel* are *not* disinterested observers. The Astrologer is akin to Berendei in some respects. Both of them observe, contemplate like sages, and take part in the action. I imagine the Astrologer to have originated as follows—if Berendei were to have commanded the clowns to perform a *deistvo* that was a satirical reflection of his kingdom, but his own role were cut in twain: with one aspect of himself as king, the other as sage and contemplative. And instead of being the "spring flower," Snow-Maiden would become more realistic: a creature commanding all the charms of feminine delight but bereft of a heart! It may be that this kingdom of *skomorokhi* is performed not by people but by puppets for the ruler's amusement. Is not the Astrologer himself the future Magician from Stravinsky's *Petrushka*?[3] A distortion of an ordinary kingdom's characteristics: of such is the kingdom of Dodon, wherein the "skomorokhi" perform their role: the role of denouncers and deriders (blasphemers), arrayed in masks, performing everything according to rank and regulation: a stylization in caricature! Masks for the king, princes, *voyevoda*, housekeeper, the folk. But the Astrologer cannot be considered a mask. Neither can the Queen of Shemakha. And the cockerel is a mechanical doll amidst living dolls.

The *deistvo* is initially enacted with humor and merriment. "Nothing pointed to a tragic outcome," as is often said in accounts of events. The "skomorokhi," in fact, are somewhat astonished by the Astrologer: this unusual character with a strange plaything, one who seems not from their midst.[4] The toy entices, beckons, diverts attention. The Astrologer is forgotten. In the second act there is a new wonder: the "skomorokhi" have only just ridiculed the demise of the prince in the fool's requiem (a *plach*-lamentation over king and army), when suddenly a tent rises up, out of which a seductive woman emerges, singing a beautiful song to the sun.[5] All take cover. In the one of them playing the clown-king, lust is aroused. He enters into salacious conversation with the queen. The charmer seduces the king, now with tenderness, now with a reproach, now with sarcasm, now like a cooing dove. The music is strangely bifurcated: in the king's characterization is heard a sustained stylization in caricature along with the phrases of an old man's pitiable and obscure passion, whereas in the characterization of the queen, everything breathes with an animated yet malicious grin, poisoned with the passion of seductive sounds in a finely wrought instrumental recasting.[6] It is sirenic song, a song passionate but heartless: a temptation emanating from a woman languishing in sensuality, yet uncognizant of the spiritual warmth of human love. In the music that permeates the queen's speech are concentrated and intensified all the charms and entreaties culled together by the great lovers and by the musicians who have captured love in sound. The hypnosis is irresistible: at the queen's command, Dodon demonstrates in his dance and song all of his clownish nature.

Believing that he has enthralled the enchantress, he takes her to the capital. There one finds a gloomy, oppressive mood. Storm clouds have gathered. The clownish folk see that the drama has begun to drag, that it has overstepped certain boundaries. The outcome quickly ensues. The Astrologer demands of the king that a promise be fulfilled. The clownish king refuses: for him, only the woman signifies reality, while the Astrologer is as much a clown as everyone else. The cockerel pecks the traitor on the crown of his head—are puppets not often murdered?! The "skomorokhi" take note of the queen's disappearance with horror and perplexity: "Where can the queen be? She's vanished as if she never existed": the frightening question and answer are expressed in a laconic yet powerful choral recitative due to its import. Perhaps, then, not a clown-king, not a mask, but a human being has been killed, and the death is real and genuine?[7] There begins a burial service, the choir's wailing for the victim. The expressivity of the choir reveals the work of genius: themes that have already appeared over the course of the action are here suddenly infused with spirit, becoming radiant and transparent.[8] The more horrifying it becomes for the soul, the greater the confusion, in relation to which the conviction grows that the events occurring against the background of foolish behavior make for a sinister truth and that the drama itself, for all its caricature, is living truth: the people are puppets and *skomorokhi* in the hands of a powerful sorcerer who participate in various *deistva* at his command; but as soon as any one of the dolls, in succumbing to the allure emanating from an evil power, wishes to break free and achieve something not foreordained for it, not decreed—death awaits that one who disobeys.

King Dodon is a *skomorokh* by calling and by station. Nothing can tempt him and deflect him from his path. He is the most experienced puppet. The demon of lust, however, can disturb even him and awaken in him feelings, which while animalistic and lustful, are yet genuine: not those of a *skomorokh*. The Queen of Shemakha attempts in every way to convince him that he is a *skomorokh* and nothing else. The king thinks more of himself. And if in fact there was no doubt in the first act, even for a moment, that Dodon was a *skomorokh*, a mask, and a doll, so in the second act one's perception becomes divided: in the king's singing one might just hear not a clown's speech, but the living speech of a genuinely infatuated, lascivious old man.[9] In the third act, with the sincere lamenting of the folk it finally becomes clear that it was not a *skomorokh* that died. The Astrologer comes out to the public to affirm that all that has transpired was a fairy tale, an exaggeration, a mirage.[10] But who would believe an official announcement, especially from such a biased witness? The question remains a question, since it is incomprehensible why such an insignificant man as Dodon and why such an obedient human herd as his people and troops can be disturbed and tempted by such clever ruses as a clear-sighted sentry-cock and a cunning woman-sorceress, one in whom all that is predatory in femininity dominates over the womanly, so that she seems a devil of voluptuousness, taking on a seductive exterior, a devil concerning which the legends about the old hermits so vividly relate. It was worthy and interesting to tempt *them*—but *here*: marvelous music woven of fragile sounds, music of china and crystal, music of the aromas and spirits of wondrous hothouse blooms, whose hues come about as a result of the multifarious hybrids, conceived in the whimsical imagination of this gardener-composer. This is the music that comes forth to face the caricatured king who is expressing his feelings in the notorious "Siskin Song."[11]

Most likely the Queen of Shemakha, no less than the cockerel, is a toy, a creation of the Astrologer. She is a sort of Coppelia (Hoffmann's goddaughter), quite perfectly bred, i.e., a woman thoroughly alive, with only a small imperfection: she lacks a heart.[12] Yet she possesses the most finely nuanced erotic sensations and a greedy lust, for whose satisfaction no limits exist, no sort of cruelty or mockery—up to the shedding of blood. From the first seemingly radiant aria of the queen ("to the Sun") to her cynical laughter at the moment of denouement, the music traverses an indescribable psychological decline.[13] If one traces the feminine characters produced by the imagination of Rimsky-Korsakov from Olga and Snow-Maiden to Fevronia and the Queen of Shemakha, it appears that the last—as a symbol of a monstrous exacerbation of female voluptuousness without any maternal feeling—will not be compensated for by Marfa's meekness, Fevronia's feats of patience and loving, Olga's sacrificial destiny, Hanna's young vernal love, Snow-Maiden's fragile sincerity, or Volkhova's devotion. Her only relative is Kashcheyevna, but even she redeems herself with the shedding of a tear. Elements of the Queen of Shemakha are found in the music of nearly all of her predecessors, for they are present in the psyche of every woman, yet how and why they would be imparted with such a sharp bias, why they are gathered together in the final work of the composer as in a conjurer's trick remains a riddle to me. If Rimsky-Korsakov were not a composer of rational intellect, if it were not all the same to him *whose* image was being realized and *how*, nevertheless the image of the Queen of Shemakha should have emerged out of observations, personal experiences, and sentiments, all of which would be assembled in the creative imagination and refined to the utmost.

I consider the creation of the Shemakha sorceress a bold effrontery after the creation of Fevronia, since right here lies the border between the higher wisdom that emanates from a loving contemplation of the world and the cold-blooded indifference of a craftsman, who with equal lack of concern sculpts the statue of a saint and the statue of a devil, imparting spirit into the finish and solidity of the work but not into its meaning. In the remarkable music that brings to life the representation of Fevronia and in the no less expressive music that characterizes the Queen of Shemakha, the composer, having relinquished any sort of hypocrisy, uncovers the veils of a woman's soul and firmly asserts as fact that in the vital fluids of a woman there are seeds that lead to heaven and to hell and that through music the two *purest* forms of these branches can be created, on which one can construct a design of enormous artistic significance. If in *Kitezh* the energy radiating from Fevronia leads to the transformation of Prince Yuri's realm and permeates the entire conception, so in *The Golden Cockerel*, the Queen of Shemakha's seductions that permeate everything lead to the demise of Dodon and his kingdom. The holy kingdom of Kitezh *should* raise a girl akin to Fevronia, while the clownish kingdom of Dodon could create either Amelfa the housekeeper in reality, or the Queen of Shemakha in a *dream*. Dream becomes reality in both *Kitezh* and *Cockerel*, but in the former fantasy and reality merge into one in the character of Fevronia, while in the latter they instead diverge: the dream becomes destructive just when it is transformed into reality. It could not be otherwise: any kingdom of *skomorokhi* akin to Dodon's kingdom, to the extent that it is lifeless and contrary to life despite a visible stability, strength of design, and an unchangeable continuity (stasis) of its existence, cannot be anything more than a superstructure onto life, a caricature of life.

People seem to think that everything created by them is unshakeable and unchangeable. But it requires only for an elemental force to direct its will to enter into a struggle with this "eternal" structure and it will collapse as once the Tower of Babel collapsed. Upon colliding with reality, a caricature loses its meaning, for it is groundless, lifeless: a mere conceit. Every person and every people are saved or perish, depending on what aspirations, what attractive ideal forms, the imagination produces. Dodon was satisfied in life with the ideals of Amelfa the housekeeper, in the imagination, with the delights of the Queen of Shemakha. He was given his due and the kingdom of *skomorokhi* collapsed upon contact with a soulless power, organized mechanistically and diabolically. The devil always demands a return or payoff of the capital that he lent. Dodon is no Faust: how might he get the better of a ghost, created by his own imagination and suddenly made real? In the end, the single living character in the entire tragic tale remains the Astrologer, the stargazer and magician, who took readings from the motion of the heavenly bodies about all that transpires and revealed it to the people in music. It must be for the sake of edification, since all that he has brought forth is far too terrifying for idle curiosity.

NOTES

1. While Rimsky-Korsakov's *Golden Cockerel* was certainly no *Salome*, it nevertheless stands apart from all his previous operas on account of the more frankly erotic scenes, the more complex chromatic passages, and the disturbing mixture of violence and satire, which may or may not register due to the consistently brilliant and distracting scoring.

2. Asafyev's comparison of the heroines from five Rimsky operas is based on the level of desire and ability in each to respond with love to the men who are attracted

to them. In the case of the supernatural figures Snow-Maiden and Kashcheyevna, loving in a human way requires an act of personal transformation. By contrast, the Queen of Shemakha withholds love by choice.

3. Like the Magician in *Petrushka*, the Astrologer is able to wield magic to bring a toy to life. Later Asafyev will claim that the Queen is no less a doll than the Cockerel.

4. The amazed crowd's initial reaction to the Golden Cockerel's first cry of "Kiriki, kirikuku!" occurs in Act 1, mm. 397–402.

5. The Queen's entrance [m. 208ff.] is heralded by a sirenic clarinet, followed by a deceptively straightforward A-major tune that is soon interrupted by destabilizing chromatic roulades.

6. The essential contrast between the Queen's more animated, more chromaticized, and more florid idiom and the King's slower, squarer diatonicism is evident throughout Act 2. In addition, Asafyev rightly draws attention to the many-hued splendor of Rimskian instrumentation, unleashed here only in service to the Queen's seduction.

7. Asafyev summarizes here the main events of Act 3, which commences with a triumphant procession into the capital and ends with the deaths of the Astrologer and King and the disappearance of the Cock and Queen.

8. Among the returning themes in Act 3's final chorus is the king's lament over his sons (Act 2, mm. 101ff.) and the noonday lullaby from Act 1 (mm. 672ff.).

9. Since Asafyev has not named the musical devices and gestures used in the first act to turn Dodon into a caricature, one can only speculate as to what in the music is responsible for the pockets of "living speech" in the second act. Certainly the formulaic phrases diminish; moreover the more halting phrases, the pauses, and the chromatic inflections would seem to indicate a new element of self-reflection as Dodon resolves to take a drastic step. The contrast registers most when the Queen turns sadistic, provoking the old King to dance against his will in full public view, thus turning him back into a caricature, a change made self-evident by the rigid, awkward, and chromatic buffo leaps.

10. The return of the Astrologer in the opera's epilogue can be construed as a resurrection, since he had been cut down with an angry blow from King Dodon's scepter at the end of Act III. Asafyev has extracted a quote from the Astrologer's final words: "Thus did the tale reach an end. / But a bloody outcome / No matter how deep / Need not worry you at all. / Here the Queen and I alone / Were the only living beings, / The rest merely deception, dream, / Pale mirage and void."

11. "Chizhik" [Siskin] is a taunting children's song.

12. The fantastic mechanical doll in E. T. A. Hoffmann's "Der Sandmann" (1815) was the inspiration for both Delibes's ballet *Coppélia* (1870) and the character Olympia in Offenbach's opera *Les contes de Hoffmann* (1881).

13. In contrast to the wide musical variety and appealing tunes of the second act, the Queen's part in the third act collapses into little more than her shrill laughter and signature pair of leitmotives (e.g., mm. 207–8, 445–47).

• *13* •

Intermezzo II

*W*hen Glinka died, those who wished to be his successors were obliged either to follow the path of his first opera, a psychological and historical drama of the everyday world, or else to set off toward that genial enigma *Ruslan*. But Russian culture is a culture of untrodden paths and good intentions. Prone to colonization in its essence, it opens up many alluring vistas and directions. Each new participant desires to begin afresh, as soon as he senses his *own* strength. Following in someone else's footsteps is also held in high esteem with us, but like any apery, it cannot create a genuine and vital culture.

Traditions are therefore inconstant. He who can sets forth a path for himself, struggles for a long time, but by the time he clears away the land, looks and finds that death has already come! Time is up! . . .

In the epoch of Glinka, such a situation was necessarily typical for any composing musician. Now, after the work of Rimsky-Korsakov and Sergei Ivanovich Taneyev, there are already methods, principles, and slogans to guide the novices. Then, everything was by happenstance. Dargomyzhsky imagined himself to be a rival to Glinka and for that reason, due to myopia, did not discern the latter's greatness. Thoughtlessly, he believed that he was in full command of his craft. And what do we see? Wherever he is an improviser of new achievements, there the music is fresh and interesting; wherever he is a follower, continuing on along a barely discernible road, wherever it is necessary to develop the craft, there he is helpless and, in comparison to Glinka, amounts to nothing. A Russian opera of everyday life can already be observed during the reign of Catherine II.[1] But if one compares *A Life for the Tsar* and *Rusalka* in this respect, it is evident where the preponderance of craftsmanship and solid foundations will turn up. Indeed *Rusalka* extends the efforts of Fomin, Cavos, and Verstovsky, but not of Glinka, either with respect to the historical and everyday world element, or in relation to dramatism and the fantastic element. Based on the nature of his language, [Dargomyzhsky's] Miller [Melnik] is a far cry from [Glinka's] Susanin, with the exception of a few instances of recitative.[2] The ensembles are "raw" in technique and in the expression of emotional states. The architectonics is naive. Wherever it is possible to surrender himself to the flow of unconstrained improvisation, there Dargomyzhsky boldly drives straightforwardly ahead, albeit helplessly and in his own peculiar way. Glinka's legacy is a dangerous legacy, with respect to both craft and spirit. The radiance of his music is blinding. Here is a clear example: the dances of Naina's magic charms in *Ruslan*. It would seem only an endearing trifle, when in fact it is the keenest and most graphic reinterpretation of the Franco-Italianate ballet style contemporaneous with Glinka, accomplished with remarkable craftsmanship, sense of color and unassailable taste, in spite of the superficial, yet piquant material and the mischievous ease of the writing! One need only compare these feathery light dances with the dances in Dargomyzhsky's *The Triumph of Bacchus*, which arose under their influence, to be convinced just how senseless it was to succeed Glinka, even in a genre of this sort.[3] Who even now has the power to grasp the conception of *Ruslan*?

Dargomyzhsky died as well. Rimsky-Korsakov was only just preparing for *The Maid of Pskov*. Tchaikovsky, evidently, broke down on *The Voyevoda*, while Balakirev had not entered the realm of opera. Between Glinka and his "grandchildren" (Tchaikovsky, Rimsky-Korsakov, Musorgsky, Borodin) stood three: Dargomyzhsky, Cui, and Serov.[4] The first was esteemed not as a follower, but as a pioneer; the second, an interloper and foreigner, created a world of detached lyrical moods. There remained Serov, to whose lot befell the crucial task of filling in the gap between the operatic creations of Glinka and his future disciples, of extending the emerging tradition of real-world opera, and of connecting the operatic-dramatic musical art of Russia with that of Western Europe, as Glinka had done in his time, associating our world of song with the West, through his first opera. Now it was necessary to connect *Ruslan* to the West as well, having built the bridge.

Serov surpassed everyone in education, in taste, in knowledge of the literature, and in breadth of outlook. By this time Wagner was already active in the West, and Serov both sensed and even comprehended the great significance of Wagner's ideas. He understood, as well, the importance of being aware of all the previous evolution of musical culture, for he sensed the necessity of disseminating it in Russia and, no doubt, felt that without this, any proponent was doomed to solitude, to becoming a "voice crying in the wilderness" of ignorance. Given his musical-creative gift, it would appear that Serov could emerge as an eclectic composer, bringing together a series of trends. Above all, this required craftsmanship. But Serov was, first of all, an autodidact; and like anyone self-taught, who attained general truths through individual effort, he conceived himself to be the sole proclaimer of indisputable values and, of course, as a master commanding the means of realizing his thoughts. Secondly, he seized upon the idea rather late, starting composition in earnest only in the fifty-second year of life. Yet he did travel along the true path. His *Judith* is a formidable project, a seriously considered effort, a broadly and deeply developed conception, that suddenly introduced Russian dramatic music into the European circle of interests. The oratorical quality of *Judith* brings it ideologically close to the finale of *Life for the Tsar* and to the first act and beginning of the finale to *Ruslan*.[5] Thanks to the dramatism and spiritual intensity, thanks to the idea of a deed, it is conceptually related to *Susanin*. Had *Judith* been created by a first-class master, instead of by a merely intelligent and talented musician, it would have become not merely a point of transition but a point of origin. *Judith* would have deserved to become a bridge between the nation-specific coloration of Glinka's first opera and the West. But a dilettantish surface ruined it! And if in the work of Serov it is the most powerful, fresh, formidable, and rigorous achievement, in the evolution of Russian opera it is merely a transitional phase, never to be a solid foundation.

Judging by the natural splendor of its steady pace, *Judith* is tied to the "Handelianism" of Anton Rubinstein, chiefly to his *Judas Maccabeus*, and furthermore to his religious operas and oratorios. Its impetus has waned for now, unless one takes into account a parallel tendency, which came about on the basis of the deep and entirely Russian religious element of Rimsky-Korsakov's *Legend of the City of Kitezh*.

Several routes led from the crossroads occupied by Serov. *Judith* led toward Europe as well as the romantic-fantastic opera (plans for a *May Night* and then a *Christmas Eve* surface periodically in his biography[6]). The historical, real-world path, together with a multitude of subsidiary paths, led to Russia.

Verstovsky (and before him, the collective effort of *The Early Reign of Oleg*), in *Askold's Grave*, revealed the path of historical romanticism.[7] In *Rogneda*, Serov became an adherent of it but would have been horrified to learn of it, since he conceived *Rogneda* almost under the inspiration of Wagner's musical-romantic legends.[8] The empty bombast of Serov's second opera (excluding a few godsends, such as the chorus of idolatrous sacrifice) places it much lower than *Judith*, nor is there reason to argue about any approximation of Glinka. There is none! Such remarkable historical nonsense it was, explainable only because of the pitiable state of culture: a genius creates a historical-psychological opera of everyday life, standing on the same plane as contemporaneous Western European craft; parallel with this, a third-rate dilettante also composes a historical romantic opera of everyday life (Verstovsky). Disciples do not tread the path of genius, but rather the path of the dilettante (*Rusalka, Rogneda*), i.e., not out of Glinka but only toward Glinka. It took the sober and practical *word* of Rimsky-Korsakov to establish (either historical-romantic or historical/real-life) the closest approximation to *A Life for the Tsar* within this sphere. Yet, however easily *The Tsar's Bride* came about for Rimsky-Korsakov later on, how much less so did *The Maid of Pskov* during an earlier creative phase: for him, too, it was necessary to pave a road for himself, in order to proceed without impedance later on. The first version of *Maid of Pskov* emerged in an epoch without roads, after Glinka, but as if he never existed! *Rogneda* is a vivid expression of having no way out: a tarantass, bogged down in the mire of nationalism, provincial Russian Wagnerism, and individual impotence. Neither taste nor logic!

An even worse situation arose with Serov's third opera, wherein he meant to embark on a new and fresh path of creating a real-life folk drama, i.e., at last, to proceed despite all along the road on which the real-life "operas" (indeed, not dramas, but vaudevilles) of Fomin, Matinsky, Titov, and others blundered.[9] Of course, a difference in epochs but not in substance was evident. In *The Power of the Fiend*, Serov gives recitatives where there was "conversation" in the earlier realists; nevertheless, its entire structure reflects a similarity with the opera-vaudeville: the forms of the arias in *Power of the Fiend* are either long-breathed folk song (harmonized according to the taste of Prach[10]) or couplets with refrains either played or sung as well as instrumental refrains, and in the intervals between, very clumsy recitatives and choruses, stylized "à la folk speech."

With respect to idea content, *The Power of the Fiend* is a great treasure, as is *Judith*. To find the path to a real-life opera through the greatest possible simplification of its language, by means of a stylization of folk speech and the introduction of the simplest of song forms in moments of lyrical effusion—is a most interesting task. Yet precisely in this sphere, in order not to tarry over a pointless reflection of reality, one must be a great artist and possess a sense of proportion and tact, and, most importantly, to discover well-defined principles and methods of stylization. There was nothing like this in Serov. He fumbled onward, inspired with "populism," and wound up in a pigsty. I am speaking so harshly because I am vexed by those moments of remarkable dramatic elevation in *Power of the Fiend*, convincing me that Serov is, without a doubt, a dramaturge and that he followed true paths, albeit blindly and deafly. The first such moment in *Power of the Fiend* is the scene in the coach house: the glorification of Shrovetide (Eremka and the chorus); next, the dialogue between Eremka and Peter; finally, thanks to an incredibly vivid, unprecedentedly fresh, truthful, and direct transformation of the everyday environment, a genuine impressionistic scene of strolling among the booths and leave-taking of Shrovetide: a scene revealing entirely new perspectives in the sense of an artistically authentic, rich "capturing" of the everyday world.

It is a crude, yet engrossingly lifelike portrait in sounds. Here the people breathe, bustle about, barter, scurry, warm themselves, peek, brawl, make mischief, delight themselves, imbibe, bawl out—yet within all the visible confusion there is something that unifies, guides, and directs. It is the great force of the composer's creative imagination, with his sight regained, looking out with a rapturous, amazed, enthusiastic gaze on the rich tapestry within the crush of humanity, hurrying to put down to the fullest each characteristic moment, striking personage, deftly animated gesture, and successful escapade; hurrying almost without selecting, trusting his avid gaze to choose what is most essential and vividly true to life. And now here before us is a magnificent portrayal, which seems for an instant to fix down a Russian Shrovetide fete: fumy, besotted, smoky, but also carefree and gay.[11] The selection taken from reality was accomplished by a genuinely gifted artist, despite the absence of premeditated structure. Serov both knew and loved painting and, himself, painted. The gift of "seeing" lay within him and therefore, when it was musically necessary for him to realize a sumptuous and vibrant true-to-life tableau, then like an Impressionist he surrendered to his imagination, which selected the most powerful and characteristic elements out of all that can be seen, united them into a single vivid reality, and miraculously made visible reality become *audible*. With this scene alone, Serov produced an entirely unique, personal, and independent artistic *phenomenon*, which was unnoticed by anyone before him. Therefore it is not necessary to disdain Serov because he was unable to do it all, or because he did things poorly. We cherish the little that is powerful and vivid, which he gave forth merely out of the strength of his rich talent and the inner culture of his soul. All around in Russia there was no one to come to his aid—he blundered about where there was no thoroughfare.

NOTES

1. During the thirty-four-year reign of Catherine II (1762–1796), significant Imperial support was provided only for foreign-language operas, which were composed by foreign-trained and almost always foreign-born composers. Nevertheless, Yevstigne Fomin (Russian, 1762–1800) and Catterino Cavos (Venetian, 1775–1840) played a role in bringing Russian-language works of Singspiel type to the stage. Alexei Verstovsky (1799–1862), a contemporary of Glinka, wrote both vaudevilles and operas, of which *Askold's Grave* (1835) became Russia's most performed work in the 19th century.

2. The Miller [Melnik] is the protagonist in Dargomyzhsky's *Rusalka*, Ivan Susanin the self-sacrificing hero of Glinka's *A Life for the Tsar*, a protagonist whom Asafyev considered to be more fully characterized in both the arias and recitatives.

3. The dances of Naina's maidens occur in *Ruslan*'s Act 3. The feathery light scoring features numerous wind solos and rapid violin passagework. By comparison, Asafyev finds the dances in Dargomyzhsky's opera-ballet (composed 1843–1848, after Pushkin's "The Triumph of Bacchus") to be heavy-footed.

4. Based on the names and works listed (death of Dargomyzhsky—1869; *Maid of Pskov*—1872; *The Voyevoda*—1868), Asafyev considers the operatic career of Alexander Serov to be the primary topic for the transitional epoch of the 1850s and 1860s, i.e., the first epoch after Glinka.

5. At the conclusion of Serov's first completed opera (*Judith*, 1861–1863), assembled soloists and chorus celebrate the triumph of Judith the Judean over the Assyrians, whereas in *A Life for the Tsar*, large forces praise the Russian tsar and nation.

6. Serov destroyed the music he wrote for an opera based on *May Night*, which he began in 1850. Sketches for *Christmas Eve* date from 1866.

7. *Nachalnoe upravlenie Olega* (The Early Reign of Oleg, 1790), the musical setting of a historical play by Catherine II, was a collaborative work of Pashkevich, Cannobio, and Sarti. Verstovsky's *Askold's Grave*, set in tenth-century Kiev, features supernatural elements as well as the interplay of paganism and Christianity.

8. Serov's *Rogneda* (1865), set at the time of Prince Vladimir I's conversion to Christianity (AD 988), mixes numerous native pagan rituals and incantations with Christian hymns sung by pilgrims that Asafyev evidently heard as Wagnerian transplants.

9. This second trio of forerunners consists of the aforementioned Fomin, Mikhail Matinsky (1750–182?), and Alexei Titov (1769–1827). Fomin's noteworthy effort in the category of folk drama was *Yamshchiki na podstave* (Postal Coachmen at the Relay Station, 1787), which sported choral folk-song arrangements. From Matinsky there was *The Petersburg Bazaar* (1779); from Titov, a trilogy of three comic countryside Singspiels incorporating peasant rituals.

10. The publication of the Lvov/Prach Collection (1790; rep. 1806) was a landmark event in the raising of Russia's musical consciousness. Later Prach's three-chord, "common-practice" harmonization reflecting the tastes of the urban and landed gentry would become controversial. For a full facsimile and commentary, see Margarita Mazo, *A Collection of Russian Folk Songs by Nikolai Lvov and Ivan Prach* (Ann Arbor: UMI Research Press, 1987).

11. Serov's depiction of the pre-Lenten "Butter Week" revelries is an obvious precedent for *Petrushka*'s setting. Asafyev provides a more vivid impression when he later praises Stravinsky's success at capturing the experience of "real life" in a popular festival.

• *14* •

The Operas of Tchaikovsky

In all the research on the psychology of musical style, form, and the evolution of musical language, I know of no problem more difficult than those associated with Tchaikovsky and opera. Wherever the composer himself makes it possible, by means of a rationally composed design, to grasp the internal architecture, the essence of the entire conception, there it is comparatively simple to find the end of the thread and untie the knot. But where the composer did not even consider how that which is visible on the surface and measurable would reflect the *music*, but instead directed its impulse into a channel delineated, as is customary, in accordance with either predetermined or spur of the moment, *ad hoc*, serendipitous schemas; where these schemas at times do not at all correspond to the true form but offer only a crude outline of it—therein lies the difficulty and the risk of making shortsighted conclusions. It is incumbent on one to seek the form not in the visible design that reflects the inner essence, but rather by perceiving the inner structure and sensing the unquestionable organicism of waves of sound seemingly flowing of their own accord, deduce therefrom the absolute justification of the actual form that is cast, one whose contours cannot be determined by the naked eye! But how difficult it is to convey what the issue is. Musicians are no longer accustomed to contemplating their art by proceeding from that which is given, from out of the living organisms. When there is talk of sonatas or symphonies, an abstract schema comes to mind, which is then applied to the music being heard in the way that one triangle is applied to another in proving a theorem; yet meanwhile the music flows along, is pulled onward. If the schema coincided with the course of the music, then all will be content (*they understood the music!*); but if it did not coincide, then disputes arise (not about the music, of course, but about the form that was violated) as well as bewilderment, and

151

even harsh verdicts for a composer without a name or a condescending pardon for the taking of a permissible liberty, if the composer is a recognized master. What is most important—i.e., finding the actual chance factor or the lack of correlation that caused the schema not to coincide with the living reality, or determining if there was a proper impulse that could produce such a discrepancy—is of no concern to anyone.

Opera suffers in particular from this familiar "research methodology," or more accurately, these offhand verdicts. The forms of so-called absolute music are *measured* nevertheless within the music itself, by means of the schemas that have been developed, whereas opera is not considered in this way at all. Having declared it a false art form, despite the stubborn fact of its existence and the living sources that nourish it, the Catos of music sternly decree that it exists in such and such a way and, in accordance with their decree, examine the right of any and all operas to exist. In view of the apparent impossibility of developing well-defined schemas for operatic composition, as is done with symphonies, sonatas, and every manner of dance forms and so-called song forms, one ought to conclude that this particular sphere of music entails an extremely individualized artistic medium, which allows generalization only *post factum*, a medium wherein decrees are for the most part absolutely ineffective. All the determinations over what can be considered opera or what opera has the right to exist are utterly insignificant when held up to Mozart's *Don Giovanni*, Wagner's *Tristan und Isolde*, Beethoven's *Fidelio*, Gluck's *Orfeo*, Glinka's *Ruslan and Lyudmila*, Tchaikovsky's *Queen of Spades*, and Rimsky-Korsakov's *Golden Cockerel*. There was a time when the Gothic period was of no concern to anyone![1] How could one not have learned from this example how fallacious and, I would say, how vulgar it is to proceed in art not from the data but from a graven image?

It is natural that a forceful creator like Wagner, after he has created the kind of opera he desired in his own imagination and hewed it out, would have the right to reject all other types as false in the name of his creation. This was for him a firm foundation and a vital necessity, for had he doubted even for a moment that his theses were in essence the only correct ones, then he would not have been the person he was. But indeed, what matters in art is something deeper than one or another set of theses from individual artists; *all* that is great, created by the *greats*, is important—and not only that which was created by Wagner. From this standpoint, it makes no difference at all whether there is a kernel of Wagnerism in Mozart as an opera composer. And never should *Die Zauberflöte* be swept aside because it was not created according to the creed of the Bayreuth reformer.

And it also makes no difference which is more important in operatic music: the word or the sound; the subjection of music to a poetic meter and the true and "proper" declamation (which, of course, means forgetting about the contingencies of the word's own truth content) or, conversely, the subjection of the verse to the lyrical wave of the music and its rhythm of ebb and flow. Indeed there is no cause for debate, in the presence of Monteverdi's *Orfeo*, Pergolesi's *La serva padrona*, Mozart's *Don Giovanni* and *Die Zauberflöte*, Glinka's *Ruslan*, and Musorgsky's *Boris*. Is it not better to delve into why *Don Giovanni* was composed in certain forms and not others, into just what constitutes its internal logic and what connection, with respect to language and style, it might have with Mozart's works on the whole and even with the entire epoch—the last being a generalization which, should it arise, would be entirely logical? Then, perhaps, it might be possible to establish one or more principles for distinguishing between various types of operatic forms, without arbitrarily doing violence to them.

If the *word* is the main thing in opera, then not one foreign vocal-dramatic work should be performed in Russian, since every translation is an approximation. Why not surround ourselves with a Great Wall and no longer take delight when Musorgsky is performed abroad: after all, can one imagine the inn scene done in French or in English?[2]

The fact is that every type of artwork will be more individualized and more flexible as to form, whenever more complex conditions produced it and less simple and fragmented elements entered into it. And certainly, the more individual one or another type, the more vital it will be, since because of this it is distinctive and *sui generis*, making it more prone to adaptation in response to changing conditions. It is evident that the requirements—or, as it is now customary to say, the artistic will (*Kunstwille* or *Formenwille*[3])—that call to life multifarious types of musical-vocal forms, united under the common title opera, were quite profound, emanating from the depths of the spirit, whenever these forms proved to be both vital and productive and, most importantly, so persistently adaptable to life under quite diverse conditions. This is not the place to set forth where and how I envision these deep sources. For me, it is important to point to the very fact of the adaptability and derive therefrom what I consider to be the one correct research methodology for operatic forms: out of the conditions of surrounding nature and the environment and out of the internal impulses of the artist; not from elevated but contrived and restrictive standards, which establish the right of existence for only one particle of the whole. I repeat, opera is the most individual kind of musical art, both with respect to the environment that produced it and with respect to the inner world of the artist.

Individual because a great variety of factors play a part in the shaping of every opera: both psychological and stylistic, especially in view of its connection with a poetic, pictorial, and tragic or comedic element,[4] since, in the process of operatic creation, extremely complicated associations in the train of thought take place, resembling chemical reactions of a most diverse concentration of elements. In order to emphasize yet more my desired conclusion, I will permit myself to make a rather obvious comparison: it is impossible to investigate a particular river, applying to it geographical concepts about rivers in general or taking the Volga, for example, as an ideal type, according to which all rivers should flow. We can dredge many canals to correspond to it, canals quite useful for stringing together systems of rivers, but it is clear to every one of us that the canal and the river, freely flowing along its own course, alive and beautiful in its meandering, are "two things incompatible."[5] Rivers vary more among themselves than do flowers of a particular kind or trees, e.g., birch trees. So, too, do operas differ more greatly than fugues, sonatas, or symphonies. On the other hand, there are, of course, operas like rivers and operas like canals. . . .

Having said this, I may return to my point of departure, to that complication that arises when a work is at issue whose logic—I can say now—is more akin to the logic in the course of a freely flowing river than the logic of a dredged-out canal. One is likely to encounter just such a difficulty when surveying Tchaikovsky's operas in general or analyzing the common traits of his operatic style. Each of them, of his operas, is somewhat self-contained, complete in itself, and self-motivated. The difficulty is further increased when the work in question is associated with numerous chance, naive, and thoroughly pointless but intractable impressions and when everything already appears to have been said and done. Naturally, this perfectly ordinary assessment is simply due to the fact that we are inundated with the music of Tchaikovsky's operas. Life often casts out paths that have not yet been explored to the end, not because they are poor ones but because nothing there needs to be surmounted, everything has laid itself out and is running its course. Thus, the violin came to play an ever-greater role in the orchestra in relation to the flourishing of instrumental music; but the finest violins were being crafted when song was everywhere and instrumentalism had only just emerged as an independent force. Therefore I am not at all disturbed by the fact that I will be speaking about artistic phenomena that have been known for some time, commenting on them as if nothing had been decided and nothing said, aside from the usual judgments: well, this is good, this is bad, or it is all bad, since *this* bears no resemblance to what is good. This, in a word, was Cui's renowned "method" with regard to Tchaikovsky.[6]

With very few exceptions, *nothing* has been said about the latter's operas, beyond reviews of the day; or if something of import has been said, then it is only in the sense of the "pigeonholing method," with praise only for that which corresponds to the pigeonhole. This much is obvious: every epoch takes from a great artist what it needs. The epoch of the 1880s and Russian society's middle class of the 1890s required only delicate, lyrical sighing and a tender sadness with a shade of indignation, or perhaps even outbursts of grief, yet not really in earnest, so that true sorrow would not tear asunder a placid life. The tragic in Tchaikovsky was overlooked. It was no wonder that the impotent and senile conservative epoch, having no desire to hear about what was or was not going wrong, craved quiet more than anything. And when people were inclined to begin "whining," then it was most often only for the sake of an "aestheticized" irritation or a feeling of intoxication ("wild gypsy decadence").

This worm of Russian provincialism ate away inside Tchaikovsky, like a grief over the dull, blind burning out of life. More than anyone, he punished himself for it, seeking through art his whole life long for a revelation of authentic tragedy without finding it. How harshly he himself castigated the [symphonic] poems *Francesca*, *The Tempest*, *Romeo and Juliet*, then *Manfred* and the Fifth Symphony; how acutely he felt everything that was not right in his works is shown in his letters (especially to Balakirev) and in the fate of the two *Voyevoda*'s, in *Undine*, *Fatum*, his loathing of *The Oprichnik*, etc.[7] Unaccustomed to tragic pathos, the epoch desired to see in the beloved composer only a "singer of elegiac moods."[8] For this, they pampered him and forgave him, like an adored child, for those whims and escapades that went deeper than their level of comprehension, as they listened to them with bewilderment.

In Tchaikovsky there glimmered an ailing, overwrought, exhausted soul. Often, perhaps consciously, he ran behind the epoch; tired and infirm, he satisfied its demands; more often, though, he himself marveled at the correspondence between his secret hidden dreams and the yearnings of the people around. So it was with *Evgeny Onegin*. At the end of his life, when he heroically gathered his strength in order to reveal at last in music something personally tragic that had tormented him his entire life, he produced *Queen of Spades* and the Sixth Symphony, which even now can become terrifying to anyone who is not accustomed to gazing at life from on high, as if it were a tilled field and nothing else. What was that element of personal and tragic terror in Tchaikovksy? An eternal unrest over the soul's not having anything to which it might attach itself. Life is not creation but self-depletion, ending with a black hole, before which stands the old hag Death.

Let us reflect on that word *self-depletion*. How tremendously frightening, if we take into account what an enormous quantity of spiritual strengths, energies, and talents have always been doomed in Russia in conjunction with abnormal sociohistorical and political conditions to deplete themselves for naught, to turn to ashes, to be frittered away in unending exertion (for the better people!) or to vegetate passively in the slime, alone, accompanied by a beating heart and a wailing over a lost life that has passed one by. What indeed, for the most part, are all of the Russian provinces with their gossip, card playing, inactivity, filth, with their monotonous interests and eternal fear that someone might stir up the swamp and life would become even worse: not better, but more troubled?! Gogol saw only a self-depletion in Russian reality, and the thought blinded him: he was unable to see a single living soul! Dostoyevsky presented us with the very same tableau, but in exquisitely voluptuous profiles of the tormenters and the tormented, among whom a few seriously thought that they were alive and accomplishing good works. In order to avoid choking in it, he enveloped this *land* with atmosphere, placing in it free birds in the form of "demons" that were free to swoop about, inventing songs that would sweetly becloud the conscience. *The Petty Demon* came next.[9] Later still came *The Twelve*, wherein a bourgeois, humdrum self-depletion was replaced by a depleting that is elemental, violent, and for moments even beautiful.[10]

Amidst a fundamental dearth of desire to live, which appeared in three-fourths of the state's population, a handful of madmen—Don Quixotes—believed in human progress, in a human soul both holy and immaculate, in the beauty of life, in creativity—indeed there is more than one type of madness! These people were also punished in various ways: some were even put in a madhouse. Or else, they merely went about their business. From time to time, the finest of the representatives would take a cruel fall from the heights of ideals, disenchanted and bitterly repentant, but after them new prophets would arrive to undertake the same thing all over again. At first there were no singers in their midst. There were lyricists of the word, whose love could inspire (the correspondence between Herzen and his bride is indeed already music![11]). But the time came and a bard was born. With what sort of song should he emerge in the world, being of the same flesh and blood as these dreamers? With songs of joyful enthusiasm, of confidence in victory? Yes, were he subject to a will that had never been despondent. But he heard something that went deeper: the rumble of rhythms convincing him that all around the Russian land, things were out of harmony; that all this depletion of the self was not happening by itself and without purpose, that neither creativity, nor constructive activity, nor faith in human decency could exist here; and the further it went, the more profound it became: no gods, no meaning to life, no joy of creation, since in any case everything rots away, etc., etc. It turned out the same historically. The 1860s had been deceptive; moreover it was no secret to the more perceptive, that the intelligentsia had been deluded, that it was necessary to live in some other manner. Apparently, this was to whine, à la Chekhov and Levitan[12]—or on a deeper level, to be resigned to fate, to "no escape from destiny," i.e., just to live any way you can for as long as you walk the Earth. . . .

Tchaikovsky was the composer of the Russian intelligentsia. For him there could not be old, sweet songs after the breaking up of the spirit of the Sixties. He stood between two extremes: dreams, reveries, the bright and pure world of humanity's youth (such is Lensky) or the deception, mirage, dull-witted onslaught of an evil power, sadness, grief, death (such is Hermann). Lensky and Hermann: here are the two poles. Neither one comprehends real life. And did the Russian intelligentsia really understand life?! They philosophized, made protests, played the simpleton, or just played themselves out: some tragically, others swinishly! . . .

This is the approximate schema of the mental states that enveloped the great Russian musician, who had no longer emerged from a genteel milieu and had lost, therefore, a direct connection with a firmly rooted existence. As it happens, just prior to this time, the old way of life was already undergoing change: the moment was approaching when a poetic restoration and stylization of it would occupy music. Tchaikovsky was already in part dealing with such a temptation, yet his unmediated emotionality would always triumph over the stylistic data. Such a line of evolution is not to be found in his operatic works. Of course, from a strictly musical standpoint, one cannot compare the mastery of *Queen of Spades* with that of *Oprichnik*, but the very essence of this mastery resulted nonetheless not from the resolution of the aforementioned artistic problems, but out of the necessity to surmount such and such complications of the "craft," since only by this means could depth of spirit and the inner world appear. It is extremely important to remember this, in order to keep to the true course for evaluating his operas.

I view the matter as follows. In the soul of Tchaikovsky, constantly worrisome and intense work was under way, which involved the consumption of a colossal supply of life energy. From day to day, it was expressed in an extremely distraught catapulting away from the awareness that it is necessary to live as everyone does and together with everyone toward the conviction that it is necessary to cast off everything and seek total freedom in the expenditure of time, in order to have the right to be oneself, at least when alone with oneself. But no one is able to *exist* alone. Hence the desire, if not found in life, then in contemplation or in creative work, to affix an image, toward which all declarations and all of the soul's confession might flow. Tchaikovsky sought [an ideal of] womanhood, sought her agonizingly and passionately. (He was not a Liszt, who knew women, knew all that they had to offer and in his dream-filled cantilenas stylized sensual delights, consciously evoking them, playing with them, and transforming them into the images both of the naive sinner Margarita and of St. Elizabeth.[13]) This is why the passionate outbursts and enthusiasms of Tchaikovsky are either naive and bright as dreams or sultry with

Italian ecstasy. Perhaps within this unsatisfied desire are found both the delights and the torments of his works: delights in attainment and torments from infinite languor. But since this is a languor out of ignorance and not the conscious languor of an aesthete of voluptuousness, chosen from desires relived, so Tchaikovsky's passion is always shrouded in a cloak of chastity, of radiant maidenhood: with a secret, not entirely disclosed and laid bare. Out of this he fashioned Tatyana's image. . . .

Amidst powerful spiritual tension and a steady stream of creative energy depleting itself (*depleting*, since Tchaikovsky never thought about how to lay down any kind of firm foundation—architectonic or ideological—underneath his compositions!); amidst a restless, uneasy search for peace and satisfaction within a new irritation, just as soon as a state resembling calm did appear—so did his life pass by. Thus, amidst this tireless fretting, either he would find a subject that would suit the next opera in turn, or he would take advice; and in those cases where the advice hit the mark, i.e., where the subject corresponded to a particular spiritual state, the labor would heat up and a magnificent opus would be created.

This raises the natural question: why was opera necessary to Tchaikovsky, from whence did that internal attraction come, so that at the times when he desired to write an opera he would convince himself of the need to rush into work on a subject that would seem foreign to him, something that he himself would later aver? Was it not the attraction to the song element that was innate to every Russian composer up until that epoch when the instrumental tendency of Western European music was taken into the flesh and blood? It is natural that Russian music would enter into the world, breathing in the atmosphere that surrounded it (i.e., that of songs and the making of songs). From this stems the persistent pull toward opera for composers from Glinka to Rimsky-Korsakov, in spite of the absence of opera theaters and a culture of opera. However, for Tchaikovsky, there were also personal reasons. Above all, they have to do with his bountiful melodic gift, which was essentially vocal and only gradually assimilated the instrumental style of thematicism. The main reason, however, was rooted in his psyche.

If we reflect on how instrumental works are performed, on the sense behind violin strokes or piano pedaling, we notice that on the one hand a performance never corresponds to what is written, and on the other, that the discrepancy is largely rhythmic in nature: a type of fluctuation occurs between the exact and even lines of strong and weak beats in regular succession and the always desirable holding back and running ahead. The latter elicits a *catching of the breath*, a sigh. Meanwhile, any sensation of emptiness or incompleteness will be unpleasant to us. We desire that the musical thread be unbroken, freely and easily spreading, enduring, extending. What else is it but a sense of life, of taking breath, of the beating of a pulse, which will always be important and dear to us to sense within the music; and without which music can at any moment become a mechanically accurate succession of pitches, yet lifeless and therefore senseless, since the meaning of music is in its vitality (I beg that this not be confused with the idea of "experience" in the everyday sense).

The spirit and respiration and breath of wind that were imported into instrumental music and are replenished in it by vocal music also inject into it the aroma and warmth of life. Only under such conditions do the violins "sing," the orchestra breathes, and the black dots of an evenly measured score turn into living sounds. In the presence of elements of a purely lyrical impulse, vocal music, without question, provides the composer with the nearest and most direct opportunity for genuinely expending himself and his life energy in sound, of reflecting in it his intense spiritual profile, especially when the culture of his native land surrounds him with song. Evidently, in Tchaikovsky's soul there arose conditions that allowed him to transform himself only within the sound of the human voice, in the warm wafting of the breath of life, in the inspired confluence of sound and word, in sound "made human."

The meaning of his life was terror in the face of the yawning black emptiness at the end of existence: inside himself he constantly felt the desire to *expend*, in exchange for which nothing visible lay ahead, nothing to hope for; he hastened to live in pursuit of a mirage of the idealized incarnation of the thing that lay hidden in his soul. It is difficult even to imagine the nightmare of such a soul state, when all around nothing stable or steadfast catches the eye. Not even his own works: he composed them, tore them from his soul like something expendable, superfluous, and unnecessary! And this incessant "onward" is no cry of triumph from the will upon encountering radiant bliss. Instead it is a cry of *departing* life, something you wish both to curtail and to curse. It is necessary to bring it to a halt, for otherwise death's abyss will rise up at your feet. Yet, once halted, all around there is nothing to grab on to! . . . In this state of mind, everything is dear that attracts unquestionable life, joy, and warmth. By contrast, fear is evoked by all that is mechanical. In the soundscape of the human voice, in song heated by warm breath, Tchaikovsky discovered a more direct, close, *familiar*, and vital element than in the orchestra. Within the colors of the latter, he devised a reliable means for conveying that which tormented him: from the freakish rustlings of invisible sounds to horrific nightmares of impending death. The human voice was indispensable to Tchaikovsky, not merely in order to sense within it the warmth of life, but to employ its warmth as a means of incantation, as a protection, as a cry, finally, amidst the oppressive gloom of fright and fear. The scenes in the countess's chamber and the barracks are therefore even more frightening than the Sixth Symphony, because in them the human voice itself is sounding the despair at one point, then flowing like a tender lifeline amidst a gradually beclouding awareness of a cold breath from the power that brings life to an end.

The song element in Tchaikovsky either signifies the desire for direct contact with the warmth of life and the pull toward a rhythm conditioned by human breath or else it is linked to the desire to intensify the nightmare by placing the voice in opposition to the onslaught of the evil "mechanical" necessity that freezes life.[14] Yet in both cases (i.e., in *Onegin* and in *The Queen of Spades*), we confront one and the same thing: the inclination to establish a more immediate connection with life by means of the song element. In song, the soul makes itself known more transparently than in the intonations of an instrument. Throughout opera, the connection with life registers all the more strongly, for in the tangible images that are surrounded by music, not only is the life of the soul heard, but the visible and real are *seen*, truly sensed. Opera seems to expand the horizon of contemplation and the limits of the world that are seen by the inner eye. The psychic necessity and need within Tchaikovsky's operatic works present themselves to me in just this light.

I approach *The Oprichnik* warily, as it was sharply detested by the composer and is unquestionably the most illogical of all his operas. It would seem that Tchaikovsky sensed in it some sort of intolerable falsity. Did it not lie with the historicism, something that held no interest for him? In *The Oprichnik* there is nothing that can be singled out as fundamental or essential, no fully formed character to follow; it is all sketches. And only occasionally do precisely sketched contours and sharp strokes attest to prior work of the imagination; yet they are still directed who knows where, except toward an ill-defined, raging dramatism. The oath scene is unquestionably the center of the opera. There an individual stands in opposition to the evil will of the human "community." The struggle is powerfully drawn, and the character of Andrei Morozov makes sense only in this moment; before and after, following the oath, he dissolves into vague outlines.[15]

As for his mother, again, in some spots, the flame of operatic dramaticism burns brightly in her characterization, but she is in essence a contrived figure, since her hatred is not directly felt. One must accept the inevitability of her thirst for revenge and then follow the music. Natasha's lyricism leaves no impression: herein one finds both the naive Russian song of the little nightingale and the passionately felt cantilena of the G-flat-major arioso, "Voices I thought I heard."[16] In order to reach the first mountain peak on the road to mastering the operatic style, Tchaikovsky progressed through the composition of *The Voyevoda*, *Undine* (lost), and *The Oprichnik*.[17] The subject for the last was probably chosen out of an instinctive attraction to the opposition of a condemned individual, writhing in the vice and the onslaught of predators (violence from outside). We already have here the psychological motive that would subsequently be developed by Tchaikovsky into every possible variant. Generally speaking, this can be expressed as follows: the composer's anxious inner world of the spirit, so acutely impressionable and highly attuned, seeks externally, in sound images, the opportunity to reveal that which disturbs it, to bring forth that *thing* that agitates it, beyond the boundaries of the personal self, beyond the limits of the agonizing soul. Of course, this kind of project could take hold of an entire life. And so it did. . . .

Nevertheless, in *The Oprichnik*, the appearance of the "thing that disturbs and agitates the soul" became quixotic, a hopeless and inauthentic undertaking, because for the psyche there was nothing to catch hold of in this atmosphere of hostility and hatred bereft of deep motivation, in a "Meyerbeerism" that was alien to Russian spiritual simplicity and sincerity. The first opera, i.e., the first genuine opera by Tchaikovsky with respect to the entirety of its content, was a work written hastily, "in one fell swoop," for a competition: the Ukrainian tale *Vakula the Smith*, which in a later version was retitled *The Slippers*.[18] In fact, this revision did not make any substantial change to the work's profile, touching instead only on superficial particulars of the style, and not always for the best. In any case, in a general survey, one can choose not to take into account the differences and speak as if there were a single work. The "thing that disturbs and agitates" is elaborated here not in tragic but in comic fashion.

The overture reveals the meaning behind the proceedings, as is customary with Tchaikovsky. The gentle caressing theme of the capricious Oksana introduces the world of *The Slippers* to the listener. In a few moments, it is fragmented and dispersed into a series of lines imitating one another; it is also characteristic of Tchaikovsky to present a theme as thesis and suddenly, without anything else to counter it, appear to scatter its elements like reflections in various mirrors.[19] As a change from Oksana's theme, a charming songful melody enters with decorum, graphically set forth by the horn over a pizzicato background; the second thesis is given here, that of everyday reality. Vakula has not yet appeared. He is the hero: he must conquer the inconstant image of a beloved girl. Therefore, after the calm presentation of the theses, that which "disturbs and agitates" the soul enters entirely logically, even though here *it* does not agitate, but only "interferes," introducing a "complication." It is the devil (the first allegro theme): an angular, nervously leaping phrase, which at a later instant in the opera acquires the piquant rhythm of the hopak for itself! The devil's theme already brings in confusion, attempting to stir up a blizzard, but then the character of Vakula enters like a radiant incantation. The entire development and elaboration of the overture are built on this contrast, although in the end the devil is "beaten," not by Vakula but by the everyday world, which takes the form of a song theme, flowing broad and deep, one which was already presented at the outset but now proceeds in a more luxuriant setting.[20] One observes that the entire opera closes with this song. Hence the conception corresponds with the denouement of Gogol's tale, not only externally in the sense of a propitious wedding, but more deeply.

Thus the entire conception becomes clear: the devil intends to interfere with and cast a shadow on the purely normal and peaceful relations of Dikanka, meddling in the romance of Vakula and Oksana (a romance, over-loaded by Tchaikovsky in the sense of a very abundant dose of psychologism). It is interesting to observe how "devilment" appears in Tchaikovsky, and how he would have an innocent and quite unspiteful Gogolian devil be transformed into a malicious, scheming demon; and how by this means, the entire modest little everyday story suddenly sheds the charm of comic simplicity, stirring up acute uneasiness. The blizzard in the first scene grows out of a remarkable and powerfully expressive incantation of the devil. Tchaikovsky exploits a serendipitous situation in order to turn a comfortable and unassuming com-munity upside down. One involuntarily desires to see the "enemy" against whom the devil sends forth such a raging snowstorm.[21] When the bumpkin Vakula enters into the action—a chap who exists in a lyrical soul state, who lays out his lover's lament in a deeply touching arioso—it becomes unclear why the devil is stirring up trouble, since the *blizzard* raised up by him has not yet been forgotten. Even though later on the devil cannot maintain a serious "role" (even though his influence in Solokha's hut mixes and mangles all the coquettish designs of Solokha herself and the plans of the Dikanka suitors), in the end the smith's confused mind, being thoroughly suffocated by the flirta-tious, incomprehensible, girlish mischief of Oksana, delivers him into the devil's hand. Roaming amidst the carolers, with a sack on his back in which the devil sits, Vakula yields more and more to the temptation to run away from people and even do away with himself. His singing at this point in the opera achieves a beautiful and ardent expressivity. The uncouth fellow vanishes and the profile of a man suffering in love is sculpted.[22] The devil does his business and the grief increases. Tchaikovsky's idea gains strength; he knew, probably from his own inner experience, that behind the spiritual woe called forth by life circumstances there is always a combination of something from within the soul and something "disturbing" coming from somewhere outside, irritating the pain ever more strongly. The devil leads Vakula into a deserted field of snow, up to a hole in the ice. By now not only the soul is moaning; someone else's moaning is sensed nearby: it is the crying of the *rusalki*, the spirits of those prevented from living out their lives. With respect to music, it is one of the most poignant moments of opera. Much weaker in expression are the sud-den beam of light and the sudden awakening of Vakula's consciousness, when he victoriously overcomes the power of evil in order to achieve his personal goal.[23] We have here an undeniable break in the flow. Tchaikovsky did not recognize the importance of the moment, and the psychological meaning of the opera lost something in its intensity.

There is still the element of everyday reality. St. Petersburg in the epoch of Catherine always held an attraction for the composer. In *The Slippers* we *hear* one of the most vivid descriptions in sound of Petersburg court festivities, in which the composer generously dispenses rhythms, each more attractive and expressive than the last. The delightful, velvety A-flat-major minuet sounds in delicate, iridescent crimson tones—yet softly, as if the sound were drooping from the overabundance of sumptuous attire. The reticent, sly, and languorous Russian dance of the maidens, with its sad theme akin to a pearl necklace, gives an expressive characterization to the song style of the epoch: a mixture of tender Ukrainian refrain and importunate Russian animation. Remarkably accurate in its composition, the hopak of the Zaporozhian Cossacks, with the cleverest of rhythmic breaks and a sharply drawn theme, is an outstanding dance *deistvo* with respect to invention and the succulence of the entwined rhythms.[24]

The next scene of the everyday world is in Dikanka.[25] Christmas morning. Here Tchaikovsky as scribe of the everyday world is revealed: he sketches simply, in lucid and distinct tones of touching sincerity, the weeping lamentation of Oksana and Solokha; describes how the crowd of people disperses after mass; how a maiden, who has done wrong and fears that her teasing has brought pain and spiritual collapse to her beloved, greets him already as husband; how the wedding ceremony proceeds; and how all of this is brought to completion with the powerful and free choral praise to the young couple: an affirmation of the everyday world.

Such is the course of the musically directed action in *The Slippers.* Tchaikovsky loved the opera. There is no more radiant opera in all his work, nor is there a more convincing triumph within the soul over "that which disturbs it." The devil has failed for the time being. . . .

Life thereafter would lead the composer toward *Evgeny Onegin.* The subject had been casually mentioned to him by the singer Pavlovskaya, but had struck him to the core.[26] Tchaikovsky quickly produced sketches, but then fell ill from a nervous breakdown and completed the opera abroad, during a period of recuperation, when he was on the verge of total freedom in his life. *Onegin* is the embodiment of the composer's dreams. At the same time, he was afraid that others would sully this work so dear, so personal, so deeply personal to him, with rough handling and coarse, insulting opinions; yet he still yearned to find an echo, a reverberation of his reveries. Russian society fell deeply in love with *Onegin.* I believe this fact was extremely valuable for Tchaikovsky's attitude to life. It reconciled him with life. When asked why Russians so love this gentle, utterly "themeless" and "undramatic" lyrical music, for me the answer is clear: for its simplicity, its sincerity, its warmth of feeling. That is all. Not because of any recollections of life on a country estate, not because of the evoking of personages familiar since childhood, not because of any kind of stylization, not due to characterization. That is, perhaps, for these as well; but they appear *post factum*, as secondhand, restated impressions. First and foremost, only on account of simplicity, sincerity, and warmth! It would seem that such words have been applied countless times to music, but when they are applied to *Onegin*, one feels complete satisfaction, as if this were the only true and accurate means of defining it. The same thing happens every summer when one stands in a field amidst the wildflowers, so familiar, so dear, and so humble. No better words will be found than the simplest and most affectionate. And the joy for the eye at catching sight of the blue of a cornflower again, after the passing of a year, is akin to the joy for the ear at hearing *Onegin* anew after a long period of time.

It is one of those rare works of art that enter so deeply into life, adhere so tenaciously to it, that they themselves become inescapable facts of life: a bit mundane, but always dear and tenderly warming to the soul. Moreover, Tchaikovsky's Tatyana is more a spiritual state or mood than a character. Liza is indeed a character, as are Maria in *Mazeppa* and Oksana. Tatyana's state of being is that of maidenhood, expressed with stunning veracity, naturalness, and at the same time with the greatest innocence (in all of operatic literature one can find nothing like the Letter Scene!). There is sublime humanity and sublime saintliness in the ability to produce life situations of such radiant intensity and within such an aura of simplicity and naturalness of sentiment, so that no vulgarity can ever dare impinge on them, regardless of how tempting the situation might seem. *This* is the matter in full, the entire essence of this wondrous music, and yet many will calmly pass *this* by in order to explain what sort of Tatyana is at hand: Pushkin's or not Pushkin's. Who cares? In the music a Russian girl is living through the sunny, blissful, and limpid time of maidenhood, when all at once she is fated to approach the most frightening threshold in life, when she is faced with taking a joyful but fearful step: that of becoming a woman. She yearns to know who the chosen one is. She awaits him. That is the simple, psychological fact, or so it would seem. But ponder over its simplicity and both the depth and the greatness will be unveiled. It is that kind of soul state before which, in a certain amount of time, everything remaining in life will be pale. We have overlaid life with formulas and pass by many such *simple* soul states, trampling on them without noticing. But then an artist arrives, a musician who captures one of these soul states, transforms it into a *poema*, and forces people to stop and think. The greatness of Russian art consists of the fact that it has loved the "simple states" and pointed them out to the West.[27] And for this they began to love us there.

The action of this opera-*poema* is all about these states. Life with its stern duty touched a dreamy girl and she became a woman and a wife. Now life wishes to tempt her with a "restoration" of the dream. How difficult to remain steadfast in spirit, when faced with the temptation to bring back spring. But the woman rejects the temptation. This, now, shows character. Nevertheless, here again is one of the *simple* states: the autumn of life. With an affectionate touch, Tchaikovsky has captured it.

No less simple—simple in a Russian sense, despite the affectation—is the figure of Lensky. Here the motif is familiar: the ill-fatedness of an idealistically disposed spirit. There is not even an attack from an evil power: it will perish out of a simple misfortune in life, from a misunderstanding—it is a kind of tragedy deeply characteristic of Russian life. Pushkin himself perished in the same way. Lensky, more so than Tatyana, is a *state of being*, not a character: the state of youthful infatuation, with sleepless nights filled with reverie, with idealized conceptions of the eternal feminine, with oaths of loyalty, with the intoxication of the first kiss, that mighty and gripping crescendo from one of life's *simple* occurrences. Like no one else, Tchaikovsky expressed in music this time of youth, so dear to all who have lived through it. Reliving it afresh, one may find happiness for life, so great is the stock of life energy, dissipated by it! There is nothing more to say about *Evgeny Onegin*.[28] For now, there can be no talk of any sort of survey or analysis. It is a set of lyric scenes, lyrical states of the soul at various levels of intensity, moments of life in its finest manifestations; here there is no need to seek out a well-proportioned structure or the development of a tragic concept, predestined from the outset.

In *The Maid of Orleans*, Tchaikovsky made an impressive attempt at a musical design based on *this* sort of concept. It was a step fully "opposed" to the *Onegin* mentality, but once again a quest to reveal the "thing that disrupts" externally, in historicism, in conflicts, not of an internal but an external "thematic" nature. In comparison to *The Oprichnik* there are, indeed, great differences: there is a heroine, a sense behind the rise and fall, a struggle and a relationship between complex elements: mystical rapture, the first awakening of passionate love, a great deed, and the obedience either to the will of God or to the will of a parent; there are striking conflicts of feelings and passions that are not closed up in the fist of Tsar Ivan; they emerge in front of our eyes and do not take place at some point in the past (as with the "history" of Morozova's enmity toward Zhemchuzhny[29]).

The essence of the entire artistic disposition of the opera lies in the destiny of Joan of Arc, the Maid of Orleans: from a maiden's exalted dream-visions to the stake. It is a task of colossal psychological difficulty. In Joan's grief-stricken monologue ("Farewell to you, oh fields, o native hills"), Tchaikovsky succeeded at capturing a particular shade of wise humility in conjunction with a perceptive stylization of the pastoral;[30] he was no less inclined, it seems, to raise up the heroine to an effective if stilted operatic heroism (the brilliant and captivatingly luxuriant ensemble-hymn of Act 1) from which in the end he cannot bring her back down.[31] Even the love duet, while beautifully flowing, does not reveal to us the soul of Joan: together with the first pastoral monologue-aria, her soul disappears from the music, eclipsed by the glare of the footlights.[32] The music affords no possibility for tracing such complex spiritual states of Joan whenever she is inspired: it presents us with a girl fated to a deed of self-sacrifice, which is all well and good except that, as a saint, she eventually becomes rather stiff. In love, she awakens and blossoms; yet she is radiant not from her own light, but from the knight's reflection. And thus this most important of moments, when a saint is transformed into a woman in love, passes without leaving a trace.[33] Therefore, the whole drama of the auto-da-fé loses its psychological acuity, leaving only the spectacle: a rather gloomy one, if theatrically captivating. Theatricality is to be understood here as a distinct and prominent pose, as spectacle, as a primitive but momentarily perceptible dramatism bedecked with lavish, imposing masks; in *Maid of Orleans*, it holds a central position. This is the background. If taken as a tableau, as a splendidly colorful episode, I believe this kind of subject appealed to the composer for two reasons: first, there was the wholly natural desire for an artist who had recovered and was at full strength to go forth along the broad European road, into the world, toward other people, to the West, away from Russian "provincialism" and scandals intermixed with blind indifference; secondly, he wished to forget about and depart somewhat from himself, from his own "aching" soul states. In a word, there was a bit of vanity involved, a desire to flaunt a grand operatic style, and also a bit of disgust toward those moods to which nature had fated him, and from which, right at this sunny period of life, on the verge of hope, he yearned to escape.

In the rhythm and melos of *Maid of Orleans* there are indications of devices that are entirely new to Tchaikovsky's style, as well as other interpretations of what had gone before. Above all, one notices the manner of juxtaposing large planes of color with strata that were meticulously elaborated and traced out.[34] One can say that the points of departure, the ascents (growths), and the attainments (resolutions, outbursts) proceed in this opera not from one personal state to another, but from ensemble to ensemble (the hymn in the first act; the scene on the square in the third act as the climax; the auto-da-fé scene). This is a complete contrast from *Onegin* and *The Slippers*, since in them the ensembles are *static* moments, points of rest, whereas in *Maid of Orleans* they are spurs or impulses toward a continuation of action. This particular trait is both fundamental and a striking change from the previous course. In accordance with this, both the melos and the rhythm take on a new aspect. They are almost entirely bereft of the breaks and capricious twists of the rhythms in *The Slippers*, flowing more smoothly, calmly, in broad, clearly formed lines, without a predominance of that favorite device of Tchaikovsky: the gradually falling line as a symbol of resigned submission. The style of *Maid of Orleans* bears the stamp of deliberation, intense scrutiny, and even a certain cold intellectualizing. It could hardly be otherwise, since there are few situations in it that relate to the composer's habitual spiritual state; it was incumbent on him to be ever watchful, so as not to lapse into the conventional deceit of decorative operaticism, but instead to harness the imagination in order to produce tableaus not envisioned by the inner eye, but surmised by an outwardly directed gaze. *The Maid of Orleans* is an organic and well-conceived opera, the value of which lies in the sumptuous and effectively picturesque element of the heroic style.

Mazeppa was the next attempt. Again there are the tableaus and the decorative quality of a historical background, but with considerably more gloominess, groans, torments, mockery, and torture. The course of action is set by a woman, just as in *Onegin*, *The Slippers*, and *Maid of Orleans*; everything rests upon a feminine image, all revolves around her. Subsequently, in *The Enchantress*, the composer would create a more finished type of such a conception, one motivated from within. In *The Maid of Orleans* the action is directed to the outside, like a superficially dramatic design. In *Mazeppa*, just as in *The Oprichnik*, there was no chance of mapping out the tragic structure and distinguishing the character who is directing the action. Maria, Mazeppa, the Cossack, Kochubei, the mother—all are characters that will rise to the surface, then disappear. Only one thing is clear: with more effort than ever before, the composer has set in motion and deployed externally, in the form of scenes, that vague something that agitates, alarms, tortures, and disquiets him inside, in the depths of his spiritual life. Clearly, by the time *Mazeppa* was composed, a monstrous amount of such "material" had accumulated. It was necessary for him to shed and expel it; and thus a correspondingly harsh subject was chosen, at the limits of which all that was foreordained found a place. In any case, if not structurally, then emotionally, all the terrors, all the onslaughts of an evil will are directed against Maria, so that in this way she is after all the center of the action, even though she does not direct it as Joan does.[35]

With respect to the intensity of the onslaught and the depth of the emotional breakdown, *Mazeppa* is the first in the series of Tchaikovsky's tragic operas. If *The Oprichnik* is dismissed as an attempt, that leaves *Mazeppa*, *The Enchantress*, and *Queen of Spades*. *The Slippers* stands by itself, while *Iolantha* inclines toward *Evgeny Onegin*. Still, *Mazeppa*, despite all, is clearly a romantic opera in the sense of amassing moments of pathos and a tendency to hold the nerves of the viewer for the full duration in a state of keen curiosity, mixed with a feeling of pity. It is with the same state of mind, no doubt, that people came in droves to witness an execution. Tchaikovsky cruelly underscored human sadism, creating an impressive tableau, one reminiscent of Surikov's "Execution of the Streltsy" in its gray and colorless palette, for the execution of Kochubei and Iskra, together with the highly expressive genre episode of a strolling Cossack.[36] The action of *Maid of Orleans* proceeds from ensemble to ensemble in the sense of a succession of "outbursts" of lyricism en masse in reference to one event or another; in *Mazeppa*, the course of action hinges on the moments wherein gloom and violence are concentrated, in which nervous energy is focused, forcing people to flounder about in horrifying despair and conditioning their actions: the cruel, the base, the senseless, and the noble. The action proceeds from the same impulse as in *The Oprichnik*: a discord between two families, with the distinction that here, the root or fundamental reason for this discord develops before the eyes of the audience, who also register its entire course.[37]

The first-act finale is the first spot, the first nerve center of insults and enmity out of which sprouts the oath and vengeance scene in Kochubei's house, which is so tremendous in its concentration of hatred; then the cruel torture scene in prison, along with the tale of the three treasures, which is somewhat unauthentic in style (a "romance for baritone!") but well motivated and intelligently developed. Further on, the mother's arrival scene, which is frightening after the sentimental, senile lyricism of Mazeppa's and Maria's dialogue; next the full summit of intensity: the execution, after which comes the bombastic and superficial yet structurally essential tableau of the "Poltavian Battle" (like the pounding of a drum at the moment of state-sanctioned murder!), and finally, a closing scene of genial dramatic expressivity with Maria bent over the Cossack's corpse ("Lullaby"), summarizing within herself the terrible sense of the opera.[38] The innocent, radiant, and pure soul of the girl was insultingly and cynically plundered, scattered about, sullied, and flooded with superhuman horrors and experiences; they drove her to madness, but could not take away her womanly caress, her woman's attachment, and tender lullabying, along with her reason. In an atmosphere of tragic destiny, such a "finale" is the only possible finale, since it reveals a sublime triumph of humanity, even in the twilight of reason.[39]

Compared to the style of *Maid of Orleans*, the style of *Mazeppa* is restless, fragmented, and confused, as if every means of expression utilized here were given in the most poignant interpretation of its possibilities. The strained expressivity of the instrumentation is crude and shrill, but I cannot agree that this quality results from a lack of taste.[40] The question of taste or the lack of it may arise wherever any artistic project is directed into the realm of "tasteful" order, where taste inspired the style. How laughable to approach *Mazeppa* with such a "weapon," in order to obliterate it. The inspiration behind *Mazeppa* is psychological: a constant changeability of the soul, an aggravation and baring of emotions. It is a matter of taste, certainly, whether someone is pleased or not pleased by the appearance of artworks, as springs or founts from the earth: from the unbroken life current of soul states! Such is the creativity or creative process of Tchaikovsky. One must accept this as a given, as a fact, just as the fully antithetical creative processes or methods in Glinka or in Sergei Taneyev.

Of great significance in *Mazeppa* are the genre scenes, suffused with the aroma of the Ukrainian song element. Tchaikovsky loved Ukraine, and in his lyrical moods one senses the wafting of the Ukrainian element more strongly than the Russian. The fine introductory girls' chorus in *Mazeppa* is slow and reflective, composed within the irregularities of a 7/4 meter and therefore piquantly flowing, even when the rhythm and the melody are on the verge of losing their calm predisposition![41] The first act also includes the well-characterized singers' chorus and the hopak; it is intricate, wild, and impassioned, yet still not as rhythmically incisive as the hopak in *The Slippers*, and, in the middle section, too florid on account of tonal shifts and, at the same time, monotonous, due to the "hammering out" of one and the same phrase.[42] The Ukrainian coloration of *The Slippers* is softer, more tender, and in relation to the meaning of the subject matter, more cunning. In this respect, the opening of the opera is indicative: Solokha's incantation to the moon, along with the impassioned five-measure phrase for her flight. There follows the caroling of the laddies: a broadly unfolding tableau of the peaceful celebratory mood of Dikanka, Oksana's ardent song about the slippers; the laments and choruses of the final tableau. In *Mazeppa* there is the same coloration, but it is used more incisively, graphically, and dramatically: such is the lament (second tableau, ensemble), and then the entire execution scene. There is no kind of deliberate "ethnographic-realistic" approach here. The Ukrainian element is introduced as an organic element, which naturally and of its own accord enters into the sound material due to associations evoked by the fabula, according to which the music runs its course.[43]

One cannot help remarking on a characteristic trait in Tchaikovsky's design of action. As I have already stated, the action is concentrated, for the most part, around feminine characters or a central feminine character, toward whom the remaining circles gravitate. In *The Oprichnik* it is the old woman Morozova and not her son who plays a dominating, guiding role, albeit psychologically unfounded. In *The Slippers*, it is Oksana, with Solokha for her companion. In *Evgeny Onegin*, it is Tatyana, for her spring and autumn are the point of departure and the culmination of the action, but not Lensky, whose love and death are still only an episode, albeit one brought to a full conclusion. In *Mazeppa* everything gravitates toward Maria, who is enchained and bound, on the one hand, by the family curse and, on the other, by love for an ambitious old man. In *The Maid of Orleans* a woman as heroine directs the action. But all of them (except for Oksana and Solokha) are fated for sacrifice. Their heroism is the heroism of the condemned, a heroism of self-surrender. All of them are ill equipped, all enchained: by an obligation to a spouse, to family, to God, to an oath. It remained for him to create a free woman, full of will, of *joi de vivre*, one not to be ruled by human beings but to play on them: to create and then, to test on her, the free woman, the tragic conception of fate.

Tchaikovsky found the prototype for such a woman in Shpazhinsky's drama *The Enchantress*: a prototype taken from everyday life.[44] The composer planned to deepen the type through music. He could never resist his regular inclination to compose operas, and the subject he had just found led him down the very path that corresponded to his soul-searchings. In the Enchantress, in this character free of a woman's duty, one seemingly not "fated" at all, the composer realized his hope in accordance with the law of contrast: in *Mazeppa*, the full power of his imagination was directed toward recreating an intensive onslaught of an evil will against a sacrificial victim; here, on the other hand, it is directed toward consolidating a woman's strength, will, and power. The Enchantress is responsible for her demise: playing with an elemental force for so long a time, she suddenly falls completely *captive* to this element, and drawing near the beloved flame surrenders herself to death without resisting. Tchaikovsky himself characterized the Enchantress quite graphically in letters to the singer Pavlovskaya, for whom he had designated the main role in the future opera, although she simply could not understand the character of Nastasya (the "Enchantress") in Shpazhinsky's drama.[45]

I transcribe the most substantive lines from the letter that justifies the composer's decision to choose this drama of everyday life for an operatic subject. . . . "I imagine and understand Nastasya quite differently than you. Of course, the old girl *gets around*, but her charm does not consist of the fact that she speaks *splendidly* and *for everyone's pleasure*. These qualities suffice to draw *le commun des mortels* into her little inn. But how, using only these means, does one compel the young prince, a mortal enemy who had come to commit murder, to become a passionately devoted lover? The fact is that in the depths of this roving old girl's soul is a *moral power and beauty*, which prior to this occasion had never been expressed. *This force is found in love.* Hers is a powerful feminine nature, capable of loving only once and for all and able to sacrifice *all* for that love. Prior to that, *love* had only been in gestation. Nastasya would exchange her vital energy for a pittance, i.e., would take pleasure from making one and all who came her way to fall in love with her. Here she is simply an appealing, attractive, albeit dissolute *moll*; she well knows that she is *alluring*. . . . But then the one appears who is fated to touch her heartstrings 'to the core,' those which had been mute up until now, and she is transformed. Life for her becomes a trifle, if she does not achieve her goal; the power of her allure, which had previously operated spontaneously and unconsciously, is now an indestructible weapon, capable in an instant of overpowering a hostile force, i.e., the prince's animosity. After this, both surrender themselves to the wild torrent of love, which leads to an inescapable catastrophe—her death, a death that leaves the audience with a feeling of reconciliation and tenderness. . . . Although charmed by *The Enchantress*, I did not at all betray my soul's deep-rooted need to illustrate with music that, which led Goethe to say: 'Das ewig Weibliche zieht uns hinan!' The fact that the *majestic beauty of femininity* lies hidden in Nastasya for so long under a loose woman's guise, intensifies all the more her scenic appeal." This letter is dated 12 April 1885.[46]

Tchaikovsky did not begin to write the opera until the early days of September, soon breaking off until January 1886. Having completed the first two acts, he took another break until June of that year. Consequently, his plan matured and strengthened for some time, so that the central act, wherein the beauty and power of the Enchantress's love are expressed, was apparently not written until a year and a half after the decision to write the opera.[47] For Tchaikovsky, such a delay was atypical. Nevertheless, the music of *The Enchantress* attests to the fact that his words did not remain only words and that the plan set forth in the letter was vividly and beautifully reflected in music.

The Enchantress is a very problematic opera. Above all, it is because this opera—which is not only the most outstanding, but in terms of concision, driving force, and dramatic expressivity, perhaps the *only* Russian opera of everyday life—contains along with its virtues the usual flaws of Russian real-life dramatic works: namely, a multitude of connected but poorly motivated everyday details (an enthusiasm for typical everyday traits and images) and a prevalence of conversations and explanations over action.[48] *The Enchantress* is an opera of dialogues and duets. One character exits, another enters, and out of this sequence of exits and entrances emerges a monotonous thread of conversations behind which hides a naive report to the audience on the unfolding drama. The second act suffers in particular from this standpoint.[49]

As for the virtues, there is an opportunity for vivid characterizations, resulting from the presence of interesting everyday tableaus and character types. Tchaikovsky exploits this, offering in the first act an idiosyncratic representation of a broadly unfolding scene of the merry "party" afoot, outside of town, at the widow Nastasya's. The young folk converge there to release their primal energy in carefree carousing, for which there is no outlet in the monotonous and proper life led according to the statutes and rules of the elders in the town itself. Against the background of gleeful unbridled youthful will, one can distinguish all the more sharply the characters of the crafty wandering monk Paisy, the stern yet hypocritical sacristan Mamyrov, Kichiga the strong man and, finally, the Enchantress herself—Nastya. In her remarkable arioso ("To gaze from Nizhny"), the unsurveyable distance of the Russian expanse resounds, devouring the gaze, where the will melts in the eye's unending, unbounded attempt to comprehend the space.[50]

In the first act the spontaneous nature of Nastya's soul unfolds. Her feigned sorcery is an inducement or provocation to a willful outburst in the people around her. All bask in the aura of her personal, freedom-loving personality, suffused with the power of a woman's beauty and congeniality, all those in whom there ferments helplessly a life force expended in vain, of the sort that has always been plentiful in Russia. This side of the Enchantress's character (directed outwardly) collides with the personality of the [elder] prince, who is accustomed to ruling without encountering resistance from other people. It is then that Nastasya's profile acquires, in the area of self-defense, the tinge of an ingratiating, flattering snake of a woman. She saves herself, her "court," and her belongings, but in the act arouses in the prince a craving, lustful passion.[51] With this the first act is broken off. We have before us, in the freest aspect known to woman, an unfolding of the powerfully bewitching and enchanting force of feminine beauty in its most elemental manifestation (turned toward nature!) in an assault against a man's strong will, an assault with the intent of self-protection. This is no longer a Tatyana or Maria. Neither Onegin, nor Mazeppa, nor sense of duty, nor conscience can oppose her (or so it would seem).

Only a love both sincere and ardent can vindicate the element of beauty, render it both tender and *ill fated* and thereby magnify it morally, for only in such a selfless and beautiful love can the value in life of a woman like the Enchantress be developed; her life goal is found in love, but behind that lies death itself. Because of this, after the vivid flourishing of vitality in Nastya's soul, nothing more remains; on the other hand, seeds of the sort that turned up at the moment of the prince's seduction or the teasing of the good-hearted lads can again emerge.

Having created a feminine ideal in *The Enchantress* who is both strikingly spontaneous and free of the conventional, Tchaikovsky came face to face with his constant internal need: how, at last, to oppose all that was disturbing and disquieting his soul and disrupting his life with that bulwark that he considered to be the strongest—the beauty and power of femininity. That "something that disquiets and disturbs" is death. Does it have the strength and the right to annihilate so mighty a bulwark? If the prince, out of his passionate malice and malicious passion, were to have killed the Enchantress as the audience envisages her either in the first act or in that part of the third where in defending herself against the prince's assault, she is prepared to slay herself, then this would leave the impression that death as a force of nature had conquered beauty as spontaneously revealed.[52] But the composer's temperament pulled him deeper, concentrating and bringing to a point the agonizing problem of life's purpose, for the sake of convincing or proving to himself its meaninglessness. He demanded of his librettist a deepening of Nastasya's character, an underscoring of the moral power of her beauty in order to convince himself and the audience that once this moral power[53] appears in a genuine blossoming of ardent love, then the force and power of death emerge as well. For one who has been flush with life, it is better to die than to dwindle into impotence. Therein lies the meaning of the Enchantress's demise; and it is so profoundly and vividly revealed in the music by means of a *bold* stylistic device that was discovered by intuition.

In the part of Nastya there are two lyrical moments, which are deployed at opposite ends, like the two extremes of life. The first, displaying the full bloom of her "roving" spirit, is presented in the expansive arioso of the first act. Here the full charm of the Enchantress's character is revealed, prior to the tragic encounter with the prince and his son, i.e., in a calm and unimpeded unfolding of the force of nature within her.[54] The musical language of this arioso is everyday Russian in the typical adornment found in Tchaikovsky's stylizations of folk song, receiving, in this case, an exceedingly plastic melos whose fine proportions are maintained throughout. However, in the fourth and final act's arioso in "anticipation" of death, the Enchantress appears in another guise, wherein all of her life energy is relinquished in *tormented bliss.*[55] If each of these instances is taken separately, i.e., removed from the unfolding of the action, one might think, given the difference in musical language between one arioso and the other, that two distinct personages are being characterized. In fact, we are confronting an essential stylistic device of Tchaikovsky: the conditioning of a musical depiction characterizing the musical speech of a given personage, approached not from any kind of external vantage point, but from within—out of the spiritual condition of the given personage and dependent upon the destination of her life's gaze, be it out toward the world or inward to the soul. In the first act, the Enchantress's entire frame of mind is directed toward life's elemental forces, which flow from outside, from a great distance, and from the temptations of an impetuous will; she sings in everyday hues, just like a Russian maiden when she leads a ritual or sings a song long ago established as communal property, one in which common thoughts are expressed and through which the feelings of many generations are poured out. However, in her last arioso, the Enchantress is alone, at one with herself. Having become impotent thanks to a desire achieved and *fulfilled,* she no longer lives, but *languishes*; she awaits her dear one but has already lost her bloom; she lacks the strength to resist any longer, for she has given to life all that she could. The revenge of the princess (the poison) only accomplishes that which is inescapable: to expel from life a beauty that is no longer necessary, just as an autumn wind chases after a yellowed leaf. The conclusion: death arrives at the proper time . . . even for an Enchantress, i.e., for a person seemingly filled with inextinguishable life energy.

The contrast between the two polar opposites is overwhelming, and it would be naive indeed to speak here of any supposed inconsistency of style. One might discuss this when analyzing a work that was knowingly intellectualized and structured with well-defined projects of stylization but not in reference to works composed by means of a deep spiritual penetration into the creation, which always occurs in the works of great artists, in which the unity of style is conditioned by very complicated interactions of multifaceted impulses. One must sense these impulses and expose them, approaching such works not from the naive standpoint of taste, namely by marking down all that appears to be "unappetizing" and therefore is false and unsuitable, but by setting forth under the belief that a creative artistic will is unavoidably present to guide the composer—provided he is indisputably a true creator—toward an intuitively sensed stylistic integrity of intention and execution.

Between the two ariosi—the one face turned outward, the other within—the drama of *The Enchantress* is disposed and the sacrament of a soul's conversion and enhancement is performed. Unfortunately, the character from whom the impulse for this transfiguration emerges is presented in the libretto as a conventional operatic stereotype: the beneficent, magnificent young prince, whose beneficence and magnificence everyone repeatedly affirms, something a spectator should accept but a listener cannot, since the young prince is musically unrealized. He sings the sweetest of tunes with the shadings of the *opéra lyrique*. Therefore, like it or not, all the organic-creative and artistic will of the composer is focused on the role of the Enchantress. This is expressed in the thoroughly atypical character of her recitatives. In truth, her entire role is based on lyrico-dramatic dialogue whose flexibility and expressivity register all the more strongly, since the Enchantress must *speak* under the dictates of profoundly different spiritual states. Great is the qualitative difference between her "seductions": i.e., of ordinary people, of the lecherous experienced prince, or of a beloved person whose hatred must be overcome and transformed into love![56]

Here Nastya's speech correspondingly changes and deepens in intensity. One might hear lyrical bravado in its most luxuriant form, then sly pretense and complaints about insults; here a flattering, insistent invitation and boasting; there, suddenly, a venomous and insinuating desire, one that appears to be tossed out by chance but is actually quite insolent. At the decisive moment in the scene with the prince (the assault), Nastasya's personage expands to the limits of the strength of a resisting will; it is a sudden and firm advance and address: a cutting address, like a blow! And after that Nastasya is yet again unrecognizable in the monologue that precedes the young prince's arrival, wherein two sentiments are in conflict: the pride of a beautiful woman, aching to bend another's will, to reverse the beloved's lack of love; and the sweet sense of doom, of surrendering oneself to the will of a dear one—even to mortal torments! As for the music, from the moment of Foka's exit to the moment when the young prince's gaze meets the gaze of the Enchantress who awaits him lies one of the most expressive moments in the opera, thanks to its state of arousal: restrained but ready to pour forth.[57] The following dialogue is but an emotional development and disclosure of this instant.

The Enchantress's recitatives—ah! but one must know how to declaim them, how to reveal their content[58]—achieve here a steely resilience and flexibility not yet seen in Tchaikovsky, a focused striving, and a convincingly laconic form so that every phrase thoughtfully expresses the desired goal in the most concentrated accumulation of sounds. It is a kind of unerring "direct hit," a continuous surmising of thoughts, a penetration into the will by the will: the young prince has nowhere to retreat ("Here you are drunk without wine").[59]

One can well imagine how unpleasant and wearisome it was for Tchaikovsky to hear Pavlovskaya's interminable requests for alterations in the role of the Enchantress, with regard to the uncomfortable tessitura and with what annoyance he conceded until finally, with uncharacteristic sharpness, he spoke out: "I am so worn out from devising alterations that, my God, I don't know how to respond to your last little letter. . . . In reference to page 78, my God, I simply do not know what to do here. Everything would indeed have to be entirely recomposed, in order to produce a free *recitative*!!! . . ." And further: "Ask Napravnik for advice. You are aware that I do not relish quarreling and shall submit to necessity . . ." (letter of Sept. 21, 1887).[60] Here again, the usual refrain: the author himself does not know what he is composing; others know better. And since it should not matter to the author whether this or that succession of pitches will appear in a particular "recitative" (so trivial!), he is obliged to submit to the orders of a capricious singer, who cannot comprehend the difference between indistinguishable operatic recitative in general and the recitative of operas like *The Enchantress*. But Tchaikovsky could not force himself to introduce changes into such an expressive and deeply characterized manifestation of musical speech as one encounters in this role.

As I have already said, the Enchantress's recitatives are quite unique on account of their expressivity. They are comparable to Natasha's recitatives in the first act of *Rusalka*.[61] In general, their "historical" line extends from Russian operas about ordinary life: from the origins of it, on to Verstovsky, Dargomyzhsky (but not from *The Stone Guest*), and from Serov in particular. Their concentrated and enhanced depth of feeling and restraint have little in common with Tatyana's lyrical agitations or the ardent "Ukrainian" emotionality of Oksana's speech, when she "torments" Vakula. In *The Enchantress* a woman speaks, doggedly and directly striving toward projected goals, and if she attains in her speech that degree where it is necessary, at last, to pour out all the bitter tears, all the despair, all the secret feeling, she does so with an awareness of the certainty of the achievement and the impossibility of a disruption (such is the lyrical shift of the "farewell to the young prince": Nastasya knows that now he will not leave and therefore releases her sorrow in an agonizing cry, while supposedly parting with him).[62]

The Enchantress is Tchaikovsky's greatest achievement in the sphere of dramatic opera concerned with everyday life. Regarding the presence of a national element, i.e., the coloration of national speech, its style is doubtless old-fashioned after the *consolidation* in this realm brought about by Rimsky-Korsakov's investigations. But here a major reservation is in order. In the heat of battle, while Tchaikovsky was composing and the Mighty Handful were establishing their style, it was possible to contrast their authentic Russian style with Tchaikovsky's European eclecticism. Now it is time to grant equal rights for "Russian *styles*" in relation to their historical consequences. The "Russian style" of Tchaikovsky emanates from a complex interaction of folk elements and "Europeanisms" as they coalesced in 18th-century Petersburg and as they reflexively merged and linked together in the works of many Russian composers, including Glinka himself. We are accustomed to calling this song style unauthentic. It is indeed inauthentic in the sense that every subsequent generation will consider its approach to any significant life phenomenon in the past to be the only correct and true, and possible, and direct one. But in fact, this style was not at all false for the people who were accustomed to thinking musically in it and through it over the course of more than one hundred years. In speaking of its immediacy, one must not lose sight of the fact that, in the cities of the early feudalistic epoch, with the presence of the "court serfs" and the extremely close ties to the countryside, the connection with folk song was much steadier and stronger than subsequently, when one began having to "travel for a song." The "stylization" of song that passes from Prach through Fomin, Kavos, Verstovsky, Glinka, Dargomyzhsky, and Serov reaches its culmination in Tchaikovsky.[63] It was profoundly vital and valuable.

In Rimsky-Korsakov's works (albeit with greater stylistic purity and perfection in Anatoly Lyadov) we observe the development and consolidation of *another* approach to song, conditioned by other tastes and other theoretical grounds. This type of stylization is near to us, but the time will come—and it is not far away, for even now the conventions of "Lyadov and Korsakov" stylization are evident from the standpoint of the new conclusions based on encounters with the art of folk song and the study of it—the time will come when even this "Russian style" that is familiar to us will become false and also imbued with "Europeanisms" that disfigure the countenance of the song, as occurred with its predecessor. For me, this is beyond question; and thus, if Tchaikovsky's "Russian style" were to be approached in accordance with the bases that were worked out in the operatic style of Rimsky-Korsakov and the song arrangements of Lyadov, then the baselessness of it all would be clear to any child and deserving of condemnation. How naive, since the previous generation cannot know the truths that are accessible to the next! Yet if the folk element in Tchaikovsky is viewed from the standpoint of a style that had yet to reach its culmination in the epoch when the composer began writing, one to which he was naturally drawn, then much about his approach to song that went undetected will appear valuable and unique. There are ample instances of such in Tchaikovsky's works, beginning even with the First Quartet. But this is not the place to discuss them in detail.

The essence of Tchaikovsky's "Russian tendency" as well as the entire "Russian style" of his predecessors constitutes the development of a unique musical language in which the material (not the national song element, which speaks for itself, but just the material), without losing its own coloring, is subjected to norms that were characteristic of Western European music in the Classical Era, which are accepted as the sole unchanging ones.[64] The attitude to norms has changed (they stood in need of being further researched or varied in response to new inquiries into the emotions or the spirit), and the approach to folk art has likewise changed.

With regard to *The Enchantress*'s "Russianisms," I would single out the finely developed diatonic introduction (based on the theme of the arioso "To gaze from Nizhny"), i.e., the roving songs of the first act, with Tchaikovsky's characteristic crescendo of ornamentation, i.e., a complication, or rather a gradual growth in the convolutions of the backing voices [*podgoloski*]; and next, the imbecilic din of the *skomorokhi* dance, so distinctive in its rhythmic diversity and its "awkward" leaps of sevenths and fourths.[65] Tchaikovsky commands complex, irregular meters with the fluency of Glinka (e.g., the choruses in *The Enchantress*, *Mazeppa*, and *The Slippers*), not so as to invent intentionally astringent ones but to freely insert rhythmic lines within them. One senses the organicism of the flow in his melodies "of asymmetrical cast." On the whole, though, Tchaikovsky's "everyday language" is not luxuriant—this was prevented by the homophonic character found in the style of the period, with a predominant ornamentation that did not emerge from the essence of the song melody, i.e., out of figurations, not from *podgoloski*.

The most notably unpalatable nuance is imparted to *The Enchantress* at those points of the opera where Tchaikovsky departs from his most character- istic personal melodic song style, there to plunge, especially at moments of lyrical elevation, into a romance style in the salon manner or into the melodic arioso design of French lyric opera. Such places find their way into the prince's part (third act), in the duet of his son and the princess (second act), and even in the final stage of the encounter between the prince and the Enchantress, at that moment of passionate outburst where the dialogue changes into a duet.[66] It is, in truth, an effective one, but still false with respect to style, since it can- not at all fit in with all the preceding development. How curious that these three lyrical disruptions in this opera are all written in the key of E-flat, one already rather foreign to Tchaikovsky, but especially sounding false here in the affected light of sentimentality à la Massenet or Gounod. These are the dis- agreeable blemishes in the background of a splendid dramatic opera about Russian everyday reality. Nevertheless, as I have already indicated, its center of gravity is found in recitative that is both dramatically expressive and intense.

Tchaikovsky's next opera after *The Enchantress* was *The Queen of Spades*. Its artistic significance and emotional intensity place it higher than all the other achievements of the composer in the realm of music for the stage. I will as- sign it to a separate article. Here I will only remark that, in relation to the re- maining operas, it serves as the outermost point along the path toward the attainment in art of the secret of suffering and death.[67] The struggle between those condemned and the force that deludes them with phantasms of bliss, love, and the meaning of life reaches its highest degree of intensity in *The Queen of Spades*, wherein a man is led into a conversation with the world be- yond in an effort to unveil *the secret*.

Based on its content, *Iolantha* would appear to be a lyric poem in which the composer's lyric impulse was taken off course, an unsuccessful work be- cause the suggested subject did not correspond to his spiritual condition. Just as in *The Nutcracker*, the first part of the ballet, so Hoffmannesque in tempera- ment, is astonishing; but the second half is nothing more than a brilliantly con- ceived ballet divertissement and not a revelation of joy and light streaming forth with sincerity, so in *Iolantha* the path of a blind girl toward the light seems only skillfully sketched, not realized in full. The Mauritanian doctor's [Ibn-Hakia] characterization is quite interesting, for Tchaikovsky possessed a peculiar talent for depicting the East in his own colorful way (one recalls the marvelous "Arabian Dance" in *The Nutcracker*); Iolantha's sadness and languor are fascinatingly outlined. It is a languor she does not understand, tenderly doleful like Tatyana's languor. But nowhere in the music is there a jubilant and ecstatic acceptance of *light* and *love* in a moment when sight is regained, in spite of all the sumptuous aural beauty of this opera's finale. Indeed there could be no light, nor could there be those rapturous delights of love, which once set fire to *Romeo* and *The Tempest*: after *The Queen of Spades*, Tchaikovsky no longer saw the light.

In the brief sketch that I have now completed, I wished to identify the psychological foundations of Tchaikovksy's operatic style: perhaps not the foundations per se, but the opportunity to *establish* the foundations, based on a close study of the structure of the operas and an assessment of their style from within, using the psychological data uncovered in the music.

Of course, there is a need for more analyses and more detailed examinations of all the means for establishing whatever it is that *expresses* a given work, i.e., its style. But I did not consider it possible to broaden the topic in this way and, out of necessity, provided only the conclusions of my observations and research. In the final result, an *opera* of Tchaikovsky (taking the word as a general concept that unifies into a single whole significant treasures within the composer's creative work)—produces in each of its manifestations the inner evolution of one or another life force or, more accurately, a spiritual datum. *The essential task of a musical realization consists of developing to the fullest the soul's most striking capability, within the character of a given individual.* More often than not, that capability is love; but it is a woman's love that awaits awakening into bloom, thus facilitating the highest ascent of womanhood (Oksana, Tatyana, the Enchantress, Joan of Arc, Maria, Liza, Iolantha). Sometimes love is replaced by hatred (Morozova), jealousy (the princess in *The Enchantress*, akin to the princess of *Rusalka*), a father's revenge (Kochubei), passion (Hermann; the prince in *The Enchantress*). But a woman's love is nevertheless always the axis, around which and under whose influence the action proceeds. Blossoming womanhood faces head on the emergence of fiendish evil power, sometimes incarnated into a particular individual, sometimes faceless, merely guiding someone's action. Stylistically, this power can be understood as a contrast and as an element born out of a struggle in order to facilitate the development of an essential spiritual capability that can counteract it. In Tchaikovsky, *it* is not a blind, stagnant, and inert mass, but the imperiously advancing element, which in the end makes nonsense out of any life-impulse, i.e., death. Hence the inescapable condemnation to death of all that lives and that fights for its own *self*.

In accordance with this understanding of the *meaning* of life, music takes on a different aspect; its structure in Tchaikovsky's operas is wholly dependent on the particular internal and external planes in which the power of love develops and on what stands in its way. In the center, therefore, stands a heroine, usually a girl falling in love for the first time. The basic flow of the melodic and harmonic fabric is designed on the basis of her moods and experiences. The thread of the musical-psychological *story* attaches itself and develops along this line. In this regard, the design of *Evgeny Onegin* is relatively simple. The first and second tableaus form a line of ascent for Tatyana's maidenly love and Lensky's youthful passion (first tableau). The third and fourth tableaus are the turning points with respect to forces. The fifth is the denouement of Lensky's "idealism." In the sixth and seventh the lines move in the reverse direction from the lines of the first and second tableaus, without being any less formidable in their tension: the "sober" acceptance of life by Tatyana, who goes on living, unlike Liza or Maria. The design of *The Queen of Spades* is the most complex, since there is reciprocal attraction of two opposites: Liza and Hermann. In addition, the power that thwarts them no longer resembles the darling devil of *The Slippers*, who is so easily tamed, nor Onegin's cold-blooded, rational speeches. The force in *Queen of Spades* is insurmountable and unconquerable, since death is acting behind it, without any embellishment as in the case of Lensky, but in the fullness of its mystical terror and inexorability.

More than anything else, the power of femininity and love drew Tchaikovsky toward life; it also *creates life* in his operas and directs their design. The lyrical instants where this power is revealed are the nerve centers, the mainstays, to which the action adheres, around which the action becomes entangled or is resolved. That which disturbed him, which caused trouble and anxiety in life, was expressed in a vague sensation that holds sway over one's every step: the sensation of an evil element ("fate!") that was in the final result a premonition of death. This mysterious *thing* emerges as a sharply dissonant interval, as an impulse toward motion, as an imperious summons from beyond the grave, something thwarting emotional arousal: mystical, threatening, and warning. From out of the clashes of the two fundamental elements, the drama is born: an action and, in response to it, the opposition of themes and moments of ascent and descent, i.e., the rhythm of the action. In *Queen of Spades* the troubling and disturbing element even enters as a leitmotif, a controlling and guiding thread! . . . Tchaikovsky's operas are therefore constructed from a succession of scenes in different moods, among which intense lyrical moments (arias, ariosi, ensembles) resound like nerve centers that pull in the forces wrestling around them.

Another tendency that produces contrast in the music is based on the opposition of the internal and the external: the I and not-I of spiritual states and their outward manifestation, the internal world and the visible world (everyday reality). It is distinctly present in *The Enchantress*, in the ball scene at the Larins' in *Evgeny Onegin*, and in the last scene of *Queen of Spades*, where the life-rhythm of the action is conditioned by the everyday surroundings in which it occurs. The absence of an externally provided plan for purely musical development imparts to Tchaikovsky's operas a coloring that is deeply emotional but hazardous with respect to design, since at the moments where the line of the composer's creative intensity falls, an impression of chance phenomena in the relationship of elements will grow (since the nerve centers or fulcrums lose all of their gravitational strength, as if they are growing feeble: thus individual numbers seem to close in on themselves, without any persistently maintained and externally given stylistic connection). Thus, for example, the action of *Iolantha* is disjointed.[68]

But since the main thread giving structure to the opera is the life evolution of a given individual who is placed in the center of the action, it is natural that the composer's intuitive inclination would produce a strengthening of the music belonging to each of the drama's *heroes*, i.e., of the language he speaks in the course of action. This tendency developed gradually, to be expressed the most clearly in *Queen of Spades*, wherein the language of each of the *dramatis personae* is unique and flexible. Tchaikovsky did not restrict himself in this regard to a strictly defined system (such as leitmotives) but instead utilized leitmotives (not in the Wagnerian sense), leit-harmonies, and sonorities, seemingly of entire planes of sound, all relating to a given character; briefly put, it is more a language of temperaments (of moments) than a stylistically predetermined manner of speech, as, for example, the speech of Sadko, the Astrologer, the devil, and other personages from Rimsky-Korsakov's operas. The emotional richness in the language of Tchaikovsky's operatic heroes yields profound, penetrating insights into their internal world, which in turn leads to the listener's impression of a compelling vitality. The characters of Tatyana, Lensky, Hermann, Liza, the Queen of Spades, Oksana, the Enchantress, Solokha, and others are offered to us as striking interpretations in sound, ever to be imprinted in the mind, enveloped by the powerfully inspired force of Tchaikovsky's music, which found the opportunity in the operatic sphere to reveal the captivating power of his imagination and to subject our will to the characters created and evoked by this power.

This power is still strong even now. Apparently, the flow of nervous energy emerging from Tchaikovsky's operatic-dramatic music, when it is interpreted in our minds and touches our feelings, calls forth a responsive echo in them, i.e., finds a mirroring environment. But at the same time, the perception of this music nowadays should no longer be the naive and immediate perception of the composer's contemporaries, who distinguished from among his musical moods only those that were accessible and familiar to them. Thanks to the greater relative distance and the fading away of the biased pro and contra from the period nearer to Tchaikovsky, we can both cherish the immediate warmth in the perception of moods that are familiar and understandable to us, and also deepen the point of view and broaden the horizon of our evaluations regarding both the artistic significance of the tendencies in his music that are alien to us and our determination of the internal connection that produces stylistic unity in various musical instants. We can see all that usually eludes the contemporaries on account of shortsightedness, for they evaluate the music of a composer that lives among them based more on the strength of the impression produced than on its essence. Experiencing the power for its own sake, we are nevertheless also in a position to strengthen or weaken its impact, depending on our awareness of the means behind that impact, i.e., the psychological foundations of the style. That is where I found my own task with regard to the operas of Tchaikovsky.

NOTES

1. The art historian Wilhelm Worringer (1881–1965) categorized style periods of art based on his conjectures of the fundamental psychological need being addressed by each. The abstraction that characterized Gothic art was an escape from real-world anxiety into transcendental forms. Yet the Gothic period was succeeded by Renaissance art's characteristic mimesis of people and objects.

2. I.e., the Scene at the Inn on the Lithuanian Border from *Boris Godunov*'s first act.

3. *Kunstwille* and *Formwille* are aesthetic terms pointing to the aesthetic impulses that emerge in response to the particular psychological needs being addressed.

4. [Author's note:] I would like to direct attention to the fact that the arts of poetry, music, painting, architecture, and theater as concepts are not at all the same as the concepts of *being* musical, poetic, painterly, and tragic. For there may be poetry that is very little or very much akin to music, as well as music that is pictorial or poetic, and so forth.

5. Asafyev alludes again to Pushkin's Mozart, opining that genius and evil are "two things incompatible."

6. As critic, César Cui was outspoken in his advocacy of a through-composed "melodic recitative" which he found in both Dargomyzhsky and Musorgsky, but not in Italian numbers opera and its derivatives.

7. Tchaikovksy's *extreme* dissatisfaction with the operas *The Voyevoda* (composed 1868–1869) and *Undine* (1869) induced him to destroy the scores.

8. Cf. Chekhov, the reputed "singer of melancholy [*súmerechnikh*] moods."

9. *The Petty Demon* (1907) is a novel by Fyodor Teternikov (pseud., Fyodor Sologub, 1863–1927), doubly satirizing the protagonist, an amoral schoolteacher named Peredonov, and the provincial milieu that he disdained.

10. *The Twelve* (1918) was Alexander Blok's kaleidoscopic, rhythmically jarring poem of the 1917 Revolution and of Russia's past, present, and future, in which character sketches, political jargon, slang, obscenities, and song lyrics intertwine as various characters tread the streets of war-torn Petrograd.

11. Alexander Herzen (1812–1870) was a socialist political thinker, esteemed writer, and editor of the influential émigré newspaper, *The Bell*. He was subsequently "canonized" by the early Soviet regime for his contributions to the revolutionary cause. While Asafyev is harshly critical of the bourgeoisie, he still keeps his specific political allegiance hidden throughout *Symphonic Etudes*.

12. Isaak Levitan (1860–1900), a painter who joined the group of artists known as the Wanderers, was also a close friend of Chekhov. Renowned for painting a "landscape of mood," Levitan explored various means for depicting the interrelationships of humanity and nature.

13. Liszt's musical portrait of Goethe's Margarete (Gretchen) is the second movement of his *Faust Symphony* of 1857. St. Elizabeth is portrayed in Liszt's oratorio, *Die Legende von der heiligen Elizabeth* (1862).

14. For further discussions of this theme, see Chapter 17, pp. 268–69, and Chapter 18, pp. 278–79.

15. In the extensive finale to Act 2 (no. 9), Andrei Morozov swears the oath of fealty to Tsar Ivan and the Oprichniki.

16. Natalya's song of the nightingale ("Solovushko v dubravushke") is found in Act 1, no. 2 (figs. 15–18); the arioso (No. 6, "Voices") contributes to the first-act finale.

17. If one dismisses the aforementioned operas *The Voyevoda* and *Undine*, then *The Oprichnik* can be considered the composer's first significant operatic work, composed at the same time as Rimsky's first opera *The Maid of Pskov*, which is set in the same historical epoch.

18. The competition sponsored by the Russian Musical Society was announced in 1873. Tchaikovsky composed the work *Vakula the Smith* [i.e., the original version of *The Slippers*] rapidly, from June to August 1874, but not in time to make the August 1 deadline. Pursuant to the composer's appeal for some leniency, *Vakula* was awarded a first-prize sum of 1,500 rubles on 16 October 1875 by a committee that included both Rimsky-Korsakov and Nikolai Rubinstein.

19. [Author's note:] Another frequent device is that of disclosing or developing a theme, after it has been given as a thesis.

20. Asafyev here concludes his program note for a multisectional dramatic overture in B-flat of medium length (273 mm.), which introduces several important themes and motives. With respect to schematic form, the Oksana and "everyday" material create a two-phase, non-tonic introduction. The devil's theme of scurrying sixteenth notes in B-flat launches an allegro at m. 63, followed by Vakula's contrasting lyrical theme in F. This is followed by an extended development (mm. 148–83), a recapitulation (beginning at m. 184) in which Vakula's theme *does* recur, and finally, a coda in which trumpets grandly state the Dikanka theme, accompanied by full orchestra, *strumming the balalaika* at full volume. (Note: Score references will be found in the full score: *Works*, vols. 7a and 7b.)

21. The snowstorm (Act 1, no. 2) is the concluding number of the first tableau. In Gogol's story, the devil causes a natural disturbance merely to keep Oksana's father at home, where he could prevent Vakula from seeing her. After the devil of the opera states his intentions, he invokes the winds at *maestoso* tempo, accompanied by the brasses and a string passage in octaves. The overpowering storm that follows is created through the devices of chromaticism, whistling piccolo, and Tchaikovskian submetrical modulation.

22. The conflicting emotions register most strongly in the ensemble sections of the Act 2 finale (no. 15), when Vakula's sad parting duet with Oksana in E-flat minor is interrupted by interjections from the strolling carolers at different tempi and veering toward different keys (e.g., mm. 41–44).

23. The scene beside the frozen river (Act 3, nos. 16–17) was Tchaikovsky's invention, providing him the opportunity to have *his* Vakula give vent to abject despair, after overhearing the sad lament of the *rusalki*. After singing his romance in E minor, Vakula outwits the devil and wins his trip to St. Petersburg. Asafyev has registered his objection to a moment of triumph announced by the hackneyed—and here anachronistic—device of a brass fanfare.

24. Vakula's visit to St. Petersburg is spread over nos. 18–23 of Act 3, most of them dominated by the meters and rhythmic gestures of the period dances that Asafyev names. The technique of allowing the plot to unfold against the background of a dance set would be further explored in *Onegin* and, of course, the ballets.

25. Act 4 consists merely of two numbers: the first is a duet-romance in A minor, the second a multisectional finale. The flow of town life is evoked through considerable use of chorus and many tempo changes.

26. Asafyev has confused two singers. Tchaikovsky credited not the soprano Pavlovskaya, but the contralto Elizaveta Lavrovskaya (1845–1919), with suggesting an *Onegin* project.

27. Cf. Asafyev's speculation over the main distinction of Russian opera in Chapter 5, pp. 51–52.

28. Actually he did have more to say, both at the end of the chapter and in the monograph that he wrote in 1942, entitled *Evgeny Onegin: An Essay on the Intonational Analysis of the Style and Musical Dramaturgy*, which can be considered a belated sequel to his chapter on *The Queen of Spades*.

29. The boyarina Morozova (mother of the protagonist Andrei) tells her son how she came to despise Prince Zhemchuzny in Act 2, no. 8 of *The Oprichnik*.

30. Joan of Arc's first extended solo number (Act 1, no. 7) is a romance in D minor. It is not clear what evidence other than the subject matter caused Asafyev to consider this song to be a pastorale.

31. The hymn "Almighty God, you are our protection" (Act 1, no. 6) expands in typical grand opera fashion from a first strophe sung by the lone voice of the heroine to a subsequent strophe in which all the assembled forces contribute.

32. Asafyev objects here to the conventionally conceived duet in A flat (Act 4, no. 22, "O wonderful sweet dream") for Joan and her English lover Lionel, in which the doomed pair trade melodic phrases and lines of text.

33. True, there is no "Letter Scene." However, an emotional transformation is laconically accomplished in the through-composed arioso that precedes the love duet.

34. The observation about the juxtaposition of large planes of color could have served Asafyev as a point of departure for demonstrating how Tchaikovsky's work differs from the French grand operas that clearly inspired it. If the use of a town-square assembly and an execution as act conclusions confirm the Western influence, elsewhere—e.g., in the march of Act 3 and the prelude to Act 4—the contrasting planes of color emerge from the orchestral choirs in passages reminiscent of the composer's kind of dramatic overture (e.g., *The Storm, Romeo and Juliet, Hamlet*, etc.).

35. A brief synopsis of this unfamiliar work will help the reader to grasp Asafyev's point. Mazeppa, the seventy-year-old Cossack chieftain, has fallen in love with Maria, the young daughter of a regional hetman (Kochubei), his friend. The father's opposi-

tion leads to a quarrel between the two, a threat, and then Kochubei's arrest, torture, and execution. The love of the young Cossack Andrei for Maria is a further complication. He dies in her arms at the end of the opera but she, having lost her mind, cannot fully return the love he expresses. Asafyev is correct that the unfolding tragedy cannot be viewed as the result of Maria's actions. After eloping with Mazeppa, she does nothing more to advance the plot.

36. The painting "Morning of the Execution of the Streltsy" (1881), by Vasily Surikov, depicts one day in the ghastly protracted series of public executions of 1698, in which Tsar Peter himself would eventually serve as executioner. The tsar, the Preobrazhensky Guards, and a tumbled mass of the condemned prisoners and their families stand out against a gray autumnal haze. The execution of the hetman Kochubei and his friend Iskra takes place in Act 3, nos. 13–14. The drunken Cossack who enters the action to sing and dance in a disconcertingly jovial G major (No. 14, m. 114ff.) is the *skomorokh* for this opera.

37. In other words, key events of the interfamilial conflict are depicted in operatic present time. Thus, e.g., the aforementioned quarrel occurs in Act 1, no. 6 (which is actually named "Quarrel Scene"); Kochubei's wife's pleading in no. 7; and daughter Maria's siding with Mazeppa in no. 8, which can be considered the high point of this finale to the first act.

38. Asafyev is here mentioning the main highlights of Acts 2 and 3. The torturer Orlik demands the location of Kochubei's treasure; in his romance (no. 9, mm. 214–81), the hetman names the three "treasures" that he values most: his honor, daughter, and God's vengeance. The revelation of Maria's mother of Kochubei's torture at the behest of Mazeppa (no. 12) is too much for the daughter to process after her preceding love scene with Mazeppa. A crowd scene followed by the execution concludes Act 2. A symphonic tableau depicting the Battle of Poltava serves as a prelude to Act 3; Maria's lullaby concludes Act 3 and the opera.

39. After the death of Andrei, Maria resumes the lullaby that she began while he was singing a last farewell; it is a lullaby better suited to a child, not to the grown man in her arms.

40. Indeed, Tchaikovsky was not one to shirk from the sure-fire effect of high, shrill winds; hammer-stroke chords in the brass; and dissonant, chromatically inflected scalar counterpoint when the situation warranted them—as this disturbing scene in his most blood-soaked opera certainly did.

41. The meter of the chorus "I weave my garland" (Act 1, no. 1) is 5/4, not 7/4.

42. The rhythmic energy flags most in the more lyrical and repetitive central section (No. 4, mm. 150–214).

43. Simply put, there are fewer independently conceived set pieces in *Mazeppa*. Thus, e.g., the part of the drunken Cossack (Act 2, no. 13) is overlaid onto a choral scene, as the crowd awaits Kochubei's execution.

44. Ippolit Shpazhinsky (1848–1917) was a dramatist renowned for the rapid and effective unfolding of melodramatic plots. The working relationship was complicated after the writer's wife confided to a deeply sympathetic Tchaikovsky that her husband intended to leave her, without guaranteeing her sufficient means to support herself and their children.

45. [Author's note:] As would later become clear, the handing over of the role of the Enchantress to Pavlovskaya was an unforgivable blunder on the composer's part; and it is apparent that the utter inability of this singer to realize this central character as Tchaikovsky conceived her would serve as the main cause for the cold indifference on the part of the public and musicians for an opera that is so remarkable in many respects. By my reckoning, the recitatives of the Enchantress herself, for example, have yet to be declaimed as they must.

46. Letter to Emilia Pavlovskaya, 12/24 April 1885. Source: Tchaikovsky, *Lit. proizvedeniia*, v. 13, Letter No. 2685.

47. Asafyev's dates can be confirmed in Tchaikovsky's correspondence. The opera was completed in May 1887.

48. Act 1 begins with two numbers designated *narodnaya stsena* [scène populaire], but the chorus remains active as well in the remaining five numbers.

49. The drama of Act 2, which centers on the family of Prince Nikita, Princess Yevpraksiya, and their son Prince Yuri, is indeed unfolded mainly in arioso duet dialogue.

50. Responding to the request of the tavern denizens, Nastasya sings the folkish, strophic song "To gaze from Nizhny," which preserves the modal flatted sevenths, melismas, and flexible phrase lengths of lyrical Slavic folk songs. The tempo *andante sostenuto*, the long-held cadential tones, fermati, and tremolo would all contribute to an impression of boundless vistas.

51. Spurred on by the aged puritanical deacon Mamyrov, Prince Nikita and a delegation from the town arrive (in Act 1, no. 6) at Nastasya's tavern, intending to shut it down. By the end of no. 6, Nastasya has convinced the prince to relent; by the end of no. 7, Mamyrov has been commanded by the infatuated prince to dance—an insult that he will not forget.

52. The threat of violence emerges in Act 3, no. 15, when Nastasya rebuffs and resists Prince Nikita's now impatient advances. Asafyev maintains that the death of Nastasya by either her own or the prince's hand at this point would have lacked the degree of tragic depth that the postponed death had.

53. [Author's note:] Apparently, for Tchaikovsky, the meaning (the essential significance) of this concept is revealed in the most intense disclosure of her life force when it encounters any *opposing* element—in this case, with hatred.

54. Asafyev has returned again to Act 1, no. 4, equating the calm and beauty of the landscape with Nastasya's spirit.

55. The through-composed arioso, "Where are you, my heart's desire" (Act 4, no. 20, mm. 35–68), is unquestionably in a different style than the first act's "To gaze from Nizhny." Beginning with gentle falling thirds in 9/8 meter, it acquires tragic power through chromaticism, sequencing, and astonishing dynamic contrasts, including a crescendo through six dynamic levels on high B.

56. Asafyev refers to three different demonstrations of Nastasya's "enchantment": (1) her enchanting (if not actually supernatural) and typically solicitous interactions with the tavern crowd (Act 1, nos. 2–4); (2) her beguiling of Prince Nikita in Act 1, no. 6 (mm. 60–165); and (3) her transformation of the hatred that her beloved initially feels for her (out of sympathy for the betrayal of his mother by his father) into love, developed in greater length in Act 3, no. 17.

57. Foka (Nastasya's father) exits at the end of Act 3, no. 16 (m. 101). The shared, untexted gaze (20 mm. in length) begins in No. 17 at m. 30.

58. [Author's note:] The exceptionally stunning talent of Chaliapine lies in this ability to declaim—to enliven a seemingly lifeless phrase. We need only recall the renowned "seducer" in *Faust* and also the flower incantations; "Roll the wine casks!" in *Prince Igor;* "Ah, evil death" in *Boris;* the addresses of Eremka in *Power of the Fiend,* etc.

59. Yuri declaims the phrase in no. 17. Thereafter (mm. 322ff.) he attempts, without success, to leave Nastasya.

60. Letter to Pavlovskaya, 21 Sep. / 2 Oct., 1887, *Lit. proizvedeniia,* v. 15, Letter No. 3361.

61. Dargomyzhsky's *Rusalka* (1848–1855), unlike his *Stone Guest,* is a numbers opera. Nevertheless, Asafyev draws attention to the expressive arioso writing that frames the set pieces.

62. Score location: Act 3, no. 17, mm. 400ff.

63. Asafyev's main point in this extended comment on the aesthetic controversy over how the composers of Russia choose to transcribe, harmonize, and arrange Russian (and other) folk songs is to deny final authority to any one approach. As he rightly notes, Tchaikovsky's eclectic approach informed by pan-European common practice cannot be assumed to be the result of his training at Rubinstein's conservatory. He alludes to Ivan Prach's early 18th-century harmonizations as the first of several likely precedents. A more extensive discussion of Prach's style can be found in Margarita Mazo's introduction to the facsimile edition of the Lvov & Pratch anthology: Lvov and Prach, *A Collection of Russian Folk Songs,* ed. Malcolm Brown (Ann Arbor: UMI Research Press, 1987): 64–76. [Author's note:] I am not speaking of song in general, which permeates all of Russian music and is the essence of its melos, but of the transformation of Russian song that is characteristic of one or another epoch.

64. [Author's note:] No one ever maimed a song on purpose. They thought they were reproducing it as it really was. One needs to read the prefaces to the anthologies of Prach and Stakhovich to be convinced how they prized the uniqueness of Russian song. But the infection of "Europeanisms" is so great that Serov, after having established in his article the "Russian style" and scolded Balakirev, committed in his operas only God knows how many absurdities. Balakirev himself provided his songs with accompaniments that had nothing in common with them, but were attractive with respect to the "dressing up" of song with contemporary pianism, just as A. Lyadov dressed it up in splendid orchestral colors from the standpoint of the "Russian style" that was contemporaneous with him. But all of this should be accepted without any certainty and represent only the continuous evolution of a national style's formation, which is not and cannot be limited to any single true point.

65. The main melodic phrase from "To gaze from Nizhny," with its characteristic ornament and half-cadence, is developed in the first part of the orchestral introduction. The vaulting leaps by a fourth or seventh in the *skomorokhi* dance (Act 1, no. 7c) beginning at m. 184.

66. Asafyev refers to three set-piece romances involving either Prince Nikita or his son: (1) the duet "God grant us bliss in life" (Act 2, no. 9); (2) the duet "I have lost

control" (Act 3, no. 15); and (3) the duet "When you calmed the anger in my soul" (Act 3, no. 17, mm. 426–536).

67. [Author's note:] I refer to the dramatic (theatrical) line within his artistic path, not the instrumental-symphonic one.

68. [Author's note:] Where many characters over a brief span, together with weak lyrical moments, which make for a faltering fundamental line.

• 15 •

The Queen of Spades

1

 $\mathscr{T}$ here is a strange Russian city. Inside it one can only dream of light, of life in all its magnificent beauty. When spring arrives, perhaps no one is more enraptured than the people of this imperial city. Timid, gentle, and fragile, it forebodes its brief existence at the moment of birth. And they who sing of spring already suffer for it. The white night, which arrives with spring, is poisoned with this suffering. The strange reflected light wearies, allures, and beckons; when the sun rises, the people no longer have the strength to rejoice in it: they have spent themselves in the process of drawing nigh to the light.

A suffering for spring and a languid, inexplicable attraction to fleeting forms—this is one sphere of moods. But in the wintry twilight and reflected light of this city's summer nights still other sentiments are engendered: the sensation of illusiveness and impermanence in all things and hence an intense curiosity for the process of destruction and death: destruction and death, not as natural laws of transformation, but rather on their own account, as if they existed for the sake of their own personal pleasure. The fantastic forms created here inevitably take on the semblance of frighteningly real phantoms, whereas real images are distorted into delusions. Maintaining equilibrium among them is difficult for one who senses that everything seen is merely appearance or for one who is predisposed to the charms of the irrational. Where [Dostoyevsky's] tale "Bobok"[1] is possible, there it is senseless to have a child's immediate acceptance of life. Even jokes and laughter are turned to derision and malicious joy.

Tchaikovsky's art is strangely connected with Petersburg and steeped in its moods. The languor of Petersburg's white nights is reflected as nowhere else

189

in Tchaikovsky's lyricism, while the fantastic coloration and humor, which stand out so in his music, are akin to the moods in the Petersburg stories of Pushkin, Gogol, and Dostoyevsky. No wonder. If Petersburg's literary art brought to life personages and visages such as the Bronze Horseman, the heroes of "The Overcoat," "The Nose," and "Portrait," and the *dramatis personae* of Dostoyevsky's "portrait gallery," so, too, Petersburg's music could not help transforming its horror and mystical spectrality into real *sounds* never heard before. And whosoever among the creatively gifted makes contact with Petersburg, even when not native to it, cannot escape the Petersburg influence. With regard to composers, Petersburg inspired Glinka but corrupted his creative instincts, relentlessly driving his healthy, sunny outlook into pessimism. Dargomyzhsky was the first to incarnate in music both the monstrous images from the "underground" world of Petersburg and the laughter: the bilious, mocking laughter of the "droll story."[2] In this city, Musorgsky progressed to the cycles *Sunless* and the [*Songs and*] *Dances of Death*, having failed with *The Sorochintsy Fair*.[3] The humor of the tragedian Musorgsky (like Dargomyzhsky's) found inexhaustible material in the life of this city of clerks with its distorted, emaciated everyday existence.

Borodin, Balakirev, and Rimsky-Korsakov were agents, but Tchaikovsky was the historian of Petersburg. How interesting that the rhythms of his musical humor are closely related to Dargomyzhsky's phantasms; his influence on Tchaikovsky, particularly in this realm, is beyond doubt. The sinister orchestral coloration, achieved thanks to a unique exploitation of timbres and the fragmented lines of woodwind rhythms (especially bassoons and clarinets), could arise within Tchaikovsky only under impressions of a distorted reflection of vitality and the monstrous phantasmagoria of Petersburg. No wonder that the subject of *Queen of Spades* would summon up a vivid influx of pitch shapes and rhythms in the composer's imagination, to be enveloped in quite specific harmonies and coloration. The scene in the countess's bedchamber, the scene in the barracks, the scene at the Winter Canal: it is all Petersburg with its hypnosis of irrationality, its augury, and incantations. An element here is taking revenge on human will and consciousness, never to forgive imperious Peter, who in defiance and spite of it raised the capital of Russia—this promontory that plunged into Europe. So many times, in returning the Neva to Petersburg, in forcing her to flow back, this element restlessly tried to sink the hated city, but in vain. Now Petersburg culture cannot be stricken from the history of Russia and humanity. In this culture, music might well play the dominating role. And within music, it is Tchaikovsky's works, imbued with the illusions of the Petersburg white nights and the contrasts of winter that have naught to do with color: black barrels, a snowy veil, and the pressing weight of granite masses, opposing the sharp definition of wrought-iron railing. Having likened Petersburg to a promontory sending Russia forth into Europe, I must extend the analogy: Tchaikovsky's music was for Europe another such advancing promontory. It brought foreigners to Russian music and established its influence in the West.

The characteristic line of Tchaikovsky's melos is a scale of pitches descending gradually or with a gentle break, usually from the third scale degree to the dominant (the main motive of Lensky's aria and the second theme of the first movement of the Sixth Symphony exemplify this).[4] Sometimes this motion is varied or disguised (the Introduction to *Onegin*; "By night or by day" in Liza's aria; the solo oboe in the opening motive of the second movement of the Fourth Symphony; the turn in Manfred's theme, etc.[5]), but the essence remains the same: a submission to fate. An upsurge (Lensky's arioso, "I love you") or point of stability (the secondary theme of the overture *Romeo*) also does not change matters: the fundamental tendency always retains the upper hand.

Not created for struggle, but feeling inside himself a sweet (Tyutchevian[6]) enticement toward chaos and the temptation to tear down the "normalities" of life, Tchaikovsky overcame this paradox within through agonizing heartache [*toska*]. A lyrical impulse dictated meek characters to him who would not face the struggle of the "doomed" ones: Juliet, Tanya, Maria, the Enchantress, Liza, Joan of Arc. A tragic impulse elicited the first movement of the Fourth Symphony, extending on from Lensky to Hermann. Composing *The Queen of Spades* "without knowing what he'd done," Tchaikovsky laid bare in the juxtaposition of Liza and Hermann the essential inclination of his inner self: an "ill-fatedness" and, as a result, a fascination with death. Being in love with life and nature (human culture he probably did not notice, since he practically never wrote of it and thought about it little), for the entire middle period in his lifetime he greedily clung to life, even to the glory of life's mundane side; but by the end of the 1880s, he had yielded to the process of self-destruction. The *Queen of Spades* is the beginning of this process, the Sixth Symphony the final end. The forces of life were exhausted. Weeping hysterically over Hermann (after completing the sketches to *The Queen of Spades*[7]), and afraid of summoning up the ghost of the Hag in his own imagination, he struggled on with the remains of the life force that had not yet rotted away in his soul. By first creating the character Hermann and impulsively including him in a circle of experiences inescapably closing in toward death, and then, with a kind of voluptuous delight, connecting the fate of Hermann both with Liza's tender maidenly countenance (an example of his meek and tender lyricism, so dear to us) and also with the character of the Hag (presenting his mystical terrors, his lack of faith that life is more powerful than death), Tchaikovsky sang for his own egress. Terrifying is his music, and blasphemous and seductive, especially for those who believe in the idea of resurrection, in eternal spring, in the triumph of love and creative energy. Tchaikovsky expended a colossal creative energy toward the gradual surrendering of himself to the *grave*. Sorrow is at the heart of his melos. Not without a fight could he give himself up. With good reason did he so love lilies-of-the-valley and his *Snow-Maiden*.[8] And if the tragic element of *Queen* and the Sixth Symphony is prized by dint of that gravitation toward destruction, then in all of his preceding work those characteristics are to be valued wherein he still shows a faith in life, giving his blessing to it, while clinging to happiness and the radiant sun. But he managed this only with effort, as did Dostoyevsky.

Music is a fearsome elemental force: its rhythms, if obedient and subdued, allow themselves to be combined so that both a music wholly abstract (sister to mathematics in the Middle Ages) and a music of the familiar, everyday world are conceivable. Yet in the abstract structures, the temptation toward psychologism creeps in from time to time, while in the rhythms of everyday music, even dance and salon music, a hypnotic seduction and rhythmic sorcery are always concealed within, plunging a person into frightening whirlpools of ecstasy: this is exemplified in the apparently innocent formula of the waltz with its head-spinning rhythm, which burst forth in an epoch that was historically assumed to be reactionary (that of the Holy Alliance) but is psychologically understood to be an epoch in which the long-lasting tense conditions of previous years were forgotten. . . .

During the epoch of Romanticism, when people bored with the commonplace allowed the forces of chaos to penetrate into the intellect's realm, the rhythms of music also became oracles of the irrational. Woe to the composer who, having summoned them, cannot control them. Schumann's insanity exemplifies this. On the other hand, if the struggle is sustained, a triumph will grant an inexhaustible supply of sounds never before used and a powerful shift in creative energy. Such was Wagner, triumphant in resisting the pull toward chaos (*Tristan* to *Meistersinger* to *Parsifal*). In Russia, Tyutchev's feat is analogous; while in the musical realm, Scriabin's tragic breakdown harbors something Schumannesque.[9] Tchaikovsky had an affinity for the language of Schumann. Many of the most characteristic lines in Tchaikovsky's melos emanate from Schumann. The pull toward the unseen and transitory, toward the force of chaos, toward "conversations with the kingdom of the dead" was innate to Tchaikovsky, but his organism was incapable of struggle. Hence the growing, grief-stricken premonition of death and destruction: he knew that if he set out impetuously toward an encounter with the irrational, the end would be near. Thus, while creative work for him meant the exhaustive utilization of his compositional gift (Tchaikovsky was a musician in full, to the marrow of his bones), his *life's* goal was to delay the advance of life forces toward insanity; from this emerged the task of adapting to the conditions of life. The middle period of creativity in Tchaikovsky's life—from after *Onegin* and the Fourth Symphony up until *The Queen of Spades*—is just such a postponement of the encounter with death. How characteristic that after *Onegin*, Tchaikovsky was so powerfully drawn to *Romeo and Juliet*. It seemed that this was the natural path for his lyrical impulse. But out of an instinct for self-preservation, he fled from this subject, extending for ten more years (from 1880 to 1890) the possibility of creating, winning back his own life but diluting somewhat the creative juices. So strong was the return to life that, as late as 1889, he could still create a *Sleeping Beauty*, wherein sinister rhythms gleam only in the prologue;[10] moreover, in 1888, in response to a suggestion from his brother Modest Ilyich, Tchaikovsky categorically rejected the subject of *The Queen of Spades*, which did not move him ("I'd be writing it any which way").[11]

And suddenly, something transpired in the soul of the composer that brought him to the music one hears in *The Queen of Spades* and the Sixth Symphony. As a result, the creative history of *The Queen of Spades* is psychologically interesting in the extreme. He began the opera on 19 January 1890 in Florence, and on 30 January in a letter to Glazunov would confess: "I am experiencing a very perplexing stage on the path to the grave. Something is coming about inside me that I myself do not comprehend. A certain fatigue from life, a disappointment: at times, an insane melancholy, but not one in whose depths there is a vision of a new rush of love for life, but rather something bereft of hope, akin to a finale, and even, as is characteristic of finales, *banal*. Yet all the while a terrible desire to compose. The devil knows what it is! On the one hand, I feel as if my own brief song is sung, on the other—this insurmountable longing to spin out either this very life, or an even better new song."[12] On 14 February he wrote to his brother: "I am already finishing the second tableau; as soon as you send the third (the ball), I will set to it. If the work progresses just as it has gone up to now—one can hope that I can actually finish on time. Whether it's coming out good or bad, I do not know. Sometimes I am quite satisfied, sometimes not—but I am not the judge."[13] And thus no analysis of the subject at all! In 1888, a simple "don't want to." Now something more realistic and sober: "I may finish on time." And earlier yet, in a letter to von Meck from Petersburg and Moscow (17–25 December 1889), one finds this communiqué: "Now it has been nearly three weeks for me of not doing anything in Petersburg. I say *doing nothing,* since I consider my true business to be composition, and all of my labors, such as directing concerts, attending ballet rehearsals, etc., are somewhat incidental, without a purpose, and only shorten my time. . . . I decided to refuse all invitations from home and abroad and go away for four months to some place in Italy, in order to relax and work on my upcoming *opera*. I selected as a subject for this opera Pushkin's *The Queen of Spades*. It happened in the following way. Three years ago, my brother Modest commenced to write a libretto on the subject of *Queen of Spades* at the request of a certain Klenovsky . . . but in the end, the latter declined to compose the music, for some reason, did not accomplish his task. Meanwhile, Vsevolozhsky, the Director of [Imperial] Theaters, was captivated by the idea of my composing an opera on this very subject and, in addition, that it most definitely be for the coming season. He expressed this wish to me, and since it accorded with my decision to flee Russia in January in order to occupy myself with composition, I agreed . . . I so much want to work, and, if successful in settling into a comfortable nook somewhere abroad,—it seems to me that I can manage my assignment, toward May shall present a piano reduction to the Directorate, then in the summer shall orchestrate it."[14]

Thus, on the one hand a yearning for work; and on the other, a subject that had come his way due to Vsevolozhsky's insistence; and finally, a desire to fulfill the commission on time. Like Mozart, Tchaikovsky preferred working toward a deadline, with urgency, and he also liked to be goaded and pressed. Concerning the subject itself, the substance of the entire affair, he is silent; and only from a letter to Glazunov do we learn of Tchaikovsky's spiritual state in connection with the material at hand and the actual work on it.[15] It is likely that he himself did not ponder over an analysis of the subject. A subject as such concerned him little: for him it was simply a means—more properly, one of several means—of realization, but not at all the main content, just like the countless Madonna subjects used by Raphael. But this time chance suggested the thread precisely suited for a *subject* dictated by the inner mood (guiding the creation of worthy artistic objects and shaping their creative purpose) and the spiritual *core* of the composer. Had another sort of subject appeared, we would have had an opera in which some moments or others that coincided with a desire that came from the heart would be entirely successful, while the remaining ones would be empty voids. Indeed this is what occurred with *Onegin:* Lensky and Tatyana are everything, while Onegin himself does not exist. In *Queen of Spades* there was a complete accord between the externally provided material and the psychological content of the given moment of life, and an accumulation of creative energy attaining a powerful level of tension. In a word, a most ideal harmony. No wonder that as a result, *Queen of Spades* was finished with astonishing rapidity.

The gradual progress of composition cannot only be denoted in detail according to dates but can also be followed in the sketches, which have been preserved in full, day by day, beginning with the earliest pencil jottings. Tchaikovsky started working on 19 January 1890 in Florence; on the 28th he finished the first tableau, from the 29th to the 4th of February, the second; from the 5th to the 11th of February, the fourth (the countess's death); from the 11th to the 19th, the third; from the 20th to the 21st, the fifth; from the 23rd to the

26th, the sixth and the introduction; from the 27th of February to the 2nd of March, the seventh; and on the 3rd of March the introduction was completed. Altogether, the sketches to the entire opera were written in 44 days. The piano reduction was produced in 22 days (March 4–26). On June 8 in Frolovsky the instrumentation was completed (with a two-week break). All the work on the opera lasted four months and twenty days.[16] Upon finishing, Tchaikovsky permitted himself, now and then, to say something about the opera. For example, in a letter to his brother, dated March 19, he said: "Either I am dreadfully mistaken or *Queen of Spades* is in fact a *chef d'oeuvre*. There are several points, for example, in the fourth tableau, which I arranged today, where I experience such fright, and dread, and shock, that it would be impossible for listeners not to feel at least something of the same."[17] With respect to the fourth tableau, he had twice beforehand communicated in letters to his brother his impression of horror. Apparently, it was the center for him as well, for it is certainly the center of the opera: psychologically, architectonically, and musically-symphonically! Concerning the entire opera, Tchaikovsky wrote to Prince Konstantin Konstantinovich: "I composed it with unprecedented fervor and enthusiasm, keenly suffering along with it and reexperiencing all that transpires in it (even to the point of fearing, for a time, the appearance of the ghost of the Queen of Spades) and I hope that all of my authorial delights, anxieties, and enthusiasms strike a chord in the hearts of responsive listeners."[18] And yet nowhere an analysis of the subject. The latter was for Tchaikovsky merely a means of expression, a vessel into which he poured the costly wine of tragic feelings that agitated his soul in his life's autumnal maturity: he would not live to see his winter, nor was he in a condition to contemplate the expiring of his creative powers.

On 7 December 1890 the opera appeared for the first time, on the stage of the Maryinsky Theater, i.e., less than one year from the moment when the creation of it began.

Entering into the analysis of *Queen of Spades*, I should say a few words about the form it will take. Originally, I had thought to divide my ideas on the creative essence, the language, and the style of the opera into two major categories: (1) the psychological foundations of the opera's style; and (2) the means by which they are realized. Beyond this, within the latter category, the texture of the work and the material would be examined with respect to the rhythmic, coloristic, dynamic, and tempo correlations and progressions, i.e., from studying the processes of sustaining, accentuation, light and shadow, intensifying and pacing: the entire *tonus* and fundamental qualities that contribute to the work's intensity and *modus vivendi*.

But it became necessary to turn away unwillingly from this method and select one that was more superficial in appearance (analysis by tableaus) but more closely dedicated in essence: otherwise there could be no revelation of the *conditions* of inner confluence, structure, and sustaining, which arise as action is developed in music and through music! Keeping in mind the somewhat complicated nature of my analysis (what a dreadful word! and how I wish that this investigation would not be taken for a formal analysis[19]) and envisioning that the broad mass of readers are not specialists, I took the risk of offering substantive conclusions, but conclusions nonetheless, i.e., the *pulp* from the juice: thus to break up and dilute the train of thought for the sake of a more perfect schema.

In order to grasp *Queen of Spades* in its crystallized aspect, in a form perceivable to the eye and tangible, i.e., as a configuration of spatial relationships, it is first necessary to perceive the pure essence of the music: as sustained in musical time, its form in the process of being created, when any chosen instant of sound is perceived as gravitating to the nearest nerve center (if it is not already such a central ganglion or a constellation of nervous impulses), uniting all within itself and conditioned by all that was created before that moment and, in turn, dictating all subsequent states. As in life, every moment is a synthesis of everything preceding and an impulse toward further processes. According to the late N. D. Kashkin,[20] Tchaikovsky—who was quite reserved in his pronouncements and rarely spoke about the inner essence of his works—once lost patience over [Hermann] Larosh's remarking that individual bits in a particular work of Tchaikovsky were good but others did not satisfy the taste and deserved to be altered. Here is the gist of the composer's reply: in his compositions, nothing was expendable, nothing could be rearranged or changed! By itself, one bit or another might not be of the highest caliber, but the entire whole develops as a tree grows and could be fixed down only after it was taken as a whole and in all of its interrelationships.

Once a certain amount of time had passed after the creation of a composition that had required a great expenditure of effort and energy, Tchaikovsky would find himself cooling toward it out of a natural nervous reaction; he would harden himself toward it, even detest it for a time, especially when he sensed any internal falseness or insincerity of expression (as occurred with *The Oprichnik*, with *Swan Lake*, and even with the Fifth Symphony). All his life he searched for simplicity, naturalness, and brevity (he berated his *Francesca* for its exaggerated dramatic pathos of expression and exposition, in comparison with the power, strength, clarity, and laconism of Dante's tercets[21]), all his life he sought *form*. Therefore he could not help but comprehend the essence of the creative process as the growth of an organism and did not venture to approach a work with a tasteful appraisal, a fleeting and false appraisal, which distorts the meaning of the concept of *style* by substituting for it the more intellectualized *stylization*; for if style is the inner unity of expressive means and the result of a complicated process of the will, then stylization is primarily a selection, a summary of expressive means determined by *taste*.

The Queen of Spades has been berated in every way, even for being an operetta (which is evidently meant to be an extreme insult). Out of habit, we take pleasure in destroying and stamping into the mud treasures of the spirit; we cheerfully analyze and underscore the failings, but are not fond of showing respect and, therefore, of constructing, connecting, and explaining. It has been acceptable to revile Tchaikovsky because the public loved his music, because the principles and methods of his creative work do not correspond with the tasks of another epoch, with other tastes. This will always occur and it is understandable, but only on the condition that loving respect and thoughtful evaluation proceed in parallel. This has not happened. Not pretending to atone for this neglect, I would only wish, by some measure of strong effort and energy, in some small way, to give a cause and impetus for worthy future works on Tchaikovsky, which if they be less high-strung and of a greater perspicacity than I myself, will fulfill the task of studying the language, style, and forms of this great composer's music.

2

The *Introduction* to the opera is structured quite compactly and laconically as a symbol of the connection between the important themes, which stems from the initial motive of Tomsky's ballade. As in Pushkin, it is this ballade, this "anecdote" that has aroused the storm and enchained Hermann, Liza, and the Hag in a mutual pact. After the vague aura of expectation in the opening bars, the threatening motive of the three cards enters.[22] The nervous pulsation of the rhythm, in whose background the progressive growth and development of the Hag's theme[23] are discernible, emanates from the appearance of this motive. The tension leads to a powerful dynamic explosion; it is then followed by the emergence of the beautiful, flowing, and enticing theme of love for Liza,[24] which for a while overshadows the Hag's ghost, serving as an excellent introduction to the first act and finding its psychological closure at the end of the second tableau of this act (in the finale's ecstatic love).

I shall now comment on the development of the drama as given in the music, excluding the setting (the everyday realities).[25] In the *first tableau* there are three nerve centers around which the action is concentrated and brought to a head: the appearance of the countess (the quintet "I am frightened"), Tomsky's ballade (a worldly-wise anecdote, related by chance, which becomes a trap for Hermann), and the storm (the scene in which Hermann's ideas are summed up and a decision comes to fruition).[26] Nevertheless, it is the ballade that serves as the center. In it the connection between the musical representation of the countess and the motive of the three cards appears for the first time, which engenders in Hermann an association of images from which he cannot escape. The quintet and all that has prepared it gravitate toward the ballade. Out of the ballade comes the storm scene with its impressive "confirmation" of the motive of the three cards.

Thus, the dramatic action is entangled with the appearance of Hermann.[27] His thoughts show a preoccupation with the image of Liza ("I do not know her name"). Tomsky's questions serve as the impulse for Hermann's lyrical effusions: the rhythm of profound contemplative content is exchanged for impulsive, goal-directed movement. Faltering breath. Nervous pulsation. Little by little, Hermann takes control of his imaginings, the image of the beloved girl is drawn more realistically, and the arioso concludes with rapturous aspiration at full volume toward the desired ideal; the originating rhythmic line, while in essence remaining unchanged, is developed with respect to an expansion in range and an increase in the intensity of the sound.

The further development of the dialogue leads to a new, impulsive outburst of feeling ("You do not know me!"[28]) and a bolstering of dynamics, yet still the musical essence is rhythmically unchanged: the basic motive, the same descending scale of tones, is quite characteristic for this stage of Hermann's experiences (passive surrender of the self to a passion). An upsurge emerges only with thoughts of a possible death, should the dream not be realized ("when I learn that I am not fated to possess her"). It is necessary to observe that the spread of death and Hermann's being fated to it are already audible in the drama's prologue, even before the moment of entanglement and the crisscrossing of paths. The prince's appearance multiplies the anxious premonitions in the soul of Hermann.[29] The canonic design of the two rivals' duet is quite interesting: the melodic structure of the lines is nearly identical but the metrical difference is tremendous. In the rhythm of the prince's lines, ascent and holding at a steady point predominate. In Hermann's rhythm the same line takes on another character: there are sharp, shorter ascents; a moderate tarrying at a point of rest; and a rapid, rolling motion downward, i.e., again a submission, a surrender of the self.[30] This rhythm well prepares and explains Hermann's agitation at the sight of the countess with Liza. The countess's theme[31]—an ascending sequence of anapests—for now, prior to Tomsky's ballade, has no significance in Hermann's life and therefore passes by in an instant. The nervous rhythmic pulsation in the orchestra summons up for Hermann the frightful awareness of the loss of Liza ("She is his bride!") and not of meeting the countess. But here the logical development of the action is sharply interrupted; in its place an irrational element enters: a premonition of misfortune.[32]

The appeal and powerful impact of opera doubtless are rooted in its giving occasion for the free use of such a highly expressive stylistic device as the unexpected appearance of a mystical power not subject to the mind.[33] In drama, either the *word* must describe the spreading of invisible forces in concepts or this spreading must be materialized into some type of image. In an opera, music achieves a transubstantiation of hidden mystery with such conviction that the visible truth of ordinary life becomes invisible, whereas the truth that is felt and grasped by instinct brightly shines, like the stars in heaven at the sun's eclipse. The quintet ("I am frightened!") is a sinister *static* moment when all participants of a *future* dramatic collision seem to be transported inside a well-marked implacable circle, from which they will be denied an exit. There is no thematic development in the quintet, for it is not an action, but only a *state of being*.[34] The ensuing action is conditioned by the already established fact of the premonition; from this it emanates. The dialogue of the countess and Tomsky is an elaboration of her misgivings. The prince's address to Liza proceeds against the background of an agonizing motive of moaning: the presentiments are the same. A thunderclap confirms Hermann's gloomy prophecy. Such a languid agglomeration of mournful thoughts and presentiments resulting from a riddle that was introduced due to the interference in the action of an irrational force, one which anticipates the course of events, eventually receives its explanation and resolution in Tomsky's ballade. A predominant E-minor triad enters in the capacity of a harmonic synthesis of all the preceding.[35] The melos of the ballade almost never steps beyond the limits of this tonality. This results in an organic correlation between the nerve centers of this scene: B minor for the introduction, quintet—F# minor, ballade—E minor, and a concluding scene that again leads to B minor [36] ("Thunder, lightning!"), that is: [b ——f# ——e ——b].

Tomsky's ballade gradually unveils the rich thematic potential of the countess's sequences, based on which her figure becomes more and more dominating. Hermann's thoughts begin to transfer from Liza to the countess, and suddenly there arises an association that Tchaikovsky discovered by instinct: the motive of the dream of Liza ("I do not know her name") nearly coincides with the ballade's refrain: "Three cards, three cards, three cards."[37] In Hermann's excited imagination, an abrupt shift is made: a reverie about possessing Liza becomes one with the greedy desire to uncover the names of the three cards. The *idée fixe* is born, the entanglement of the drama completed. Hermann has fallen into a death trap. The ensuing romantic storm scene develops and confirms the emerging idea amid the turbulence of nature. Hermann's prophetic oath ("She shall be mine . . . or I will die") is the perfect cadence that seals the entanglement.

Second Tableau. Under the enchantment of a crazy idea, Hermann will naturally dream of acquainting Liza with it. Passion for the girl is linked inside him with solving the perplexing secret of the cards. These are two sides of the same intense pulling toward destruction. Depending on the circumstances, Hermann shows first one, then the other side to the audience. The scene with Liza is inundated with the passion of love. At the ball, there is an imbalance: an oscillation. During the scene in the countess's bedchamber, the other side is brought out—and from then on to the end, to the delirium preceding his death, Hermann remains in the power of the Queen of Spades. The second tableau (at Liza's) is remarkably well constructed. Strictly speaking, the musical development commences with the phrase in the *cor anglais* (a motive from the aria "Whence these tears?").[38] Everything that precedes is a scene from the everyday world. In the present case, however, this sojourn in everyday realities is unquestionably necessary to balance the high-strung atmosphere of the preceding tableau, wherein the interference of an unseen evil force had already delivered everything visible, all of life's ordinary equilibrium, over to the power of the irrational. This everyday tableau is also important for another reason: the inveigling of the maidenly Liza into the whirlwind of passion is yet to come. Will she go willingly or does a struggle lie ahead? Furthermore: if she does become involved, will she plunge into ruin by inertia or hold firm? As the world surrounding Liza unfolds before the listener in a scene of intimate girlish merrymaking, the music nevertheless mirrors Liza herself and does so with such keen perception, that even prior to the moment when the inner countenance of the girl bares itself in a languid response to her tears and in a passionate hymn to the night, it becomes clear that the fruit has ripened, that there will be no resistance and that Liza is doomed.

This is achieved through sharp contrasts in musical moods, thanks to which peaceful, idyllic, everyday reality becomes frightening and disturbing. According to appearances, life here is passing by naturally and contentedly: a pastoral duet gives the impression of a quiet spring evening; thereafter Polina's romance in a sentimental style; an impassioned Russian [folk] dance and governess's scolding.[39] But appearance is deceiving. The pastoral mood that opens the scene is the premise that Liza is obligated to maintain. Polina's innocent romance already presents an abrupt juxtaposition: G major (3/4), through E minor to E-flat minor (4/4), thus destroying the illusion. Any such abrupt motion away from the center elicits a reverse tendency toward the restoration of equilibrium: the tempo, coloration, meter (2/4), and dynamics of the Russian dance *nervily* shift the mood, but the initial calm is not regained: the governess's "minuet" (again a tonal shift: from A major in the dance to E-flat major) is only a misty curtain, which serves to hide the "simple change of scenery."[40] Thus the abrupt tonal shifting, the jumps in tempo, the changeability of coloration—the entire style of the everyday music does not express well-being. But as I have already said, the interrupted development of the action commences only with Liza's monologue. Her mood is at first communicated by the orchestra; gradually it becomes clearer, more stable, and more defined, eventually to be transformed into the sound of the human voice and words (with the aria "Whence these tears?"). Nonetheless this music is still not a declaration but a *question*. Maidenly shyness and shame prevent Liza, even when alone with herself, from being fully conscious of the reason for her sorrow.

It is striking how the rhythm changes at the moment when Liza attempts to mesmerize herself with the thought of her husband's nobility: a full resonance, solidity, and strength in the sound momentarily replace the unsteadiness and the faltering hazy indistinctness.[41] But the question remains a question. Only the passionate inner anxiety is betrayed. Over the restrained, tender, quivering throb of thirds, the breaks in the melodic line register more strongly and sharply. At last they interrupt the flow of music (at the words "It burdens and frightens me!"). Liza has sensed that concealment is useless: "But why deceive myself?" The phrase is uttered atop a sustained altered chord with a double meaning: a double meaning, since it can lead to C minor and to C major, i.e., both to the pathos of suffering and the pathos of rapture.[42] The music chooses the latter path; and the passionate maidenly confession, this sincerest of declarations of a girl in love, takes flight, wave upon wave, in maidenhood's magnificent impulsivity, in a hymn to the white night.

This is the focal point, the central attainment of the second scene. C major was a brilliant find. It synthesizes the previous tonal instability, yet is not perceived to set a tone of sunny radiance: its whiteness is *reflected*.[43] Moreover, Tchaikovsky does everything possible to soften the coloration and dampen the wave of passion; the agitated whispering of the strings, the oboe's entreaty, and the harp's glissando establish a supple, translucent background. The crystal purity of the lyricism, the rhythm's combination of restraint and intensity, the breathtaking constant ascent in the melodic line, and the effusion of radiant sincerity, simplicity, and impulsive directness throughout the full duration and prolongation of the sound achieve a supreme level of artistic beauty. The chaste and holy regard for womanhood and the idealization of the Russian maiden have ensured in Russian art the presence of unforgettable female characters. The very manner of their revelation in literature (Gogol, Turgenev, Chekhov) could be compared with these miraculous pages of Liza's confessional address.

And yet, this is a turning point. This confession is at once the highest attainment of saintliness and a temptation. Were Hermann not to appear at this

moment, Liza could become a Tatyana: she is only capable of a feat of submission to fate, but the course of it depends on an impulse. The psychological acuity of the moment (a man in love happens upon a maiden ardently confessing a passion) is expressed in music with the benumbing of both Liza and
Hermann (a sustained sound and underneath, a sliding, flickering burst of
tremolo); it is as if the breath has stopped, frozen still (the sigh at "O night!"
is powerful, and the exhalation is held out to the utmost possibility).[44] The dialogue begins with the alternating rhythms, the tonal instability, and the faltering tracery of the accompaniment as indications of Liza's indecisiveness. Of
course, Hermann at this moment is the romantic knight of passionate love. His
addresses breathe ardent rapture. At the sight of Liza, he is consumed by her;
and from the moment when the orchestra begins to sing the motive of passionate love (F major, Moderato agitato),[45] he is transformed. In the music that
characterizes him an abrupt change is made: the major mode appears and ascending melodic lines predominate; the sighing ascent, rapture, and intensity
all hold sway over the descents; a productive, active lyricism is audible in the
gradual accumulations; a firm masculine will awakens, and in the occasional
gentle dips in the melodic line are heard again the impassioned musings of a
lover intoxicated by beauty. The strong nervous intensity elicits a reaction: a
tender, languishing entreaty ("Forgive me, celestial creature"), but even here
passionate sighs and active desire dominate.[46] In gazing at Liza, Hermann
draws in vital fluids and imbibes the air; in this moment he is youth, knight,
husband. Yet he need only hearken to the call of death to become a vampire,
sucking in his bride's blood to postpone his own demise.

The minor-key theme of the prayer is transformed into the tonality of
the white night: Liza is prepared to surrender herself (Andante mosso, C major): perhaps Hermann's rebirth might be achieved![47] But they have indeed
fallen into a hexed circle, under a bell jar, separating them from every living
thing: for the countess / Hag is with them. A knock at the door. Ominous
progressions of rising anapest sequences in thirds, the sinister coloration of
specific timbres (a mixture of clarinets and bassoons) announce the interference and onslaught of malicious and ironic deviltry: the smell of decay and
whisper of fallen leaves! The theme of the Hag, this Baba-Yaga of legend, here
rises up in little hops, there growls with scorn, there moves by menacing
leaps.[48] One can only marvel at the inventiveness of this particular flight of
Tchaikovsky's imagination: not in the letters and nowhere in reminiscences
about him are the traces of such a dread to be found.

Only the music reveals what "Hoffmannesque" monsters swarmed in his
mind and what frightful countenances and phenomena he observed in life.
The leaping theme is sometimes accompanied by the knocking of a skeletal
hand or else replaced with a persistent stamping. The icy cold seizes one dur-

ing listening and even while glancing at the score. As in the quintet of the first act, here, too, the meaning of the opera is revealed and a conception of the opera is discernible.[49] From the standpoint of operatic realism, nothing could be more trivial than such a scene: a grandmother comes to her granddaughter who is offering herself to her officer lover almost on the eve of her wedding. The lover hides himself; there follows a stern parental reprimand and then the order to go to sleep. But the music implants this scene with such "content" that it becomes impossible to dwell on the banal melodramatic situation. The Hag makes a timely arrival, as a messenger of death. Hermann senses this and, in a recitative that is overwhelming in its expressivity, laconism, and particular choice of timbres, speaks the words "Of the one who arrives, passionately in love," achieving with the words "Cold from the grave blows all around!" a maximum of horror (tremolo in the low register of the clarinets over sustained *pianissimo* chords in the trombones)!

Generally speaking, the opinion that Tchaikovsky had no mastery of timbre and that his orchestration is crude and incompetent is based on a misunderstanding or on academic pedantry, which only allows for one or more recipes for instrumentation, conceived *in abstracto*, for their own sake, apart from dramatic expressivity. The score of *Queen of Spades* deserves and, no doubt, will one day receive a special study in this regard, since the composer's mastery found therein—in the sphere of discrimination of colors and shadings that are dependent on the development of the action and the dramatic situations—presents a series of exemplary solutions to the problems of operatic instrumentation. Only a cursory regard for the monuments of art and a compulsory praising of selected works at the expense of others could encourage the obstinate ignorance and dull-witted myopia. Otherwise, the treatment of Tchaikovsky is incomprehensible. Either people have confused beauty of sound with expressivity of sound or else, because of a lack of correspondence between certain devices and personal or fashionable tastes, have negated the significance of a major artistic phenomenon.

The action that has been disrupted by the interference of the irrational (as in the first tableau) now with all the more intensity draws Liza and Hermann toward an encounter with a preordained destiny. Liza impulsively exerts all of her will to preserve her girlhood and with it her life. A *bride* up until this moment, since she had managed *not to comprehend* the full horror of her situation; now out of instinct she senses misfortune. Hermann, on the other hand, in possessing Liza, instinctively thinks to find an escape, a protection, a delay of death. The struggle is short-lived. Brief but emotional upward surges, an acceleration of the rhythms, the persistent pounding of triplets in the basses,[50] the impassioned appearance of themes, the dynamic contrasts, and the change of nuances, until a crescendo into fortissimo halts the motion—the complex psychic process, occurring in the soul of Liza. After this come the passionate exhaustion and triumph of Hermann in a sumptuous, rapturous E major: it is the third appearance of the theme of passionate entreaty, "Forgive me, celestial creature," uniting the entire course of the material in the second half of this tableau and sounding like a refrain. A highly idiosyncratic rondo!

The *third tableau*'s design is somewhat akin to that of the first: just as genre scenes there alternate with scenes that develop the plot, so, here, with yet more consistency, contrasts are established between the external visible action and the internal, with the former here dominating:

(a) Contredanse	(a) Dialogue of Surin and Chekalinsky. The prince and Liza. Hermann's monologue and hallucinations (the joking of Surin and Chekalinsky)
(b) Intermezzo: "The Faithful Shepherdess"	(b) The meeting of Hermann and the countess. Surin's scorn. *Scene with the key.*
(c) The Reception of Catherine II[51]	

It is characteristic that, as in the first tableau, the impetus influencing Hermann the most was the ballade of Tomsky, which had been related by chance (as Gershenson expressed it in an article on Pushkin's *Queen of Spades*: "An anecdote heard indifferently by others but bursting the soul of Hermann"[52]), so, in the third, the role of the "spark cast into the powder magazine" was fulfilled by the quite ordinary friendly joking of Surin and Chekalinsky, who in the midst of a masked ball's frivolity tease Hermann by slyly whispering to him snatch phrases about the cards. For Hermann's shaky will, any firm suggestion heightens the shift in the direction that *fate* desires. Therefore the course of action in the music logically develops toward a crisis in his soul, toward the thought of winning at cards. After having possessed Liza, he naturally arrives at this thought out of a desire to secure his bond with riches. An as yet unused syncopated rhythm in thirds that accompany and creep along after the nervously meandering, supple, orchestral phrase whenever Hermann appears to express his unrest introduces a marked element of contrast into the material that is developed in this tableau.[53] Hermann's music in general for this situation reveals in full the refinement of the composer's dramatic instinct, presented here with an economy of means that is unusual for him. The phrase just mentioned is continually contrasted under the most varied lights with the motive of the three cards. The doubt that troubles Hermann's brain resonates vaguely and restlessly, here rising up, there symmetrically subsiding, there solidifying into a question. In its wake, the cards' trace of a tune cuts through everything, relentlessly and insistently, still anticipated by the "limping" sequences of the countess's motive, which are combined with a scrap from the ballade ("Are you not the third?").[54] The confusion of Hermann's imagination is expressed at all times with fragmented motives and ideas, melodic phrases rendered by the orchestra, recitatives that are disjointed and, so to speak, irritable. Unrest reigns also in the rhythm: stability is nowhere to be found, other than in the importunate declarations of the sinking line of the cards' leitmotive or refrain. Relentless and horrific thought! It obsessively pursues Hermann, sometimes sounding from without, sometimes welling up from within, inside his brain; here distinctly and markedly cutting through, there coldly and mockingly squinting, and always, like a phantom, gradually dissolving and evaporating (in the bassoon's thirds, during the adagio before the *intermedio*).[55]

The mute encounter with the countess decides the matter: Surin's voice ("Look, there is your beloved!") sounds to Hermann like a mysterious sentencing. His reason and will harden into numbness: the sustained note E and the receding flicker of the strings underneath are heard to resemble the moment of Hermann's appearance before Liza in the second tableau.[56] But there it is the bright countenance of a beloved girl that arrests him, whereas here the power of an unseen force is casting a spell. Consequently, there one finds a diminuendo, but here a growth in the sound, a crescendo; it leads to *fortissimo* and to a formulaic phrase, obedient to death's call: "O, how pitiable and laughable I am!" (the phrase is quite similar to the initial motive in Lensky's aria before the duel).[57] An overpowering scene ensues.[58] Liza, aflame with passion in tremulous anticipation of the rendezvous, hands over to the nervously agitated Hermann the key to the secret door *of the countess's bedchamber.* She does not, however, notice that Hermann's thoughts have taken another course, and it is only the music that betrays the essence of the situation: the motive of passionate love that sounds in the orchestra is already shown in a patchy and perverted aspect.[59] Receiving the key to the countess's bedchamber, Hermann at last falls under the power of the idea that is hypnotizing his will: "Now not I but fate itself wills that I will know the three cards!" In response to this, the countess's sequences sound glaringly and imperatively in the trombones and trumpets: a delusion has finally captured the soul of a man.[60] The entire development of this tableau's internal musical action is built on the gradual hypnotizing of Hermann's mind. The parallelism with the external action (everyday realities) also demands its resolution: thus begins a triumphal reception for the Empress.[61]

Fourth Tableau. In the preceding tableau, the growth of the inner action proceeded intensely and logically, despite a whole series of scenes interfering with it. Now comes a moment of stasis, albeit a frightening one. The music no longer diverts the listener with tableaus drawn from everyday life, but concentrates exclusively on manifesting spiritual states; even when an everyday scene in essence is being sketched (the poor relations' greeting to their mistress), it continues by means of rhythm and coloration to establish a fundamental oppressive mood of doom, depression, and illusion.[62] Neither air, nor light! The horror of death! The quiet of the tomb, interrupted only with sighs that turn the soul to ice and the firm stamp of a *basso ostinato* ("Es muss sein").[63] It is the stubborn struggle of someone's fettered will against the laboring of the grave digger: a sensation that must be known to the one sunk into lethargy as the coffin is nailed shut; that is what sounds in the steady pizzicato of the cellos and basses. The monotonous rustling of the violas serves as the background, like a rivulet from an underground spring or like a blinding fixed idea that slays all resistance from mind and will. In this way the silence sometimes *speaks*: such is the state of the human soul given expression by Tchaikovsky in the entr'acte to the fourth tableau of *Queen of Spades*. Deep and distant, far from life, the sun, and human vanities, this terrifying music beckons. Indeed, all the preceding was merely a premonition of terror and of death, a description of the underworldly kingdom of the shades, but now its very self is here. From here there can be no escape. Up until now, the music was subject to the action and to the will of human experiences, now it is reversed: any action is the result of the condition dictated by the music. It is the herald of fate and destiny, itself the action and the realization. The countess, Hermann, and Liza are marionettes. What remains unknown is whether the countess's evil will was an active one, or whether she was merely a capacitor in which the energy[64] from the electrical charge was concentrated, from whose contact arose the current that entered into Hermann and Liza. The latter is more believable, since the countess nowhere displays her will and does not even speak with Hermann. When she attempts to defend herself, she cannot, for she is the transmitter of commands from an invisible power. The fourth tableau is the *center* of the opera. Here the drama's heroes are entangled into a mortal knot. Here Hermann and the Hag have their fateful encounter.[65]

In all there are six such encounters in the opera, and the intensity of the impressions increases from the first to the fourth tableau.[66] In the first tableau the countess merely has a presentiment of woe from a close encounter with Hermann; in the second his presence is only intuited; in the third, she is gripped in fright at the sight of the delirium that has inundated Hermann; and in the fourth, during the encounter with him, she dies, taking with her the secret. Indeed, was there a secret? Perhaps there was, but not the one that Hermann sought to uncover ("And if there is no secret at all?"). The problem of the existence of evil: this is *The Queen of Spade*'s thesis. Is it nominal or is it real? Merely the delirium of a pathological, pitiable, and as it was once acceptable to

say, *servile* human soul or else a power existing externally, outside a human being, into whose sphere a person is drawn by chance or by predisposition?
For Tchaikovsky, apparently, the solution was evident: if there is death
then there is evil. Its cold breath and clinging skeletal fingers were felt by him
all his life. In *The Queen of Spades* he brought out this sensation both intensely
and ecstatically. *The Queen of Spades* is a symphony, a cantata, and a great poem
of death. Only Musorgsky and Tolstoy can be compared—the first in his glo-
rifying of death, the second in his fear of it (hidden but beyond doubt)—to
Tchaikovsky. In the fourth tableau of *The Queen of Spades*, which provoked
dread in the composer himself, he boldly attempted to translate into music the
sensation of the reality of death's existence, imagining it for himself not as the
negation of life and not as a null and void, but as an active force, parallel with
life but acting in the opposite direction. He managed to bring it into existence,
but quite evidently with a colossal loss of life energy.[67]

Hermann's monologue proceeds against the background of the music for
the entr'acte. The scene before the countess's portrait and the joining of the
human (speaking) voice with the word all the more emphatically underscore
the meaning: the motive of the depressed sighing predominates ("By some
mysterious force, fate has joined me to her"), which in its rhythmic structure
is intimately fused with Liza's plaintive motive, "Whence these tears?"[68] There
is a clear purpose to the depressing mood: an unbreakable inner connection
between Hermann and the invisible world has been created. He is enchained:
"I should like to run away but have no strength. . . ." A rustle and a whisper
of steps are heard: against a steady background of the strings' rhythmic figure
♪♪♪ ♪♪♪, which is so typical of *The Queen of Spades*, the bassoon plays a little phrase of evil mockery.[69] Again the familiar coloration of decay and coldness with the knocking of skeletal fingers on the slab of the grave. The little
phrase is imitated by the contentious woodwinds, fussily flitting about. The
maidservants and poor relations, creeping along like shadows, greet the Hag-
countess. Cruelly and *blasphemously*, the music describes a sort of funeral
march, or else molds a fantastic "scherzo"—a bit of merry twinkling of animated ghosts or the ghostly reflection of life.[70]

The scene with Liza and the chambermaid underscores the horror of the
situation, as it *prolongs* the scene with the key at the ball: the music still sings
the motive of Hermann's passionate declaration, since Liza still does not suspect a turnabout in his consciousness.[71] Again a rustling of steps, and the procession resumes. The coloration turns yet gloomier, and again there is a wafting of a severe autumnal snowstorm scattering about dead leaves and breaking
off dry branches and twigs, as the strings slither and the woodwinds patter. But
this is still only the beginning to the crescendo of horrors and frights.

The countess's monologue—the reminiscences of a corpse—unfolds against the background of a languorous and wearied snatch of a "minuet" (bassoon, then muted violins). With the words "But who was it that used to dance?" a *sinodik* [prayer list] for deceased royalty is read out, for which corresponding timbres are selected: a stopped horn supports the psalm tone; underneath, from the depths, ribbons of clarinet trills are strung, the violins whisper a tremolo *ppp*, while pizzicato celli and bass clarinet hold fast to the rhythm. The memoirs (weird authentic memoirs of the 18th century, *promulgated for the first time in music*) proceed to the description of the successes of the heroine herself: a cold wind (muted violins) traverses the crypt. With "I see all that was as if before me now," two flutes enter in a low-register third (D, F#), signifying with their entrance the *translation* of the dominant of G minor into the tonic of B minor, while emotionally, with their icy cold breath, they uncover the portal to the world beyond.[72] It is one of the most brilliantly intuitive moments in the entire opera and an ideal example of dramatization through instrumental color. All turns stock-still, and a sentimental air by Grétry sounds like a sinister voice from the other world.[73] Coming out of her reverie, the countess shoos away the servants and falls asleep (the "minuet" phrase is now in the clarinets, with flickering shudders in the strings). Again the air appears as if through a dream. The "minuet" phrase is heard for the last time in the strings (in basses at *ppp*). The silence of the crypt settles in.

As long as the countess was singing, the Hag's sequences were not recalled. Now once again, the secret hidden essence of the *Hag* comes forth (the bass clarinet strikes up her sequence heavily against a background of cellos; the bassoon continues on).[74] Hermann appears (while in the strings, the phrase for the three cards in the rhythm of the third tableau appears).[75] Hermann's recitatives—fragmented and disjointed—pass by against a background of frightful music: syncopated triplets with grace notes in the bassoons and arpeggiated roulades in the clarinets engender feelings of a gripping horror as a terrified person faces the agony of impending death: the teeth chatter, the body grows chill, and the heart, flaring up with abrupt intermittent pulses, approaches a breakdown. Seized by an insane idea, Hermann does not hear this, does not notice the spread of death approaching. He even becomes more assured, singing a rather sentimental, engaging arioso, which is sincere, however, in feeling: "If you have ever known the feeling of love."[76]

In its middle section he touches on secrets and sins. Immediately, the coloration makes an abrupt change: again a stream of cold air flutters as the Hag's characteristic rhythm appears: 𝄽𝅘𝅥𝅯𝅘𝅥𝅯𝅘𝅥𝅮 𝅘𝅥𝅯𝅘𝅥𝅯𝅘𝅥𝅮 .

Suddenly, she straightens up and her penetrating glance compels Hermann to be silent: in the trombones and trumpets a new, menacing theme sounds, like a proclamation of the Last Judgment.[77] Possessed, deprived of his reason, Hermann draws a pistol, intent on slaying the "witch." Again, there are syncopes in the bassoons, a sinister "gurgling" in the clarinets; then cold shudders from the flutes, two *pianissimo* attacks from the trombones and trumpets, resembling a shift or a collapse of something, and silence can enter—the terrible gaping maw of the abyss is uncovered (a low-register seventh chord in third inversion: cor anglais, clarinet, stopped horns, bassoons, and bass clarinet).[78] Another series of prolonged, sustained chords, provoking terror due to the *blackness* of their color, and only then does Hermann begin to understand what has happened. However, as a *living* corpse facing the dead, he has no concern for death, but only with one fact: "I did not learn the secret!" Meanwhile, in the orchestra, the frightening finale of this tableau is being prepared: a rhythm ♫♩ ♫♩ rattles vehemently in the double basses along with a timpani tremolo, as waves of sighing from the music to the entr'acte well up.[79] Liza enters: the full horror of the preceding is now uncovered to her. That which began in the scene with the key is now brought to a conclusion. A wild chase takes off in the orchestra (Vivace, alla breve): as if a swarm of demonic beings rushes by in a blustery whirlwind, with a regular and ponderously resonant stamping. Against the background of this syncopated regular rhythm, all the more gripping and powerful, like a victory fanfare, the triplet motive of the three cards resounds, until it claims for itself a final triumph! . . .[80] Every hope can be set aside. The ascent of the action has come to an end. Now from the uttermost height begins a rapid descent by inertia into the abyss of death (with the pyramid as a symbol).[81]

The scene in the barracks (Fifth Tableau): an encounter between Hermann and the ghost, along with the deceitful insane delirium of the trey, seven, ace. This is the first line of descent. From a musical-symphonic standpoint, the entire tableau serves as an example of the most graphic descriptiveness and craftsmanship. New thematic material is brought into play here: the singing of an offstage choir ("I will pour out my prayer to the Lord") during the delirium over the funeral; the roll call for a patrol; and the whole-tone scale with the appearance of the ghost. Previous themes[82] receive new idiosyncratic rhythmic and coloristic variations and hues as they enhance the rather perilous romantic situation of a conversation with the next world to a maximum of expressivity and conviction.

One cannot help believing in such a state when both the fusion of elements and the growth of energy occur so organically. Psychologically and structurally, the sense of the tableau can be understood to be a development of the mood of the quintet ("I am frightened!) of the first tableau—a mood concentrated now entirely on Hermann like the crescendo of a delirious nightmare; rhythmically and dynamically, this scene is firmly connected with all the musical content of the opera.

The introduction (entr'acte) lays bare Hermann's emotional experiences from the moment of the countess's death to the raising of the curtain, at which point we might view him as a man rooted in a position, sensing his transgression with respect to Liza. With good reason, the rhythmic profile of the outcry preceding the scene with the key in the third tableau ("O, how pitiable and laughable I am!"), surfaces both in the orchestra (entr'acte) and in a phrase from one of Hermann's recitatives.[83] Emerging from the funereal tableau that is so firmly fixed in Hermann's imagination, the music of the entr'acte delineates Hermann's confusion of thoughts and feelings against this background. An echo from the external world (the military fanfare of a patrol's trumpet, initially from a distance) seems to summon his confused brain to concentration and self-analysis! Fragments of themes, disjointedness, and distortion of them seem to signify that oppressive spiritual condition when a disturbed and agitated person, deluged with horrors, endeavors to cast away from himself the fetters of delusion and give himself a clear account of what came to pass. The sound of the trumpet (everyday life once again) is subordinated to the inner progress of the action and, in piercing through the agonizing sphere of delirium, seems to restore equilibrium in Hermann's soul: we find him (at the curtain's raising) to be *reading* a letter from Liza. His reading (not *singing*, so as to emphasize the complete reality, the everyday aspect, ordinariness, and normalcy of matters at hand with the intent of heightening the contrast with the subsequent denouement of the present situation) is accompanied by a most expressive recitative in the bass clarinet, sliding down to the note D in the great octave, a godsend (so astounding to Rimsky-Korsakov) comparable to the remarkable appearance of a third in the flutes before the air "Je crains de lui parler la nuit" in the preceding tableau.[84]

But the return of Hermann to the real world is only apparent: he has gone too far, been drawn in too deeply, and is not to be released. The conversation with the Hag while alive has remained unfinished and needs to receive closure. The fact that Tchaikovsky did not finish off the given situation through superficial description but enhanced it to a high degree of psychological and structural refinement reveals a terrible truth: the fear of death and, as a result, the greedy curiosity to know "what lies beyond it" drew him into conversation with *that* world by means of the power of musical autosuggestion and incantation. For a religious person it is blasphemy, since one should not attempt to comprehend that which is not given to be comprehended and which is pointless (for the needs of life) to comprehend. But for a Russian thinker, there are no limitations: Dostoyevsky progressed to an enigmatic cynicism in his tale "Bobok," Tchaikovsky to a blasphemous intensification of Pushkin's theme in *Queen of Spades*.[85]

The approach to the moment of Hermann's encounter with the *dead* Hag is prepared in logical structural increments, which emphasize all the more that it is an unavoidable *fact*. At first a struggle ensues: the singing at the burial (or the wind's howling?) again sounds in Hermann's brain, but simultaneously the image of Liza is still passing through (fragments of the love theme maintain the attraction).[86] A sudden burst of wind scatters everything, aside from the singing (it is finally now clear both to Hermann and the listener that this is *indeed* singing). It is exchanged for a rustling and whispering of violas with ironic undertones from the winds, but all quiets for a moment so that, once again, like a *Dies Irae*, it can burst into the most resolute fortissimo and, with that, place Hermann's mind under total eclipse. He now unwillingly awaits the ghost. Now begins the scene of incantation—the summoning of the Hag (just *so* does Hermann's unwilling will take action; or perhaps, by now, *someone else's* will trustingly setting forth to encounter *itself*). Vague indefinite reeling, trembling, and the terrifying upward surges in sequences from when the Hag was yet alive. To them the motive of the three cards responds: it proceeds, as always, in contrary motion to the sequences and with syncopations cleaves the rocking and reeling harmonic background.[87] For the moment we are still in the real world. But with the words "No, no, I can't bear it!" the motive of the three cards crashes down in regular triplets to the abyss of the lower octaves. There in the quivering agitation of the harmonic background, pierced by upward gliding scales like lightning bolts, the music seemingly congeals. Amidst this frightful, reeling sound mass the ghost's eventual theme makes a prophetic and pompous announcement of its appearance: a theme, consisting of five descending tones, moving still by semitone, with the third note syncopated. Without a doubt, it has sprouted logically from a variation of the three cards' theme, which has been distorted within Hermann's brain.[88]

Upon analysis this variation—and, as a result, the apparent fusion of the three cards' motive with the ghost's motive (more motive than theme, for it lacks development and only appears statically)—makes a staggering impact. Above all, the breathtaking structure and developmental logic of sound material within a genuinely organic artwork are revealed here once again: transformation, dissolution, rebirth in a new guise, development, compression—all types of physical reactions in the most varied relationships and displacements are conceivable in so-called musical developments! Like the elements, the music that is guided by the organizing mind of man is controlled by the laws of mechanics that rule the universe.

With respect to *Queen of Spades*, the present example reveals important stylistic and psychological details: the amazing gradual transformation of the theme joins together and justifies, while enhancing all the factors of the dramatic situation. The ghost's theme is born not from the Hag's sequences but from the "three cards," for from the moment of its appearance, the threatening sound of the five notes separated by semitone changes into the yet more sinister sound of five notes separated by a whole tone, i.e., into a petrified, inert whole-tone scale enclosed in the space allotted to it.[89] But now the five are sounded more broadly, *marcato, pianissimo*, and grouped by threes (a fusion of fragments): F, E-flat, D-flat; then D-flat, B, A, etc. Since even in its diseased state Hermann's brain functions in accordance with logical norms, it is therefore entirely logical that he would associate the theme of the cards with the "dead" Hag, and that at the moment the ghost's theme is extracted from the cards' theme, the character of the Queen of Spades is already anticipated.[90] Just now, in this terrible instant, is born the otherwise incomprehensible outcome of the tragedy in the final tableau—when Hermann, having lost the stakes, sees in his hand not the ace but the queen of spades. That it must be so from a psychological standpoint is confirmed by yet another important circumstance: the deep distinction between the concluding musical moments of the first (in the barracks) and the second (in the gambling house) conversations of Hermann with the ghost. The tableau in the barracks concludes with the vanishing and dissolution of the ghost and the *peaceful resolution* of the restless wandering harmonies, which came from the whole-tone scale into a radiant, "pastoral" F-major triad. Hermann's brain is drugged and bewitched. On the other hand, in the final tableau's closing scene, the appearance and conversation with the ghost directly after the loss at cards leads to a six-four chord left hanging in the air, to resolution by way of a shift to a secundal chord [i.e., the dominant seventh in third inversion] of another tonality, i.e., into a yet tenser dissonance![91] However, when Hermann's mind again clears up and the charm loses its grip, the whole-tone progression of the ghost's motive is exchanged for a semitonal progression, i.e., reversing the path that Hermann's clouded brain had taken before the encounter with the ghost in the barracks scene.[92] Again we can marvel at that profoundly stirring gift of an organic union of elements, a gift that is so characteristic of the creative power of intuition!

The Scene at the Winter Canal (Sixth Tableau) was incorporated in the opera due to the firm insistence of Pyotr Ilyich himself.[93] In this way he demonstrated the instinct of a dramaturge and the intuition of a great musician. The full second half of the opera (from the death of the countess), if examined on the basis of its rhythmic structure, presents a continuous *decline*; but from a dynamic standpoint, shows a *growth*, a crescendo of Hermann's delirious nightmare, and from the key scene onward is no longer restrained by the worship of the maidenly personage of Liza.

From an architectonic standpoint, the amatory encounter with her in the second tableau demands a response, just as Liza's giving away of herself requires an outcome. In the end, Hermann's delirium itself, when transferred from the scene in the barracks directly to the gambling house, would not justify its own advance. It grows from subduing the calls of conscience and the feeling of love. In the scene at the canal, Hermann finally overcomes these callings, having become convinced that Liza will not follow him into the gambling house.

Thus, the sixth tableau completes and offers resolution to the second. By contrast, it begins in E minor, whereas the second had closed in a triumphal E major. The intimate interconnection between the tableaus of the entire opera can be graphically represented in this way:

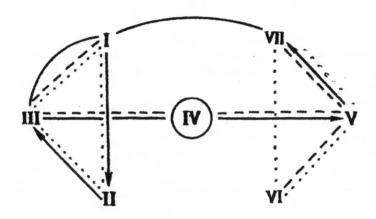

——————→ 1. increasing tension of the action with each new encounter between Hermann and the Hag (in the fourth tableau, the moment of the terrible turnabout);

— — — — — 2. the development of Hermann's delirious idea;

· · · · · · · · 3. from the first to the second and third is shown the development of passionate love for Liza (in the fourth tableau: obliviousness); from the fifth to the sixth and seventh is the empathy for Liza and, momentarily, the arousal of feeling;

⌒‿ 4. the link of the everyday scenes and personages framing the intimate tragedy of the *three*.[94]

The introduction to the sixth tableau is based on the heavy beating of a pulse (accentuato—unison flutes, oboes, clarinets over a rocking string figuration). It is both a call of fate and a resolve: nothing is left in Liza's life that might be grasped for. Judging by this music, which is dominated by the sensation of firmness and rock steadiness, Liza's attempt once more to see Hermann—to convince herself of his innocence and most importantly of his love for her, a love ardent and true—ends with the death of that hope. In contrast to that mood are the dreariness and sorrow of the well-known aria, "Ah, I languish from my woe." How mistaken are all the singers who treat this aria with the pathos of Aida's aria, as she awaits Radames. This is a complete misunderstanding of Tchaikovsky's style in *The Queen of Spades*.

Not a romantic heroine, but a simple, quiet, and meek Russian girl stands before us, fated by life to suffering and ruin. She intuits her doom, her fate, just as every Russian girl intuits the bitter lot that all maidenly Russian folk songs have expressed since ancient times. The makeup of the aria, both rhythmic and melodic, indicates a kind of lullaby, an appeasement, a lamentation or lullaby for one's own self. Only in the middle section do we ponder a rise in the drama; there Liza is captivated by the desire to resist and, apparently, determine her fate for herself, but not for long: the agitation quickly subsides and the outburst of feeling again is transformed into an epic lament. On the other hand, in the instant just after the aria, there is an attempt at struggle, but that instant is risky. The entire musical characterization of the figure of Liza up until now did not unveil before us the will of a heroine, of Pushkin's "maiden on a cliff."[95] The arousal of this will turned out to be excessively demanding, even for Tchaikovsky: in the insincere, pompous Meyerbeerish pathos of the "patetico" Allegro giusto ("Then it's true") there is a certain strain, an offense against style and measure. One is even embarrassed for Liza while listening to such melodramatic wailing, which completely distorts her image. We have here a tawdry operatic protest *an und für sich*, one fruitless and unnecessary! This spot is a [hidden] reef for all performers; to overcome it requires an ample sense of proportion and artistic tact, so as not to destroy all of the illusion that has been created.

Fortunately, the moment of Hermann's appearance, along with the duet, counts as one of the greatest and purest pearls in the string of Tchaikovsky's lyricism. Liza has been created anew before us: genuine and alive! For the true paradigm of the composer's dramatic intuition one must direct attention to Hermann's role in the duet. In the arrival of her beloved, Liza already sees the blissful rebirth of bygone hopes and obliviousness to grief. She begins the duet, whereas Hermann at first only joins in, unconsciously imitating her singing. Under the influence of Liza's affections, however, a moment comes when his mind seems to return to him. The duet closes with full harmony.[96] But it is only for a moment, only for that digression after which the basic incline of the action becomes steeper. Hermann begins to rave, and a distortion of the duet's melody sounds in the orchestra. Liza is at a loss. Finally, Hermann seizes onto his idea and makes it concrete: "To the gambling house!" There follows remarkably inspired music for the ravings about gold: the three cards' theme, like a pedal point, flickers in the bass clarinet against a background of bassoon harmonies and upsurges from the remaining winds.[97] Again that specifically sinister and phantasmal coloration, with the hovering stench of decay and the images of a sarcastic dance of death, emerging out of ancient sources! The crescendo of delirium grows. Liza is powerless to stop it.

Enter the whole-tone scale of the ghost! But the reprise of the horrifying deceitful Allegro ("Then it's true"), now with countermelodies from Hermann, furthers the development of the action and disperses the tension. Only with a rhythmic change and the appearance of the Hag's imperious alternating sequences of anapests in a galloping rhythm is the previous level of impulsiveness reestablished. In delirious ecstasy, Hermann sings the ballade motive ("Are you not the third?") while in the orchestra, against the background of a galloping accompaniment, the rising sequences of the Hag expand. In a wildly insane outburst, he pushes away the girl he loves and flees. "He is doomed, doomed, and I with him!" is the cry of Liza.

In response to it, a powerful and triumphal rumbling sounds in the orchestra: over a formidable yet peculiar arpeggiated tremolo in all the strings, trombones and horns majestically intone at *fortissimo* the deciding motive of Liza's terrible fate.[98]

Seventh tableau. Hermann's insane delirium is still not exhausted. On the eve of ruin, he has yet to carry out his primary idea. The action is transplanted into the hot-tempered milieu of the gambling house. We hear the carousing of Hermann's companions. As in the first tableau, the genre creates the background, against which the dramatic action develops. In the wild, wanton song, "In bad weather days," Tchaikovsky succeeded at expressing unrestrained and frightening Russian revelry. Enter Hermann. Unaware of the presence of Liza's betrothed, Prince Yeletsky, he announces his wish to lay down a card (the Hag's sequence slithers in the orchestra).[99] Two wins in a row agitate his mood into delirious ecstasy. In a drinking song, he pronounces a toast to death and a challenge to fate. It seems he has overcome the decree of fate: Hermann is intoxicated with nervous energy; a march rhythm, along with constant flights and ascents, upholds the illusion of victory! At his newest offer to lay a card, Liza's suitor responds (in the orchestra, the Hag's theme seems to confirm the significance of his decision). Confusion and doubt arise within Hermann. He loses. The Hag's theme establishes the incontrovertible fact: the queen of spades and not the ace remains in Hermann's hands! Still not coming to, Hermann raves over the card (with the ghost's scale!) and stabs himself.[100] In the agony preceding his death, his mind attains clarity: the motive of Liza's adoration sounds caressingly and, just after the choir promising Eternal repose,[101] the image of the loving Liza floating over the corpse gently concludes the opera. It is the sole easement to the dramatic situation allowed by the composer. Indeed we are paused over the yawning black hole, prior to a collapse into the abyss of despair, ever at risk to be carried down into the accursed circle of the doomed.

My goal has been to vindicate *The Queen of Spades*, an opera of profound wholeness in its conception, organic in the outlay of elements. It has been deeply harmed by popularity and by distorted, careless performance. One may also doubt, with respect to the 1890s (the years of the opera's earliest productions), whether either the connoisseurs or the masses could see in it something of value, which can be so clearly revealed today: namely, that inclination, so characteristic of Russian creative thought, to solve the problem of evil, i.e., of death and the mortal dread of it. In general the 1890s imprinted Tchaikovsky's works with a false, clamorous pathos in addition to a ubiquitous, senseless affectation and *tempo rubato*. The salons of the capital and the provinces definitively affirmed and, moreover, even exaggerated the "Figner style."[102] The tragedy in Tchaikovsky's music disappeared without a trace, overlaid with a syrup of sentimentality, while its purely Russian sincerity and simplicity were suppressed by the strange, purposeless "gypsy" style. In order to understand how Tchaikovsky's image was conceived in the 1890s, one needs to listen to Napravnik's *Dubrovsky*:[103] here is an exact reflection of the taste of that epoch. Now the time has come to approach Tchaikovsky as a Russian classic and to uncover the essence of the tendencies and goals of the "artistic will" (*Formenwille*,[104] as defined by German researchers of the psychology of style), which helped bring about one and not another sort of creative intents and attainments. I have initiated this, perhaps initiated it unsuccessfully, but with sincere trepidation and worshipful respect for the memory of this great musician.

The opera *The Queen of Spades* deserves to become a classic. It is irreproachable in its technical mastery (the *intermedio* alone establishes this), deeply truthful in the presentation and resolution of psychological problems, organic with respect to architectonics, intense and replete in its *temporal-musical* duration and flow, all of which results in a firmly fused form that attests to thorough mastery of complex and varied material and to a light beam of creativeity strong enough to melt metal. The richness and novelty of its rhythms delight no less than the intelligence, freshness, and expressivity of the orchestral writing. The chiaroscuro of the "Petersburg coloration" in the music to *Queen of Spades* is, from the standpoint of dramatic intensity, an ideal worthy of continued study. The use of the characteristically sharp timbres in the woodwinds so beloved by Tchaikovsky reveals indescribable mastery and acuity. The sole blunders—blunders only in the choice of material (for example, those moments in the scene at the Winter Canal and others indicated by me)—in the end are smoothed over amidst the precious body of the whole and the well-planned connection of the details. One need only discover an authentic performance practice and distinguish the nerve centers, the internal harmoniousness, and the rigor of the action. However, up until now, there has not been a worthy performer for the role of Hermann—a tragic artist, who could create the role as Chaliapine created Boris Godunov. Without a Hermann, there can be no *Queen of Spades*; therein lies all the hopelessness of dreaming about an authentic realization of this opera.

There is still another painful question, which concerns the fate of *Queen of Spades* abroad. It could not hold its place in the repertoire there, and, judging by the descriptions, was performed either in the style of a boulevard anecdote or, in the best case, in the spirit of a pompous melodrama. In a word, the approach to the subject was from the outside in, from events, from the escapades of a hero in a romantic novel. Of course, such an approach to the plot of *Queen of Spades* ruins everything, by turning it into a trite anecdote while the music goes to waste by remaining unnoticed! . . .

A man of sharp intellect, high-strung and *exsulté*, falls into a circle of ideas, notions, and facts that condition the course of his behavior and present to him imperatives that he cannot avoid following. He sees that which others do not notice and hears that which others do not hear. Fateful coincidences exist for him, of the sort that elude many others; and for him, no less than nature for a lover, evil magic comes alive, since it truly is real for him in his existence. Is he a hero of an ancient, tragic sort? No, due to the fact that he neither achieves a victory, nor commits a crime in the name of an idea; thus, he does not affirm himself. For him there is no atonement. Does he act perhaps in the name of his own annihilation, by his own will, going to meet death-as-night, like Tristan? No. Once again, for the West, Tristan is a tragic hero, since he must commit his crime against Mark, just as Orestes must kill his mother.

But for us Hermann is also a tragic hero, particularly when his life is conducted through the prism of music. It unfolds such a list of inner obstacles and collisions that Hermann, while trying to overcome it, like a doomed man, *unwillingly* commits a great sin: *exchanging the ends for the means*. In this case, the idea of getting rich for the sake of passionate love is exchanged for the idea of getting rich for its own sake ("There lie chests of gold and to me, to *me alone*, they belong"[105]). The three cards' theme acquires a predominant significance over the themes of ardent love, adoration, and entreaty. We might imagine Orestes killing Clytemnestra not for the sake of vengeance, but for the sake of a voluptuous feeling of matricide as a goal in its own right, and committing such a sin *unwillingly*, after being enticed by the force of a powerful whirlwind of ideas and facts. Hermann kills Liza,[106] his supreme ideal, his purest idea, his joy, his light; and he does so *unwillingly*. Of course, only music could affirm, using all its force and the magnitude of its devices, the unquestionable tragedy of the situation and elucidate its most profound truth. It is difficult to reveal in words the psychological distinction between *willed* and *unwilled* tragedy.

Apparently, this distinction cannot be translated into another means of perception. Is this not the reason for the West's inability to comprehend our operas: in particular, *The Queen of Spades?*

If now we might recall the magnificent work of our genius and sage Pushkin, *Mozart and Salieri*,[107] the distinction just now drawn turns into an abyss, separating two poles of *psychological* outlook (that may however be conquered by the intellect): Salieri murders Mozart because he is required by conscience to destroy a blasphemer who has committed a transgression against the divine gift attainable only by one chosen for the sacred blessings of beauty, creativity, and genius. By his thoughtlessness, Mozart has desecrated something holy. Moreover, Mozart is a criminal who crazily squanders a treasure, for the possession of which honest toilers and virtuous souls labor their entire lives. Salieri is the hero. And without question he is in the right according to the commandments of formal justice. But the worm of conscience or perhaps merely his own mind shakes up the significance of the conclusions of reason. Is this not envy? Is this not an exchange of means for ends? Furthermore, can Mozart be in the right, if "genius and villainy are two things incompatible" and if the latter reference to Michelangelo's being a murderer is an empty fabrication?![108] What is most frightening is that there is not even an atonement in the form of suicide: oh no, we know for certain that a person like Salieri does *not* kill himself, nor does *music* interest itself in his fate.

3

The composition, connection, and progression of musical relationships of rhythm, key centers, color (harmonic, tonal, and timbral), dynamics, and tempo, i.e., duration, accentuation, chiaroscuro, colors, the force of sounds, and velocities—taken altogether, these comprise the language of music. After such an extended analysis of the psychological and the musical-structural lines of the opera's development, I shall permit myself to characterize in brief the most important traits and particularities of the just-mentioned process of constructing musical speech in the present work.

Only a little remains to be said about the purely rhythmic relationships. To begin with, one must note in general the plasticity of rhythmic transformations of themes and motives in accordance with the dictates of the action. The fundamental rhythmic lines are essentially these: a lyricism of calm undulations predominates in Liza's speech. Tortuous wends, impulsive upsurges, ascents in moments of decisiveness or horror, entreaties, and either moans or else an intense incline in the melodic line with an insignificant tarrying at the top comprise the language of Hermann's "fateful" instants and of the moments of self-surrender to passion. The countess's speech is made up of unstable and fragmented phrases of recitative. Even the language of her "reminiscences" (fourth tableau) is one of broken lines (in Hermann, sharply curved ones predominate). For the countess's lyricism a melody was taken from Grétry. The authority of her will is expressed in the constant reinforcement—amidst the fragmentation—of the main word's main stress on the strong beat of the measure. Speaking of the accentuation of the three main personages, I must comment on the predominately high vocal tessitura used in the moments requiring emphasis, i.e., more stress on the high-pitched [sounds] than low ones. Thus if one sets off from the fundamental line as well as any kind of psalmody (i.e., the regular alternation of syllables on one tone with an insignificant raising or lowering of the voice within stressed syllables and words), then ascent will dominate over descent.

In *Onegin*, however, the feminine ending predominates (Lensky's "I love you," Tatyana's "Onegin, I was younger then"). Evidently, the nervous agitation of language here is of another sort. One sees this when comparing the phrase "Come quickly" in *The Enchantress* to the phrase "To gaze from Nizhny"![109]

Among the metrical feet of *Queen of Spades*, a leading role is played by the anapest (the Hag's sequences) and the dactyl with an anacrusis (the ballade and the "three cards"). All is entirely in accordance with the sense of the action: the motive of the ballade and the cards is a *thesis*, emanating from the legend, from the tale, while the Hag's sequences are *an aggressive principle*, whose essence is already contained in the legend itself:

Od - nazh - dy vVer-sa - le "aux   jeu   de   la   Reine...."

The sequence's *anapest* separates itself from the *dactyl* of the tale, hence, consciously willed activity from contemplation.[110] This is a remarkable secret of creativity.

Mention was made of the coloration and the particular characteristics of timbres during the course of the analysis. Only observations made while listening to the opera can reveal the full evocativeness of the composer's imagination in this sphere and, most importantly, in the use of sinister (taunting and rustling) timbres of the woodwinds. The coloration of *blanc et noir*[111] predominates over the coloration and, without a doubt, there can be no talk of the self-sufficing significance of a color unless it be subordinated to the basic conception of the work, wherein subject, rhythm, and color are only means of expression and not the goal. *The Queen of Spades* was reproached for lacking a style—evidencing no awareness of an understanding of style as a unity of expressive means, but rather as a replacement with *stylization*, i.e., a unity in the choice of material with a predetermined goal. From the standpoint of construction and form, *The Queen of Spades* is unquestionably a work of the best style. From the standpoint of taste, much in it is debatable: although the material and its elaboration (for example, in the *intermedio*, in the duet of Liza and Polina) are generally irreproachable, Tomsky's song nevertheless may seem excessively naturalistic. With respect to harmony, *Queen of Spades* is more of a confirmation and development of previous content than a new discovery in the work of Tchaikovsky. But if the harmonies of *Queen* (as static entities) are indeed no novelty for Tchaikovsky, their rhythmic interrelationships do reveal an unprecedented gulf: the Hag's sequences out of secundal chords alone are indicative of it! Thus, in the choice of harmonic material the reproductive imagination predominates, while in the process of its coming into existence, it is the *associative* imagination. The quality is characteristic of Tchaikovsky's works, whose harmonic vocabulary presented itself almost immediately, from the earliest *opere*. Quite the reverse for Wagner! . . .

The dynamism of *Queen of Spades* is quite idiosyncratic. There are few of those extended accumulations in sound that are found in *Onegin*, in the overture *Romeo*, in *The Storm*, etc. In this respect, *Queen of Spades* is more laconic and restrained. The shadings of *marcato e pesante*, the *fortissimo* disruptions, the frequent *sforzando*, the heaving, accented, arpeggiated string tremolo seem to serve the goal of grounding, stamping, and hammering down the sounding material. The free flight of lines, their spiraling, the prolongation of an impulse, and mere delight are foreign to the main process of the action. Romantic ecstasy is short-lived; languor is restless. The peaks of dynamic increases are brief moments. Just then, the descent, the subsiding of the waves of sound can sometimes be sharp and sheer. A frequent device is the accented drumming or abrupt, caustic hammering away (of *pianissimo* bassoons, for example, before the greeting of the countess in the fourth tableau). I would employ the notion of "dynamics of coloration" to denote the essence of it in this tableau. A flat and regular plane of sound predominates, almost entirely set out at *pp* and *ppp*. The accumulation is scarcely increased at all. And it all, as it were, ensures that in the scene's finale, in abrupt contrast, with a marked rhythmic instability, the accumulation can be brought up to the blackest *fortissimo* during death's wild flight. Yet another sinister device: *marcato pianissimo* over a yet quieter whispering background. Or: a brief unchecked outburst of *crescendo* that suddenly is exchanged for gloomy, expectant quiet. The lack of extended dynamic progressions in the sound and the predominance of outbursts and abrupt changes over smooth dispersion of the sound energy corresponds in full to the nervous, confused course of the action, while the frequent *sforzandi* and the weighing down to earth signify the frightening will of a mysterious power stubbornly achieving what it desires.

Just such an impression emerges from the outlay of the chiaroscuro: night, twilight, shadows and half-shadows, the gloom of the crypt, the twinkling of icon lamps[112] all hold sway. Only once does the dawn spread its rays: the duet of Liza and Hermann in the scene at the Canal! Still, this is not the dawn, but a mirage of the white night, well matched to the A major of the shepherds in the *intermedio*. The soft evening light in the duet of Liza and Polina is a calm before the storm. Smoothly and quietly lingering daylight is just as inconceivable in *Queen of Spades*, as a calm *piano*. We may recall the dynamism and coloration of late autumn in Peter's city in *The Bronze Horseman!*[113] We can recall the twilight of the Petersburg winter and its terrible snowstorms and blizzards. Hence it is all the same in *Queen of Spades*: quiet is conceivable only as a quiet of the tomb. Even the chanting of the Last Rites sounds like the howling of the wind. On the other hand, in the everyday scenes can be seen a calmer and clearer (normal) distribution of dynamics and light, particularly in the stylish *intermedio* of the third tableau. But this is unable to change the main course of dynamic instabilities. The dynamic aspect of *Queen of Spades* is analogous to a prolonged stay within the sound of the interval of an augmented fourth.

The change of tempi and the relationship of speeds are less unstable. Perhaps this is a more becalmed sphere of action with quite insignificant fluctuations on the side. Such "basso ostinato" tempi as the beginning of the fourth tableau are fairly characteristic of the entire opera, creating a morose background of hopelessness and cold, diabolical observation of the gradual approach of sacrificial victims to ruination. The median rate of tempo for the first tableau wavers between *Andante mosso* (quarter = 84) and *Allegro moderato* (quarter = 112). The most serene moment, in the tableau's center, is the promenaders' chorus in F major, at *Allegro giusto* (quarter = 126); the nerve center for the action, the ballade, is at *Allegro con spirito* (quarter = 116); for that most gloomy midpoint, the quintet, *Andante* (quarter = 60). In the second tableau, the main tempo rate is *Andante* (quarter = 60—66) or *Andante mosso* (quarter = 76) with rare disruptions of *Allegro* (for example, by contrast: the countess's arrival is at *Allegro vivo*, quarter = 152). In the scene at the ball, a serene, sustained, and noble *Allegro* prevails, since many spots are taken over by genre scenes. In the distribution of keys,[114] too, this tableau is the most serene in the entire opera. The tempo of the fifth is slower and more somber than the tempo of the fourth tableau: from *Largo* (quarter = 50) to *Moderato* (quarter = 112). Then there is a progression in speed in the fourth tableau: from *Andante mosso* (quarter = 76) to *Vivace alla breve* (quarter = 92). In the sixth tableau the tempo deviations are, if not more abrupt, then at least more nervously impulsive, with the tempo's main character registering as an initially leisurely but convincingly resolute tempo of *Moderato assai* (quarter = 88). The last tableau is the reverse of the first, fourth, fifth, and sixth, in that the progression of rates proceeds in descending order: from *Allegro moderato e con fuoco* (quarter = 120), attaining *Allegro vivo* (quarter = 160), then to *Moderato, Andantino,* and, finally, *Andante sostenuto* (quarter = 69). The extreme limits of speed for the entire opera fluctuate between *Largo* (quarter = 50) and *Allegro molto vivo* (quarter = 160) and *Vivace* (half = 92, i.e., quarter = 184). *Allegro moderato* (quarter = 102—112) can be considered the median tempo with a greater inclination toward deceleration (toward *Andante mosso,* quarter = 76) than acceleration.[115] Given the supple and skittish rhythm, the capricious dynamics, the complexity of accentuation and metrical design, one must recognize the shady twilit coloration and restraint in tempo as the most stable elements in the opera, establishing a background amidst clashes and changes of durations, force, and accents.

The train or process of thought in *Queen of Spades* is guided by what might be called the principle of *integration,* i.e., of continual transition from fragmented, differentiated sound material toward a reconstruction of it, toward concentration.[116] The first stage of integration is fulfilled in the unconscious: we do not know how flowing, fragmented sound matter is transformed in our mind into material from which sound patterns can be differentiated (cells, motives, tempi, melos, rhythms, timbres). The creative process in general begins with a choice and the refining of it, i.e., already from the differentiation of some material at hand. In the ensuing stage, there is already a connection of sound patterns, a new reunification; moreover, as in living organisms, when there is a common connection, a "specialization" of function develops among the individual parts and elements and, in addition, yet more definition. In certain composers, the process never reaches this stage: the elements join together so that the ear continually perceives them only by their differences, despite the sometimes markedly vivid coloration of these "individuals." In language, through the process of integration the opportunity is created to present a word as a whole, as indivisible, and in the next stage, a series of words as a unit of expressed thought. It is the same in music. Of course, the whole style of music takes on a quite different character from that which predominates in the creative process: dismemberment or reunification, indefiniteness (in the sense of importunity of separate and seemingly independent ideas) or definition (in the sense of a connection of elements with the whole and the significance of their intent and function).

The differentiation that prevails during the course of musical speech makes the texture translucent and the schemas easy to grasp. But in order for the listener to perceive the inner essence of the action, its intentionality, flow, and the ceaseless coming into being, an effort toward further integration must occur in one's own brain. The process is interesting and compelling for musicians, who will find continuous delight while listening to the synthesis that is being produced. The value lies not in the fact that the musician immediately takes note of how the composer creates and takes apart elements, but in how, upon seeing the dismemberment, his mind concentrates them. On the other hand, while listening to music in which the process of integration prevails, it is unnecessary for a musician to synthesize, for a synthesis is already present in every moment in the musical flow. This leaves analysis, which is a reverse process, a process of differentiation. This requires more effort, since it is difficult not to make a simple surrender of the self to the power of music—as is done by every sincere listener, to whom music speaks only as an emotional force. But it is more difficult for such a listener to listen to music that is more differentiated: the process of integration is not easily affected, and therefore the Philistine's reproach toward this kind of music as boring becomes rather commonplace. But musicians in turn are often unjust toward that music wherein the texture is continuous, where unbroken continuity, prolongation, and flow—as in the life process—appear to be a synthesis of all the preceding, in every subsequent moment. When under the impression of this music, one is unlikely to say: how delightful the instrumentation of that chord, how clever the approach to that suspension, etc. Even though, in a process of unbroken development, a halt in the motion results in a dearth of those moments of mastery that provoke amazement! But the value of the music is not harmed, nor does it depend on the use of one or another principle for realizing ideas. Only the usual Philistinism, pedantry, as well as the habit of unverified judgment and the desire to make a quick unverified reaction to everything could induce people—specialists and nonspecialists alike—to mistake their personal attraction toward one or another principle for the music itself.

The process of differentiation can be quite complex and quite far removed from the initial stage; while on the other hand, the process of integration can remain at the first stage of combining the simplest correlations. How often have the followers and detractors, say, of Wagner, Tchaikovsky, Rimsky-Korsakov, Richard Strauss, Debussy, and Musorgsky hammered away at each other, out of a predilection only based on personal taste and a personal inclination to blame the music of the disliked composer for something undeserving of blame. For some, Tchaikovsky's sin lies with his emotionality; and therefore, foaming at the mouth, they will deny him any right to the title of master. On the other hand, for others, Rimsky-Korsakov is a dried-up pedant, feeling nothing, experiencing nothing. To this end, terribly muddled ideas are invoked: e.g., objectivity and subjectivity or, even worse, classicism and romanticism; meanwhile, it appears that Rimsky-Korsakov is a classic for his mastery of technique and a

romantic in his choice of subjects, as if subject is existing only for itself and is
not merely one means of expressing thoughts and creative concepts, guided by
the *will* toward artistic creation, to the creation of *form*.

I wonder how the perception of nature and the embodiment of the
Russian spring in *Snow-Maiden* could *not* be subjective? One might boldly
state that in Russian music there are Rimsky-Korsakov's "sea," Glinka's
"Spain," Musorgsky's and Tchaikovsky's "Ukraine," and Borodin's "vast
steppes." It is the same in the spiritual sphere. Are the wondrous ariosi in
D minor and G minor from *Snow-Maiden*[117] and the moving melodies of *The
Tsar's Bride* less *emotional* than Tchaikovsky's melos? And why must emotion
be feared and the eyes be closed to the enormous significance of psychology
in music? No. The whole matter comes down to this: to the habit of relating
too simplistically to the mental process—to artistic creation—there you have
it! Next comes the narrow-minded custom (affecting the specialists as well!)
of "analyzing" everything from the selfsame formulas, approaching the *work*
with *them* and not starting from *it*. Next comes our bondage to criticism according to taste and emerging from taste. If the "gourmands of art" unite behind the proverb *de gustibus non est disputandum* in order to protect the invio-
lable tranquility of their contemplation of the "beautiful," then it is time to
realize that this principle is *res privato*, just like the classroom habits of a pedant
or the untalented "Beckmesserism" of people accustomed to following the
beaten path, who despise and shower suspicion on anyone who will not go
their way: misunderstanding your neighbor is indeed easier than acknowledging one's own spiritual poverty. But all these natural little sins and human
vices must not obstruct the *idea* of seeking out firm foundations in the evaluation of creative achievements. Even if certain foundations may be unattainable as an ideal, still in this is found the delight of all seeking and the
meaning of life itself. Otherwise we impede the growth of our consciousness
and also restrict our own frame of reference, marveling at the flowers of our
personal garden and not seeing the sumptuous beauty of our neighbor's. Spiritual blindness and deafness—what could be worse?

In concluding my sketch on Tchaikovsky and his *Queen of Spades* with a
digression so important to me, I would merely wish to direct attention to my
credo. I believe that artworks, once born into life, in turn give birth around
themselves to energy of thought. Criticism, therefore, cannot be a permanent
censure. Its value and meaning come from the elaboration of a thought *emerging from* a given impulse. However, in seeking firm foundations, the critic will
not become an omnivorous eclectic, provided he senses within a burning desire for art. Any firm foundation is a stage toward a future, more firm one; but
only the passion of worship and love helps one to see what is hidden and hear
the unheard amidst the vanities of life and the grip of a classroom tablature.

The Queen of Spades 225

Having heard things of value in something dear, I learned to hear it, too, in what was *not*. Therefore I cannot help bowing to the memory of Pyotr Ilyich Tchaikovsky, whose music compelled me to ponder over *music*.

NOTES

1. *Bobok* [bó-bok] is a nonsense word (with a possible etymological link to *bob* [bean]) and also the stuff of trifling conversation. The protagonist in Dostoevsky's short story of 1873 (published as one installment of his serial work *A Writer's Diary*) is a failed writer who becomes attuned to the conversations of St. Petersburg's recently departed. After burial, he learns that they all resume venting from a surfeit of St. Petersburg gossip, envy, malice, and trivia until decomposition eventually reduces each corpse's discourse to "bobok, bobok, bobok. . . ."

2. Asafyev considers Dargomyzhsky to be a forerunner of Musorgsky, thanks to his composition of a number of satirical character sketches for voice: "The Miller" (1851), "The Worm" (1856), and "The Old Corporal" (1858). "A Droll Story" is another short fictional work by Dostoyevsky.

3. *Sunless* (1874) is Musorgsky's setting of verses by Golenishchev-Kutuzov; *Songs and Dances of Death* is another cycle based on verses by the same poet. *The Sorochintsy Fair* (1874–1880) was a comic opera based on one of Gogol's Ukrainian village tales left incomplete at the composer's death.

4. In Lensky's second-act aria "Whither have you fled," the line descends from G to B in E minor; in the Sixth Symphony, from F# to A in D major.

5. In the Introduction to *Onegin*, the pitches descend from E-flat to G in G minor; in Liza's aria, the descent is from F to A in A minor; in the Fourth Symphony, second movement, the descent is from D-flat to F in B-flat minor; in *Manfred*, first movement, from D to F# in B minor.

6. The poet Fyodor Ivanovich Tyutchev (1803–1873) authored only about 400 poems and was not broadly read until the 1850s. A tragic, dualistic worldview in which the cosmos is subordinate to chaos underlies his metaphysical nature poetry and love lyrics.

7. On 2/14 March 1890, the composer wrote in his diary: "Finished the seventh tableau (the aria is left). Cried terribly when Hermann breathed his last. The result of fatigue or, perhaps, because it is indeed good."

8. Eight years before Rimsky's opera, Tchaikovsky composed incidental music for Ostrovsky's play, consisting of nineteen numbers.

9. Asafyev's comment may be an indication that the enormous prewar veneration of Scriabin was waning, especially in post-Revolutionary Petrograd.

10. Chromatic inflections, grace notes, and spasmodic rhythms characterize the evil fairy Carabosse, who first appears in the prologue's finale (no. 4).

11. Letter to Modest, 28 March/9 April 1888. The texts of this chapter's letters would have been available to Asafyev from Modest's biography, published 1900–1902.

The text of this letter (which Poznansky lists as No. 3539) was not, however, reprinted in the Soviet-era *Literaturnye proizvedeniia* of Tchaikovsky.

12. Letter to Glazunov, 30 Jan./11 Feb. 1890. Source: Tchaikovsky, *Lit. proizvedeniia*, v. 15B, letter no. 4018.

13. Letter to Modest, 2 Feb./14 Feb. 1890. Source: Tchaikovsky, *Lit. proizvedeniia*, v. 15B, letter no. 4022.

14. Letter to von Meck, 17–26 Dec. 1889/29 Dec. 1889–7 Jan. 1890. Source: Tchaikovsky, *Lit. proizvedeniia*, v. 15A, letter no. 3985.

15. See n. 11.

16. Asafyev's dates for the compositional history are based on the Julian (Old style) calendar.

17. Letter to Modest, 19/31 March 1890. Source: Tchaikovsky, *Lit. proizvedeniia*, v. 15B, letter no. 4072.

18. Letter to Konstantin Romanov, 5/17 August 1890. Source: Tchaikovsky, *Lit. proizvedeniia*, v. 15B, letter no. 4195.

19. Asafyev echoed this concern elsewhere, which is central to understanding the subsequent course of his career.

20. Nikolai Kashkin (1839–1920) taught at the Moscow Conservatory and was an influential critic. His memoir of the composer was published in 1896.

21. Asafyev is paraphrasing Tchaikovsky's self-criticism of *Francesca*, found in a letter to Balakirev of 12/24 Nov. 1882. Source: Tchaikovsky, *Lit. proizvedeniia*, v. 11, letter no. 2158.

22. Hanging dominants contribute to the aura (cf. the analogous theme from the Fifth Symphony, where they are absent). The motive's genesis occurs in m. 2 of the Introduction; sharp rhythmic definition arrives in m. 16.

23. Trombones and trumpets introduce the Hag's theme atop pulsating dotted rhythms, forming three grating tritones with the accompaniment already in the first statement.

24. Score location: Introduction, mm. 34–57, designated *molto espressivo* and fully scored using a familiar Tchaikovskian palette, albeit here with a disconcerting "late style" compaction. Cf. second tableau, no. 10, m. 178.

25. Asafyev's gambit deserves comment. Here he abandons a main concern of the Rimsky-Korsakov chapters and a main focus of Western criticism (i.e., Tchaikovsky's degree of success at evoking the 18th century and the music of that time) in order to direct the reader's attention away from the stage spectacle toward the "invisible" yet audible psychological drama.

26. Readers familiar with Asafyev's dualistic doctrine of musical form will see the obvious parallel. The clearly identified, enumerated, and harmonically demarcated musical "numbers" for each act correspond to musical form construed as an architectonic *schema*, while the succession of independently plotted musico-dramatic climaxes with their respective approaches, departures, and cyclic elements (e.g., melodic motives, rhythms, chord, and timbres) serve as fulcrums for musical form conceived as an ongoing musical *process*.

27. This paragraph presents Asafyev's interpretation of the first tableau's second vocal number: a through-composed scene and arioso, whose main thematic content is the previously mentioned descending sixth and whose shifting emotions are underscored

with a harmonic process that fails to stabilize any of the main tonalities (D, A-flat, F) for any significant duration.

28. Asafyev is still responding to Hermann's arioso (mm. 109–10).

29. As promised, Asafyev leaps past the scene-setting "everyday" element of the promenaders' chorus (no. 3) to the arioso passage (mm. 103–10) in which the prince's appearance furthers the drama.

30. Score location: first tableau, chorus, mm. 123–48. "Rhythm" refers to the quicker pacing of Hermann's phrases; deviations in pitch and duration disqualify the passage from being considered canonic.

31. As the prince points to Liza, exclaiming, "There she is!" the clarinets play the countess's theme, which had been previously introduced by trombones.

32. In a mere 10 mm. at the end of no. 3, the "irrational element" manifests in three ways: (1) in the clarinets' statement of the countess's theme; (2) the "pulsating rhythm" in the horns; and (3) weird scalar flourishes spanning a ninth. Taken in context, the event registers both as an incursion into the unfolding interpersonal drama and an anomaly within the form-schema.

33. Asafyev's chief interpretive task from here on out will be to establish the independence of his "mystical power," i.e., to keep it apart from any one character's conscious or unconscious emotional state and from the plane of visible action portrayed on stage. A charting of its musical/textual interpolations into the melodrama would reveal further independence: from the conversation of the moment, from precise labeling or attachment to any one motive, from key signature, and from the actual (local) key.

34. The sense of stasis fraught with anxiety is enhanced by Tchaikovsky's typical device of an extended pedal point on the dominant (here, C#). Weakly resolved in the immediate context (Quintet, m. 18), the chord of the dominant will play a prominent role in the characters' later tragedies, whereas the key of F# minor will conclude two acts.

35. The E-minor triad does hold sway throughout most of Tomsky's ballade (i.e., no. 5, mm. 24–105), which is the first solo vocal number to have that harmonic stability.

36. Asafyev's key assignments for his psychological nerve centers can be substantiated. The main keys for the "everyday" scenes that he omits (D, G, F, B-flat, F) make for a pointed tonal conflict.

37. Cf. no. 2, mm. 53–55. (pitches: D E D C B-flat A G D C) and no. 5, mm. 41–43 (pitches E F# E D C B A D C). An alternative hypothesis: not Hermann but Tomsky makes the shift, since he sings the latter phrase, which does indeed echo back something that he *heard.*

38. Score location: second tableau, no. 10, mm. 31–32. The statement of the *cor anglais* occurs in the *scena* portion.

39. The duet in G major ("'Tis evening") and the romance in E-flat minor ("Dear girls") that open the second tableau are both accompanied by pianoforte, signifying that they are songs to be heard by audience and characters both. Asafyev is correct to consider "Well now, Masha" a dance, since the girls will promptly be scolded for engaging in unmaidenly Russian dancing.

40. The E-flat minor tonality and the "rococo" gestures suggesting a minuet found in the governess's brief arioso do indeed function as a diversion, one that fails, however, to dispel the underlying anxiety.

41. Score location: second tableau, no. 10, mm. 64–76.

42. The chord in mm. 103–4 is an ordinary diminished seventh, spelled with B natural as the root and bass.

43. The key of C major "synthesizes" only in that it is a midpoint between the previous flat- and sharp-side keys. Asafyev's reference to the weak reflected light of a St. Petersburg summer night applies as well to the fragility of C major in this operatic context, lying as it does on the periphery of the main key scheme.

44. Liza's cry "O night!" culminates in m. 139, after which Hermann and she confront each other wordlessly.

45. Score location: second tableau, no. 10, m. 178.

46. Score location: second tableau, no. 10, m. 235.

47. Score location: second tableau, no. 10, m. 281 (Tempo I = Andante mosso!).

48. A diminished-seventh chord appearing just prior to the countess's knock interrupts the love scene and launches 60 mm. (mm. 288–347) of grotesque dissonant music, mainly in the low register. The theme that Asafyev had previously associated with the countess is now renamed the "Hag's theme," i.e., the evil entity that inhabits, possesses, or somehow controls the countess. Meanwhile, the theme itself sheds its previous tonal stability and is subjected to weird intervallic mutations.

49. It is likely to be the sudden shift in timbre that would cause one to sense an "icy chill." In an instant, the lyrical warmth of the love theme (scored for massed upper strings over a full tutti accompaniment, all directed toward a projected C-major cadence that never appears) is exchanged for a dissonant tremolo and fragments of the aforementioned macabre motives.

50. The dominant pedal on B enters in m. 349 with timpani (not basses!) repeating the triplet figure. Twenty-seven measures of dialogue (Liza's confession of love) separate the dominant from the resolution to E at *fff*. [Author's note:] On the note B, i.e., the dominant of E major, which closes the tableau. It is a rather typical device in Tchaikovsky to bolster the dramatic intensity: to prepare the conclusion of an act for a long time and somewhat in advance by means of a pedal point, setting it aside prior to the conclusion itself.

51. The contredanse begins when the second-act curtain rises (third tableau, no. 11, m. 62). Nos. 12–13 (including the prince's aria) correspond to the first item in Asafyev's right column. No. 14 is the intermedio. No. 15 (mm. 1–64) corresponds to the second item in the right column, with the remainder of no. 15 concerned with empress's arrival (left column).

52. Mikhail Osipovich Gershenzon, *Mudrost Pushkina* (Moscow: Knigoizdatelstvo pisatelei, 1919), 103. Gershenzon (1869–1925) was an intellectual historian, philosopher, critic, and lifelong Pushkinist. His psychological study of Pushkin's story (mainly concerned with how Hermann's predisposition influences events) differs sharply from Asafyev's view of the opera.

53. Syncopated eighths launch no. 13 (Scena) and recur frequently throughout it.

54. To the aforementioned syncopes, Tchaikovsky adds the Hag-countess's theme (mm. 15ff.), the cards' theme (11–13), and the quoted phrase from Tomsky's ballade (mm. 25–28).

55. Score location: no. 13, mm. 42–45.

56. After skipping over the entire intermedio, Asafyev resumes his psychological commentary with the final scene (no. 15). The passage in question with its triplet figure more closely resembles a later passage in the second tableau (mm. 349ff.), which he mentioned earlier.

57. Cf. *Queen*, third tableau, no. 15, mm. 31–32; and *Onegin*, Act 2, 5th tableau, no. 5, mm. 58–59 (fig. 2 + 9–10). (Note the tonicization of Lensky's key of E minor!)

58. [Author's note:] It is the germ of the scene at the Winter Canal, when Liza becomes convinced that Hermann is devoted not to her, but to the fateful thought of winning.

59. Shortened and with a jerky dotted rhythm, the echo of the love theme is introduced by oboe in m. 34 over swirling chromatic sextuplets.

60. Score location: no. 15, mm. 63–64, with a return to the scoring of the opera's introduction.

61. The A-major chord following Hermann's last outburst constitutes a half cadence for the D-minor tonality of the final phrase. The D-major chorus thereafter is harmonically logical, but leaves the outcome of the tragedy pointedly unresolved.

62. [Author's note:] And in this constantly maintained subordination of everyday scenes to the rhythm of the inner action, the solid, strict, and harmonious construction of *The Queen of Spades* is expressed.

63. Tchaikovsky assigned the rhythmic ostinato at the beginning of the fourth tableau to violas; their repeated C#'s serve as dominant to the entr'acte, the opening scene, and the close of the tableau.

64. Score location: no. 16, mm. 177ff.

65. After acknowledging some ambivalence, Asafyev again attributes the root cause of the central tragedy not to the countess but to a separate entity whose "evil will" or "electric charge" enters the character.

66. In the first encounter (first tableau, quintet), Hermann and the countess were visible to each other; in the second (second tableau, no. 12), Hermann was hidden; in the third (third tableau, no. 15), they again lock eyes in a shared state of fascination and fright; in the fourth (fourth tableau), Hermann will speak to the mute countess who is incapacitated by horror; in the final two encounters (fifth and seventh tableaus), the Hag *herself*—i.e., no longer in coexistence with the now dead countess—returns twice more as an apparition.

67. A continuation of Asafyev's musing from the previous chapter (pp. 159–60). [Author's note:] In mechanics there is still no success at carrying through an experiment with the reversibility of motion. Either it does not exist in nature or nature is opposed to it. Is this not in fact death, provided it be understood not as the cessation of life's functions, but as an extended process of degenerating and self-destructing, in opposition to that which is vital and creative?

68. Cf. fourth tableau, no. 16, mm. 68–70; and second tableau, no. 10, mm. 54–55.

69. The bassoon's chromatic motive will be developed in dissonant canonic stretto (mm. 95ff.), weirdly voiced and articulated to accentuate the distinctive timbre.

70. The impression of a macabre march coincides with the entry of the chorus of the countess's retainers, due to a metrical stabilization and the unusual marking of *pp pesante* (mm. 113ff., winds). [Author's note:] More precisely, it is a *scherzo funebre*.

71. Score location: no. 16, mm. 135ff.

72. The pair of flutes appear in m. 212, just where the countess loses her train of thought. Unaccompanied, the flutes trail off—tone dissolving into breath—and the strings add the pitch B to D and F#, thus establishing the tonic triad for the countess's reverting to the French of her youth.

73. Tchaikovsky's arrangement of the operatic air ("Je crains de lui" from Grétry's *Richard Couer-de-lion* [1784]) is scored for strings, suggestive of the 18th century, albeit with the addition of 19th-century wind writing.

74. We have reached the beginning of the fourth tableau's final scene (no. 17). Asafyev speaks again of the familiar anapest sequences, now chromaticized. From now on, he will associate them only with manifestations of the Hag, not the countess.

75. Score location: no. 17, mm. 11–13. The theme must now conform to a 12/8 meter.

76. Score location: no. 17, mm. 39–40.

77. Score location: no. 17, mm. 69–73.

78. Score location: no. 17, m. 84 (G7 chord in third inversion).

79. Score location: no. 17, mm. 92–107. The pedal F# sounds the cadential tonic prematurely.

80. Score location: no. 17, mm. 162–72 (brasses).

81. While the fourth tableau is central, the succeeding measure count shows that the descent will occur more quickly than the ascent.

82. [Author's note:] The leit-rhythm [Asafyev's example shows a pattern of triplet sixteenths plus an eighth note], the Hag's sequences, and the three cards' motive (in particular); with the motive of Liza's adoration used fleetingly.

83. Score locations: Cf. third tableau, no. 15, mm. 32 (Hermann), 34, 36 (oboe) with fifth tableau, no. 18, mm. 19–25 and 55–58.

84. Score location: fifth tableau, no. 18, mm. 39–45.

85. After the death of the countess in Pushkin's story, Hermann attends her funeral, during which he believes that he sees her wink. Although shaken, he manages to leave, gets drunk, and attempts to sleep it off. The countess's apparition in the barracks is per-functorily dealt with: she shuffles in through the *door* (!), names the three cards, and leaves, after which Hermann writes down what he has witnessed. In his libretto, Mod-est neither altered nor added to the basic visible events during the countess's visit. Thus the harrowing musical details that mark the specter's arrival (fifth tableau, no. 19, mm. 25–41)—e.g., brasses at *tutta forza fff*, free dissonance, complete harmonic disorienta-tion, and a six-octave range—are intended to be *felt*, not *seen*.

86. Score location: fifth tableau, no. 18, mm. 57–58.

87. The first entrance of the Hag-countess's sequences in no. 19 is in m. 3. The call-and-response passage of the two themes occurs in mm. 19–30.

88. Score location: fifth tableau, no. 19, mm. 34–39, with the distortion involving both rhythm and pitch (to semitones).

89. Score location: fifth tableau, no. 19, mm. 41–44 (clarinet, in dotted halves).

90. In simpler terms, Asafyev is claiming that from here on out, Hermann's fate lies not with the formerly alive countess, nor even with the Hag (as represented by the ris-ing anapests), but with the mysterious power of the cards themselves—trey, seven,

ace!—their full power having finally been revealed after their long-awaited naming. [Author's note:] The motive of the *dead* Hag, when combined thus inside Hermann's synthesizing imagination, could simply not emanate from the sequences of the *living* Hag-countess. Indeed the secret of the three cards took on the role of chief impulse for the combining, i.e., in a creative sense and not merely as the mechanical production of a lunatic's imagination. In creating and summoning the ghost, Hermann's imagination, in response to that "anecdote," to Tomsky's ballade, and to the unfinished conversation with the Hag before her death, is attempting to *prosecute* its demand that the cards be shown and to communicate by means of this demand with *that* abstract unknown world. The controlling idea of the three cards' secret enshrouds the newcomer from *that* world within the form of a herald of the secret's revelation, in this way linking it with the cards but not with the enigmatic figure of the countess, who was the bearer of the secret while alive, but with whom Hermann has no concern now!

91. Score location: seventh tableau, no. 24, mm. 185–86. The second-inversion F# chord moves to a third-inversion dominant seventh of G, thus denying closure to the important key of F# minor.

92. Score location: fifth tableau, no. 19, mm. 62ff. (bassoons). Asafyev's three-note (ascending) chromatic motive is prominent; basses, however, continue with wholetone material.

93. "You [i.e., Modest] and Larosh are undeniably against [the sixth tableau], whereas I—despite wanting to have as few *tableaus* as possible and desiring concision—I fear that without this tableau the whole third act will be without a woman—and that would be dull." Letter to Modest, 2/14 Feb 1890. Source: *Lit. proizvedeniia*, v. 15B, letter no. 4022.

94. The reproduction of Asafyev's diagram is taken from the second Russian edition.

95. The reference is to the unnamed female figure in Pushkin's short poem, "The Tempest" of 1825, which closes with these lines: "But believe me, the maiden on the cliff / Is more magnificent than waves, heaven, and storm."

96. Score location: sixth tableau, no. 21, m. 88. The duet's final cadence on E does not, however, resolve the duet's tonic key of A major.

97. Score location: sixth tableau, no. 21, mm. 101ff.

98. Asafyev has summarized the concluding musical events of the sixth tableau, beginning with the reprise of the whole-tone scale (mm. 116–18). The march in F# minor (beginning in m. 181) comes in response to Liza's suicidal leap.

99. Score location: seventh tableau, no. 24, mm. 35ff.

100. Score location: seventh tableau, no. 24, mm. 177ff.

101. [Author's note:] The choir is natural here, taking the place of a sign of the cross and prayer for Heavenly repose.

102. The elegant Nikolai Figner (1857–1918), who premiered the role of Hermann, was indeed a popular stage figure in the 1890s, despite a rather limited vocal instrument.

103. The Bohemian-born conductor Eduard Nápravník (1839–1916), a central figure in the history of Russian opera, tried his hand at setting Pushkin to music in 1894. In *Dubrovsky*, his adaptation of the writer's unfinished novel of love, revenge, murder, and banditry, he showcased the particular strengths of Nikolai Figner, his wife Medea

Mei-Figner, and Fyodor Stravinsky and indulged the Late Imperial taste for spectacle on the grandest scale.

104. See Chapter 14, n. 3.

105. The quotation is taken from Modest's dialogue for the final encounter between Hermann and Liza (6th tableau, mm. 102–5).

106. [Author's note:] When he insisted on introducing the fact of Liza's demise into the opera (the scene at the Winter Canal), Tchaikovsky knew intuitively that he had redeemed the full intention, the entire libretto of his brother.

107. Pushkin wrote both *Mozart and Salieri* and *The Stone Guest* in the fall of 1830. After assisting with the completion of Dargomyzhsky's setting of *The Stone Guest*, Rimsky-Korsakov himself set *Mozart and Salieri* in 1897.

108. Just after Pushkin's Mozart raises the question, Salieri poisons him. The play ends with Salieri wondering if the claim was true that the genius Michelangelo was also a murderer.

109. The two vocal numbers from *The Enchantress* differ in the general melodic contours of their phrases. In "Hasten here" (Act 4, no. 20), the phrases descend to downbeat emphases; in "To gaze from Nizhny" (Act 1, no. 4) they rise.

110. Three motives of three notes each are under discussion: (1) the cards' motive ("tri kár-ty, tri kár-ty," etc.); (2) the dactylic rhythm of the ballade; and (3) the Hag's anapest (illustrated in Asafyev's example).

111. [Author's note:] But the shadings of this *noir* of Tchaikovsky are countless! We need only to recall the minor-key tonal coloration of the scene in the countess's bedchamber where even the G minor of Hermann's address sounds like a ray of light.

112. The quotation from Asafyev's note is a stage direction appearing on the opening page of the fourth tableau. [Author's note:] An astonishing comment in the fourth tableau: "The countess's bedchamber illuminated by lamps"—and not a peep more.

113. "O'er darkened Petrograd / November breathed autumnal chill" (Pushkin, *The Bronze Horseman*).

114. [Author's note:] With a predominance of D major and A major.

115. Orlova noted that Asafyev had made use of an 1890 edition of the score. The metronome markings appear as footnotes in the full score found in the *Complete Works*.

116. Underlying Asafyev's fairly straightforward explanation of how the mind comprehends a sophisticated musical work through a process of *integration* is the assumption that an opera in all of its multiplicity of individual sounds, patterns, forms, characters, "character-states," emotions, conflicts, experiences, etc, etc. is indeed best construed as a *living organism*. Behind this viewpoint one is right to suspect that fundamental concern of the pre-Revolutionary Russian Idealist tradition—from Vladimir Solovyov to Nikolai Lossky—with explaining an unconditioned and eternal "All-Unity" spanning all the apparent material and phenomenal diversity of the universe. See also Chapter 19, n. 8.

117. Snow-Maiden's D-minor arietta "I heard, I heard," with its delicate chromatic appoggiaturas, is found in the opera's prologue; the G-minor arietta "How painful here" is in Act 1.

· *16* ·

Modest Petrovich Musorgsky (1839–1881)

Toward a Reappraisal of His Works

In rereading the article that I wrote (but did not publish) in early 1917,[1] which outlined new paths toward the perception of Musorgsky's music and hence established new guideposts for defining the foundations of the style and spiritual (emotional) makeup of his compositions, I realized that my essential views on the works of this great "psychologist" and musician have yet to change. Refinement and elaboration occurred in certain respects, in others partial corrections came to mind, but the core, or rather, the bases of the idea content remained the same. By the same token, the issue of Musorgsky had somehow neither advanced over the course of this period of time nor yielded new perspectives. Its present-day lack of progress also permits me to turn back, in order that subsequent judgments of Musorgsky might commence from a point of departure established in the distant past (the experiences of these years justify that "distant past"—with regard to psychology, of course, not chronology). I am reissuing the article on the strength of what I have just confessed, practically unaltered but with *post factum* remarks. In addition, I am introducing the article with a comparison between the works of Musorgsky and those of a great Italian musician of the 17th century—a comparison that may seem rather bold (but then every comparison is always bold if one takes into account the permanent changeability, inimitableness, and indivisibility of every self-contained phenomenon!) yet one that appears unavoidable to me, on account of the thoughts that came to light over the course of the exposition.

A likeness in the psychological foundations, character of the epoch, and spiritual makeup of artists elicits a commonality in stylistic undertakings. The musical and artistic culture of Italy at the beginning of the 17th century brought to life (or utilized like a vessel) the genius of Monteverdi. In a similar way, the much less intensive and not so "civilized" Russian culture of a romantically and idealistically minded society during the middle of the 19th century nurtured the genius of Musorgsky. By Monteverdi's lifetime, the church had ceased to be the master controlling the minds of its subjects: a chosen few among them withdrew from under its guardianship. This is understandable. It was not reason that dispelled the charm, since reason itself was still swaddled in scholasticism and insufficiently "positivistic." The church had ceased to express the soul's truth, the sincere feelings of a spirit blazing toward heaven. The church, sensing demise, turned to music for help; Palestrina's style gave support to it, a highly moral support, in comparison to that "amoral" support rendered not by music but by the Jesuits. But the establishment of secular society could not relieve the wants that until then had been satisfied by religion: it remained for some human capability to express the truth, a truth not of the intellect, but of the soul. Music, being summoned to this responsible post as an art form not yet infected with sybaritic and aestheticist ills, has been maintaining its reputation with honor then and now. It was natural that whatever the church could do in a temple, music, conditioned by the growing demands, would achieve only in the theater. Thus did opera emerge. It emerged from deep psychological foundations, not out of a mere wish to amuse. An invention of the Florentine nobles was only one means of expressing the soul's awakening. Corseted in its stylization, namely a resurrection of ancient tragedy, opera quickly broke out into the open air, since everywhere it had instinctively been awaited (that's why it was to everyone's taste!). Two powerful impulses opened the floodgates: first, the romantic genius of Monteverdi; and next the vocal genius of the Italian people (the Neapolitan School).[2]

Something similar occurred in cold, faraway Russia. The powerful song element within the Russian people persistently drew Russian composers to opera, despite the absence of any broad and deep theatrical culture, but benefiting from an inclination toward the theater and the theatrical impulse. From the time of Peter I to Nikolai I, Russian society managed to become sufficiently "Voltairean": they demanded the catechism of Filaret to be a bridle, but not a pillar of fire leading the faithful to the promised land.[3] The official church had ceased to express the truth of life: music had taken on this mission for itself. Folk song had always been created in this way. But as soon as Russian music, having associated itself with Western norms through the creative achievement of Glinka, became resilient and felt itself capable of resolving the problem of opera independently, it attempted to reject classical norms and meet the dream of romanticism head on. It began to express a life truth, the truth of the soul, posited as a thesis: a vocalized sound = a *word* that has been experienced, captured emotionally, and felt. Dargomyzhsky was the apostle and pioneer; his ardent pupil, follower, and the one who came to make so powerful a realization of his own conceptions enhanced by the ideas of Dargomyzhsky—was Modest Musorgsky.

An extreme realist, even a "naturalist" in the view of his contemporaries, a scarecrow to the schoolteachers of music, and the destroyer of the logical foundations of voice leading—Musorgsky, through the power of the richest of imaginations, revealed and introduced into music worlds of sound never before heard, governed not by the abstract structures of so-called absolute music but by the great romantic dream of truth both immediately and authentically expressed in sounds drawn from the soul's experiences, as if in the free speech of prose, outside architectonic norms and only *by ear*, i.e., from listening to the voice of the soul. That is why his recitatives are so expressive of life. That is why he has an Impressionist's voice-leading: a coloration emerging from spots of harmony, a chiaroscuro that enhances the line of the melos, which all the more graphically and sharply stands out against an emotionally animated harmonic background. It appears that Monteverdi was striking out for the very same thing: one needs only to take in the style of his harmonic accompaniments and his endeavors to characterize with color. Such are the recitatives of *L'Orfeo*. Even more indicative is Seneca's death scene (the conversation with his pupils preceding his death in *L'Incoronazione di Poppea*).[4] Hearing these pliantly expressive recitatives, one unwittingly thinks of their intimate connection with the recitatives of Pimen and Dosifei: it is as if one composer was an heir to the other! It could not be otherwise, since Monteverdi was indeed a prophet of factual certainty and the deeper truth of words put into sound in order to express the truth of the soul through sound.

How characteristic was the duality in his conception of the universe: along with scenes unquestionably worldly, which even anticipate the erotic lyricism of 18th-century French composers, Monteverdi did not abandon the composition of Catholic hymns. His musically expressive language is suffused with the idioms of ecclesiastical language, which approach the level of an anachronism astride the poignancy of his emotional harmonies. A similar occurrence is noticeable in Musorgsky: in place of God, there was a yawning black hole of death and unenlightened annihilation, while his discord and spiritual nihilism were fouler and deeper than Monteverdi's contrasts. Nevertheless, he did create *Khovanshchina*, a tragedy nourished with a religious impulse, the tragedy of a woman's soul, divided between flights of spiritual ecstasy and a carnal lust seeking appeasement in an immolation of the flesh of herself and her lover for the sake of raising souls up to heaven. Still, it is quite likely that Marfa had no faith in heaven: her divination is far too convincingly realistic. All in all, Monteverdi gravitates more to Apollo, Musorgsky toward the Black Goat[5]—therein lies the terrible distinction between them.

In recent times, the interest in Musorgsky's music has greatly increased, both in Russian society and abroad (especially in France).[6] It obviously holds mysterious and invisible threads within, linking it with present-day intuitions, hopes, and dreams. There must indeed be something in Musorgsky's works that appeals to our epoch, since it seems to have made contact with the refined music of the proponents of Impressionism (it may even be a source of it in certain respects[7]) and in Russia has commanded the attention both of musicians and the public, alongside the growth in the appeal of the works of high-strung, ecstatic Scriabin. This interest, while parallel and equally charged with vitality and not merely the product of fashion, would seem to be out of place for two such dissimilar composers.

Scriabin lived entirely in the present, was imbued by it and engulfed in contemporary philosophical and religious striving. As a musician, he absorbed both the elegant sentimentalism of Chopin and the white-hot eroticism of Liszt. In the fullest and finest sense of the concept, Scriabin was a refined, cultured, and modern European Russian, a Westward-leaning *intelligent*. His technique was faultless, his thought always strictly logical. Musorgsky created his works, filled with vivid Romantic impressions of fundamentally Russian life in the 1870s, when amidst the Russian intelligentsia there predominated— along with a nationalistic gravitation toward the Russian everyday world and Russian antiquity—the *romanticism* of the People's Will,[8] the still undampened idealism of the 1860s, the social sentimentalism of the Wanderers[9] and either the half-scornful or crudely utilitarian views of art as something useless. Musorgsky would have been the first to ridicule a perception and understanding of the world akin to Scriabin's, with its isolation from concrete real-world existence and shunning of the populist element and the ideology of "utilitarianism," wherein art was relegated to a servile and subordinate role. With a bold sweep, Musorgsky rejected the foundations of European musical culture, along with musical problems of a merely technical sort. He himself made everyone marvel at his astringent musical uncouthness and deliberate sloppiness in voice leading as if intentionally, out of spite, he wished to act differently from all the rest. He subordinated his own musical thought to the tendencies and purposes of *another* extramusical sort: he craved to express the *truth* in the sounds.

The small circle of his admirers seized on this slogan, yet without entirely making clear which truth was under discussion: was it a truth in the realization (i.e., a *realization* of something *lived through* and grasped by "instinct") or a phenomenological truth, i.e., a correspondence between the images realized and the given reality? At the head of the most frenzied adherents of Musorgsky's symbols of faith stood that fervid and convinced supporter of his, the ardent prophet of Russian art from that lustrous period: Vladimir Vasilyevich Stasov. With his help, the *truth* of the composer was quickly adapted to the understanding of art's servile-subordinate role that characterized the epoch, and Musorgsky acquired a superficial label that said nothing about his importance as a profound psychologist-musician: the label of *nationalist-realist*. Evidently he took the name to heart. He composed "national musical dramas," striving to present everyday life and historical data "truthfully" (i.e., graphically), to sketch (to record) not only the soul's experiences, but the full profile, habits, and customs of people. He seemed to be suffused with a civic sorrow and craved to soften hearts, composing marvelous vocal works and romance-dramas which, as snapshots of reality, could be accurate documents revealing social injustices. The subject matter, utilitarianism, and external occasion sometimes suppressed the direct intuitive instinct of the artist in Musorgsky, directing his creative energy along a path unworthy of its true importance and vocation: instead of realizing life's essence, it was a realization of life's surface, up to the point of composing out musical anecdotes, stories, or naive caricatures, which had and have only a fleeting and insignificant right to success.

Being a man endowed with brilliant talent, Musorgsky expressed himself even in trifles with remarkable outbursts of sincerity and immediacy. Thus his "Seminarist" [1866], "Song of the Bedbug" [i.e., "Mephistopheles's Song in Auerbach's Cellar," 1879], a bit of "Rayok" [The Peepshow, 1870], and later on "A Society Tale: The Goat" [1867] elicit a smile even now. Meanwhile the highly talented music of *The Marriage*, which is descriptive yet fussily captious as to external characterizations, has significance only for being the richest of experiences—a project carried out by the composer for the sake of achieving a flexibility of musical declamation—which attains the nuances of psychological character that are already in *Boris Godunov* and *Khovanshchina*.[10]

And yet, the title of nationalist-realist was necessary for Musorgsky at the time. Spurned by the musicians of an orthodox academic persuasion due to technical "uncouthness" and for his contempt of conservatory scholasticism, he could enthrall his contemporaries only within the realm of an artistic credo that was considered progressive for that time: otherwise he would not have found that support amidst the intelligentsia, especially among the young, albeit for other reasons than those of his brothers in art.

When Stasov depicted Musorgsky in his biography as a "Wanderer" composer and compared his works to those of the painter Perov,[11] he instinctively sensed an image of Musorgsky that his contemporaries could bear; consequently, he created a schematic and narrow characterization of the composer that is profoundly unacceptable in our time.

Stasov surely sensed and understood Musorgsky's works more deeply and powerfully than he was able to express in words. He loved his music fervently and passionately; he was not frightened by it but esteemed it and promoted it with his characteristic energy and directness. Yet he could not grasp the significance of so many of the most important and remarkable compositions of Musorgsky, especially those from the final (i.e., Stasov's third) period of the composer's creativity, i.e., from 1875 to 1880. With astonishment and unease Stasov noted an apparent change of direction in the creative work that he saw as a decline: a deep-seated departure from superficial description, a burdensome pessimism and painful self-analysis. Parallel to this direction, Musorgsky distanced himself from his former musician comrades in the Balakirev circle. There is nothing to hide now: for them he had already become a bitter failure and pitiable alcoholic, endowed with the proud self-assurance of an ignoramus. At least this was the gist of the harsh, pointed and direct judgment over the last years of Musorgsky's life as expressed by his friend Nikolai Rimsky-Korsakov in his *Chronicle*.[12] As a result, practically no evidence remains for a judgment about the true essence of the composer's spiritual experiences in the years prior to his death: for *judgments*, not speculations. A psychologically based biography of Musorgsky does not exist, nor will it apparently for a long time.

The impression emerges that no one among his friends and admirers cared about the soul, the *worldview* of the composer.

He lived. He composed. As he composed, something drew favor; he was praised and issued the diploma that designated him a "people's artist." When something did indeed take place in the man—an incomprehensible or grave spiritual shift—and, in response to the spiritual breakdown and flagging will, the compositions then became more impulsive but also more inherently profound and imprinted with a frightening specter of loneliness, alienation, and dying: some proudly turned away from Musorgsky, others regretfully sympathized. Friends could not comprehend the complex spiritual impulse in Musorgsky that painfully took in the monstrosity of Russian life while poisoning itself through self-analysis. The character portraits presented to us by Stasov and Rimsky-Korsakov are too simplistic and direct, too constricted by an attitude derived from the ideals of a nationalistic art and from populism on the one hand (Stasov) and corrupted by stern judgments from a highly disciplined man on the other (Rimsky-Korsakov).

In his letters, too, Musorgsky submits to deciphering only with effort. He constantly plays the fool, twists meaning, plunges into dull-witted pathos, and proclaims prophetically with magniloquent verbs. Ever prone to submit to an influence (especially to Stasov's), with delight and rapture he would be seized by each and every subject in turn that gave him pleasure (from *The Marriage* to *Khovanshchina* and *The Sorochintsy Fair*), would then fuss about the material, always igniting and burning in the realm of fabulously effective projects (for example, in the letters on the creation of the character of Marfa![13]). And yet one could never state definitively that Musorgsky truly was as he portrayed himself in the letters. Either he used his verbal "oddity" and "eccentricity," his intense pathos as armor, as a "camouflage," i.e., was consciously reserved and allowed no one into his "inner sanctum"; or else he did not know himself and was protecting himself from some inner contradiction [by escaping] into a realm of preaching and holy foolery. Fortunately we have the music of Musorgsky, which indeed may have been edited in significant measure by Rimsky-Korsakov, but does preserve the fundamental defining traits of its nature. It speaks of its creator and *for him* with a more convincing sincerity than Stasov's tendentious rapture. Moreover, it gives a deeper and more accurate portrayal of this turbulent individual—more than the wry epigrammatic style of a crafty bibliophile, which is found in the letters.

Only in music can we who cherish Musorgsky's musical legacy seek out the answer to the many *trajectories* of his art and explain to ourselves why this staunch opponent (based on his own words) of music for music's sake (i.e., apart from any requirements, and freely developing by its own power) became so dear and near to us. Wherein lies the effect of his works on us, how did he go beyond his era, or why do we find an affinity with him and understand him? Might not the reasons for his rapid self-consumption, his self-immolation, thereby be explained? . . .

First of all, we can point out several salient traits of Musorgsky the composer. Vocal music was his primary sphere of composition; with respect to instrumental music, he generally wrote so-called program music; it seems that Musorgsky was ever in need of a stimulus, an impulse, and a guiding thread or outline from outside, whether it be an opera libretto, a poem, or a simple description to evoke in the imagination some image or picture and then, already out of these, musical patterns and characteristics. To prevent himself from being suspected of aestheticism or even of creativity for creativity's sake, he announced: "Art is a means for conversation between people, but not the goal."[14]

A creative ardor (accompanied by an unquestionable predisposition for the creative process in the depths of his soul) caught fire when confronted with an incentive, a stimulus, a support from outside: it did not proceed according to its own logical evolution. "He saw the task of the music to be not merely the reproduction in musical sounds of a single sensate mood, but most importantly, as a mood of human speech."[15] What does this mean? Is it not merely a superficial worry over correct declamation? Certainly not. It is apparent that Musorgsky wished to express in this way that music must impregnate and nourish the word with a "felt" (emotional) content, *must pour into the abstract envelope of the word, into its intellectual content, the direct data of perception.*

In this aspiration, one not realized in full (since Musorgsky himself both went astray and was led astray in his understanding of the idea of truth in music that he held so dear), is contained the real significance of the attraction for

Musorgsky in our time. The struggle for an organic worldview is occurring now in the realms of religion, philosophy, and science. A philosophical movement is now on the rise, which establishes as the basis of its cognition of the world the doctrine of intuition, of immediate perception as opposed to discursive knowledge of phenomena. It stands to reason that if art is understood as creative work both organic and free, aimed toward the creation of unique concrete forms that are indivisibly interrelated and dependent on impressions of the senses, then it should find a strong basis for opposing the dominance of utilitarian materialism and rationalism in the teachings on the importance and value of intuitive thought.[16] On the other hand, since intuition is the opposite of intellect, just as knowledge drawn from life is to lifeless abstraction, intuition seeks out a basis for its aspirations in the synthesizing and all-embracing activity of art.

Since music is the most intuitive art, it touches upon the life of the spirit and the immediate sources of *life* more directly than anything else; since it takes control of perceptual content and, in addition, is even more malleable, being both imageless[17] and developmental over time (moreover, in time filled with sounds, i.e., in time that is *organized* by the music itself in an instant, over the course or in the period of its sounding)—music, beyond doubt, must hold sway over the consciousness of contemporary humanity and exercise its influence on all spheres of the remaining branches of art. This influence is easily seen by anyone acquainted with recent tendencies in modern poetry and painting. The essence of modern poetry lies in its "musicalization," in the tendency to use the word not as a concept or figure of "thought," but as a conceptual "consonance" of instrumental sound. In art, Impressionism's scorn for the intellectual schemes of academicism and its inclination toward vivid colors and Futurism's ceaseless striving to create the illusion of three-dimensionality on a plane and to destroy the impression of stasis in formal design led to quasi-musical projects involving the direct harnessing of the senses (i.e., through the [artistic] substance and material). With creativity headed in this way, Musorgsky's music could not help attracting attention; moreover, the significance assigned to the music of this composer now has an entirely different basis than in the past.

Musorgsky is important because with unbelievable clarity, imagery, and plasticity he was able to implant the ideas and relationships that were either revealed to him by the poetic text or were seized from life with an unusually intense musical content, i.e., to react to every given impulse from word or image through a creative musical reconstruction. He relived all that he wished to translate into sound as a perception *taken from life*. One can understand why Musorgsky so detested academicism and the musical scholasticism of the conservatory, why any prepared formulas and schemas worked out long ago nauseated him: he did not wish to think in abstract concepts, and if he intuited "temperaments" in human speech, then this was all the more reason he was unable to bring to music anything that might be reminiscent of intellectualized structures! Undoubtedly, Musorgsky's inclination toward vocal and programmatic music was the result of this deeply organic hatred of discursiveness. In musical forms that were abstracted away from the "subject matter" he sensed ossified schemas, which were filled in by the play of abstract sounds that for him lacked purpose, which deprived sound of its essence—to be the exponent of living perceptions and to fill the *word* with a direct quivering taken from the life of the soul. Vocal music gave him the possibility of lavishly enlivening the word and the outline on which he could embroider psychological ornamentation. Without a text to guide his musical thought, Musorgsky became helpless and timid. His single major symphonic effort, *St. John's Night on Bald Mountain*, was shaped by a program; was then meant to serve as an operatic intermezzo; and, in the end, was completed by Rimsky-Korsakov.[18] Yet how powerful and great was Musorgsky in the operas, especially when he did not limit himself to the goal of descriptiveness but brought forth the soul's *stream* of life in sounds, within the process of "making music" out of human speech.

It is interesting that in *Boris Godunov* Musorgsky nearly everywhere accompanied a recitative of wonderfully flexible declamation with marvelous harmonies that even now (since 1874) show a vividness in relationships, a freshness in juxtapositions, and a profoundly impressive clarity, despite the relatively simple makeup of the chords themselves. When one examines the makeup of the harmonies, taking each of them in isolation, their charm may seem strange to the refined modern ear: the chords are so extremely simple, but the harmonic structure on the whole is extremely complex and conditioned by an inspiration not defined by musical logic. And if one looks beyond the individual chordal complexes, in an attempt to examine the texture and structure of *Boris* and *Khovanshchina* purely from the standpoint of the musical *material*—it turns out that the accompanimental line does not shine either in refinement or novelty (the harmonic and melodic figurations are of a quite ordinary sort), that the rhythm at times is crudely schematic and sluggish, that with an absence of polyphony the connection of elements can be quite conditional. Wherein lies the enchantment?

Yet one needs only to begin playing it, and the enchantment returns.

The full delight of this music lies with its unique kind of motion (sometimes taken to an extreme, to a self-contradictory slowing down, as in Pimen's cell in *Boris*) and with the linkage and succession of these apparently simple harmonies. But they are linkages, I repeat, not based on purely musical expressivity but on internal motivations: i.e., out of a change in the soul's experiences! Like no other Russian musician, Musorgsky can follow every twist and turn as he pursues the changes of mood dictated by the text. His changes of harmony (a shift that is often hardly noticed!) have the same force as a change in perceptions, so that the word is never left to become a lonely abstraction of an *uninspired* idea. With a remarkable acuity, Musorgsky could impregnate into sound whatever was most essential, profound, and necessary in the text. By means of this trait, he creates form and avoids the danger of a trivial pursuit of details in the verbal shadings of the tale, which would lead to a loss of integrity and to an undifferentiated, indistinct (since it is arrhythmic), and groundless succession of instants that are of equal value but no real worth. Musorgsky sensed a similar danger in *The Marriage* with its *verismo* tendencies coming at the expense of proportion and clarity of material. As he evolved, he attained such an indivisible union of word and sound that one needs only to say that in his works, the word becomes flesh! Only Dargomyzhsky in *The Stone Guest* managed to anticipate Musorgsky in this regard. And yet the latter's tasks were incomparably more complex and difficult, since Musorgsky's conceptions were *tragic* ones, requiring considerably more concentration of energies, especially in view of that *fundamental* quality of Musorgsky's talent and his *creative* ethos: invent nothing—all must be experienced!

The psychological aspect of the harmonies, or rather the psychological parallelism that can be discerned between the tonal and harmonic changes on the one hand and the ever-changing stream of spiritual experiences on the other, can be followed over the course of nearly all the scenes of *Boris* and *Khovanshchina*. Moreover, in several of them, the musical-psychological characterization of individual moments, phrases, words, and situations reaches a strange and terrible level of saturation and intensity in their expressive and representational "veracity" (examples include the monologue of the clerk Shchelkalov, "My soul is sad" of Boris, the scenes in the monastic cell, at the inn, Boris alone, Boris and Shuisky, Pimen's miracle tale, Podiachy and Shaklovity, Podiachy and the Streltsy, Dosifei's monologue, etc., etc.). In such moments, the attention is *tightly* focused: nothing can divert it. Not a single harmony, not one passage exists that is not the result of a psychological dictate. Hence the colossal wealth of *new* sound combinations and permutations and an absence of purely musical refinements for the ear, for it is not the principles of voice-leading that drive Musorgsky's music and not the music that preconditions them, but something that unites them both: his insatiable craving to remove the protective veil of the human soul through music. Boris's monologue ("I have achieved the highest power"), his scene with Shuisky, the hallucinatory mysticism, and his death are all miraculous and matchless models of saturating the word to the utmost with tragic musical content, yet with a remarkable economy of means, since in the end the harmonic material is by no means sumptuous.

If one can but comprehend the sense behind the appeal produced by the music of *Boris Godunov*, i.e., the continuity and organicism of the musical material (its movement and dynamism) along with the ebb and flow of soul experiences that the *dramatis personae* undergo, then one step taken by Musorgsky, so strange at first glance, will come as no surprise. He did not set Pushkin's text in its entirety, but pretty well tore it apart, crafting the libretto on his own, stitching verses into it, sometimes of a quite vulgar operatic sort (e.g., the scene at the fountain).[19] If such a step cannot be justified from a purely artistic standpoint, then with regard to the psychological dynamic, Musorgsky was in the right. Pushkin's design, so self-assured in its intellectual integrity and self-containment, would have led Musorgsky into a blind alley. He could produce only under a state of rapidly changing, highly expressive sensory perception (which again brings him closer to our own time). Wherever the text would demand a slackening in the tempo of *lived experiences* for the sake of momentary reflection, there Musorgsky could still make do; but wherever reasoning entered in its own right, wherever music needed to take over completely, starting from the internal data contained therein, there he found himself at a loss. He could not comprehend music apart from the outbursts of spirit whose time and place were marked by the narrative chain; he detested musical development for its own sake, one that merely emerged from the dynamic possibilities and the inclination toward motion that were stored up in a given theme. Musorgsky thrived on the change in musical perceptions: any so-called conceptual structure in the music, any autonomous development of a musical idea, was foreign and incomprehensible to him. Only once was he inspired by a strong and passionate female character (Marfa in *Khovanshchina*), and he imbued her with a purely song-based, independent, and rapidly developing lyrical content, having subordinated the words to the music. Its inspired expressivity verges on the miraculous.

Khovanshchina is, in essence, much less saturated than *Boris Godunov* with harmonic content. In this respect it is more ascetic, transparent, "unisonal," and perhaps static. Yet for all that, one observes within it another remarkable phenomenon. In Marfa's part the musical speech (i.e., recitative or *skaz*) is developed into melos, into the pure song element. This development proceeds gradually, in *crescendo*, over the duration of the whole opera; and in the final tableau, when Marfa's character is revealed in all its tragic greatness, her melos achieves something never before seen in Russian operatic music: a beauty, force, and lyrical expressivity linked with a passionate, sumptuous, and intense erotic ecstasy. In Marfa's character, the composer achieved a sublime synthesis, which once could not have been more than a dream (his letters to V. V. Stasov bear witness to us that he intuited and was conscious of the significance of the creative act he accomplished for this character). In the scene of the love "duet" and prayer for her beloved's passing, Marfa's melody expresses on its own, without graphic reinforcement from either harmony or coloration, the direct incarnation of the life of the human spirit that is so characteristic of Musorgsky's art. Here it is not recitative but melody that enlivens the "word," subordinating the latter to its structure, while the harmonic accompaniment is nearly brought to a complete standstill. For me personally, this wonderfully pliant, sculpted melody of Marfa represents the most lifelike vocal melody in all of Russian music, on account of its poignancy, its saturation with the soul's warmth (even the heat of passion!), irrespective of the beauty of the sound, which resembles the velvety aromatic spirit of a well-preserved strong wine.[20]

However, even apart from his operas, in each of his romances,[21] Musorgsky remains true to himself and painstakingly follows through so that the poetic text is permeated with musical content. In addition, both the aforementioned harmonic-psychological correspondence and the highly acute declamation achieve a tremendous intensification and, one may say, real ecstasy. Especially remarkable in this regard are the two cycles on texts of the poet Golenishchev-Kutuzov: *Songs and Dances of Death* and *Sunless*.[22] So, too, is *In the Nursery*, a series of vocal scenes that present a remarkable musical recreation of a child's world. With any undertaking of Musorgsky one may say in general: "Incipit vita nova" (Dante), for it was a new life, a new world that he created in sounds. The cycle *Sunless* is additionally interesting because the composer departed almost entirely from plot and narrative and presented strictly musical-lyrical moods that were not conditioned by external action or an externally attached program. Musorgsky achieved his goal: his music began to *speak*. But doing so came at the costly price of a breakdown of willpower and a surrendering of his soul to alcohol.

Indeed, could it have been otherwise? With regard to vitality and intensity, a small excerpt from Musorgsky's music can stand up to several of the major symphonic structures of a more intellectually minded composer. Such an earnest and elevated creative disposition demanded an enormous expenditure of energy, health, and spiritual equanimity. In every musical moment, Musorgsky materialized a part of his soul, his *self*; he neither reasoned out nor constructed a musical train of thought but relived his musical thoughts and feelings, lived them out with the full might of the organism. Musorgsky's music is characterized by an almost complete lack of the customary formulas, structures, and devices that allow a work to be mechanically connected whenever the imagination requires respite. The artificial joints, continuations, passages dictated by form, cadences, stereotypical periods, and even sequences that make possible a motion by inertia are rare, practically nonexistent among Musorgsky's compositional devices.

The sharply elevated sensitivity and the powerfully dramatic perception of life make themselves known everywhere and unwittingly give rise to the question: was Musorgsky then a visionary? Of what do his notorious, naive, populist realism and the accurate recreation of visible reality consist—i.e., that very fundamental quality that has been attributed to him, because of which some praised him and others criticized and maligned him, with taunts and teasing?

Could this nervous, impressionable, and finely attuned human being who reacted so intensely to everything ever have a sober and clear attitude to life as a given reality? Could that attitude be one bereft of both an exaggerated attentiveness to some phenomena and an indifferent bypassing of others? Did every phenomenon of life—whether it be an encounter with an interesting person, or an impression of nature, or a passing infatuation—draw out the observer and recorder of the everyday world in Musorgsky? Whence, where, and how was he inspired? Were both the ability to observe the external world and the memory to preserve the impressions highly developed in him? Many such questions arise. But let us first return to the subject matter that so enthralled Musorgsky—and do so without strongly exaggerating the influence of Stasov since, in the end, Musorgsky remained who he wanted to be and how he wanted to be, to the point where Stasov even commenced to complain about this quality in the composer (in connection with the frequent changes of plan during the creation of *Khovanshchina*). Did these subjects truly have historical reality? Did Musorgsky have a correspondingly sober and realistic attitude toward them? Judging by the letters from the period of *Khovanshchina*, work proceeded as follows: a vivid scenic image of some sort was conceived, or an interesting clash of characters, or an effective situation, and everything else was driven toward it and a close connection made, albeit one that was often rather far-fetched and extremely conditional!

In his youth, at age 17, the composer attempted to write an opera on a typically hot-blooded subject of French Romanticism: Victor Hugo's *Han d'Islande*.[23] The next operatic attempt was *Salammbô*, after Flaubert, during 1863–1864.[24] In the period from 1858 to 1865, in addition to sketches for *Salammbô*, he composed the romances "Saul," "The Beggar" (from Goethe's *Wilhelm Meister*), and "Night" (based on a bowdlerized text of Pushkin); and the instrumental works *Intermezzo symphonique in modo classico*, *Prélude* [lost], *Menuet-monstre* [lost], and *Ein Kinderscherz*; and finally, music for Sophocles's tragedy *Oedipus Rex*.[25] Stasov claims that this period was notable for its focus on ideas. Such a focus, though, assumes a state of spiritual equilibrium, calm, contemplation, concentration, and thoughtfulness.

One need only acquaint himself with the "restless" scenario for *Salammbô*, as noted by Musorgsky himself, to be convinced that Musorgsky could no more be labeled an idealist than Victor Hugo. The fact is that the entire projected structure of the opera *Salammbô* points to the influence of Romanticism on Musorgsky and, moreover, to the French character of the school. I would compare the ardor of Musorgsky to that of Delacroix, although one would never see any sort of ideally balanced design with a careful weighing and assigning of each element's function in his art and thought! In order to reveal his heroes in their full splendor, Musorgsky was primarily concerned with placing them in the most effectively exciting and dangerous dramatic situations. An approach from without, from events, set the stage for a certain enhancement in psychological experiences, but not the other way around: i.e., an approach from within, from the psychological foundations for which stunning external spectacle might not even be necessary. But an approach of this type did not yet interest the composer. It was necessary for him to pile up events and crowd scenes; to elaborate the entire mold of the scene, the movements, and the gestures; to describe in detail the entire *mise en scène*; and finally, to fill the text itself with despairing romantic verses, for example, Polezhaev's "I die alone" or Heine's "Tear out the heart, this source of evil!"[26] The individual was completely crushed by the melodramatic situations! And then, later on, a portion of the music designated for *Salammbô* was brought over to the opera *Boris Godunov* by this "rigorously" consistent realist!

Of course, Musorgsky had the complete right to *take* such a step, precisely because he had found a state of mind in *Boris* that held for him a psychological correspondence with those in *Salammbô* or else was heard to be musically identical (in an expressive sense). Nevertheless, this fact, along with this yet ultraromantic elaboration of *Salammbô*'s subject, suggests that for Musorgsky "truth" had a quite different character than that which is ascribed to it, while the presence of a romantic element in his juvenile works is connected to the elevated and high-strung perception of life, which has been frequently noted above.

The romance "Saul" on the composer's own text also attests to an impulsive and high-spirited temperament.[27] "Night" is imbued with a highly characteristic trait of Musorgsky that has gone unnoticed by everyone: the contemplation of a phantasmal feminine image conceived in the imagination.[28] The significance of the visionary quality and the passionate dreams that fed it (both of which are present in Musorgsky's early output) is self-evident, since youthful impulses and aspirations do not easily vanish or fade later on. Neither did they vanish within Musorgsky. If we leap to the third period of his works (that of the decline, according to Stasov) we observe that the entire cycle *Songs and Dances of Death* from 1875 is imbued with romantic pathos in its devices of realization as well as a romantic perception of the world, albeit one that is already stained with the black streaks of an impenetrable depression, with cruel laughter, and sullen grief. Amid the vocal portraits only "The Field Marshal" is adorned with an externally bombastic pathos, bringing it near to the emotionalism of the youthful "Saul." In the cycle *Sunless* a mournful romantic acceptance of the world (rather, a rejection of joy) has been developed, finally and inescapably, into a fully tragic temperament. It is the groan of a lonely soul, hiding away in shame. These are lyrical-dramatic monologues filled with self-analyses and a shy craving for quiet contemplation; yet they are poisoned almost everywhere by the wounds and the tragic strain of consciousness.

If we trace the type of subjects and Musorgsky's attitude toward them in the middle and most productive period of his creative life (1865–1874), then the "deviations from the beginning and the end" will have a more formal and superficial character, while the essence remains the same. At first glance, the abundance, so to speak, of "unlovely" subjects in the romances (vocal scenes) is truly remarkable, no less than the reputed realistic historicism of *Boris Godunov* and *Khovanshchina*, even though in actual fact these are only new heroes and objects for an incorrigible dreamer and visionary. The "truthfulness" of Musorgsky lies not in the precise depiction of the peasant sorrow and tears of all the downtrodden, but in the sincerity of his music, so saturated with the directly conveyed sensory data. It is the truth of sincerity and immediacy, which can either exist or not in the realist, the romantic, or the classicist: at issue is the nature of the art, not its coloration. Musorgsky's passionate approach to the subject and to the conception and presentation of it are clearly *romantic*. Musorgsky creates his world and endows it with *his* world of harmonies, but he does not occupy himself with recording previously discovered worlds as do the classicists. The force of his talent has seen to it that, ever since Musorgsky, we believe in precisely *these* unfortunate and aggrieved, those that he depicted for us in sounds. But can we trust his objectivity? Never. His heightened sensitivity announces itself at every step, and the world of sound that he created is a real world no more and no less than that of any work of art, which gains its right to be real by means of its own *environment*, its own existence.[29]

A nervous perceptual acuity induced Musorgsky at times to don the mask of deformity and buffoonery, here maliciously exaggerated to the point of cruel insult ("Ozornik" [The Ragamuffin, 1867], "Darling Savishna!" [1866]) and caricature, there verging on the clownery of *skomorokhi* ("Rayok," [1870]), there remaining within the confines of sly humor ("Hopak" [1866], "Po griby" [Mushroom hunting, 1867]), and there adapting the form of satire, naive on account of its crude approach to the theme (e.g., "The Song of Mephistopheles in Auerbach's Cellar" [1879], "Kozel" [i.e., "A Society Tale: The Goat," 1867]).[30] Musorgsky's laughter does not reveal a simple-hearted human smile trustingly and joyfully gazing at the word; his laughter is always "prickly," with an undisguised goal of getting under the skin. It is the humor of a hurt pride, through which the world is viewed, as in the devil's cunning mirror of Hans Christian Andersen's "Snow Queen." Only in "The Seminarist," in this clever genre-tableau, is something akin to light and freedom uncovered; it seems to glow with kindhearted infectious and merry laughter, without the grimace, without a secret thought to wound.[31] Such is Varlaam in *Boris*, too, in the scene at the inn. His antipode is the grimacing and shifty Podiachy in *Khovanshchina*. But one could never agree that the humorous acceptance of the world as it is revealed in the relevant works of Musorgsky supports the view of him as a leader and vehement proponent of realism and even of naturalism: in this respect his world is nothing other than a peepshow!

Now let us turn to that sphere of Musorgsky's art where he revealed himself with particular brightness and where, it would seem, the true reproduction of reality should be evident unconditionally and directly: in the concrete realization of the history of the Russian people, as it is set forth in the "national music dramas" *Boris Godunov* and *Khovanshchina*. We just now established Musorgsky's humorous acceptance of the world. To know his song cycles *Sunless* and *Songs and Dances of Death*; the ballade "The Forgotten One" [1874]; the romances "Evil Death (Letter from the Grave)" [1874] and "The Leaves Rustle Cheerlessly" [1859] is to see that his humor was rooted in the same deep recesses of the soul in which it (humor) dwelled at the time when artistic depictions of the "dances of death" were made in the West, i.e., that along with the "laughter" there occurred in Musorgsky a steady deepening or cleansing of this humor of specific elements of mockery (insults) and a transformation of it into a *tragic* acceptance of the world. From studying the characteristics of the dramatic material favored by Musorgsky and the devices for its elaboration that were typical for him, it becomes clear that he was not to be satisfied either with *life when it is inwardly focused but outwardly inexpressive*, nor with a human personality as merely a kind of spiritual entity.

Briefly stated, life without events that have a sharp external profile and a human being without the influences of an affect and of dramatic collisions from without held little interest for Musorgsky. He always made the individual dependent on the events that pulled at him, toward which he would have to define his attitude in one way or another. Such a characterization in accord with events and on the basis of events was a technique highly characteristic of Hugo and of French Romanticism in general: a technique that found the broadest employment in French Romantic opera (it is instructive in this regard to compare the handling of the plot of *Queen of Spades* in Halévy[32] and in Tchaikovsky) and, finally, achieved its greatest flowering in Meyerbeer's action-adventure operas.[33] It was once believed that the individual would reveal his heroic essence only if he was put in the vice of highly melodramatic conflicts (does this not reveal the psychology of *l'aventurisme* of the 18th century?). In his youth, Musorgsky was inculcated with the influence of the romantic school and since it was connected to his nervously excitable nature, it sank deep into his soul for his entire life.

On no account are the operas of Musorgsky national musical dramas in essence. The people do not exist as a freely acting collective in them, nor is there a dramatic development in which the people could truly play a major role.[34] We are merely dealing here with a whole series of dramatic situations to which the people somehow respond and under the narcotic effect of which they now rage (the brilliant Kromy Forest scene in *Boris*), now groan (the prologue to the opera), here rejoice (also there), there pray (the Streltsy before Khovansky; the Old Believers), here take to drinking (the Streltsy enclave), there cringe (the prologue to *Boris*, the coronation, the greeting of the Pretender), but at no time create anything or act productively. What kind of drama lacks an active force and a heroic element (for indeed, the Old Believers who are processing backstage, those to whom Dosifei points during the "conversation between the princes"[35] are not yet actual heroes who participate in the plot)? What sort of dramatic characterization is it when the role of the people is reduced to reflex actions, to passive submission or revolt? When revolt immediately changes over into servile docility? Such a characterization of the folk through melodramatic conflicts does not bring to light an authentic national drama; the essence of the spirit of the people is revealed here only incidentally and inconsistently.

If Musorgsky's dramas are nevertheless vivid and seemingly nationalistic, this occurs on the strength of the hypnotic power of the genial music, a power that emanates from its emotional saturation and because Musorgsky, despite his romantic attitude to history, was always a remarkable psychologist. With great acuity he realized his perception of the world in sound, one in which he believed profoundly, considering it to be an authentic *expression* of the world. How typical that this populist and realist found it necessary to escape into history, to the distant past, indeed into an epoch marked by the greatest awakening of passions, into a chaotic confusion of moods and demands. And there amidst this stormy milieu, the composer piled stone upon stone, encounter upon encounter, and murder upon murder. Remaining at all times a sincere and amazingly accurate conveyer of psychic experiences, Musorgsky gave them a concrete realization in the framework of operatic melodrama. He conceived history through the images created by the romantic imagination.

Accompanied by a lavish entourage of everyday details and scenic effects, these stand out in nervous relief against the background of a historical perspective, completely inundated with the afterglow of romantic passion. *Khovanshchina* in particular abounds in rather naive "melodramatic" characteristics to emphasize baseness, villainy, dullness, wildness, ferocity, hypocrisy, etc.

Such are the machinations of Shaklovity, the blind ambition of old Khovansky, the crudity and vulgarity of the Streltsy, the cynicism of Golitsyn in relation to Marfa. Lastly, we may direct attention to the choice of situations: the scene with Khovansky's murder, Marfa's divination, her impassioned amorous taunting of Prince Andrei, the horrors of the execution of the Streltsy, the Old Believers in their act of self-immolation.[36] Blood, murders, executions, denunciations, betrayals, the outbreak of lust and bloodthirsty instincts—what a nice selection of data for the representation of true reality, and in the form of national drama no less! . . . For the most part, the human characters are portrayed as Musorgsky was wont to interpret them: with distortions, bad consciences, spiritual and physical poverty, animosities, and fanatical cruelty. It is remarkable how the stock of creative energy in Musorgsky sufficed to characterize with unfailing and stunning brilliance all of these tortured souls, tormenting and tormented by each other! The composer's power of expression was such that he could induce us to believe in the reality of hallucinations and even in the appearance of death itself. It is no wonder, given the presence of such graphically realized experiences, that Musorgsky's heroes carry on as if alive, that they live before us, whereas with any composer who does not possess the power to reincarnate his life energy into a character, nor such an impassioned imaginative vitality, nor control over the gift for transforming perceptions of life into musical representations sated with feeling—these same heroes, when placed in such ultraromantic "operatic-theatrical" conditions of existence on stage, would inevitably turn into walking windup toys or would stay frozen in the excessive pathos of costumed actors.

The great significance of *Boris Godunov* and *Khovanshchina* does not consist of the fact that they are realistic national dramas. It is not in the concrete manifestation of the historical reality that supposedly characterizes them that the effectiveness of these remarkable works is revealed. Beyond the purely musical brilliance, freshness, and originality, their significance can be traced to a solid psychological foundation. Within them, Musorgsky, perhaps wholly unconsciously, touched on the depths of tragic experiences in the solitary human soul. In them he presented the problem of the tragic Russian awareness of life, which was partly his very own problem, to be set forth and resolved in music. By this means, he may have found the only possible way for constructing the musical tragedy he was building on the basis of the song element (i.e., not the *instrumental* element).

The center of *Boris Godunov*, its dramatic axis, is not the people at all, but man's tragic experience (here, Tsar Boris's) of his inescapable guilt before his own conscience and before the terrifying unknown power called death. The meaning of *Boris* is unveiled in a pair of "outcries" acting as fulcrums, toward which Musorgsky typically synchronizes all the preceding musical momentum:

"Oh cruel conscience, how heavily you punish" (after the scene with Shuisky in the second act) and "Oh evil death, how brutally you torment" (in the final struggle preceding death).[37] To achieve the expressivity he needed, Musorgsky did not even spare Pushkin but mercilessly tore to pieces his well-proportioned design for the sake of underscoring or strengthening one moment or other, a certain experience of the soul, with some melodramatic phrase. The same occurs in *Khovanshchina*, where Musorgsky, in his craving to capture more fully a world of passions both of individual people and of the masses, at times loses the dramatic thread of the work.

At the center of this opera is a woman (Marfa) who loves, passionately and *powerfully*, whose covetous and greedy love is transformed through the prism of the religious worldview of the Old Believers into a peculiar *vengeance*, a sacrifice of herself and her beloved for the sake of an idea that unites all and cleanses them both of sin: for the sake of a victorious martyrdom for the faith. Marfa is a divided soul: her conscience is broken. With a pure heart, she confesses her sin, her carnal love, to Dosifei; but in the end it remains unknown whether she is suffering for the Faith or because there is *no other means* for her to keep Prince Andrei to herself, no other union other than a union through a martyr's death. The loving woman sings the requiem for her beloved—what a flight, what a composition, what a course for an imagination seemingly seeking reality! Like Tsar Boris, Marfa feels herself to be guilty before God and before her own conscience (I recall her overwhelmingly powerful monologue-prayer, "We've done it, oh Lord!").[38] And death is the escape for her.

The same could also be said for Dosifei. He is no brazen fanatic! He is forever doubting and by himself accomplishes essentially nothing, instead delegating to others so as to retain for himself the right to contemplate, sermonize, and persuade. He burns because in the act he seems to see an eventual resolution to agonizing questions, because this is the only escape from his vacillations. "How many woes, how much suffering the spirit of doubt has visited on me"—in this way he confesses, remaining alone with his thoughts.[39] Dosifei's fifth-act monologue, "Here, at this holy place," which is so remarkable in conception and in economy of means, carries a hint of sadness, torment, and vacillation.[40] Passive contemplation and self-confession ("Am I right or am I wrong?") are far more characteristic of Dosifei than those moments where he must prophesy and be a guide to others. In the latter instance the music is agitated and sated with an unpleasant pathos in another, seemingly non-Russian style. Such are the exhortations: "Trumpet of the Eternal! The time has come to accept the crown of eternal glory in fire and flame" and "Be gone, carnal snares of Hell." These could never be compared to Boris's cries prior to his death.

Groaning emanates from all of Musorgsky's music, and this groaning stretches from the cradle to the grave: from a mother's sad and tender laments

over her child to the horror of death. Yet it would dishonor Musorgsky to at-
tribute his moans and groans to complaints for the *destitute* and unfortunate.
They were the result of a much more profound and incurable pessimism. Musorgsky was indeed poor, but poor *in spirit*: a man with a broken conscience.
His sorrow was a sorrow that came from an awareness of a general guilt borne
throughout the world by all for the sake of one, and by one on behalf of all.
Out of this emerges ceaseless self-torment: is not every human being (every
"I") guilty merely by being alive? If it is necessary to live amidst pain and to
feel oneself guilty by nature, then how can one not fear death?! No matter
when, no matter where, it is behind you, disrupting any semblance of an active life, destroying hopes and aspirations. Never does death enter as an element to pacify or bring to a natural end. It is a blind alley, impenetrable and
senseless. It is brutal and omnipotent. Though seemingly idyllic, the ending
of "Trepak" is an evil mockery. It offers not peace but a threat: a man has
ceased to be, while everything in the world proceeds along its normal course,
calmly and indifferently, and—even more painfully—as if at peace and not
without beauty.[41] There is nothing whole that anyone can achieve that death
will not tear asunder.

In the motley series of characters created by Musorgsky there are suffer-
ers, tormenters, villains, even monsters—but not a single human being joyfully accepting life and achieving his calling, having found his life purpose.
Actually there is one, but even that one is a pretender who will change his
countenance several times over the course of the opera (in the cell, in the inn,
with Marina, in the Kromy Forest) so that in the end it is unclear whether he
was real or a phantom: an illusion of the popular imagination.[42] And what of
the Dmitri-Tsarevich "theme" that follows his path and accompanies him?[43]
The course of action is as follows: in his conversation with Grigory, Pimen
points out the crime of Boris Godunov. In his monologue Grigory lets us
know that the time of God's punishment of the criminal has arrived and that
he will not escape the carrying out of divine justice. Is he not thinking of
himself here as the emissary, the executor of a Higher Power's behests?
Thereafter begins the peculiar "biography" of Grigory as Fugitive Dmitri. In
the inn he is a state criminal (and Dmitri's theme reinforces his growing belief of being on a mission); in Poland he is a passionate lover; and at the conclusion [of the act] under the impulse of passion, intoxicated with Marina's
beauty, a visionary who has convinced himself of his imperial ancestry. In the
Kromy Forest he is the people's choice, the tsar accepted by the people (if indeed the *people* actually do function here as previously with the choosing of
Boris, acting as a bearer of an intuited and historically established ideal of a
kingdom, which to me is doubtful). Then suddenly, in Pimen's tale of the
miracle, the face of the genuine Dmitri the Miracle Worker rises up. Who

then is *that*? . . . Pimen, it seems, has also found his calling, but at the price of withdrawing from life and rejecting any aspirations and achievements. Hence all the delights in the world are deception and mirage, sent by some cunning entity; a protective cover, spread over a terrible descent into the unknown. And those people who believe in the world groan, weep, and *cry out*, impotent in their sin and with each other.

It is a salvation from suffering and horror up until the moment of death's arrival that lies in the attempt to create a *dream*: to sink into reverie. Hence from time to time Musorgsky came to compose tender, illusory romances filled with impulsive longing for affectionate, unknown, ghostly personages: romances such as "Night" [1864], "Softly the Spirit Flew" [1877], "Desire" [1866], and "Vision" [1877]. Catching fleeting glimpses of light, the sun, and affection, he would create such things as the simple-hearted, transparent, idyllic piece "Along the Don a Garden Blooms" [1867], wherein a girl's lively, palpable form glimmers; or the firmly rooted down-to-earth "Peasant's Feast" [1867]; or the sketches to *Sorochintsy Fair* [1874–1880], which, of course, he *never* could have completed! Conceived in 1875 [*sic*], this everyday operatic tale remained a beautiful dream never to be fully expressed. Though given to perceiving the world from a gloomy perspective, the visionary composer decided to produce an *opèra characteristique,* part genre piece and part idyll, in order to recreate in the realm of sound sincere, naive, and simple-hearted relations between people who were not gripped by a spiritual struggle. Strength was lacking for this feat, since it would have been a feat indeed for Musorgsky in his declining days to realize in sound a worldview to which he was completely unaccustomed, i.e., the one contained in Gogol's tale.

Musorgsky's high-strung, impressionable nature and his highly elevated perception of life phenomena had a dual effect on his creativity: together they produced the psychological inundation of his musical structures and simultaneously imbued his attitude toward reality with a restless and unbalanced character that even reached the point of delirious visions. Musorgsky built his perception of the world on the shaky footing of poignant personal experiences, on the deepest empathizing with every phenomenon, to the point of forgetting entirely that external phenomena did not constitute his inner world. Sensing the pain and sadness of others, Musorgsky made them his own, deepening them of course. To love is to pity. Reconceiving the world with love and sympathy, he endowed his *own* embodiments of tormenters, torment, and the tormented with the semblance of indisputable reality. This was due, of course, to his enormous creative talent. Hence the musical world created by Musorgsky was filled up, like no one else's, with a vital nerve; Musorgsky strove for a direct, intuitive knowledge and manifestation in music of everything around, of life in its entirety. Not only did he not produce *formalized* musical structures, but he desired that every pattern of human speech given to him would be sated with music and that music itself be filled with the energy of life experiences.

The element of music was for him an immediate fact of life with which he desired to reproduce in sound the temper of human speech, the course of action taken, and the stream of human feelings. It was due to the *songfulness* of the word and the *"speech-like" disposition of musical sound* based on immutably given perceptions, on a faith in the *truth* of the soul's testimony, that Musorgsky became so well cherished in our time, when the influence of intuitive thought is everywhere apparent and when music as the most intuitive[44] of the arts is attracting particular attention and, itself, is influencing other spheres of art. And if Musorgsky in his intellectual views professed the principles of utilitarian and tendentious art, thanks to intuition he showed in his works an artistic approach of greater depth and content.

His art bears the undeniable imprint of a romantic artist's characteristic approach and not that of the idealist-classicist or the realist-nationalist. Or, more probably the *essence* of Musorgsky's nationalism was romantic, for it was dreamy, illusory, and unreal to an extreme, if *still* profoundly lifelike. Proof of this is found, first, in the one-sided concrete manifestation of history tinged with pathos and melodrama; secondly, in the predominance of a personally tragic element over the national element in both operas;[45] and thirdly, in the constantly distorted and exaggerated reflection of all that pertains to the nation throughout all of Musorgsky's works. Moreover, the romantic element in Musorgsky's characters is expressed in his choice of subjects (beginning with the youthful effort *Han d'Islande*), in his attitude toward them (the characteristic elaboration of *Salammbô*), and in the role of the vision, illusion, and dream in his works. The musical world realized by Musorgsky overwhelms with gloom, groaning, and suffering. And since Musorgsky is always sincere and truthful with respect to the correspondence between the music and the psychological moment being expressed in each individual case, in every characterization, we cannot help but believe in his art on the whole. The musical realization of Musorgsky's ideas is unquestionably sincere and truthful; but it is by no means based on a realistic artist's powers of observation, for it is exaggeratedly one-sided and limited by a highly subjective selection of impressions and constantly colored with a strong dose of hyperbole and magniloquence. It is the world of a romantic, a visionary, a dreamer.

Within the romantic worldview overall and the romantic approach to art, two characteristic traits stand out, which are inherent in Musorgsky's perception of the world: the humorous and the tragic. Musorgsky's humor at its core is imprinted with pity toward people; but often, wearing the mask of a holy fool, the composer cast aside compassion and ridiculed in a malicious caricature that which he himself detested in the human whirlpool of lies, cynicism, and cruelty. Musorgsky's laughter sounds the weakest in his satires that deliberately denounce society; strongest of all is the scene at the inn, so remarkable for its flexibility of language and accuracy in "delineations," a scene where bitter humor in some moments burns itself up, to be transformed into vigorous, healthy, good-natured laughter.[46] This astonishingly well-integrated, characteristic tableau of everyday life even leaves one with a regret: why was Musorgsky not destined to complete his comic opera of the commonplace [i.e., *The Sorochintsy Fair*]?! Perhaps light and salvation and a release from the tragic view of life's phenomena that so seized the composer's imagination might have been revealed in it. True enough, this viewpoint gave Russia *Boris Godunov* and *Khovanshchina*, two unprecedented historical chronicles, but it also deprived the person who created them of will, courage, self-esteem (despite a blatant conceit!), and stability in life.

Judging by the characterizations of Boris, Marfa, Dosifei, by the hopelessness of the cycles *Sunless* and *Songs and Dances of Death*, the root of Musorgsky's tragedy lies with a broken and divided conscience ashamed of itself and in his acceptance of the burden of shared suffering and common guilt of all people toward all. It is something eternally Russian: the shame of not living like a human being, but the even greater shame at living well when for others it is difficult. A conscience in pain and ashamed of itself is worried at times by self-analysis that is constant, importunate, and excruciating; at times by a chain of external events, which typically squeezed the human individual in Russia until his life was transformed into a "Tale of Woe-Misfortune."[47] An outwardly insolent and provocative behavior of boorishness and cynicism then emerges as a protective covering for inner shame of self: it is an opportune escape for those natures that do not surrender easily to fate. That the suffering soul might only be hidden! The face of death looms ever larger as the unavoidable final exit, a sinister and irreconcilable necessity. Its ghostly form is present here and everywhere, so that at the prescribed moment life will be cut short and the existence of any kind of consciously willed project curtailed, unless it be directed toward death and destruction. Even the suicide (the self-immolation on wings of religious ecstasy) in *Khovanshchina* cannot remove death's senseless and cruel aspect. Presentiments of resurrection and a transfigured spiritual life in paradise, whether on Earth or in Heaven, did not exist for Musorgsky; therefore, the self-immolation of the Old Believers is presented as a horrible and flagrant transgression: an annihilation that insults the element of life and not a martyrdom. Hence *Khovanshchina* with its tragically divided religious consciousness has such a stunning effect on us; hence it was necessary to bring an end to all this "commotion" with a blasphemous, high-falutin' "European" firework of a march!

The concluding scene of *Khovanshchina* obtains its profound meaning not through its nationalism but through the tragic character of Marfa, as a *consummation* of this woman's burning passion. Only from a romantic point of view can one accept the entire opera as an artistically unified structure: as a conception for uncovering the secret of how religious ecstasy can be permeated with erotic content, and a mystical love with the love that is carnal lust. It is evident that the composer could not find a secure foundation either in *Boris* or in *Khovanshchina*: in one and in the other one there are merely the torments of a suffering conscience. A ground for his imagination glimmers only in a few romances of contemplative character, wherein he dreams of a beautiful vision of a woman. But this is hardly a dream of love.

One can only guess about the effect of feelings of love and of a woman's psyche on Musorgsky's psyche, since both his life and his art give only the strangest of indications about it. For all its stylistic logic, the characterization of Marina is unusually conventional and formalistic.[48] Her love duet with the Pretender is splendid at the moment when the pliant, noble melody in E-flat major enters ("O prince, I beg you"), but love plays no role at all here. This is music characterizing the proud, rapturous outburst of a woman in response to the angry outburst that she herself had provoked in a beguiled lover. This leaves Marfa. Her passionate feeling of love is complicated and enhanced by experiences of an ecstatic sort and by visions that deceive. Her elements are fanaticism, pride, and mysticism. One cannot speak of Musorgsky's perception of amorous feeling as infatuation, with the exception of an idyllic "objectification" of this feeling in "The Peasant Boy's Dumka" and "Parasya's Dumka" [both from *Sorochintsy Fair*].[49]

Based on the romances "Night," "Vision," "Desire," and to a greater degree on Musorgsky's chaste letters, one can speak with certainty only of the deep reverence that he had for woman and femininity. As a testimony of this there is the touching and poignant lullaby "Sleep, go to sleep, my peasant son" [1865], which the composer dedicated to the memory of his dearly beloved mother.[50] Musorgsky showed equal reverence for the memory of Nadezhda Petrovna Opochinina. Could she have been his Beatrice?![51]

If one speaks about those of Musorgsky's emotions that accord with their *manifestation* in his works, I would single out the following as fundamental: a reverential *attraction* to the feminine and to a ghostly unknown, *compassion* for people, and a *shame* of conscience on account of human monstrosity, physical and spiritual poverty in the world, and the states of holy foolery and malicious mocking that emanate therefrom. These are the spiritual "bases" on which the experiences of the composer seem to be grounded. Out of these, compassionate love in particular permeates nearly all of his compositions. The character of the Holy Fool introduced in *Boris Godunov* is a kind of metaphor—a unique synthesis of the compassionate moods that characterize Musorgsky's sad soul. The external bulwark or support for him was *everyday life*. In his operas as well as in his vocal and instrumental compositions, he devoted much music to the depiction of everyday scenes, tableaus, and phenomena. Even in his excursions into the fantastic, Musorgsky proceeds not from a perception of the mysterious and fairytale element as such, but rather from the appeal of everyday and national color that is revealed in this sphere (*Night on Bald Mountain*, "Baba Yaga"). A perception of anything intangible, i.e., not found in the direct experience of inner spiritual life *in connection with external reality*, was in all likelihood foreign to Musorgsky's nature. Thus there is practically nothing to be said (for now, in any case) regarding the immediate religious sentiment of the composer. Without a doubt, a perception of religious ecstasy through the mediated sphere of human character (the schismatic element in religion) was a given to him, but this was religion as interpreted through affects, a religion as reflected in the psyche of an ailing soul. It is not the same as the shining and radiant "acathistus" to Heaven and Earth of the maiden Fevronia in the first-act "forest mystery" of *The Legend of the City Kitezh*! How interesting that contact with the religious sphere of folk beliefs from two great representatives of Russian music as Musorgsky and Rimsky-Korsakov would elicit such substantially different results.

Impressions of the visible world had an irresistible power over Musorgsky; they suggested to him striking images of profound musical description. One encounters examples at every step in the operas and everywhere else: bell peals and clock chimes in *Boris*; dawn, the clatter of hooves (the cavalry), and the procession taking Golitsyn into exile in *Khovanshchina*;[52] masses of characteristic, superficially descriptive detail in *The Marriage*, *Pictures at an Exhibition* for piano, and a whole series of little pieces for piano—"The Seamstress" [1871], "Nanny and Me," and "First Punishment" [both from the piano set *Childhood Memories*, 1865], *A Traveler's Crimean Sketches* [i.e., "On the Crimean Southern Shore" (1879) and "Near the Crimean Southern Shore" (1880), both for piano], and nearly all of *In the Nursery* [1872]. Self-contained depictions of nature, of course, occur more rarely, which becomes entirely comprehensible and predictable if one keeps in mind that Musorgsky's creative gaze was directed more often and with greater intensity toward the perception of a human being in his spiritual world—a perception, however, conditioned by the constant presence of the visible world surrounding the human soul and the experiences of human beings. It was as if the perception of phenomena crystallizing in visible and palpable things gave Musorgsky a footing in life or firm foundation. In the musical realization of it all, Musorgsky found his calling as a composer and a justification for his art.

Musorgsky's *greatness* lies in his compassion for humanity, for the sufferings of the human soul. From this stems his inescapable sorrow, the blind alleys of his aspirations; from this, too, come the spiritual instability and corresponding sketchiness of thought as well as the ineptitude for purely musical, self-animated, organic conceptions. Musorgsky's *weakness* is due to the fact that his "intuitions" were not enlightened and unified by an idea and not deepened by either a religious or a philosophical awareness. Emotions and vital impressions elicited in him only reflexes of ingenuity and paradoxical flickers of an idea, but not thought. From feelings and mind alone, Musorgsky found neither justification nor atonement for human sorrow, ugliness, and spiritual emptiness. In *the final end*, there arose before his spiritual gaze only a single *entity*, one both evil and cruel in its inevitability and inescapability, by means of which the human tragicomedy was brought to a close: *death*. Faced with this dead end, Musorgsky would come to a halt, bereft of strength and will, focused on the horror (listen to the death of Boris!!!), without any hope of overcoming it and emerging from it.

This raises a question: did Musorgsky lack the wisdom, the faith, or the will to tear away from the hexed circle of creative experiences and conflicts[53] to which he was drawn and enticed, and that his own creative imagination set before him? In his *Pictures at an Exhibition*, inspired by the *death* of the architect Hartman, amid a series of musical realizations so remarkable for their descriptive acuity and graphic outline, the gloomiest is "Catacombs." Do we not have here a symbol of the spiritual state within which the composer passed by his entire life, never finding an escape to the light and perhaps not even certain that the light existed?

In lieu of endnotes, I will now extract the moments from Musorgsky's letters that vividly restore the countenance of this composer-psychologist before me as I sense and imagine it to be.[54]

From the letter of 16 and 22 June 1872: "The past in the present—here is my task. '*We've progressed!*' is a lie. '*Same spot!*' The paper and the books have progressed—but we are in the *same spot*. Until the people can believe *for themselves* what is being concocted, until they want it for *themselves* that one thing or another be concocted from it—*same spot!* All sorts of benefactors know how to become famous, to strengthen their grandiloquence with documents, while the people groan or, in order not to groan, drink themselves into a stupor and groan all the more: *Same spot*" (p. 209).

In the letter of 13 July 1872, after writing out a brilliantly expressive Old Believers' legend about the Antichrist, Musorgsky continues: "Much can be done with such an outline: pictorially, mystically, and with a delightful *caricature* [my emphasis—Igor Glebov] of history. There is much substance in the materials" (p. 215).

This letter contains more interesting and graphic ideas on technique and its significance in art. An example: "I, for instance, cannot stand it when there is a fine *pirog* that's been cooked and, more particularly, *eaten*, and the hostess says: 'One million pounds of butter, 500 eggs, a whole bed of cabbage, 150

1/4 fish . . . You eat the *pirog* and it's tasty and because you've heard about the kitchen, you imagine the man or woman cooking, always untidy, severed head of the capon on the bench, one gutted fish on top of another, and sometimes nearby, the intestines of something or other staring up out of the sieve (like Prussians honoring us with a visit!), and often enough, a greasy apron shows itself, with snot all over it, put into the apron that later they will use to wipe the edge of the plate with the *pirog* so that it'd be cleaner . . . well, by then the *pirog* has become less tasty" (pp. 203–4).

In regards to how incisively Musorgsky sensed depth of feeling and the vital sap of intense passion, the following excerpt from a letter of 18 October 1872 says: "If a strong and passionate and beloved woman gives a powerful squeeze to the man she loves while embracing him, even though the violence registers, there is no desire to break free, since this violence is 'boundless bliss,' since it is from this violence that the 'young man's blood starts to boil.' I am not ashamed of the comparison: no matter how you twist and flirt with the truth, whoever has experienced love in all its power and abandon, has *lived* and will remember that he lived *well* and will not cast a shadow over bygone bliss" (p. 217).

The letter of 2 August 1873 concerns the death of Victor Hartman:[55] "The thing of it is, we only sense danger for another when he is sinking or prepared to die. Idiot! And still a fool even with a king-size brain, a hopeless idiot! And every last little man's just such an idiot, not excluding the pompous doctors like turkeys wiggling their tails—spreading the fan as they decide matters of life and death.

"At such times, it is the sages that usually console us idiots: *he* does not exist but that which he managed to do does exist and will exist and, well, it's not many people that have such a happy lot not to be forgotten. Hamburger again (with horseradish for tears) made from our dear human pride. Devil take your wisdom! If *he* did not live in vain, but *created,* then what kind of a rascal must one be to take delight in the consolation and make peace with the fact that he has *ceased to create*. There is no peace nor can there be and there should not be consolations either—how hapless . . ." (pp. 212–13).

From the same letter, amidst the information about *Khovanshchina*: "For now, three pieces of news: first, the incantation 'to the wind' of the Old Believer woman is getting drowned out by the Old Believers' song about the 'Alleluia woman' as they emerge from the forest in shrouds and with green candles; during one of the choir's periphrases, one Old Believer woman pierces the scene with the cry: 'Death approaches!' and follows the brethren 'to cloak herself in white raiment and take up the light of the righteous.' Meanwhile, Andrei Khovansky shows himself at the cell's little window, where the fräulein is concealed, and sings a 'nightingale's song.' Hearing this, the Old Believer woman in a shroud and with a candle emerges from the hermitage and steals up to Khovansky, but he, as if hit on the head with a shovel, like a fool, does not notice what is underway in the hermitage. To the love theme from the incantation, the woman whispers to him: 'The hour of your death is nigh, my beloved; embrace me for the last time; you will be dear to me unto the grave; to die with you is to fall into sweet slumber. Alleluia!' (walking round him and bowing). This lover's requiem *pleases all without exception* and is pleasing also to me . . ." (p. 212).[56]

From the letter of 19 October 1875, in contemplation of the portrait of Vladimir Stasov: "Many thanks to you. The hale and hearty *faraway!* and *forward!* urge me onward as well. As I think of certain artists stuck behind the gate, it's not longing, but something akin to *delusion* that takes place. Their entire aspiration is to *drizzle* one little drop on top of another and all these droplets are all alike, all cherished; they are amused but for the common man there is only longing and boredom; why don't you break through, my dear, as living people break through; show whether you have claws or webbed feet; whether you are a beast then or some amphibian? How could you! But what about the gate! Without reason, without a will they surround themselves— these artists—with the traditional paths, affirm the law of inertia, thinking they are accomplishing a great deed . . ." (p. 201).

In the letter of 23 November 1875, concerning Saint-Saens's "new playthings":[57] "It's not music that we need, nor words, nor a palette, nor a chisel— no, devil take you all, liars, hypocrites, *e tutti quanti*—give us living thoughts, start up a lively talk with people, no matter what you choose to discuss with them! . . ." (p. 214).

From the letter of 29–30 December 1875, concerning the marriage of the poet Golenishchev-Kutuzov:[58] "Such matters nag me to work all the more. When there's just one left—I shall be alone. It behooves one to die alone; it's not as if everyone else will come with me . . ." (p. 217).

From the letter of 15 June 1876: "By the way, I thank you that we have understood Marfa and will make this Russian woman pure. But pathos is fine and fitting for Marfa's tragedy and, truth be told, it is profitable for a musician that the sin is concealed . . ." (p. 217).

From the letter of 25 December 1876: "You know, before *Boris*, I offered tableaus of the people. My wish now is to produce a *prognostic* and this is how the prognostic will be: a *living* melody instead of a classical one. Through working with human speech, I came to a melody that was created out of this speech; I began to turn recitative into melody (aside from dramatic actions, *bien entendu*, when one can even go on to interjections). I would like to call this an intelligible/justified melody. And work gives me pleasure; suddenly something unexpected and unspeakable and inimical to classical melody (so highly favored) will be sung and immediately be understood by one and all. If I attain this—I will count it as an achievement in art, and it is indeed necessary to achieve. I would like to submit a few tableaus to try out. By the way, there are already a few inclinations in *Khovanshchina* (Marfa's sorrow before Dosifei) and in *Sorochintsy*—both are at the ready" (p. 204).

NOTES

1. Orlova notes that the unpublished article, dated February 1917, was titled "Musorgsky (1839–1881): Toward an Understanding of his Creativity."

2. The heyday of Baroque Neapolitan opera occurred in the late 17th and early 18th centuries, as represented in the works of Alessandro Scarlatti. The development of recitative, da capo aria, comic, and dialect operas all set important precedents for later 18th-century opera.

3. The erudite religious leader Filaret (adopted clerical name for Vasily Drozdov, 1782–1867), who became Metropolitan in 1826, made it his mission to revitalize Orthodoxy during embattled times; his *Christian Catechism* of 1823 was widely read and admired for its high literary style.

4. The death of Seneca occurs in the second act of Monteverdi's *L'Incoronzaione di Poppea*. The philosopher's recitative is notable for its free, expressive dissonances.

5. The metaphor of the "black goat" carries associations with Russian and other satanic rituals.

6. A catalyst for reawakened interest abroad would be Diaghilev's staging of *Boris Godunov*, beginning on 19 May 1908.

7. This frequently asserted claim is typically substantiated on the evidence of Debussy's employment in 1880 by Tchaikovsky's patron Nadezhda von Meck; Debussy's acquaintance with the scores of *Boris* and several of the song cycles (at least by 1893); and his attendance at the concerts that Rimsky-Korsakov conducted in Paris for the Exposition Universelle of 1889.

8. *Narodnaya volya* or "People's Will" was a political protest group that favored terrorist action, led by Andrei Zhelyabov and Sofia Perovskaya. Their planning and execution of Tsar Alexander II in 1881 prompted mass outrage and led to the group's dissolution.

9. See n. 11.

10. The project of adapting Gogol's comic play *The Marriage* resulted only in a one-act operatic torso, composed in 1868. The work is a through-composed, line-by-line setting of the play, using a flexible recitative style replete with caricature and comic interjections.

11. Vasily Perov (1834–1882) joined the group of late 19th-century Russian painters known as *Peredvizhniki* (Wanderers), who were known for their itinerant

annual art showings and for a more or less shared commitment to making art relevant to the issues of contemporary life. Perov's depiction of urban and rural poverty was indicative to Stasov of a social conscience akin to the one he sensed in Musorgsky.

12. Two years before his death, Rimsky was already complaining in his personal "Letopis" (i.e., "Chronicle," published in English as *My Musical Life*) of Musorgsky's "fatuous self-conceit and conviction that the path he had chosen in art was the only true path," noting in addition a "complete decline, alcoholism, and, as a result, an ever befogged mind" [Rimsky-Korsakov, *My Musical Life*, trans. Judah Joffe (New York: Tudor, 1936), 206].

13. In his letters of 1873 Musorgsky described several scenes with Marfa. He was especially pleased with the material that would eventually be used in Act 5, scene 3 (i.e., the duet of Marfa and Andrei Khovansky, preceding the immolation scene). In a letter of 2 Aug 1873, he reported to Stasov: "*Everybody without exception likes* the love-burial-service and even I like it myself. [Musorgsky's note]: This duet: the powerless struggle of Andrei, his horror, the scathing words of the dissentress about both the German girl and self-immolation—this pleases me no end" [Leyda and Bertensson, *The Musorgsky Reader* (New York: Norton, 1947): 235.]

14. Musorgsky's celebrated dictum appeared in the "Autobiographical Note" that the composer wrote in 1880 for a music dictionary being compiled by Hugo Riemann. A full translation appears in Leyda and Bertensson, *The Musorgsky Reader*, 416–20.

15. Another excerpt from the "Autobiographical Note."

16. The "intuitive" and "process" philosophies of Bergson and Nikolai Lossky that so preoccupied Asafyev during the writing of the *Etudes* cannot easily be reconciled with the Marxist materialism of the young Soviet ideologues. In a note for the second edition (p. 261, n. 9), Orlova finesses the difficulty by equating Asafyev's unqualified derisive reference to "utilitarian materialism" with "vulgar sociologism," a catchall euphemism from the 1920s, employed whenever it was necessary to show that what looked like a blanket condemnation of Marxism was in fact only a criticism of a distorted interpretation of it.

17. [Author's note:] In the sense of images that are visible and tangible in their three-dimensionality (sculpture) or in imitation of three-dimensionality on a plane (painting).

18. Musorgsky completed his version of *St. John's Night on Bald Mountain* in 1867. Rimsky's more familiar revision dates from 1886.

19. The so-called Polish act, centering on the cajoling of Dmitri the Pretender by Princess Marina and the priest Rangoni was scored to lines written by Musorsgky, including the text of the love duet "O Tsarevich, I implore you," which is sung at night, with a moonlit fountain in the background.

20. In the version of *Khovanshchina* that Asafyev likely consulted, Rimsky had created the scene in question (Act 5, no. 3) using a combination of actual sketches and his own memory of Musorgsky's rendition at the piano. In this penultimate scene preceding the immolation, Marfa's "wonderfully pliant" melodic line might, in another context, call to mind Bellini's *melodie lunghe*, thanks to its slow unfolding and the careful avoidance of a conclusive cadence. As Asafyev correctly observes, this is not Mu-

sorgskian recitative, but rather a periodically phrased lyrical melody, set to a skeletal harmonic background of tonics and dominants. Hence it is with pitch and the singer's inflection alone that the intensity is sustained and the previously conflicting religious and erotic impulses in Marfa are fused into a single extended vocal line.

21. [Author's note:] This designation (the notion of the *romance*) is naturally too superficial and narrow to characterize the vocal pieces or scenes of Musorgsky, which are so rich in dramatic, brilliant expressivity and representation.

22. Arseny Golenishchev-Kutuzov (1848–1913) became a close friend of Musorgsky in 1873. Four of his poems were used in the cycle *Songs and Dances of Death* (1874–1877), six more for *Sunless* (1874).

23. Victor Hugo's *Han d'Islande* (1821) is a gory novel of rebellion set in 17th-century Norway, involving the supernatural figure of a cannibalistic dwarf. At age 17, Musorgsky considered basing an opera on it.

24. Musorgsky's sketches for an adaptation of Flaubert's novel *Salammbô* amount to 90 minutes of music.

25. Not Sophocles but Vladislav Ozerov! Only one scene survives of a projected opera based on Ozerov's play *Oedipus in Athens*, written in 1804.

26. Alexander Polezhaev (1804–1838) was ordered into the military by Tsar Nikolai I on account of his satirical narrative poem *Sashka*. Asafyev quotes from his poem, "Song of the Captive Iroquois." The original German source for Asafyev's Heine translation is unknown to me.

27. The text of "Tsar Saul" is by Byron, as translated by Kozlov, not Musorgsky. The song is a battle piece with fanfares and thundering octaves.

28. Musorgsky dedicated his youthful (1864) setting of Pushkin's love poem "Night" to Nadezhda Opochinina. The magical night hour is evoked with tremolos, delicate arpeggios, and the use of the unusual key of F# major.

29. It would be nearly impossible to reconcile this view of Musorgsky as an artist of romantic sensibility with the precepts of socialist realism as defined by the ideologues of the 1930s. Consequently, Asafyev and various generations of his apologists (including Orlova! See her introduction to the second edition, pp. 9–10, 13) were obliged to distance themselves from the fundamental viewpoint articulated in this chapter.

30. Asafyev here names several of Musorgsky's most familiar solo vocal works. "Rayok" (translated either as "The Gallery" or "The Peep Show"), a setting of the composer's own text, is a five-section lampoon of Musorgsky's musical foes.

31. In "The Seminarist" (1866–1870), the young student interrupts his tedious recitation of Latin declensions with erotic fantasies centering on a priest's daughter.

32. The premiere of Fromental Halévy's *La dame de pique*, using a Scribe libretto, occurred on 28 Dec 1850.

33. In Chapter 5, Asafyev had suggested that in general terms, Russian opera is distinguished from other traditions precisely because its drama is not primarily defined by external events.

34. Yet another strong position that would become anathema for subsequent Soviet scholarship.

35. The *argument* between Prince Ivan Khovansky and Prince Golitsyn begins in Act 2, scene 3; the chanting of the Old Believers is first heard at fig. 89.

36. It may be appropriate to note that the alleged complexity of *Khovanshchina* does not lie with the melodramatic plot. Broadly speaking, Musorgsky has utilized some standard plot devices of grand opera to depict aspects of late 17th-century Russia at the time of Peter the Great's violent consolidation of power. Ivan (father) and Andrei (son) Khovansky are in command of the Strelsty, an Imperial guards unit of uncertain loyalty. Both of them, together with the priest Dosifei and Marfa (Andrei's jilted past love) belong to the Christian sect known as *Raskolniki* ("Schismatics," a.k.a. Old Believers). All the principals fall victim in one way or another to Tsar Peter's targeting of the groups to which they belong for annihilation. Of considerably more complexity than the plot is the astonishing succession of passions, lusts, motivations, allegiances, and concerns that the main characters grapple with over the course of the opera's five acts.

37. Score locations: (1) Act 2, fig. 97 + 7ff.; (2) Act 4, scene 1, fig. 65 + 7ff.

38. In her prayer at the beginning of Act 5, scene 3, Marfa asks forgiveness for the sin of having loved a fellow human being.

39. Score location: Act 5, scene 1, fig. 191 + 5ff.

40. Score location: Act 5, scene 1. Dosifei is consecrating the house of refuge that will become the site of immolation. A line of running eighths, frequently in unharmonized octaves, pervades the short scene.

41. At the conclusion of "Trepak" (third song of the *Songs and Dances of Death*), the hoofbeats and frequent dissonances yield to a subdued cadence in D minor.

42. As Asafyev proceeds to explain, Tsar Boris is obsessed not with one but with two nemeses: the murdered Tsarevich Dmitri and the renegade monk Grigory, who is masquerading as a resurrected Dmitri. Pimen's miracle story (Act 4, scene 1) suggests to the psychologically vulnerable tsar that the true Dmitri is more than a figment of his imagination. Regular quarter-note motion and a rising sixth define the Dmitri-Tsarevich theme, which attaches itself to both the real and the false Dmitri.

43. The Dmitri theme first emerges in the accompaniment as Pimen responds to Grigory's questions about the Tsarevich's murder (Act 1, scene 1, fig. 41 + 11).

44. [Author's note:] I.e., an ability of the spirit or of a condition of the soul to know the world by means of intuition.

45. [Author's note:] One must distinguish between the dramatic and the tragic situation or condition of the people (as in *Khovanshchina* and *Boris*) from a national drama or tragedy, where the nation is the hero: a collective entity manifesting itself.

46. The scene entitled "An Inn at the Lithuanian Border" takes place after the scene in Pimen's cell (Act 1, scenes 1 and 2 of the 1874 revision).

47. *The Tale of Woe-Misfortune* is an anonymous 17th-century prose narrative about a prodigal son, whose dissolute behavior and boasting conjure up an evil spirit (Woe-Misfortune personified) that hounds him until he repents.

48. Much of Marina's characterization is tied to dance idioms and periodic phrases, as opposed to the arioso passages assigned to the Russian characters. While the andante duet in E-flat (fig. 72) that concludes Act 3 fulfills the basic criteria for a love scene (exchange of endearments and a kiss), Asafyev is right to doubt the depth of feeling, in view of her political agenda.

49. Asafyev names two vocal numbers from *The Sorochintsy Fair.* "The Peasant Lad's Dumka" (transcribed in Lamm's vocal score, pp. 53ff.) was intended for Act 1, "Parasya's Dumka" (Lamm, p. 235) for Act 3.

50. Asafyev must be referring to the traditional nurturing role represented by the woman's singing her grandson to sleep.

51. Both Nadezhda Opochinina (1821–1874) and her brother Vladimir were close friends of the composer. The sister's death on 1 July 1874 greatly saddened Musorgsky.

52. The celebrated tritonally linked bell chords from *Boris* are found in the Prologue's second tableau; the clock chimes tormenting the tsar occur in Act 2 at fig. 98. *Khovanshchina* opens with an orchestral prelude depicting dawn on Red Square; the hoofbeats (a rhythmic ostinato of six sixteenth notes) occur in Act 4, scene 5, as Prince Golitsyn is led off under an armed guard.

53. [Author's note:] A strong hold on reality but still an imagination that in the end led him into the thrall of death!!

54. Asafyev found his quotations in a 1911 edition of Musorgsky's correspondence and gave the appropriate page references (preserved in the text). For the second edition of the *Etudes*, Orlova used an edition of 1932. An earlier English translation of the full text of all nine letters is found in: Leyda and Bertensson, *The Musorgsky Reader* (New York: Norton, 1947): Letter nos. 87, 89, 93, 109, 156, 160, 164, 177, 187.

55. The artist and architect Viktor Hartmann died on 23 July 1873; within a year he was immortalized in *Pictures at an Exhibition.*

56. Musorgsky is outlining the events of Act 5, scenes 3–4. It is Marfa who sings the "Alleluia."

57. Musorgsky's comment came in response to a concert he attended, featuring Saint-Saens's *Danse Macabre* and Third Piano Concerto, the latter performed by the composer.

58. Golenishchev-Kutuzov's marriage in 1875 brought an end to his sharing of quarters with Musorgsky, leaving the composer doubly despondent over the loss of his friend's company and of an agreeable living situation.

• *17* •

Intermezzo III

*J*n 1889 Tchaikovsky composed his celebrated fairy-tale ballet *Sleeping Beauty*. This fact is of considerably more importance than is usually thought. We have become so accustomed to it that we do not take note of its significance for the history and psychology of style, which is enormous on both counts. With this lavish work that was so influential in opening up new possibilities, vistas, and perspectives for Russian choreography, Tchaikovsky *revealed* the dance impetus that has so long been the source and constant companion to Russian music: i.e., the realm of the lyrical-instrumental-dance element. In Russian folk music, it has from ancient times been realized in the songs of *khorovody* and games, in the tunes of *skomorokhi*, in buglers' improvisations, the spirited Cossack dances, and the lively Ukrainian hopak.

The role of dance rhythms and tunes is yet more significant for Slavic music in general: Can one imagine a characterization of Polish nationality without any mention of the rhythms of the polonaise, mazurka, and krakowiak?

What then is dance music or the rhythm of the dance?

It is, of course, a stylized rhythm, i.e., a rhythm contained at all times in a predetermined metrical scheme. Apart from a metrical scheme conditioned by gesture and the eurhythmics of dance, there is no dance music. Melody, too, is subject to this scheme, for its presence and beauty are less significant for the dance than a regular, lockstep rhythm. Serving as evidence of this are the national dance tunes of Spain, wherein a tune in our understanding is missing, but a "rhythmic tune" executed by the percussion instruments is present, which is sometimes notable for an extreme refinement and whimsicality of contour.[1]

In Russian music, of course, even before Tchaikovsky's efforts, a fiery strain of the dance element and of rhythmicized dance had not only smoldered but caught fire. Polish, Russian, and Spanish choreography had been brilliantly realized by Glinka. Borodin's Polovtsian Dances had an elemental power. The rhythms of the *skoromokhi* had been stylized by Rimsky-Korsakov in *Snow-Maiden*, and the *khorovod* dance in *May Night*. In the symphonic poem *Sadko* he unfolded an entire choreographic tableau: the incantation of the sea element by the power of song and the elemental dance of the underwater kingdom accompanied by Sadko's gusli tunes. This dance powerfully expresses the rhythmic monotony[2] of masculine Russian dancing seemingly constrained in movement, since it is rooted in the stamping and trampling of the ground.[3] It can be demonstrated that all of Rimsky-Korsakov's symphonic poems are permeated with stylized dance tunes and dance meters at their rhythmic core, to say nothing of the special case of *Capriccio espagnole*. We need only to recall the episodes in *Antar*, nearly all of *Scheherazade*, the dance rhythm in *Russian Easter Overture*, and finally, the important role of dance in nearly all the operas, *Mlada* in particular. It was not long ago that crude generalizations of thought kept us from making distinctions between the dance element and vulgar ballet music. Since the latter was considered to be somehow disgraceful in general for the serious musician, one took offense when the presence of a "ballet element" was indicated in the music.[4] I believe that this time is gone forever and that the signs of an undeniable predominance of the dance element in Rimsky-Korsakov's music, i.e., a stylization on behalf of rhythmic elasticity, should no longer offend anyone.

When Tchaikovsky created *Sleeping Beauty* based on a suggestion from Vsevolozhsky,[5] thereby deigning to appear as a ballet composer in *spite* of the gossip, he took an important but entirely natural step: he consolidated within a specialized sphere—in the realm of ballet—those trends and inclinations that had for a long time typified the Russian element in music, toward which Russian composers beginning with Glinka (and even before him) involuntarily inclined.

The Russian musical element has two fundamental branches: a purely lyrical song element and an instrumental one. Within each of them, one can distinguish between artistic creation based on the principle of prosaic speech (free rhythm) and that based on the principle of poetic stylization (meter). Long-breathed, flexibly flowing lyrical song born of the wide-open steppes is certainly created on different bases than that of a sprightly dance tune. Russian opera absorbed both tendencies. However, the powerful dance element, although no less powerful than the song element, was too constricted within the confines of opera. Thus it found acceptance in the symphonic field (in Glinka and Rimsky-Korsakov). Tchaikovsky infused it into the ballet and thereby changed the course of it.

The thought would certainly never have occurred to any Russian composer before 1889 that such a highly scorned artistic field would be fated to bring glory to Russian art in general throughout Europe and that the finest Russian musicians would make such valuable contributions to the ballet. Now it is a *fait accompli*; it remains only to marvel at the evolution in style accomplished by Russian ballet music from the rhythms of *Sleeping Beauty*, conditioned by the French-Italian structure of classical ballet, to the elemental power in the national rhythms of the dance and the mimed recitative or pantomimed *skaz* of Igor Stravinsky's *Petrushka* and *The Rite of Spring* (in the period from 1889 until 1910, i.e., slightly more than twenty years).[6]

Sleeping Beauty was an attempt to create an engaging choreographic fairy tale. Tchaikovsky intuitively enhanced the entire project and offered a series of interesting instants of the fabulous in instrumentation and timbre (the variations in the Prologue, the characterization of the evil fairy Carabosse and the fairy-tale personages who figure in the final tableau of the ballet, namely: Little Red Riding Hood and the wolf, Puss in Boots and the White Cat, the Blue Bird, Tom Thumb and the Ogre, etc.). In addition, he greatly expanded the lyrical and dramatic sphere of the ballet, creating an enchanting world of poetic visions, sometimes on the basis of pure dance (the Adagio and variations), sometimes in the form of instrumental-symphonic moments (the Panorama, the Kingdom of Sleep, the Awakening), sometimes in the form of songful instrumental cantilenas (of the Lilac Fairy).

The Nutcracker is cast in an entirely different mold. In the first half it is filled with the sinister "lightning bolts" of Hoffmannesque mysticism. The music brilliantly intertwines a realistic bourgeois milieu, the delight of a child's naivete and daydreaming, the mysterious kingdom of the mice, and the life of toys infused with spirit (far more expressively than the life of objects and animals in Maeterlinck's *L'oiseau bleu*).[7] How marvelous and direct is the link between the real world and the unreal, since the boundary is set using the world of children, who can simultaneously be attached to real surroundings and to the fantastic and have the ability to anthropomorphize the objects that surround them. The second part of *Nutcracker* is a kingdom of toys brought magically to life, a fairy tale in instrumental colors. The road leading from the mysticism of *Nutcracker* to the trials of Petrushka is not a long one: Is the warmth of life not at hand where one blindly senses merely the mechanical? And, on the other hand, is not a malicious mechanistic causality operative where only free will seems to be present?[8]

Goethe addresses this very well in *Werther*: "Ich stehe wie vor einem Raritätenkasten, und sehe die Männchen und Gäulchen vor mir herumrücken, und frage mich oft, ob es nicht ein optischer Betrug ist. Ich spiele mit, vielmehr ich werde gespielt wie eine Marionette, und fasse manchmal meinen Nachbar an der hölzernen Hand und schauders zurück" (am 20 Januar 1772).[9]

The puppet element in the ballet allows the composer as never before to develop such a theme; therefore *The Nutcracker* is by no means the naive work for which it has been taken. The peculiar relationship between rhythms and colorations obliges one to engage in speculation. Beneath the surface of living people, sinister phantoms can be sensed. Underneath an apparent vitality are wound-up puppets and mechanisms. And if one might speak of the creation of *Sleeping Beauty* on the verge of *Queen of Spades*, using the words of Anna Akhmatova:

> Eshchyó na západe zemnóe sólntse svyétit
> I króvli gorodóv v eqó luchákh blestyát,
> A zdyes uzh byélye domá krestámi myétit
> I klíchet vórony, i voróny letyát.[10]

> [The earthly sun still shines in the west
> And the roofs of the cities sparkle in its rays,
> But here the white houses are marked with crosses
> And the ravens are called and the ravens fly.]

—then we can fully apply the epigraph from Odoyevsky's "Ball" to *The Nutcracker*. "Le sanglot consiste, ainsi que le rire, en une expiration entrecoupèe, ayant lieu de la même manière."[11]

If we recall, this excerpt from *Russian Nights* describes a strange orchestra under the direction of a no less strange *Kapellmeister*, with the music for the ball chosen by him, containing "something strange, enchanting, and horrible" . . .

There is a quite different world to be found in the three "baroque" ballets of Glazunov, which are as sumptuous as Rastrelli palaces:[12] *Raimonda, La serva padrona (Les ruses d'amour)*, and *The Seasons*.[13] Though differing in plot and choreographic aims, they share this master's characteristic manner of composing with rich strokes of sonority that exceed mere dictates of color, with an application of layers of tones one on top of the other and a dense draping of harmonies, against which the melodic line moves calmly and assuredly ahead. Within the ordinary schemas of dance music, Glazunov can discover a broad expanse for the carrying out of his characteristically unique goals: the adorning of a fundamental tune with subsidiary offshoots and counter-voices, which in their branching out challenge the predominance of the melody that engendered them, like the branches of an acacia enclosing its trunk. But the dynamics of the *dance* in Glazunov are contingent not as much on the density of the offshoots, but on the pulsations of the rhythm, pulsations that are not frenzied and nervous, but jubilantly aroused, intoxicated with hops. The elemental power of the Russian's soul is revealed in his dance music: a tramping, an impulsive stroke, a sharpness of accents, the force of a body weighted to the ground, and suddenly an apparent breaking away from the ground—a leap, a caper, a swoop! From the standpoint of the subject matter of *Les ruses d'amour*, French *paysannes* of Watteau's epoch are dancing *la fricassèe* in nuptial revelry.[14] Yet with respect to the real sense and rhythmic essence, it is a Russian dance with that dance's most basic trait: a ponderous stomping of the ground, as if unable to leave it or break away. Meanwhile in the very stomping there is growth—a crescendo—as if strength were passing from the earth to the body, just as juice flows in the roots of a plant. Suddenly a man is torn up from the ground, torn away with a daring and bold impudence, to whirl about in a frenzied *prisyadka*!

The most characteristic example (and one of the finest moments in Glazunov's ballet music) is the Bacchanale from *The Seasons*. A broad, wild, and free melody lights up into a beautiful flame and spreads forth over the rhythmic ostinato of chordal *passages*. It is a feast of autumnal prosperity, a festival of harvest and maturation, satiety and ripeness. In this music, a youthful sunny sparkle, froth from the juice of grapes, and an Eastern Russian devil-may-care drunken revelry seem to converge. Scenes from Alexei Koltsov's "The Harvest" and images from Pushkin's *Triumph of Bacchus* come to mind.[15] Above all, one recalls Blok:

> *Tam s posvístom da s prisvístom*
> *Gulyáyut do zarí . . .*[16]
>
> [There with a whizzing and a whirring
> They roam until dawn . . .]

The artistic substance and beauty of dance music are contained in that most interesting contrast between the tautly stretched rhythmic pattern (the conditioning metrical schema of the dance) and the melody, which strives at every instant to destroy the meter and emerge from the boundaries that fetter the span. Therein lie the nerve and the intensifying impulse of the dance tune, its range and trajectory, and also the psychological effect, from a quivering and stirring in the body, from a readiness to break into dance, reaching ecstatic rapture, out of zeal, out of whirling about. In Russian music, the elemental might of the dance found its complete expression. Over the enormous span between the aforementioned endpoints, Russian composers have transformed the most subtle nuances of the dance, beginning with the most rudimentary forms of the *khorovod*—*choreia*—to the amatory languors and raptures of the *pas de deux*, from the simplest ornament in character dances to the head-spinning ecstasies of mystical dance in Scriabin's poem-symphonies.

In the works of the contemporary composer Igor Stravinsky the elemental power of the dance is communicated with such intense force that I could not resist the temptation to conclude my book on Russian music's richly dramatic and descriptive vein with a sketch of his most eminent compositions. In advance I will remark that Stravinsky's innovations, especially in *The Rite of Spring,* are aroused, from my point of view, by the involuntary emergence in his works of the elemental forces themselves, which have now been granted the opportunity to express themselves in Russian music, thanks to the flexibility of a contemporary idiom. From Glinka's *impressions* of Spain, from his *Kamarinskaya,* and even earlier, from the choreographic third act of *Ruslan,*[17] an element of rhythmic, revolving motion emerging from the spontaneity of folk dance music took root in Russian music: an element of rhythmic stamping (hopak, trepak, *prisyadka,* etc.) and a wavelike, rhythmic pacing (the dances of maidens). In Stravinsky we confront the most striking emergence of the dance instinct at its very core: elemental, spontaneous, and stripped of all stylization.

NOTES

1. The *baile de Ibio* or "stick dance" from the Santander province of Spain is traditionally accompanied only by tambourines, sometimes with the addition of a large conch shell.

2. [Author's note:] Rhythmic monotony, or rather, rhythmic monothematicism, yet with a florid intricacy of melodic ornament in the most diverse variants and transformations (for example, as in the Kamarinskaya dance-song of the hornists from Vladimir).

3. In his footnote [no. 2, supra], the author makes reference to Russian horn bands. The *rozhok* can be considered a folk version of the straight cornett made of birch bark and with at least four finger holes. The *khor rozhechnikov* of the Vladimir region incorporated instruments of different sizes, allowing for playing in parts.

4. In his response to Taneyev's criticism that every movement of the Fourth Symphony contained a balletic element, Tchaikovsky pointed out that a dance element is observable in nearly all of Beethoven's symphonies.

5. Ivan Alexandrovich Vsevolozhsky (1835–1909) was the director of the Imperial Theatres from 1881 to 1899. He suggested the project to Tchaikovsky in a letter of 13 May 1888 and himself drafted a libretto based on "La belle au bois dormant."

6. The date 1910 can be used in reference to the *composition* of *Petrushka,* but not to *The Rite,* whose earliest sketches date from 1911.

7. Maurice Maeterlinck's *L'Oiseau bleu* of 1908 is a dream quest play, whose inspiration the author accredited in part to Barrie's *Peter Pan.* Anthropomorphically depicted animals and substances include a dog, a cat, sugar, fire, bread, water, light, and milk.

8. The theme of free will and mechanistic causality is further explored in reference to *Petrushka*; see Chapter 18, pp. 288–90.

9. Asafyev (or his editor) quotes from a recent edition of *Werther*, with the 18th-century spellings modernized. Translation: "I stand as if before a peep show, and see the little mannequins and horses scamper about in front of me; and I often ask myself, whether it is not an optical illusion. I play along, even more I am played with like a marionette, and I clasp sometimes my neighbor's wooden hand and pull back with a shudder."

10. Asafyev quotes the last stanza from the poem "Has this century been worse," which was written in 1919 and included in the fourth book of the already celebrated, still young Anna Andreyevna Akhmatova (1889–1966).

11. Orlova notes that the quotation in French to the chapter "A Ball" from Vladimir Odoyevsky's prose cycle *Russian Nights* (1844) was eventually replaced. The prose sketch describes a macabre ball, following a bloody victory; the music for the event was all somehow associated with suffering and thus relevant to Asafyev's overriding theme of soulless, malevolent mechanization. Translation: "Sighing, as well as laughing, consists of a choked-off expiration, taking place in a like manner."

12. The Italian architect Bartolomeo Francesco Rastrelli (1700–1771) designed various buildings in the Winter Palace complex as well as several others in and around St. Petersburg.

13. In less than five years, the reliably prolific Glazunov completed his three ballets: *Raymonda*, op. 57 (1896–1897); *Les ruses d'amour*, op. 61 (1898); and *Les saisons*, op. 67 (1899).

14. *La fricasée* is actually a category of 16th-century French song, not dance. The culinary reference reflects a primary trait: the songs' polystilistic hash of recognizable preexisting ingredients, e.g., phrases from Janequin or Sermisy.

15. Aleksei Vasilyevich Koltsov (1809–1842) was the first of Russia's "peasant poets." The poem "Urozhai" ("The Crop," 1835) ties the lives of villagers to the rhythm of the growing season, culminating in the harvest home celebration. Pushkin's "Triumph of Bacchus" is a celebration of wine, women, song, and the wind god Bacchus; its frequent references to the singing and dancing of individuals and groups inspired Dargomyzhsky to adapt it first as a cantata (1843–1846) and then as an opera-ballet (1846–1848).

16. The lines are from the poem "Harmonica, Harmonica," found in the cycle *Incantations*, which Alexander Blok (1880–1921) included in the "second book" of the great trilogy he compiled to span his career. The intoxicating poetic alchemy of music, magic, eroticism, urban misery, and unexpected epiphanies of transcendental grace and beauty, most of them occurring in and around pre-Revolutionary Petersburg, earned Blok broad new acclaim as a poet of the modern city and his second book the reputation of being a Russian Symbolist's *Fleurs du mal*.

17. The main point of the following author's note is to add a defense of Glinka's use of the waltz to his previous defense of Tchaikovsky. Ruslan's rival Ratimir sings of his lusts in his Act 3 cavatina "Heat so sultry." The waltz-like cabaletta and the Italianate bel canto idioms had previously elicited unfavorable critical comment. [Author's note:] Indeed, every manner of *choreia*. I may point to the abundance of the *waltz* in

Russian music, which is far from accidental, especially with regard to the "waltzes" of Glinka's Ratmir and those of Tchaikovsky. Only narrow-minded critics would see "Italianisms" in the role of Ratmir and vulgarity in the symphonic waltzes of Tchaikovsky. In the organic artworks of composers of genius accidents do not occur. This is only our habit of trifling with treasures of the spirit and incomprehension of the fact that thought spawns thought, idea spawns idea, so that once a thought or idea is expressed, a trace remains and when it arises, it does so according to a basis unknown to us, but not at all accidentally. This incomprehension leads to a crude treatment of an artistic legacy and to a reluctance to explain for oneself its essence and the interaction of forces concealed within it.

· 18 ·

Igor Stravinsky and His Ballets

1

$\mathcal{I}$gor Fyodorovich Stravinsky was born on June 5, 1882. His father was the renowned and preeminent artist-singer of Russian opera, Fyodor Ignatye-vich Stravinsky (1843–1902), a thoughtful and sensitive artist and a man deeply dedicated to the art of music.[1] From his very childhood, Igor Stravin-sky found himself in close contact with music and with people who served and worshiped music.

In 1902, as a youth, Igor Stravinsky became one of the most fervent and hardest-working pupils of Nikolai Rimsky-Korsakov; after five years he began to emerge as a talented, sensitive, and perceptive musician. The first of Igor Stravinsky's compositions to be presented in concerts and published (in 1907, the Suite for voice and orchestra based on Pushkin's text *The Faun and the Shepherdess*; in 1908, two remarkable songs: the penitential song "Rosianka" and the monastic song "Spring"; Four Etudes for piano and *Pastorale* for voice and piano) drew attention to him, thanks to the foretaste of something un-usual, something not in accordance with acquired rules, and thus different from the majority of the pupils and disciples of the Rimsky-Korsakov school.[2] The First Symphony (composed in 1907) simultaneously attested to the at-tainment of technique and to the fact that the young composer stood at a crossroads under the influence of three Russian masters: Rimsky-Korsakov, Tchaikovsky, and Glazunov (the concluding movement of the symphony). Yet along all the paths, the traces of an unaccredited craftsmanship were visible and a spirit of willfulness was in the air.

In the Symphony's scherzo one finds the countenance of the future Stravinsky: the ingenious sovereign of orchestral hues and wizard-prankster.

The realm of the scherzo, i.e., music of a joking, capricious, fantastic, and magical character, clearly attracted the youth as it did many Russian composers. Yet although examples of this type of music did exist, Stravinsky right away found his own paths, his own techniques: as evidence of this there are the *Fantastic Scherzo*, composed in 1908, and after that *Fireworks*—two of his unique musical tableaus, opening up boldly new and vivid sound combinations and a play of light and shadow in orchestral sound.

The development of Stravinsky's talent is brilliantly revealed in the ballet *The Firebird*, a work commissioned from him in 1909 by one who shrewdly divined his abilities, that major figure in the propagandizing of Russian art abroad: Sergei Pavlovich Diaghilev.

One may consider *The Firebird* to be the first Russian fairy-tale ballet-soundscape. Stravinsky managed to provoke a gasp from the leading Russian and French musicians after the very first orchestral rehearsals for the music of *The Firebird* in Paris, June 1910, so fresh and immediately impressive was the spellbinding vision in sound of Kashchei's kingdom and its inhabitants!

In his treatment of orchestral sonorities, Stravinsky showed himself here to be an expert conjurer and refined master of sonic matters.

But within a year, the first general wave of astonishment and amazement were replaced by a second even greater one: on June 13, 1911, Stravinsky, in cooperation with the painter Alexander Benois, emerged in Paris with the ballet *Petrushka (Amusing Scenes in Four Tableaus)*.

Strongly developed technical ability, skill, and flair at mastering all the properties of the newfound sonorities; but most of all, a young man's inspired ardor and imaginative richness, drove Stravinsky to create an astounding tableau of the promenading of the Russian people at Shrovetide in connection with the mysterious and frightening experiences of the *dramatis personae*: Petrushka, the Moor, the Magician, and the Ballerina.

It would seem that the music of *Petrushka* is, first and foremost, vividly theatrical and could only achieve its fullest effect in connection with scenic action. But the force of the sincerity and expressivity, the graphic nature of the musical images, the clarity of the ideas and the pungency of their interweaving achieve a miraculous feat: even apart from scenery, without actors and decoration, the music itself depicts one tableau after another and evokes them in the listeners' imagination. A soul-stirring, intoxicating impression is born out of surging waves of life—as if, in the fresh, cold air under the light of the sun, human merrymaking were broadly and freely spreading forth. As the raucous festive day hums and buzzes, deep inside within it, an uncontrived but fearsome drama of jealousy crouches.

Only a bit of music is devoted to depicting a certain strange "magic trick," but it expresses much, convincingly and indisputably; one feels that amidst life both radiant and warm, dark and dismal forces always hide: fervently spun webs of evil. Just now they catch up one of the people or hook several of them and entangle them with each other in some cleverly conceived game. The people strike out and collide with each other as if in a hexed circle, having neither the strength nor the imagination to break free; in blind hatred they live, devouring each other until death comes to assist and abducts one or more. Then the knot of malice is pulled asunder and a few of the participants, like puppets, are taken from life, like useless rags, at the wave of the unseen magician's hand. The rest, however, remain alive, waiting their turn.

In their haughty blindness, people do not sense that all of their affairs and actions are not free, that they act according to the predetermined *whim* of an invisible elemental force and, like puppets in a puppet theater, obey the hand of the master magician that moves them about. But the joy and strength of the force of life surging all around result in a forgetting of man's hard lot: under the light of the sun, one does not want to believe in an evil fate. And in the music of *Petrushka* the hale and hearty scenes of the real world of the folk engross us entirely and fill the spirit with bold, steadfast courage and the will to live.

The first performance dates of *The Firebird* and *Petrushka* in Paris (June 25, 1910, and June 13, 1911) perhaps will be considered as historically significant and beneficial for the development of Russian music as the first performance dates of Glinka's operas in St. Petersburg (*A Life for the Tsar*: November 27, 1836; *Ruslan and Lyudmila*: November 27, 1842). They signify not only a triumphal introduction of contemporary Russian music to the West but also a *turning point* within Russian music itself toward new tendencies and, in the music of the Russian ballet, toward a complete renewal. The significance of Igor Stravinsky in *this* regard is not less than that of Glinka in the creation of Russian opera and the dispatching of Russian music along a new path. Glinka, with his *Ruslan*, certainly, seemed no less a revolutionary composer to his contemporaries than Stravinsky now seems to a majority of people.

After *Petrushka* came yet another remarkable but still entirely *unappreciated* work: that mysterious *deistvo*, *The Rite of Spring* (with a first run in Paris, summer of 1913). Once again, just as in *The Firebird* and *Petrushka*, like an ancient mage or sorcerer, the composer summons forth into the world, invokes, and subjects to his will the invisible elemental forces that reign over life.

In *The Firebird* these forces appear in a bright and colorful depiction, in *Petrushka* they conduct a kind of malevolent, intricate game behind the backs of the merry revelers. In *The Rite of Spring* they themselves rage unchecked: the luxuriant vernal growth of nature, the mighty shudders of Mother Earth, and the quivering of all creation before elemental calls and commands—this is the essence of *The Rite*'s music. Nothing like the numerous pitiful plays and the sensitive romances in various keys singing of a sickly spring will you find in Stravinsky!

Unfortunately, this most modern and elementally Russian music of Stravinsky, concealing within it presentiments of great struggle and terrible rhythms of the spirit of music breathing freely—is practically unknown in Russia.[3]

In 1909 Stravinsky composed a scene from Hans Christian Andersen's well-known fairy tale "The Nightingale." By the summer of 1914 he had developed and expanded his original plan into the dimensions of a small-scale opera. In it are juxtaposed the world of music freely flowing in nature (the nightingale with its songs signifies this powerful vital force) and the sphere of humanity, associated with the circumstances of everyday surroundings and with stylized, fabricated art. The palace of a Chinese emperor is portrayed as an example of all fenced-in dominions, thanks to which people disassociate themselves from unrestricted life and creativity, from an unmediated joy in accord with the call of nature. At a formal reception given by the Chinese emperor, in a peculiar contest between the "mechanical and organic elements," the song of the living nightingale meets with disapproval, while the artificial windup toy nightingale is received as a welcome guest.

All of Igor Stravinsky's works reveal to us an irrepressible rush toward the free element of music, a fervent drive to burst free of the framework and barriers of conventional forms and the sound combinations used thousands of times. It is not without reason that in all of these works he *never exalts* a human personality: people are playthings (puppets, "Petrushkas")—caught in the grip of an elemental force—who love all that is artificial and toylike and surround themselves—out of fear at gazing into the depths of harsh and cruel life—with a multitude of conditions and rules. To tear free of them—this is the task of this artist-composer's unhampered thought! Igor Stravinsky summons and invokes the elemental forces of nature. Will the strength and *elan vital* inside him suffice, in order to subject the terrible and willful new arrivals to the proud will of human consciousness? Sometimes it seems that the world of wild sounds has controlled the composer's will, that a rupture threatens his striving. Yet another woe: in Stravinsky, in his projects and sonorities, one finds much delicacy, refinement, and effeminacy. What if he were to confine himself to the realm of nice and warm, cunningly *tasteful* "hothouse" music, refined and recherché examples of which are to be found in *The Nightingale* and in other vocal works (songs) of the penultimate creative period? "Penultimate" period indeed, since the last period is unknown to us: from 1914 on, we know neither what has become of the music of Stravinsky nor how it has developed. Who knows if the elemental Russian soul of the composer withstood the acute temptation from the side of the highly refined, contemporary music of France, under whose influence he found himself—or, indeed, whether he was tempted to become the complete master of the "modern" Western art of music, *at the very moment when in Russia* new songs are being sung, which are *yet more modern*, gazing *forward* into the distance?[4]

2

Intricacy of design and vividness in instrumental ornament: these are what attracts the attention of the listener who is taking in the music of *The Firebird* for the first time. This impression, being both general yet unquestionably pronounced (for the talent behind the venture and its realization, in spite of all of the capriciousness and keen wit, is bursting with novelty and freshness of invention), remains the same, even under a more detailed and thoughtful penetration into the sphere of this work's *soundscape*. It is a fairy tale, but a fairy tale which, in essence, is entirely devoid of a smooth narrative: everything left untold or not wholly told in sound is realized in the elastic representation of the scenic gestures, i.e., in the action of the ballet. The music strives to "narrate" the tale in its own way and extract from the plot everything that offers the possibility of revealing the musical element in its deepest essence: as ante-emotional, ante-narrative, and ante-formal/architectonic. Music's spiritual essence nevertheless amounts to an influence at once strong-willed, bewitching, and enchanting. The influence develops in two directions: it stupefies, even petrifies, or rather freezes: but then, on the other hand, it makes a hubbub in both feelings and thoughts, i.e., commotion, confusion, disarray, snowstorm and blizzard, and other such bits of devilry. Which of the two conjured-up courses is predominant depends on the fermentative elements that seem to elicit the chemical-acoustic reaction. It appears that the most significant role is played by one or more regular or irregular durational relationships, i.e., the rhythmic element in its simplest manifestation. Contemporary music, however, has elicited a no less powerful hypnotic power of harmonic and coloristic intertwining, juxtapositions, and correlations. In *rhythmicizing* the sharp and pungent sonorities—the most intricate timbral inflorescences—an intensity is achieved no less than that of the most exquisite and pure rhythms of Spanish folk dances![5]

In each of his three ballet dramas, Stravinsky plumbed the depths of his understanding of a primal essence—the spirit of music—passing through successive stages born out of experience and the creative act, penetrating into the immeasurable spheres wherein forces are at play, assembling a visible order in the world. From the stupefying coloristic aroma of *The Firebird*, through psychological intensification (in *Petrushka*), and the terrible conveyance of the *mechanistic* element that guides the world and humanity, he reached the mysterious boundaries of *The Rite of Spring*, which, alas, remains uncomprehended and unappreciated. The radiant and joyous festival of spring, the resurrection of life, the stimulation of *growth*, the increase of energies is directed therein not toward the sun, but toward the Earth. Opposed to the energy of heat is the dark and gloomy power of the bowels of the Earth, of forces that produce and generate, yet greedily demand sacrifices, since the seed cannot come to life unless it dies. In a complete opposition to the inspired resurrection of Kitezh, the music in *The Rite of Spring* displays the *dark* life of the inorganic world, which man in his proud striving toward the sun and expansion of consciousness nearly denies, forgetting his own attachment to the Earth and of his dependence, not yet overcome, on its calls and commands. The contrast between the organic and inorganic worlds, their struggle, but also their mutual connection and interdependence through the imperious usage of the hypnotic charms of incantation (such as are known to man, to the snake, and to priceless gems!)—these are the fundamental paths and the creative crossroads of the enormous talent of Igor Stravinsky.

Of course, he did not always proceed along these paths in his compositions with an equal intensity of effort that was grounded in an intuitive preconception of the ultimate significance of his creative activity. Nor could he escape the influence of the human element inside him or surrounding him: at times *all too human*? Nevertheless, he follows the true path. In the seemingly naive *The Nightingale*, akin to a Chinese doll, that same great "quarrel" resounds that arose long ago between the mechanical element and the organic. Death is implicated in this quarrel. And life, the energy of life that emanates from *living* song, from *inspired* sound triumphs over death because it arouses within it the greedy, unslakable craving to hear the nightingale's songs and to imbibe their life current. And thus, with radiance and joy, the first creative period of Igor Stravinsky that is known to us came to an end.

In *The Firebird* the aforementioned problem is resolved with youthful fervor and freshness, but also naivete. The musical structure of this tale is quite simple. The captivating and, on first encounter, even somewhat stupefying complexity of the sonorities proceeds externally, in the details, not at the core. Rhythmically, the music of *The Firebird* is not complex: neither in the relationship of the tiny cells nor in the juxtaposition of the so-called rhythmoforms can anything remarkable be discerned.[6] And even the orchestrationally resourceful, evil, "grimacing" Infernal Dance, if compared to the wild dances of the horde of the steppes in *Igor* or to the rhythms of Sergei Prokofyev's *Scythian Suite*, will only sound clever, not elemental. The rhythmic "curlicues" that barely surface in the "piecemeal" planning of the material (for example, during the Vivo episode in the scene of the magical chime ringing, at the moment when the meter changes from 3/2 to 12/4 and the theme appears in tubas and bassoons[7]) most often serve as clever and timely means for setting in motion the essentially static diminished or augmented modes,[8] but not as independently developing rhythmic enterprises.

The simplicity of the structure is clearly expressed in the uncomplicated realization of the juxtaposition of the enchanted *chromatic* world and the real knightly world; or rather, the everyday *diatonic* world of the fairy tale (the recitatives of Prince Ivan and the *khorovod*). One can only marvel at the rich, spicy aroma and the rustling of the Firebird's flights or the wild permutations of thirds in the slippery advances of Kashchei, which resemble the advances of a toad! Yet at the same time—one must show sympathy for the conceptually weak and flaccid implementation of diatonic melodic phrases to characterize the world of radiance and light, from which will come the victory over the frigid kingdom of evil Kashchei the Deathless, i.e., over the inorganic world.[9] One cannot comprehend this complete absence of dynamism in the diatonicism of *The Firebird*, when compared to the brilliant diatonicism of *Petrushka*! Even the "chromatic structure" of the tale—when it is removed from the just-noted juxtaposition (which should be the dramatic element of the *musical* action) and taken on its own—conceals within a simplistic mechanical design: nearly always, only simple oscillations, for the most part not involving the rhythm. How unfortunate that moments rife with possibilities (for example, the sequences of the Firebird's flights[10]) usually come to an impasse—at times cut off, as a contrast, by the appearance of diatonic "Russian" themes; at times spreading out, melting into the stasis of the sustaining harmonies that restrain them. The magic and charm of this ballet's sonorities are not contained in its structure. The effect does not stem from the rhythm of the form, but from the juxtaposition of timbres and the highly refined ornamentation of the intoxicating and bewitching orchestral sonorities. Here within this sphere, Stravinsky's intuition creates truly magical images of a ghostly reality.

The musical action of the ballet unfolds as follows. In the oppressively gloomy introduction, which is akin to the muffled rumbling of invisible wellsprings in the bowels of the Earth, we hear a winding ribbon of harmonic figurations, which immediately introduce us into the world of Kashchei: into a world of inanimate life, into a kingdom of an everlasting "living death," into a petrified, congealed genetic state. I use such contradictory epithets to express the strange and remarkable impression engendered by the music, which, despite the stasis and immobility, nevertheless does *move*, within the confines of this immobility.[11] It does not so much move as flicker and sparkle, or rather, does not shine as much as glimmer, as if in the depths of the Earth a certain mechanical force was compelling an axial rotation of precious gems. Simply but ingeniously, Stravinsky underscored both this iridescence and inconstant glimmering, as well as the motion of congealed energies, incorporating as the basic content of the cyclic motion the alternation of two thirds connected with an inner chromatic motion![12] Such a highly characterized invention gives birth to a sensation of illusoriness and instability—a sense of motion going nowhere, since the ear is all the time listening intently but in vain, sensing itself to be on the verge of a triad that is constantly changing its color and composition; to apprehend them all in their slippery succession by means of a direct impression (and not a reflection) is senseless and unnecessary! . . . With regard to psychology, in this succession of thirds (I repeat: in a sliding, slipping succession, which occurs at the lower voice's upward leap of a fifth, while the other voice creeps *chromatically* a half-step lower[13]) lurks a malevolent ironic grin: make a guess, is it life or death within the sonority? If death, then why the glimmering and moving forward? If life, even "undying" life, then what horror lies hidden in this "death in life," without desire, without aspirations, without hopes and goals, and most importantly, without love? It is the deathlessness of inorganic nature, aggravated by the law of gravity, but not a deathlessness understood as a process of ceaseless evolution of Universal Mind wherein, perhaps, in reality the transformation of matter into energy stands to be accomplished, as has been forecasted by modern science! . . .

The introduction leads into Kashchei's enchanted garden. All is frozen. For an instant, inorganic nature reveals the secret of its life and then again closes up, sensing the approach of a man. There follows the grand scene of Prince Ivan and the Firebird. Its intent: to encapsulate the splendid power of air, ever in motion, ever taking flight. This power reigns both in fire and in wind: two elements that are controlled by a mechanical, nonliving power, but that contend against the sluggish gravitational pull and "corpulence" of the "mortal" inorganic forces. Thus within the music characterizing the magic, enchanted other world, a contrast of its own emerges. Again one must rue the fact that the fundamental (primary) contrast, the dramatic contrast—an opposition of man and nature—is established not according to an intense struggle, i.e., heroically, but within a superficial, stylized technique: through the introduction of static themes *à la russe*![14]

The secondary "internal" contrast, a contrast within the "chromaticism" itself, is carried out more graphically and vividly. The dull, inert, petrified mass of harmonies of "nature" under Kashchei is opposed by every possible type of gently seductive stirring and rustling, by the ebb and flow of sonorous airborne waves of modern orchestral timbres. There is no need to speak here about the melos, since the indistinct element does not become concrete therein; only the people, i.e., only Prince Ivan and the princesses, receive a tuneful characterization (though unfortunately not a vivid one). The entire structure of the flights of fire and the wind, i.e., for the Firebird, is created out of something of a diminished mode, which emerges from a fundamental symmetrical opposition of chromatic "tetrachords."[15] The motion of "segments" gradually ascends and broadens: each of them is followed by seconds contained within, which slide in a downward motion or the reverse, then by a leap of a third, so that on the whole, a taut *spiral* of augmented tetrachords is assembled, coiled up like a snake. This foundation remains essentially unchanged in various ingenious instrumental exchanges, and thus it is a mechanical, not a living force that inspires the motion of the Firebird, "setting it in motion" for the entire time. Within this large scene, one can distinguish the episode entitled "Dance of the Firebird" for its colors and interesting depiction in sound of the bird's flights and whistling. Stravinsky's instrumental inventiveness astounds. Having overheard the magical sounds in nature by which our feelings are enchanted and bewitched, the composer conjures up the element itself. Certain sonorous instants of *The Firebird* make for a stunning hallucination of radiant timbres. No matter how simple it might be for the modern mind to decipher the actual technical craftsmanship nowadays, eleven years after the publication of this fairy tale, still a powerfully captivating impression remains.

Of course the sources of the chromatic motion and modal schemes of *The Firebird* need not be searched far afield: they are audible in Berendei's cavatina and in the turns of phrase by which this wise elder "orates" his speech.[16] But the common origin of the language (of which kinship there are many cases in *The Firebird*, especially in the languorous effusions of the princesses, which are nearly "Korsakovian," in the sequence of Kashchei's thirds, similar to the thirds of the opera *Kashchei*, and in the borrowed harmonies of *Christmas Eve*, found in the *Poco meno* episode of the bell ringing, from which emerges the theme of the "Infernal Dance!"[17])—let me repeat—the common origin does not prevent Stravinsky's *skaz* from voicing a *new word*. So strong indeed are the vivid (coloristic and timbral) transformations, within which shine the *pupil's inventions*, even when they have clearly emerged from prior ideas of his great teacher! . . .

The scene with the Firebird is juxtaposed with the tender and beguiling episode wherein the thirteen spellbound princesses appear, with their languorous cries and laments tenderly interwoven into imitative ornamentation.[18] I consider this moment to be the most noteworthy with respect to drama: here a femininity is brought into the music, a passive and captive humanity to balance the sonorities developed up until now, which have characterized the world of inorganic nature, mechanistically controlled by an elemental power. The feminine groans and complaints of the captive maidens, and then the gracious yet mischievous "Princesses at Play with Golden Apples" (a charming scherzo) are episodes whose music seems to enliven and blanket with warmth the cold sphere of "malicious mechanicism." A crescendo—an enhancement of the human element—is the dramatic point of this moment, assuming that it be taken in earnest and Prince Ivan treated as an active hero. Unfortunately, instead of the anticipated appearance of a human spirituality, instead of the organizing and active life force and an intensity, which could call the evil forces to battle or bring them to life, the action is unexpectedly interrupted (in the music). The appearance of Prince Ivan is a series of recitatives "stylized in a Russian mode," with an inconsistent diatonicism (with that wretched use of a B natural amidst the pure natural minor G mode![19]); these recitatives lead once again into a stylized *khorovod*. The emergence of morning (trumpet fanfares in the harmonies of the augmented scale) brings the games to a halt. Again the charming, languorous complaints of the captive princesses are heard. Suddenly unleashed scalar ascents signify Prince Ivan's intrusion into Kashchei's castle.[20] Thus the crucial dramatic moment of a man's entrance into the castle of an evil, mortifying power is characterized with a purely superficial device. Neither a heroic intensity nor an intensification: from the first complaints of the princesses to their repetition, the action is enclosed in a circle of balletic frolicking!

But now the kingdom of Kashchei has come alive. The enchanted fairytale chimes ring and buzz, spreading the sound into sonic space. Again a moment of enchanted hallucination and magical influence is made audible: Stravinsky is in his sphere. Now the musical action of the tale develops without a break in tension. The rumbling grows. In the midst of it, forcing its way, the strong-willed, "ferocious" theme of the infernal kingdom manifests itself. The ringing transforms into a wind, into a malevolent but also pathetic and plaintive howling of the forces of material nature, enchained by the law of gravity.[21] Determinism, the "foreordained power" of Kashchei's death-inducing will, compels everything to fall silent; in the orchestra, thirds made sinister by virtue of their "inanimate animation," which are already familiar from the introduction, begin to sound, but here are bent to a powerful will. Kashchei's incantations make for terrifying music, terrifying on account of a fervent denial of the possibility of growth, of a rising toward the light, to the sun (subsequently, in *The Rite of Spring*, Stravinsky will use maximal expressive means to transport this sort of mood into sheer terror!). The prayers of the princesses are set in opposition to Kashchei's recitative, like the soft babbling of a crystal spring; of course this babbling is not fated to overcome the power of morbid inertness. Once again an enchantment stemming from the elements of air and fire becomes involved in the action; the sorcery of the Firebird appears to confront the incantations of Kashchei that are deadening all life.

The power of the force that animates the world gradually draws all of Kashchei's "infernal" kingdom into its orbit. The music is transformed into a wild and dismal, ponderous, sharply rhythmicized dance.[22] The swarm of "faceless" forces, infinitely varied in their disfigurement, attempt, under the influence of the charms of the air element, to overcome their natural gravitation downward, toward the Earth, to the very bowels of the Earth—by means of the theme's syncopated rhythm. Blindly and clumsily bursting forth, the wearied "captives" strive to spin about in a diabolical *khorovod* and escape in centrifugal motion. Although there is something in the main theme of the dance itself that crushes, enchains, and confines, although the sharply accented attacks of the ponderous chord, which regularly appears every four measures, fervently pin down any tendency toward flight, still the power of the Firebird's incantations is stronger than the power of Kashchei. Despite all, her animating force "enlivens" the petrified monsters and coaxes them into furiously agitated zeal.

The bold resolution of this wild attack of evil forces is of the sort that only a musician of enormous talent would allow: Stravinsky brings the dance to a halt with the sharp commanding chord of the trumpets[23] and takes the music to a new level, entirely different in mood: to a *lullaby*; to the most tender, sweetly lulling undulations of the violas and harps, against which background the bassoon sings the sort of touching melody for which Musorgsky's songs are venerated. The bold contrast calls forth marvelous music: it is the delicate and tender pearl in all of Stravinsky's lyricism, a musical design like the most precious and refined openwork. The translucency of the lullaby's airy background astounds, no less than the "realism" of its melody's sad complaint. It is a conceptually profound conclusion, without question the most beautiful musical moment of the entire ballet. In the fading twilight of the lullaby, the action comes to a standstill. But humanity's warmth and kindness registering through the flickering light are already melting, foretelling the destruction of Kashchei's kingdom: within his power, something is wavering; within his deathless state, resulting from a deadening denial of life with its passionate self-immolation in a constant rush toward the sun—rays of light, warmth, and vitality have crept in. Convulsive upsurges and splashes of sliding thirds no longer frighten and terrify as before, at the first appearance of Kashchei. Life condemns all that is inert to death, so as to liberate the radiant forces of life energy that are concealed and enchained therein. The *deistvo* concludes with a festive and joyous hymn-finale,[24] "operatic" in character and stylized within a Russian mode, whose main organizing melody seems to brighten and grow, though born out of the gloom and chaos that set in with the death of Kashchei.

A harmoniously developing organic element without a doubt directs all the action of the tale; but only in the finale, in the concluding song, does it emerge in its fullest power. Prior to that moment it emerges as a deep-seated element, emerging somewhere deep inside to struggle and collide with elemental wills, marked by the power of the incantations. Thus music, with its modern-day might, in its full command of hypnotic forces, wields the miraculous gift of transforming a tale into myth: an intricate *deistvo* rendered verbally—into a sincerely felt rivalry between the elements. And it seems that at no time will the organizing will of human consciousness have the power fully to oppose their onslaught, since on their side sits a powerful support from the principle of mechanistic causality, to which people also are subjected. But Stravinsky proclaims this in *Petrushka*.

3

A divertissement of clowns. A drama of puppets. A stylization of the puppet show of the 1830s. An enticement for the debased tastes of the Parisian gourmands of art. Illustrative music of the theater absent any genuine music (but with an exception made on behalf of the "magic trick"). Yet another crude Russian "masculine" environment! A ploy by the *enfant terrible* composer, drunk with the success of *The Firebird*, "with a need to invent something never before seen to draw attention to himself once again." In a word: "Stravinsky has turned himself loose." Such was the opinion of one eminent Russian musician (expressed, however, in a more cynical manner), an opinion that appeared to encapsulate an endless series of findings that have uselessly encumbered a healthy attitude and forthright approach to this highly individual composition: findings that I have just now transcribed in part. In essence, the debates of 1912 concerning the just-published score of *Petrushka* centered around two focal points. Is it indeed a joke, a prank, a wish to taunt, or, in the best case, a vivid theatrical stylization? Or is it a genuine work of art? The majority were confused. A minority, among whom could be numbered that prominent patron of music, sagacious Kashkin, welcomed this impressive new work of Russian music.[25]

Russian theater of bygone times was maintained on the one hand by the *skomorokhi* and on the other by church-related individuals: in the churches, schools, and academies. For the former, the theater was a mirror of life (a mirror of the Devil in Hans Christian Andersen's "Snow Queen") in which faces and mugs were monstrously distorted; for the latter it was also a reflection, yet not of life, but of abstract virtues. The intelligentsia brought their suggested improvements to the theater from every manner of ideology: patriotism, "back to the people" romanticism, everyday realism, symbolism! But the essence remained as it had been: Gogol assimilated the *skomorokhi* tendencies, whereas in *Kitezh* there were a resurrected Oven Play, tales of holy martyrs and righteous maidens, and legends of demonic hallucinations and possessions. Most likely, there was yet another path: the path of the seekers of life, which was indeed an overgrown path. From afar it comes and always leads into dense thickets. According to the most recent research, there was always a concealed action in spells and incantations, which was accompanied by a verbal formula. Already in the *Stoglav* there are indications, vague to be sure, concerning certain "soothsayers and sorcerers of demonic lore who offer assistance using magic, and gaze into *The Gates of Aristotle* and the *Raffle Book*, and interpret the stars and heavenly bodies, and observe the days and the hours and by these diabolical actions deceive the world and turn it away from God."[26] In a word, there were people who were seeking both gods and nature, as well as Fausts and people of the Black Book. There are grounds for claiming that magic found acceptance in theatrical *deistva* and exerted pressure on the development of the plot. Hence the Astrologer in *The Golden Cockerel* was no chance newcomer, but an old theatrical disguise! Indeed, even spellbinding songs and dances of the Queen of Shemakha are unquestionably rooted far in the distant past.

The musical style of *Petrushka* is, without a doubt, conditioned by the magic of rhythm. It is the fundamental line of action and the primary key to the essence of the music. In the hands of one human being among those seeking out their fate (i.e., the Magician) are found the strings that control the movements (the life aspirations) of three creatures: Petrushka, the Moor, and the Ballerina. They are not individual personalities but creatures, endowed with instincts and corresponding reflexes that are characteristic of the human types to which each of them belongs. In the first tableau, just after the mysteriously resonating harmonies of the "magic trick," with harp and celeste figurations that strew about tiny beads and a flute cadenza to interrupt them, there comes a sharply delineated mechanical dance of the three puppets. The rhythm of this dance is strikingly distinct from the rhythm of the "trick," in which the hollow thud of pizzicato basses was followed by a splash, as if from a stone thrown into the water; the attention of the audience is hypnotized by the regular succession of the thud and the splash or by rings therefrom. In the dance, however, the rhythm becomes rigidly tense and clenched, as if the Magician is straining all of his will in order to subordinate the instincts of the three puppets to the mechanical movements of the Russian dance. But through the will of the "master," a distinction in the type and temperament for each of the three "puppet" creatures creeps in. First it is in the gestures and the appearance, soon in a half-conscious aspiration as well. It is indeed difficult to distinguish where rote learning ends and individual instinct begins. The love of Petrushka for the Ballerina emerges and also her attraction for the dull-witted and self-satisfied Moor. Their rhythms begin to differentiate: the Ballerina's coquettish grimaces, Petrushka's jealous lunges, and the crude footfalls of the Moor, irritated by the pestering.[27] Thus, in the rhythm of the dance itself, we already have the crux of the drama: a type of prologue, wherein the lines of the future conflict and the prophesied demise of one of the participants is discernible. One may well surmise that death will come to the unrestrainedly nervous, perceptive, and touchy Petrushka! But the Magician, sensing misfortune and fearing that he is not in a position to restrain the puppets' instincts to his will, brings the performance to a halt.

In the second tableau, a miracle of music is achieved: whimsically and ingeniously joining, combining, and developing the leit-rhythms that are characteristic of Petrushka, the composer's imagination displays to us the entire "mechanical" structure of the puppet. But at the same time, in a way that we ourselves do not quite understand, we cannot help surrendering ourselves to the appeal of psychologism and thus to begin sensing in each anxious, impulsive movement of Petrushka a wounded and agonizingly suffering living soul. When is the moment when the automatic mechanism becomes a psychological state? It is undetectable, just as the instant of the transformation of the tiniest particles of matter into a current's energy is undetectable, or the partition dividing an inorganic entity from the organic process of life is imperceptible. In the music, the characteristic rhythm of Petrushka was set apart; having been further designated and set apart for an independent development, the rhythm disseminates into the tiniest bits; in the linkages of these, as in a process of cell division, new organisms (rhythmic shapes) are born, arousing in us new impressions and evoking new images. Such is the mechanical process—but at the same time, in parallel, the emotional essence of this process is convincing and true to life to such a degree that one does not wish to think about its structure and tendencies, about the course of the reaction itself; but instead only take in the spiritual drama of the unfortunate, pitiful freak and, with agonizing empathy, follow the quivering of the life force that is flickering inside him. The musical rhythm convinces us of the unquestionable existence of Petrushka's "real" being. The hypnosis spreads. Having sensed the concrete being of Petrushka and felt his suffering, we cannot help becoming observers and participants in his drama: the more aware we are of the character of the "puppet" Petrushka, the more ardent we become.[28]

The third tableau is psychologically more complicated. Not only are detailed characterizations of the Moor and the Ballerina developed here, but the theme of the Ballerina's attraction to the sensual Moor and the awakening in the latter of voluptuous and lascivious instincts are elaborated as well. A love duet between this extraordinary pair takes place and then, finally, the clash of the Moor with Petrushka, who has gained access to him. Thus the development of the dramatic action is rapidly condensed and set in motion, its denouement quite evident. But the style of the play, this complex of expressive means, demands another, more impressive location for the denouement than the Moor's chamber. Hence there is a stylistic necessity for the fourth tableau that is not only stylistic but, as we will see later, one conditioned by rhythm, too.

The leit-rhythms of the Moor are sharply opposed to the leit-rhythms of Petrushka. His movements are lazy, dull, stubbornly sluggish and slow; yet should he be irritated, he will strike the victim with his sable, fervently and fiercely. The interchange of Petrushka's "rhythmic melodies" is elastic and fluent, in spite of his "puppet" nature and "bony" knocking about. It is a peculiar device: in Petrushka's orchestral "part," the sound of the piano predominates, albeit in a highly unique toccata-like transformation, both as a solo and in unusual combinations with the harp, clarinets, and the stridently "hysterical" cries of the trumpets, so that a sinister timbre emerges, as if to represent a musical toy—a box of knuckle bones, which upon rapid rotation would play whimsical-sounding arabesques, without losing the basic "skeletal" coloration.[29] In general, the music of Petrushka—there, where it recreates the gestures and bustling about of the "hero"—is characterized by a nearly continuous sensation of being lifted off the ground as if suspended over it, turning and revolving in the air. This is achieved through the absence in such moments of a bass background, a foundation, as if in the chord the lower tones of a chord were removed so the chord would sound from the seventh on up. This technique has a significance in the everyday world scenes, but of a different sort.

Returning to the rhythms of the Moor and to a comparison with Petrushka's rhythms, we find a complete polarity: Petrushka is supple, springy, and overstrung. The full meaning of life for him is to break free of a "puppet's lot," to escape from the strong grip of the Magician, now that a consciousness of his individual self is already pulsing within him. Petrushka could indeed evade the Moor's saber, if the springs controlling his movements did not keep him attached and if they were not two-dimensional movements but a spiral motion that could infuse him with the strength to make the crazy leap into another, more desirable plane of experience. The music underscores this at every step: while not at all static, its motion is either one of helpless, "clawlike" scratching or flailing about within a closed circle or a pitiful breaking apart and wailing.

Amidst this chaos of spinning about and impotent attempts at breaking free of the automatism, one can follow an idea that is implemented quite consistently over the course of the four tableaus: to lead the listener toward a horrifying denouement (the death of Petrushka) without offering him the possibility prior to this moment of ascertaining whether there is humanity in Petrushka, and only by occasional hints indicating the possibility of genuine sympathy for the unfortunate creature. And suddenly, at the minute of death—

a lento of ten measures' duration[30]—the music begins to show warmth and twinkle quietly; no more puppet, no more howling of a tortured animal, no convulsions! In this minuscule moment, just as life is slipping away, waning, and, like a shadow, disappearing, Petrushka *is alive*, like a naive, childishly helpless human being. Through love he began to be drawn to the light, for it was love that ignited the desire in him to break into freedom and the flicker of consciousness; in love, too, he met with destruction. There is nothing remarkable in the fact that the crowd does not want to believe that it was a puppet that died. The music of this briefest of scenes rises to a dramatic peak. They are ten measures of constant tension and a holding of the breath.

I can think of no other music for the stage with such a realization of the cold breath of death and such an experience upon the moment of its approach of an entire drama of life, so that the entire form of the dying creature stands before the listener in his full being. That most intense agony of Tristan is, in essence, a triumphant procession toward death and night: he thirsts for them. Siegfried's death is the struggle of a hero at full power with life melting away. Petrushka's death is the death of a creature in whom consciousness and an attraction to the joy of life have only just begun to blossom. There arises the painful and perplexing question: for what? and also a doleful submission, that very submission with which the Russian soldier dies in Tolstoy's *Hadji Murad*.[31] I am amazed at the reproaches that are heaped on the defenders of *Petrushka* because they accept a most typical stylization, intended for the delectation of distorted Parisian tastes as a genuine, vital, and sincere work, an imitation pearl for the gem, found on the sea bed—I am amazed at how these reproaches can appear in the face of even just a single musical moment such as the death of Petrushka! The brevity proves nothing at all, for time in music is measured not in distances, not in quantitative duration, but by the quality of the tension. A minute of life, in which an *epoch* of life is concentrated, is experienced in musical time as having lasted longer than an hour's worth of prolix schemas (the latter, however, are measured by the tedium of awaiting the end). Petrushka died but the *puppet* remained. Again one hears the howls of a tortured creature. The Magician is afraid. He, for one, knows what's the matter!

The music of the "Amusing Scenes" comes to a halt with a unique and unprecedented cadence invented by Stravinsky—a unison leap of a diminished fifth, like a question mark: the drama may begin all over again.[32] If all of our culture is movement within a closed circle and only a spiral motion (Andrei Bely)[33] that is conceivable for the future can promise a new rebirth of humanity, then Stravinsky was brilliantly correct in his intuition. For now, we are all in the hands of some "Magician" and can live in peace provided we do not strain and break the spring wires by which we are suspended or hooked. We are permitted to run about the circle, but the tight longe remains in the hands of the groom with the whip, who stands in the center of the stadium covered with sand! . . .

To the Moor, it makes absolutely no difference. In his animal nature he does not suspect that his movements are automatic. If he were to be aware of his situation, he might consider himself endowed with a free will: if God does not obey him, he beats him up! Stravinsky discovered extremely successful fixed timbres and rhythms in order to represent the primitive psyche of this "beast." The music is structured on a motive with a shade of orientalism (clarinet and bass clarinet at a distance of two measures) to characterize the Moor's ritual dance (worship of an idol).[34] The dance is exchanged for exasperated outbursts of the savage: the rhythm becomes fragmented, and out of the monotonous *tune* a transition is made to clumsy leaps and malicious swoops; the original timbres alternate with the beast's savage roars over a querulous buzzing. . . . The leit-rhythm of the Moor's saber blows would seem to introduce an automatic regularity into this confused instrumental recitative. Suddenly growing calm, apparently from an instinctive sensation of some mystery present even in his primitive religion, the Moor begins to pray. Again the monotonous rhythm of an Oriental melody. Enter the Ballerina with a *cornet à pistons* in her hands.[35] The profile of her that is rhythmically revealed indeed cannot compare conceptually to those of Petrushka and the Moor, but her musical sketch is nevertheless clever and intricate.

Why the dull and obstinately capricious Moor would be dearer to her than Petrushka is not expressed in the music. We know only the "ballerina" and that she is already infatuated. Like a pure coquette, she will not balk at any rhythmic arabesques in order to reach her goal of ensnaring the Moor. Here the rhythm of an ardent Viennese waltz from an organ-grinder's music, there a sly and mischievous tawdry chansonette tune played by trumpet and accompanied by a drum! The cantabile of a sweet adagio of the Lanner type in the end wins over the Moor and arouses in him a crudely lascivious sensuality.[36] In all of this scene the musical action unfolds in a remarkable way, with the play of rhythm in its astonishing pointedness and tension unquestionably giving definition to the psychological truth of the "romantic" collision taking place. It should not be forgotten that a pantomime is at issue, that in this case the composer has managed without support from the timbres of human voices and that, in placing the three characterizations in continuous motion (the Moor, the Ballerina, and at the end Petrushka, who jumps into it), he had to base the links and the contrasts of rhythms and timbres exclusively on the instruments, since the actors are mute. The more difficult it is, the more interesting the task for a master of the orchestra like Stravinsky. Out of the struggle of leit-rhythms and instrumental timbres emerges the most profound incarnation of emotions. Two very distinct worlds collide: those of the savage and the product of "culture": a coquettish ballerina.

In their natures something is nevertheless revealed that can promote the attraction, and in this attraction arises the current of sensuality that envelops the two creatures. In the music two very distinct rhythmic and timbral planes are juxtaposed: at first they are sharply disjointed; then, in an instant, the Ballerina's four-bar waltz rhythm is ingeniously linked with the three-bar rhythm of the oriental tune.[37] The Moor's fright and confusion are transformed into lust—at first timid but then, in proportion to the Ballerina's coquettish teasing, impatient. Whether by an intuitive achievement or a conscious action, it is equally remarkable how Stravinsky transforms an adagio, originally designed to be humorous (a vulgar tune stylized as organ-grinder's music) into an eerie "ballet" duet, realistically handled, thanks to the inlaying of music dear to the Ballerina's heart with contrapuntal inner voices out of the Moor's rhythmic-timbral sphere! The howls of Petrushka, which are initially choked with wheezing, shatter the amorous mood, which was by no means harmonious, but wavering over a shaky relationship.

Then a new juxtaposition: the rhythms of the Moor's saber blows and the spasmodic rhythm of "Petrushkian" flight, with the frenzied wails permeating the background figurations.[38] An impression is created of the inescapableness of death for the victim caught in a trap. Petrushka is restrained by someone holding strings that do not allow him to run beyond a predetermined distance. Even though the Moor's blows are blindly automatic, since they are expended in a space dictated by the incantation during the "magic trick," they will sooner or later reach their goal and the awakening in Petrushka of the temptations of consciousness will be quashed.

With this unusual "scherzo," the third tableau is brought to an end and the action again transferred from the intimate life of "puppets" to the expanse of the square before the puppet show.

At evening time, amidst Shrovetide revelry, in the heady fumes and smoke of Russian merrymaking, cries and an uproar spread out from within the Magician's little theater. Tearing into the rhythm of the dance in general, Petrushka's cry is terrifying, like a spell that in a certain moment brings all motions to a halt, even the spontaneous automatic motion of the crowd.

The "scherzo," i.e., the Moor's pursuit of Petrushka, continues here, on the square before the theater. The Moor slays Petrushka![39] The profound transformation in the music upon his death is, I repeat, unusual and unprecedented in its laconic intensity.

True to the typical device in Russian music for the stage, in *Petrushka*, too, the action is played out against a background of richly colored tableaus of everyday reality, which in Stravinsky's elaborations receive new tints, new rhythms, and new contrasts of elements. The sharpness of outline, the complex coloristic and dynamic effects, the unique contrasts and associations—in the course of inventing it all, the composer's rich imagination found in this subject a long-sought foundation and a point to apply itself. I will proceed to an analysis of those brilliant discoveries in sound that were created by Stravinsky in the broadly deployed "Shrovetide *deistvo*," since here the everyday milieu plays not only the role of a background but also that of a "puppetlike" action, developing in parallel, albeit raised to a human scale. This transition demands an explanation of the significance of Stravinsky's music with respect to its coloristic riches. In analyzing the characterizations of the three puppets with respect to rhythm, it already became necessary to point out the timbral solutions to one set of tasks or another as well. The fact is that if the concept of rhythm is broadened from the correlation and balance of elements of duration and accent to the correlation between elements of light and color and the correspondence with them of dynamic nuances, then the issue of the role of rhythm in *Petrushka* will reveal to us new riches in this so very laconic and, in essence, "stretto" sort of work.

I will not be touching on the dynamics, but will dwell instead on the special role of timbre. Its enormous significance with respect to one or another emotional influence is evident: neither the Moor, nor the Ballerina, nor Petrushka would hold that psychological persuasiveness nor the clarity of characterization for us if Stravinsky, this master of timbral contrasts, had not attained such a flexible control of them, so that all the pantomimed, rhythmic recitatives acquire over their course coloristic shades that correspond to the characters and language of the *dramatis personae*. It is unthinkable to cite the numerous examples from the score; but for a remarkable model, I will point out that the mysteriously glimmering light in the music for the death of Petrushka is achieved through a mystical flickering (tremolo) of viola harmonics, just about to die away, which tie together severed elements from Petrushka's motives that sound first in the flutes, then in clarinets, then in violin solo and bassoons in the most varied timbral guises, but in a single mood of exhaustion, feebleness, and timid sorrow.[40] The breath weakens—the violas' tremolo ceases abruptly under the influence of cold, slithering currents: falling chromatic motions by minor thirds in the *con sordino* tremolos of the first and second violins. Against this background a solo violin dauntlessly plays—in augmentation—the chief motive of a once nervous, frenzied howl. The flute in the low register recalls the motive of Petrushka's complaint. Everything is waning. Sarcastically distorted and fussy movements in the bassoon (leaps of a fifth) take the place of a trembling in the face of death: it is the Magician who hurries to resolve the perplexity of the bystanders. It is all so easy to explain!

The stunning collection of colors in the death scene is valuable for its own sake, but their worth with respect to the development of all the action is increased all the more when we recall that in the death scene all that we know about Petrushka from the preceding is heard in a thoroughly transformed aspect. It means that in this case one finds a well-proportioned organic and harmonious relationship of individual episodes, conditioned by the rhythmic balance of timbral plans and realizations. The entire work is structured on such relationships, which alter only the direction (sometimes contrasts, comparisons, or the connections called forth by the laws of associations) but not the architectonic essence.

In the folk scenes, in the characterization of everyday reality and action, the coloristic relationships have a primary importance for Stravinsky. The beginning of the fourth tableau is a vivid spot, sounding continuously in full color. Here the music does not progress: it merely *overflows*. There is a somewhat similar moment in the fish-catching scene in Rimsky-Korsakov's *Sadko*, when the orchestra sounds like sunbeams streaming forth in rivulets of gold![41] Stravinsky expands the moment into an extended state of being and characterizes the festive roar of the crowd by means of a sparkling effusion of a resounding metal: the orchestral figurations are atop a D-major chord of molten gold! The most primitive type of variation schema acquires here a dazzling assortment of colors, whose spinning around yields a single lighting and a single mood. With respect to rhythm, one can compare this spot with the depiction of the Shrovetide promenading in the first tableau: here, a general rumble, there, an individualizing of separate shouts, entrances, exclamations, and pranks against a more transparent and motley-colored background, as if the Shrovetide revelry had still not been set right, had not changed into a spontaneous possession. In this respect, a definite relationship is visible between the first and last tableaus of *Petrushka*, whose implementation is based on the principle of rhythmic progression. The sound material in the first part of the revelry is more sparse and dispersed.[42] In the last tableau, he heightens the concentration and sharpens the rhythms more and more; the coloration grows thick; strong, heavy pedal points appear in the basses. The sense that higher overtones are sounding without a fundamental vanishes. An elemental whiff of the crowd, of the masses—the ponderous force of human beings akin to the earth—pervades the music and results in the most grandiose growth of powerful sound in the ingenious creation of the coachmen's dance, the likes of which have never existed in Russian music.[43]

In the relationship of the durations and in the dynamism of this dance, in the wild and stormy accentuation, Stravinsky set down the very essence of masculine Russian dancing, in which the very persistence of accents is reflected, like an incantation of the Earth: a chaining to the ground through regular, rhythmic stamping. It is a betrothal of the active strength of the male, both *effective* and mature, with Earth's *virginal* fructifying strength, stored up in potential. Of course, there can be no talk here of a dedication of the self to the gods of the underworld. Mother Earth is a beneficent nurturer. Amidst an agrarian people, "dance" incantations can arise, leading to a symbolic betrothal to the Earth and a bonding to the soil. Not a single Russian dance in opera has had this meaning (though there is a hint of it in the dance of the *skomorokhi* in *Snow-Maiden*[44]), and one can only regret that in no production yet of *Petrushka* has the sacred, ritualistic significance of this remarkable dance been clearly emphasized and brought out. It is the center of the Shrovetide scene. To it are adjoined the sly and alluring dance of the preening nursemaids (with yet another discovery in the orchestra: a rustling or chirring of the strings resulting from a unique use of grace notes[45]); after this are the genre scenes: the bear with the trainer, the merchant with the gypsy girls. After the coachmen, there begins a confused flight of the mummers and a general uninhibited dance. The coloration darkens, the rhythm becomes strongly accentuated and ponderous; and in the end, each individual chord receives a stroke and the heavy pile of accented chords in wild succession leads to the yelp of the pursued Petrushka. The gregarious preoccupation of the crowd (also a type of "puppets," with automatic movements that are subject to some kind of Magician) collides with the unexpected incident, which to all appearances is completely incomprehensible. The noxious fumes dissipate under an impression of the horror of death.

The dance of the coachmen and the death of Petrushka—these are the two overwhelming moments of the fourth tableau, in comparison to which the remaining escapades, while not lacking in poignancy, do not at all compare in depth of concept and realization. It must also be noted that Stravinsky's prodigious instinct for counterpoint allowed him to make ingenious and bold linkages and combinations of motives and their components into a most unexpected and seemingly capricious blending. In essence, such a use of the idea of subordinate voices produces a harmoniously organic connection and a strong inner fusion of parts that are separated at times by significant gaps.

With respect to purely schematic form, *Petrushka* is quite simple. The major divisions are these: (1) the dances; and (2) the pantomimes (choreographic recitatives). The dances, of course, are divided into character (genre) dances and dramatic ones, emerging from the essence of the drama itself. The pantomimes encompass recitatives, monologues, duets, trios, and other ensembles; in addition, in the recitatives certain moments are distinguished for having not an active but a contemplative character (a type of arioso). The entire second tableau (*chez Petroushka*) is structured in such a recitative-arioso style. The first and fourth tableaus approximate a rondo in their design, for which the role of main themes—or according to the terminology of French scholars *refrains* (*choruses*)— is played by an initial twisting and turning motive of modal type (typically a flute against clarinet and horn figurations) in the first tableau; and, in the fourth, music of the festival's roar, grounded in a D-major triad, tying together all the individual entrances as if the crowd, in its improvisation, creates and distinguishes group after group, dance after dance! . . .[46]

For its inner rhythmic cohesiveness and logic, for the emotional truth of the action itself and its musical realization, finally, for its innovative achievements in the spheres of rhythm, timbre, coloration, as well as the freshness of the brilliant contrapuntal and harmonic combinations—*Petrushka* is an outstanding work. But, even though it introduces new techniques into the structure of ballet, with respect to pure architectonics it creates nothing exceptional to surpass the schemas developed in Russian music for the stage. As for its connection with Russian music in general, and with the devices of folk artworks, there can be no disagreement: the diatonic and typically Russian cast of nearly all the music of *Petrushka* is evident to every scholar, even upon superficial acquaintance. Moreover, Stravinsky's works possess, as their most worthy quality, the intuitive display of a forgotten and vanishing element of folk creativity: instrumental improvisation, which—no less than the vocal element—conceals a marvelous residue, even when judged by the fragments. In *Petrushka*'s style can be seen the devices and qualities of this fresh tendency.

Just as a chemical reaction of various substances can yield a dissimilar substance with unique properties, so in music, the juxtaposition of elements can engender new sounds, and with them new sensations and experiences. Hence any analysis of details is meager in comparison to the living perception of music that emerges within the intense magnetic pull, the coupling, and the gradual animation of the particles of sound.

In relaying my impressions from listening and investigating the music of Stravinsky's *Petrushka*, I strove to move closer to a grasp or even an understanding of the language and style of one of the most unique works of Russian music. My personal experience of the perceptions has always convinced me that the significance of this piece exceeds the limits of descriptive music that has been created for a stylized theatrical presentation. For me, *Petrushka* is thoroughly acceptable even in a purely symphonic performance. But the issue is not whether this music is for the theater or not for the theater. It is first of all *music*. Based on the testimony of one of *Petrushka*'s collaborators, it was revealed to me that the basic kernel of the action in *Petrushka* was developed first *in music* and that it was on the basis of the music, according to the vestiges left by it, that the psychological phases of the subject and its scenic realization were elaborated.[47]

NOTES

1. Stravinsky's father became the principal bass for the Maryinsky Theater in 1876, where he would portray 64 different characters. Among his significant Russian roles were Farlaf (*Ruslan*), Rangoni and Varlaam (*Boris*), the Village Head (*May*

Night), Grandfather Frost (*Snow-Maiden*), Mamyrov (*The Enchantress*), and Panas (*Christmas Eve*).

2. Among the half dozen or so songs that preceded *The Firebird*, Asafyev singled out the Two Romances, op. 6, both settings of verses by the poet Sergei Gorodetsky (1885–1967). An early performance of the latter song—with its unprepared dissonances simulating bell peals—at one of the St. Petersburg Evenings of Contemporary Music provoked a response from Rimsky, recorded by Yastrebstev: "The middle of this song is very good and expressive in some places, . . . but the beginning is frenetic and harmonically senseless" [V. V. Yastrebstev, *Reminiscences of Rimsky-Korsakov*, trans. by F. Jonas (New York: Columbia, 1985): 429].

3. Prior to World War I, Sergei Koussevitsky had conducted the Russian premieres in both capitals: St. Petersburg, 12 February 1914; Moscow, 18 February 1914; Asafyev is bemoaning the lack of performances since the revolution and Koussevitsky's emigration.

4. In a controversial essay that Andrei Rimsky-Korsakov had refused to print in his *Muzykalnyi sovremennik* (Contemporary musician), Glebov/Asafyev had named Stravinsky, Prokofyev, and Myaskovsky as musical pathfinders. In the essay "Paths to the Future" (1918), he urged Russian contemporary composers to take their bearings from Beethoven and Tchaikovsky. The reader should take note that even here, the apolitical author has deliberately avoided making any comment about the new regime under which the "new songs" were destined to be composed.

5. See Chapter 17, n.1.

6. "Rhythmic patterns" would be an alternative translation, the juxtaposition of which produces a polyrhythmic composite structure.

7. Score location: fig. 101. Asafyev suggests that the interplay of motives and ostinati does not sufficiently counteract the effect of the episode's static harmonic content.

8. The terms *umenshennyi lad* [diminished mode] and *uvelichennyi lad* [augmented mode] were introduced into Russian theory in the early 20th century as theoretical constructs to explain aspects of Rimsky-Korsakov's harmonic practice. The diminished mode of eight tones results from the combination of two diminished-seventh chords; outside of Russia, it is more typically called the "octatonic" scale or collection. Augmented modes result from the combination of either two or three augmented triads separated by a half step, resulting in modes of six or nine tones.

9. Music associated with the captive princesses occurs, e.g., at the first tableau, figs. 48–54, 61, and 115, where delicately scored leitmotives of arpeggiated chromatic seventh chords appear. [Author's note:] Only the delicate melting cries and complaints of the captive princesses serve as a marvelously beautiful link between the two worlds and thus diminish the impression of incommensurability with regard to the artistic merit of the two components of the *fundamental* dramatic opposition.

10. See, e.g., figs. 8 and 119.

11. Asafyev's metaphors aptly describe the slowly flowing eighths arranged into a basso ostinato, two measures in length, with which *The Firebird* begins.

12. In the opening ostinato, an A-flat/F-flat third is chromatically linked by the pitch E flat to a D/F third.

13. Asafyev must be referring to the voice-crossing bassoons of m. 7 involving leaps of a diminished fifth.

14. As is generally known, the bland and nonmagical Prince Ivan is assigned diatonic themes throughout the ballet. His initial appearance at fig. 6 is accompanied by short, staggered phrases in muted horns and bassoon.

15. Asafyev has taken note of the inversionally symmetrical four-note motives at fig. 8: the first consisting of the pitches F#, E#, E, and C; the second of pitches B, C, C#, and E#. He hedges about the "diminished mode" content, since the full collection is not present.

16. In Tsar Berendei's Act 2 cavatina in the key of A major ("Mighty nature, full of wonders") from *Snow-Maiden*, the vocal line is diatonic, but an obligato accompaniment for solo cello is based on the same four-note chromatic idea used for the Firebird's flight music.

17. Cf. *Kashchei*, second tableau, mm. 170–75, 181–86; and *Firebird*, first tableau, figs. 106 + 2 and 110 + 4. The claim for common ground is based on both composers' arrangements of chromatically linked major thirds to produce *nondiatonic motives and scalar passages. The poco meno* episode [labeled *Meno mosso* in the Jurgenson score] occurs at fig. 103. Asafyev spotted a similar pattern in the "demonic carol" of Rimsky's *Christmas Eve* (sixth tableau, mm. 6–28).

18. Score location: figs. 48 to 55.

19. The solo horn representing the prince faultlessly maintains the mode. The offending B naturals enter first in the cellos (fig. 73 + 5), where they tonicize C with the customary leading tone of European common practice.

20. The scalar flourish (*Vivo assai*) occurs at fig. 97.

21. As noted above, the theme of the subsequent *Danse infernale* emerges first at fig. 103, as an aftermath of the magic carillon's ringing.

22. The result of the Firebird's spell is revealed in a brief allegro dance episode at fig. 126, which makes prominent use of the bird's motivic material and offshoots from it. The "sharply rhythmicized dance," i.e., the familiar *Danse infernale* (figs. 133–82) is the next phase of liberation, which Asafyev credits to the air element.

23. The augmented sonority is first sounded by the three trumpets in the pit at full volume, then sustained by three muted trumpets offstage.

24. The famous pentachordal tune is introduced at fig. 197 by Prince Ivan's usual orchestral counterpart, the horn.

25. Richard Taruskin has translated excerpts of reviews by Nikolai Myaskovsky, Andrei Rimsky-Korsakov, Nikolai Kashkin, and others that well represent the range of opinions voiced in the pre-Revolutionary Russian press. See Taruskin, *Stravinsky and the Russian Traditions*, v. 1 (Berkeley: University of California Press, 1996): 759–70.

26. The *Stoglav* [lit., "Hundred Chapters"] is a fascinating manuscript consisting of a set of church resolutions drafted by a council that convened in Moscow early in 1551. They provide a wealth of information on the lifestyles, customs, and rituals of medieval Muscovites, as well as details on church and government administration. The quoted passage on Russian occult practices attests to the circulation of Western European occult books and practices. The report on these suspect practices was a preparation for their prohibition.

27. Asafyev's commentary concerns the musical gestures of the Russian Dance (beg. at fig. 33), in which the simple, repetitive, periodic, and "rigidly tense" tune alternates

with the sharply differentiated gestures that create episodes. At fig. 34, the Moor's sabre blows (octave leaps at fortissimo), the Ballerina's cornet, and Petrushka's grotesque advances are easily discerned.

28. Asafyev seems to ask (without entirely answering) a central question about the second tableau: how do these 110 measures of vivid, unforgettable, yet heterogeneous gestures amalgamate into the portrait of a sensate (or not, . . . or not entirely) puppet character?

29. The characterization of Petrushka by means of toccata-like piano writing in combination with harp, clarinets, and trumpets occurs in the second tableau.

30. Score location: fourth tableau, fig. 129.

31. The novella *Hadji Murad* was Tolstoy's last major work of fiction, completed in 1904 but not published until 1912, i.e., a mere nine years before the *Etudes*. From the outset, it is evident that the central issue is to be the death of the wise and fearless Chechen chieftain Hadji Murad, who is portrayed from a wide range of viewpoints. The Russian soldier Avdeev dies early on, a few hours after he is shot, in full acceptance of and submission to fate; his parting words: "Bring a candle. I am going to die."

32. The scalar flourish of C to F# in contrary motion occurs in the strings as an ornament to the second beat.

33. Asafyev's second reference to the paradigm of the spiral. For comment, see Chapter 11, n. 50.

34. Asafyev is describing a passage in the third tableau at fig. 65. The compact, lugubrious legato tune in woodwinds is accompanied by unharmonized strata of B-flat pedal points, provided by pizzicato strings.

35. Score location: third tableau, fig. 69.

36. The waltzes of Joseph Lanner (1801–1843), a contemporary of Johann Strauss the elder, were popular throughout Europe and Russia.

37. Score location: third tableau, figs. 72–73. A contrast of superimposed meters—the Ballerina's music in 2/4, the Moor's in 3/4—heightens the contrast between tunes and phrase lengths.

38. Score location: third tableau, figs. 78–81.

39. Score location: fourth tableau, fig. 128 + 4. The Moor's sabre blow is depicted with a *sul ponticello* glissando for massed strings.

40. Score location: fourth tableau, fig. 129.

41. Cf. *Sadko*, fourth tableau, mm. 512–29. Rimsky-Korsakov's triadic oscillations in D major and use of pianoforte (!!) make the link to *Petrushka*'s fourth tableau indisputable.

42. [Author's note:] The presence of organ-grinder's music of an *automatic* sort due to a frequent use of witty transcriptions of motives from the street creates the smack of a stylization of the everyday environment, but also prepares well for the appearance of the "puppets."

43. Score location: fourth tableau, fig. 108.

44. Cf. *Snow-Maiden*, Act 3, no. 3. While Rimsky-Korsakov's "Dance of the Skomorokhi" differs in many particulars, Asafyev could have in mind the passage beginning at m. 219, featuring down-bowed low-range octaves and chords doubled in the low brass—all at *fortissimo*.

45. Score location: fourth tableau, fig. 90. The grace notes alternate between upper and lower notes of the staccato thirds played by *divisi* first violins.

46. Asafyev implies that the triadic oscillations (not actually in D at all points!) representing the crowd as a whole act as a refrain to demarcate the series of dance and pantomime episodes that attract the crowd's attention.

47. On the evidence of a sketch from 1910 and the composer's later reminiscences, it is now accepted that *Petrushka* was initially conceived as a Konzertstück for piano and orchestra.

· 19 ·

In Lieu of a Finale

My Symphonic Etudes emerged gradually, from January to July 1921. Initially (some time ago), a lengthy article was planned, whose goal was to vindicate Russian opera as an artistic legacy of enormous value, undeservedly insulted by the frivolous judgments made by the advocates of techniques and devices that are foreign to the psychological foundations of the language and style of Russian operatic composers. The dimensions of the planned "vindication," combined with the ever-increasing wealth of material, convinced me to prepare a research study on the essence of Russian theatrical music in regards to its musical nature, particular means of realization, and philosophical significance. Along the way, the present etudes appeared, as concrete case studies from the theoretical "Essay on the Structuring of the Psychological Bases for Russian Musical Style," which was coming to fruition in the background; indeed, a portion of this work was once synthesized by me into a concise prospectus, as part of a lengthy lecture entitled "Foundations of the Russian Operatic Style."[1]

The life circumstances that are forever diverting me from focusing energy on a single major project oblige me to publish these *Etudes* in the form of an interconnected, thematically unified survey of the most significant moments in the evolution of the Russian musical mind in the intimately connected realms of operatic and ballet music. I could not shed light on all the phenomena in detail (for example, toward *Prince Igor*); a few were entirely omitted for various reasons. Sergei Taneyev's *Oresteia*—a most interesting interpretation of the ancient tragedy through an operatic prism, an interpretation that served as a unique creative test for this composer-symphonist—received no treatment here for purely extraneous reasons. Several years ago, I devoted a separate monograph to the analysis of this operatic trilogy, which was somewhat differently conceived (a detailed thematic analysis with musical examples) than the articles in the present book.[2] It was not possible, due to formal considerations, to cover Rachmaninov's operas, in particular the poetic *Francesca*, or Rebikov's operas, or the operas of Cui and Rubinstein from the previous generation. All of this would have required a separate introductory essay with any number of digressions, both psychological and historical, as a result of which the book would have been transformed into a bloated survey in which thoroughness of scope would take precedence over the elaboration of essential *tenets*. As it happens, the latter are the most admirable quality of the sets of "symphonic etudes" by Schumann, Chopin, and Liszt, distinguishing them from "collections of etudes" that may exhaust all technical problems but do not raise these problems to the level of artistic necessity, which alone should be the precondition for their technical expediency.

I did not tarry over the details of Stravinsky's opera *The Nightingale*, but merely emphasized its significance with regard to how it enhanced the vitality of the idea of a song element: song inspired by life that overcomes mechanical reproduction is a symbol of the struggle of song (songfulness), or the melos of music, against a mechanism that oppresses the instrumental element in music. Stravinsky's *Nightingale*, along with Prokofyev's *The Gambler*, a work omitted by me entirely (despite an obvious connection of this opera with the idea behind *The Queen of Spades* and with stylistic devices of Musorgsky), constitutes a contemporary trend of Russian theatrical music that is still not fully defined; I would prefer to await "different songs," in order to form a sharper image of the essential character of the new period and of the degree to which it is connected to past achievements.

Russian ballet was touched on only to the extent necessary to indicate the relationship between the instrumental-dance element predominating therein and its emergence and presence in operatic works, and with that particular direction that defined Russian dramatic music of the period just prior to the Revolution: the trend toward choreographed action. Superficially, this can be explained as resulting from the "Parisian spectacles" and reforming work of Fokine,[3] although, in essence, a similar tendency has for some time been concealed within the continual rivalry between the pure rhythm of song and the rhythm of dance, which can be observed in the operas of nearly all composers. The dramatism (internal-psychological) of Glinka's *A Life for the Tsar* is the result of the reflexive opposition of the Great Russian song element and the Polish dance formulas, which Gogol correctly noted with great depth of insight.[4] The "choreography" of *Ruslan* was sufficiently emphasized by me in the first etude of this book, but a detailed analysis of the dance meters of this brilliant opera from a dramatic standpoint provides the opportunity to reach very intriguing conclusions regarding its structural peculiarities. I shall merely point out the remarkable introduction of a three-beat polonaise pattern during the nervous, elevated excitement at the moment of bewilderment after the enchanted sleep (the canon) in the finale to the first act of *Ruslan*.[5]

Dances in Russian opera do not hold the superficial place that is characteristic of them in the schemas of the so-called grand opera style, which long ago has divulged the main effects of its content. Respite from singing and a diversion for the eyes are one matter, but choreographed action is something quite different: both the meaning and the intent are different. The third and fourth acts of *Ruslan*, the second act of *A Life for the Tsar*, Dargomyzhsky's remarkable and idiosyncratic attempt at designing a choreographic cantata: *The Triumph of Bacchus*;[6] the scene in the underwater kingdom in *Sadko*; the folk games and dances in *May Night*, in *Snow-Maiden*, in *Mlada*; the clowns' activity in *The Enchantress*—all are organic elements of the action, not arbitrary and pointless ballet numbers. It is high time to realize that the action in a Russian opera is not determined by this or that schema and does not depend at all on whether an opera was composed in the old manner of fragmentation into arias, ensembles, etc., or in the new "Wagnerian" manner of division according to scenes and episodes. This is a question of style and its versatility, but not of the psychological essence of the action: Gluck and Mozart are more dramatic than the endless column of "Wagnerians," and Debussy shaped the drama in *Pelléas* on the basis of an entirely different internal experience and external expression than those from which *Tristan*'s drama was structured.

But even the design of the Wagnerian dramas could not quash the fermentation of "Meyerbeerisms." The vague accusations of unstageworthiness and lack of drama made against the foremost Russian operas speak to what extent many people have become accustomed to "action for the eye" of a *L'Africaine* sort. They bow to the name of Wagner, having been mesmerized by the shadow of Meyerbeer, from whose precepts it is easier to disavow in words than to overcome in reality.

Had Wagner himself not justified the scenic and musical design of his dramas on the basis of ideological premises, many would have had difficulty detecting their genuine dramatism and averting the charges of unstageworthiness ("boring to hear!"). On the other hand, had Glinka thought to produce a preface to his *Ruslan*, how easy it would have been for many to criticize other operas that lacked *Ruslan*'s design, in accordance with this standard appended by the composer himself.

There remains the question of influences. Literary criticism would be naive if it only took note of influences in an accusatory tone, and not in the sense of the evolution of language and subjects or as an indication of their ancestry. It has been customary in music, especially in regard to certain Russian operas, to pass on determinations of absolutely no significance: this, apparently, is from Wagner, this from Meyerbeer, this from Verdi. Nevertheless, the real and indubitable influences, i.e., not the superficial infiltrations, those influences deeply hidden in the instrumentation, the techniques of characterization, in ornamental embellishments, etc., remain undetected in spite of their sharp relief. No one has shown how deeply and substantially Tchaikovsky transformed both the Italians and Meyerbeer, or, more importantly, how the genius of Mozart reflected on him (on him and also on Glinka). No less idiosyncratic and, in essence, no less of a "true-to-self" interpretation, was Rimsky-Korsakov's transformation of the ideology and musico-poetic element in Wagnerism. These are complex issues, not to be resolved by simpleminded references to influences and borrowings. It is necessary, just as in poetry, to invent a theory of influences and a theory of borrowings, tied to the history of "migrating subjects."

Enormous and multifaceted is that sphere wherein research on Russian opera should circulate on account of its distinct artistic value. It calls forth ever-new problems, one after another, and demands resolutions to a series of essential questions, among which the matter of explaining and defining the principles of scenic realization and the performance practice for the great works of Russian operatic composers[7] is vitally important. Without an "interpretive culture," we shall live to see the already historical riches vanish without a trace, shall cut off barely traceable traditions, and remain in a broken-down trough: we shall have to start from scratch. Russian art is a series of oases in the desert, like 15th- to 17th-century monasteries amidst impassable forests and bogs. Is it possible that Russian music, and especially Russian opera, has been fated to develop in the same way? The universal deafness to its beauty of design and emotional depths, in relation to the utter "facelessness" of its style in certain stagings, leads to an eventual neglect and incomprehension of one of the finest pages in the history of Russian art. I fear that the time is coming when those who are interested in the monuments of Russian operatic music will feel as if they are in Novgorod, in a musty provincial town, amidst the priceless and splendid creations of Novgorod architecture and iconic art, peacefully sleeping in *soundless*, museum quiet. Does not that same feeling appear when, amid the masquerade-like emptiness and the simpleminded connivances, you view productions of *Ruslan* and *Igor* that are deaf to the music, presented on a stage once held to be exemplary? I will say no more, since from this point on my requisite formal conclusion on the actual scenic conditions of Russian opera would only proceed into moaning and groaning of no use to anyone.

The goal of my *Etudes* was to demonstrate the necessity of careful and thorough research, with respect to the psychology of creativity and the questions of style, of this extremely important field of Russian music. For this reason I have frequently led the narrative in two directions, providing purely stylistic analysis with respect to some operas, permitting a psychological approach with respect to others, and sometimes combining both the one and the other method (as, for example, in the study on *The Queen of Spades*) in order to examine a given phenomenon by studying the psychological foundations of both the language and the style. In this way I have at all times attempted, by varying the methods and techniques, to remain within the confines of an etude format, i.e., underscoring one or another tenet of importance to the etude and to the *comprehension* of the artistic idiosyncrasies of Russian opera, transferring it into a plane of discussion based on a concrete, given example while striving to make a particular case meaningful in constructing a theory of knowledge covering the full range of Russian musical art. This method is that of the great creators of "symphonic etudes" (Schumann, Chopin, and Liszt). They took a particular technical matter within the realm of pianism for their starting point and through creative intuition raised their stylistic intention to a level of profound artistic significance—achieving, in the process of transforming "technical expertise" into the living tissue of music, the surmounting of and *infusing of spirit into* the inert element within instrumental music, an element whose essence and source are found in mechanical principles. This process is called *symphonism*, which was first comprehended in its full profundity by Beethoven.[8] But this is a task exceeding the limits of the present work. Here I will merely add that the melos of Russian opera occupies a significant and elevated position in the struggle and the interaction of the instrumental and the song elements, and that it imparts a quite exceptional expressivity to the grandest of Russian operatic conceptions. As an example of this phenomenon, I can name the *bylina*-opera *Sadko*, wherein the spiritual transformation of Volkhova symbolizes the entire process that I have just now identified. In this work, the composer reinterprets an influence of Wagnerian instrumentalism by affirming song in the act of liberating from the power of the dark element the person of Volkhova, the girl who selflessly submits to fate (betrothal to her beloved).

The musical-aesthetic problem of how melos and instrumentalism interact is linked in Russian operatic music with the distinctly discernible psychological problem concerning the tragic lot of an individual who is condemned to perish (which applies especially to the fate of a Russian woman).[9] The dramatic intensity that emerges in the process of bringing out both the above-mentioned interaction and the problem of fateful condemnation produces a somewhat atypical design in the majority of Russian operas. Justifying their design was a further intention of mine.

Pro domo sua, I will say that, as a musician, I feel that my *Symphonic Etudes* are akin to Schumannesque striving, i.e., constructed in variation form, with an expansive symphonic development and contrasting themes that are juxta-posed with the main theme. However, with respect to psychology, my aims are the reverse of Schumann's: in his time, when music was spreading its wings, it sought out support in the great contemporaneous literary-philosophical move-ment and "poeticized" its ideas with the aid of words, sometimes even fixing its form in a definite "program." Now a reverse process has emerged: a trans-ference of the rhythm of music into the realm of the Logos, for at the root of modern philosophical searching and the endeavors to construct an organic worldview lie elements that have been inherent in the spirit of music since time immemorial.

"In the beginning the whole exists, and *elements* are capable of existing *only within the system of the whole.* Therefore, it is never possible to explain the world as a result of attaching A to B, to C, etc.: multiplicity does not shape the whole but, on the contrary, is born out of a single whole. In other words, the whole is more primary than the elements; the absolute must be sought as arising within the realm of the whole or, more accurately, *lifting itself above it,* but by no means among the elements; elements are in any case derivative and relative, i.e., capable of existing only in relation to the system, in which they serve as members" (Nikolai Lossky, *The World as an Organic Whole*).[10]

NOTES

1. Orlova noted that the typescript of the prospectus was stored in a private Leningrad archive, as of 1970.

2. The essay "The Oresteia: A Musical Tragedy by S. I. Taneyev" (1915) appeared in four numbers of the journal *Muzyka.*

3. "Parisian spectacles" is a reference to Diaghilev's productions, of which *Scheherazade* (1910), *The Firebird* (1910), *Le Spectre de la Rose* (1911), and especially *Petrushka* (1911) exemplify the reforming work of Mikhail [Michel] Fokine (1880–1942).

4. Gogol made his acquaintance with Glinka's first opera in both rehearsal and pub-lic performance. His renowned *aperçu* appeared in a survey of St. Petersburg's 1835–1836 theatrical season printed in the journal "In his work [Glinka] successfully fused two Slavonic musics, and you may hear where the Russian speaks and where the Pole: in one there breathes the free melody of Russian song, and in the other the rash tune of a Polish mazurka" (cited from Alexandra Orlova, *Glinka's Life in Music*, trans. Richard Hoops [Ann Arbor: UMI Research Press, 1988]: 166).

5. Score location: *Ruslan*, Act 1, no. 3, fig. 47 + 25. The destabilization due to me-ter is further enhanced by the modulatory character of the passage, which begins with a feint toward G and concludes with a feint toward C.

6. See Chapter 17, n. 15.

7. [Author's note:] And indeed, only a few were not opera composers, which suggests a peculiar, I might say, even superstitious attraction for opera, undoubtedly having deep psychological roots, which deserve contemplation and a show of greater respect for what is valuable in Russian musical thought, without pointing to Germany as the eternal ideal. . . .

8. Like *intonatsiya*, Asafyev's better-known contribution to the theory and philosophy of music, the coinage *simfonizm or* "symphonism" opened up a vast field of inquiry and changed in its connotations over the course of his career. By the time of *Symphonic Etudes*, he had concluded that a certain quality of musical flow on a very large scale that was most evident in Beethoven's symphonies and in Tchaikovsky's Sixth was not unique to these works or even to a larger number of symphonies, but was entirely conceivable in the realms of opera, chamber music, and—somewhat surprisingly—in the long lines of that lyrical developmental category of Russian folk song known as *protyazhnye pesni*. Asafyev's most extended discussions are found in the essay "Paths to the Future" (1918), the monograph *The Instrumental Works of Tchaikovsky* (1922), and the second volume of the book *Musical Form as a Process* (1947), wherein the explication of symphonism functions as a countertheme to the main concern of explaining *intonatsiya*. Prior to his forced adaptation of a Marxist conceptualization of music in the late 1920s, he frequently suggested that symphonism was the "stream of musical consciousness," hinting at affinities with the thought of Bergson and William James.

9. The concept of an individual's resignation to a dark fate or "ill-fatedness" [*obrechyónnost*] is indeed a recurrent theme in *Symphonic Etudes* and, in Asafyev's view, central to an understanding of Tchaikovsky's creativity and works. While the nature of human suffering is addressed by various philosophers and writers, a tragic worldview rooted in an ultimately pointless, nonredemptive, and pathological *obrechyónnost* of the sort espoused by either Grishka Kuterma or Hermann is alien to the thought of most of the significant 19th-century Russian philosophers, with the exception of the existentialist Lev Shestov (1886–1938).

10. No less than Vladimir Solovyov (1853–1900), the patriarch among Russian Idealist philosophers, Asafyev's teacher Nikolai Lossky (1870–1965) was a system builder and discipline bridger. His lifelong philosophical project was an attempt to complete several Herculean tasks, including the reconciliation of idealism and materialism; a bridging of the Kantian gulf between noumenon and phenomenon; and an explanation of how the universe in all of its multiplicity nevertheless owes its genesis, its evolution, and its past, present, and future organic interconnection to a Supracosmic Principle that both antedates any philosophical system and cannot be explained by its terms. This last project was the main concern of *The World as an Organic Whole* (1917), from which Asafyev quotes.

Index of Russian Operas, Ballets, and Principal Roles

General Index

About the Author

David Haas is professor of music at the University of Georgia. He received a bachelor of music degree in horn performance from the Cincinnati Conservatory and a master's and doctorate in historical musicology from the University of Michigan. His book, *Leningrad's Modernists* (1998), was concerned with the new music and musical thought of Leningrad in the 1920s. His essays on the music of Shostakovich and Tchaikovsky will be published in forthcoming volumes of the Cambridge Handbooks series. He is currently at work on a study of the 19th-century Russian symphony and a novel about an American symphonist.